BETTER PLACE

Duane Murray
and Shawn Daley

Top Shelf
PRODUCTIONS

For Laura and Emblyn, who make my place better. –D.M.

For Molly and Edison. –S.D.

BETTER PLACE © 2021 DUANE MURRAY

Published by Top Shelf Productions, an imprint of IDW Publishing, a division of Idea and Design Works, LLC. Offices: Top Shelf Productions, c/o Idea & Design Works, LLC, 2765 Truxtun Road, San Diego, CA 92106. Top Shelf Productions®, the Top Shelf logo, Idea and Design Works®, and the IDW logo are registered trademarks of Idea and Design Works, LLC. All Rights Reserved. With the exception of small excerpts of artwork used for review purposes, none of the contents of this publication may be reprinted without the permission of IDW Publishing.

IDW Publishing does not read or accept unsolicited submissions of ideas, stories, or artwork.

Editor-in-Chief: Chris Staros

Edited by Leigh Walton & Chris Staros

Based on a story by Duane Murray and Shane Belcourt.

Additional art by Matt Kindt (page 19), Jeff Lemire (47), Farel Dalrymple (57-58), Tyler Boss (117), Jim Rugg (117 box), and Nate Powell (123).

ISBN: 978-1-60309-495-5   24 23 22 21   4 3 2 1

Visit our online catalog at topshelfcomix.com.

Printed in Korea.

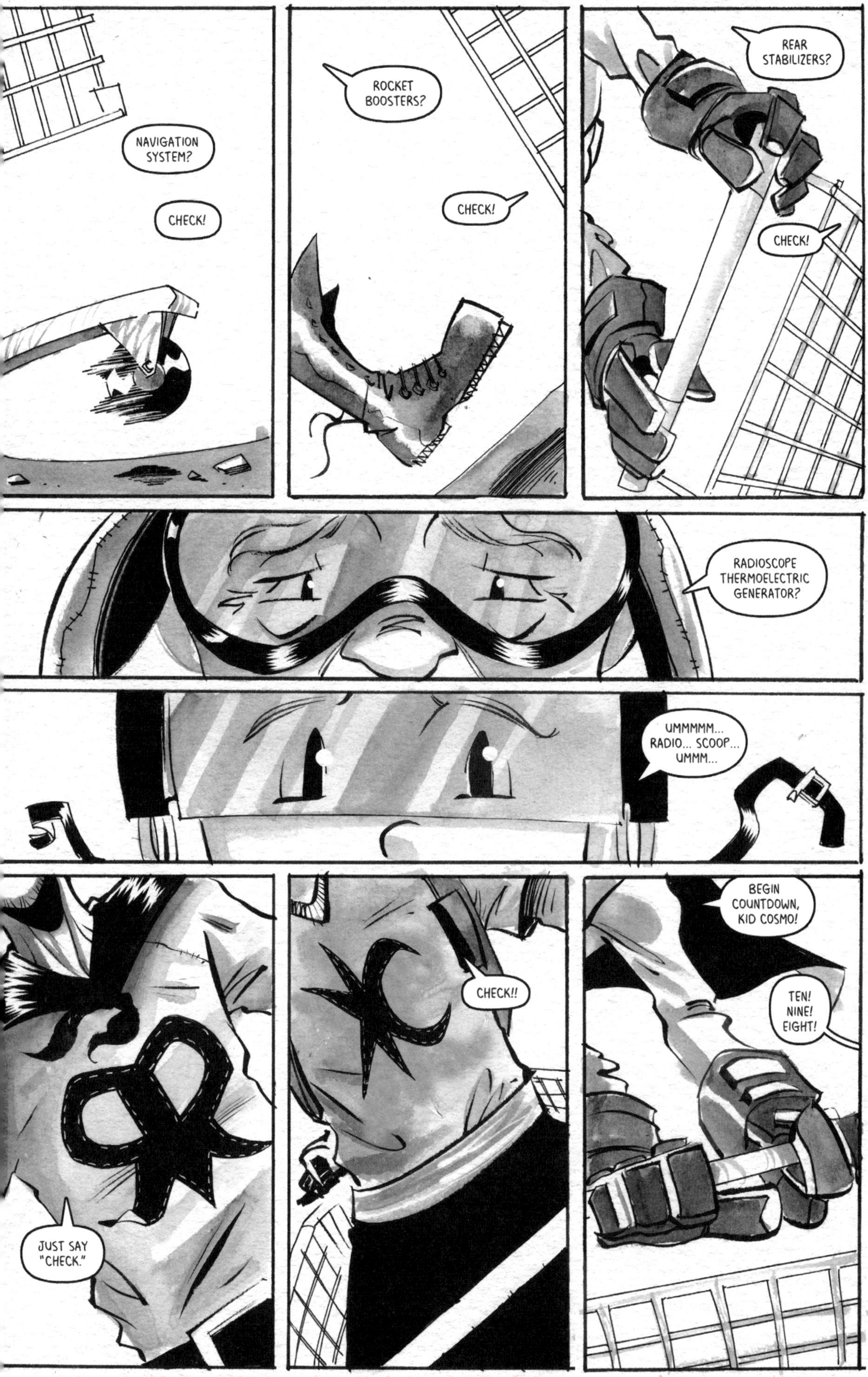
NAVIGATION SYSTEM?
CHECK!
ROCKET BOOSTERS?
CHECK!
REAR STABILIZERS?
CHECK!
RADIOSCOPE THERMOELECTRIC GENERATOR?
UMMMMM... RADIO... SCOOP... UMMM...
JUST SAY "CHECK."
CHECK!!
BEGIN COUNTDOWN, KID COSMO!
TEN! NINE! EIGHT!

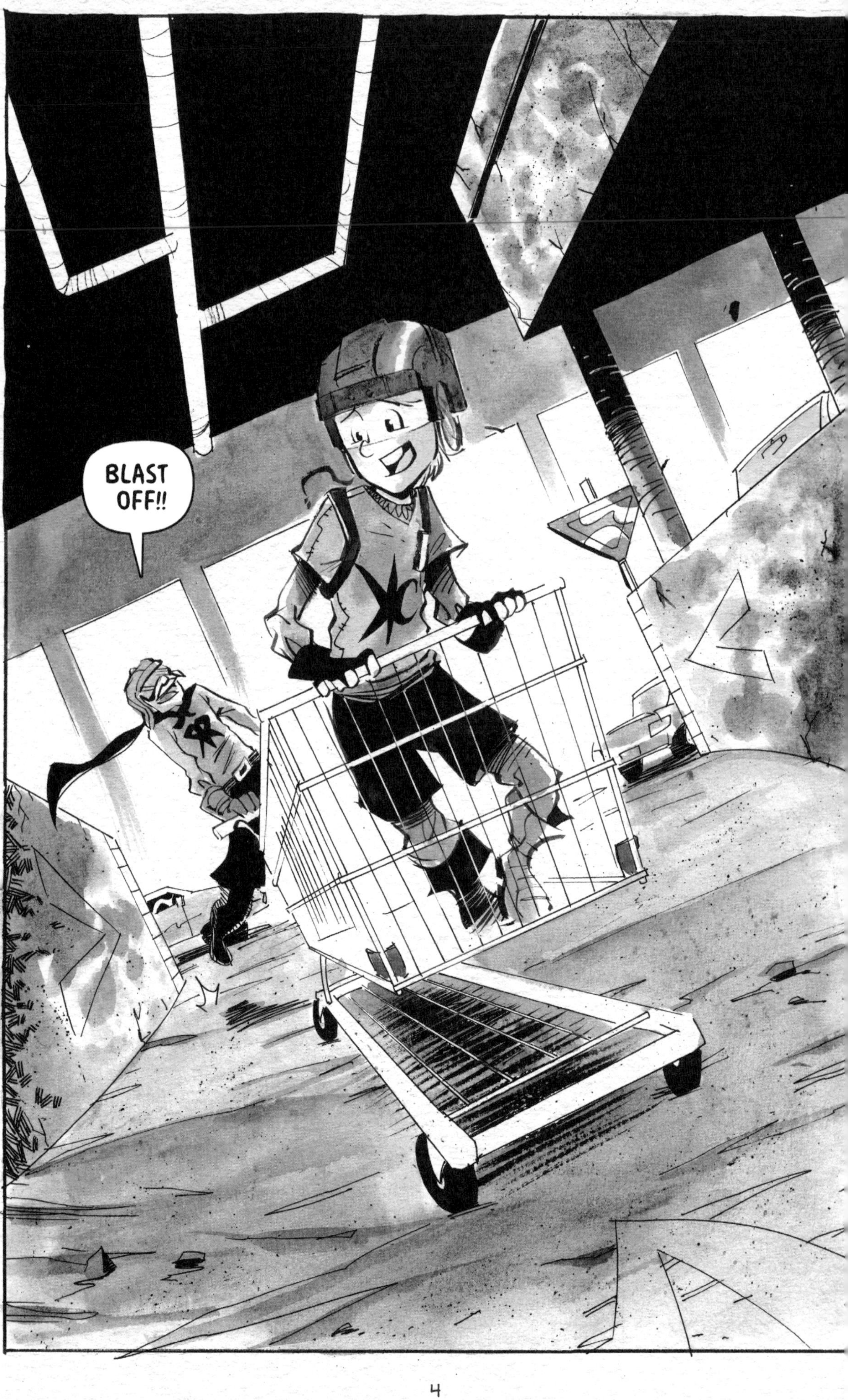
BLAST OFF!!

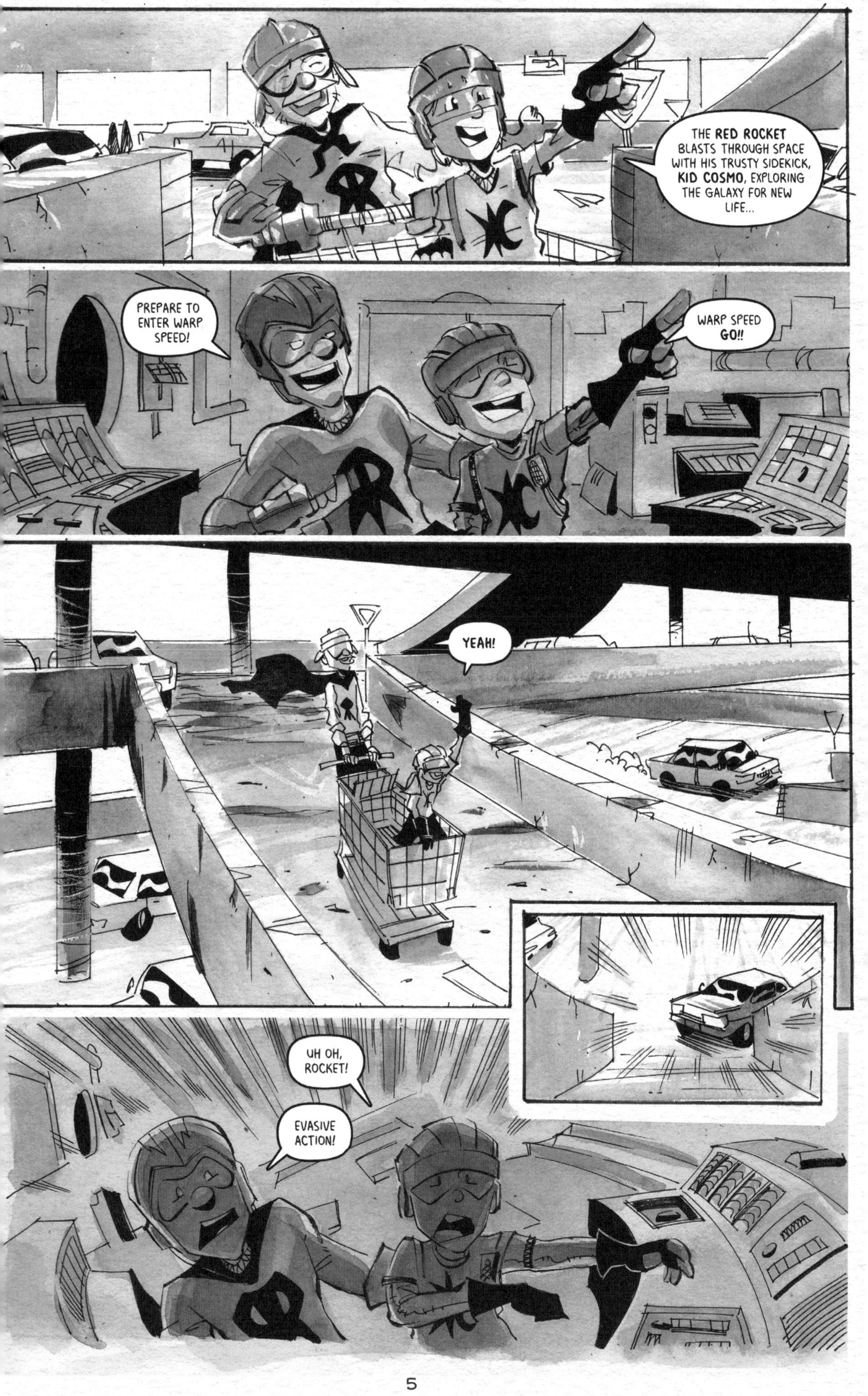
THE **RED ROCKET** BLASTS THROUGH SPACE WITH HIS TRUSTY SIDEKICK, **KID COSMO**, EXPLORING THE GALAXY FOR NEW LIFE...
PREPARE TO ENTER WARP SPEED!
WARP SPEED **GO!!**
YEAH!
UH OH, ROCKET!
EVASIVE ACTION!

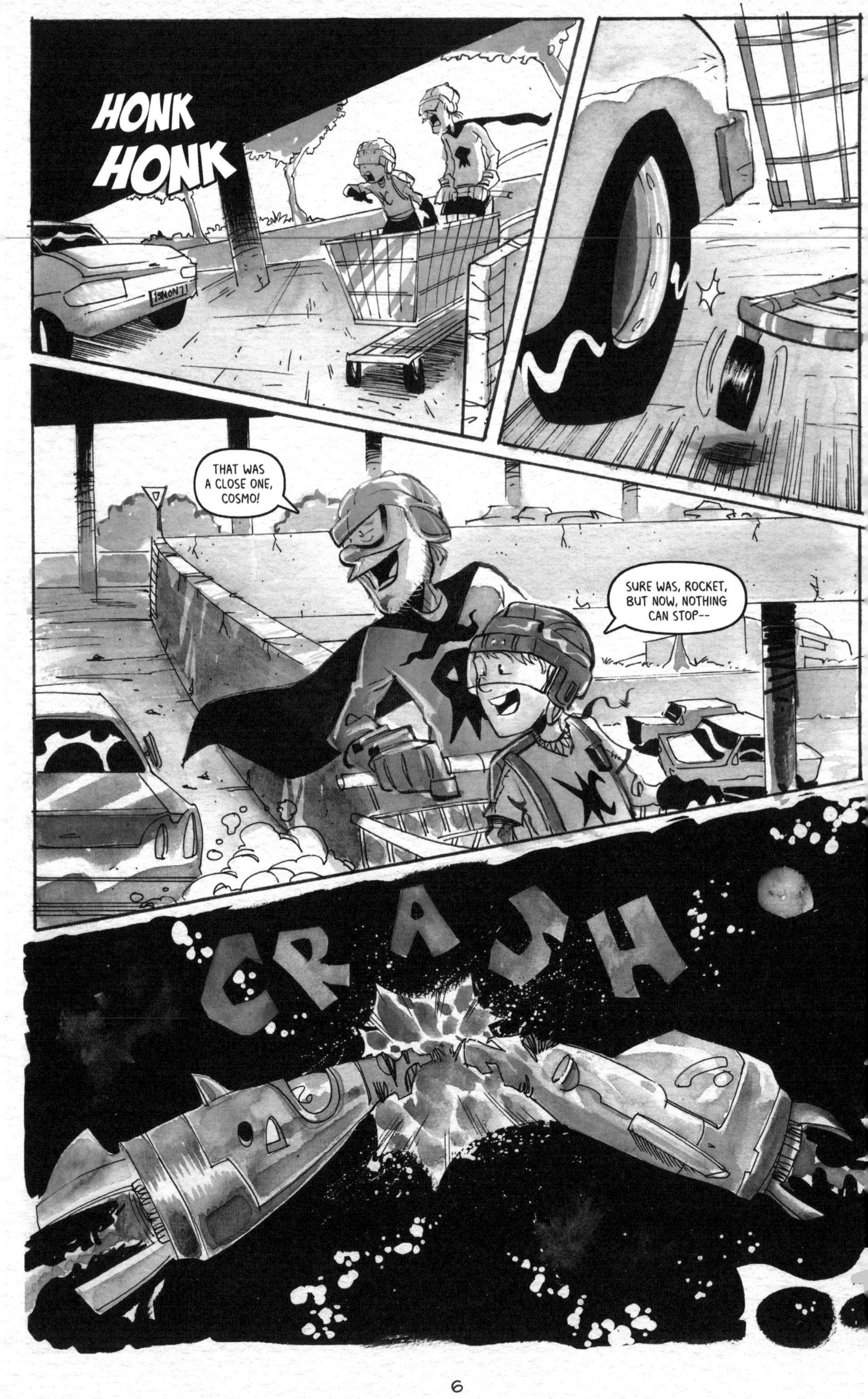
HONK
HONK
THAT WAS A CLOSE ONE, COSMO!
SURE WAS, ROCKET, BUT NOW, NOTHING CAN STOP--
CRASH

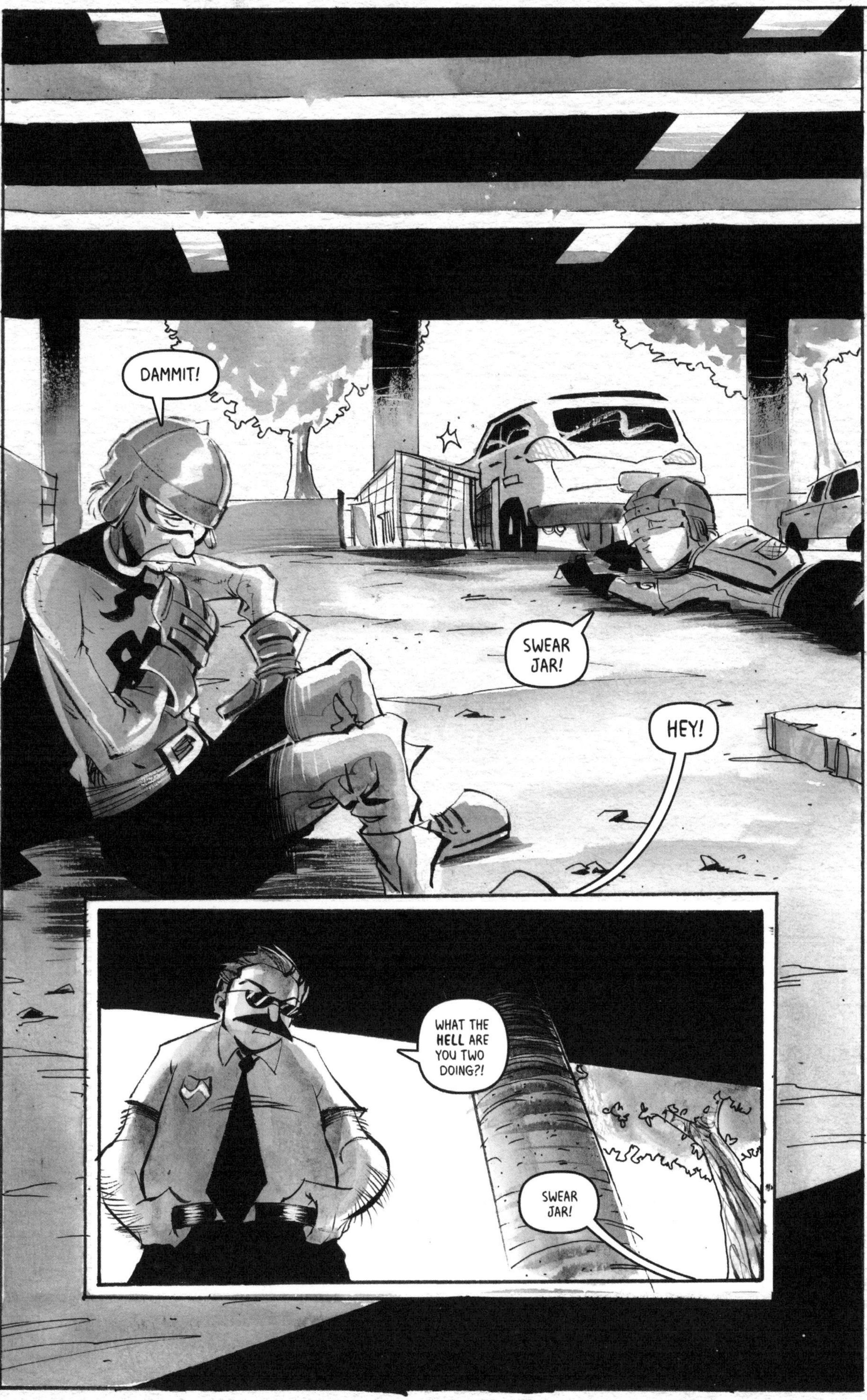
DAMMIT!
SWEAR JAR!
HEY!
WHAT THE **HELL** ARE YOU TWO DOING?!
SWEAR JAR!

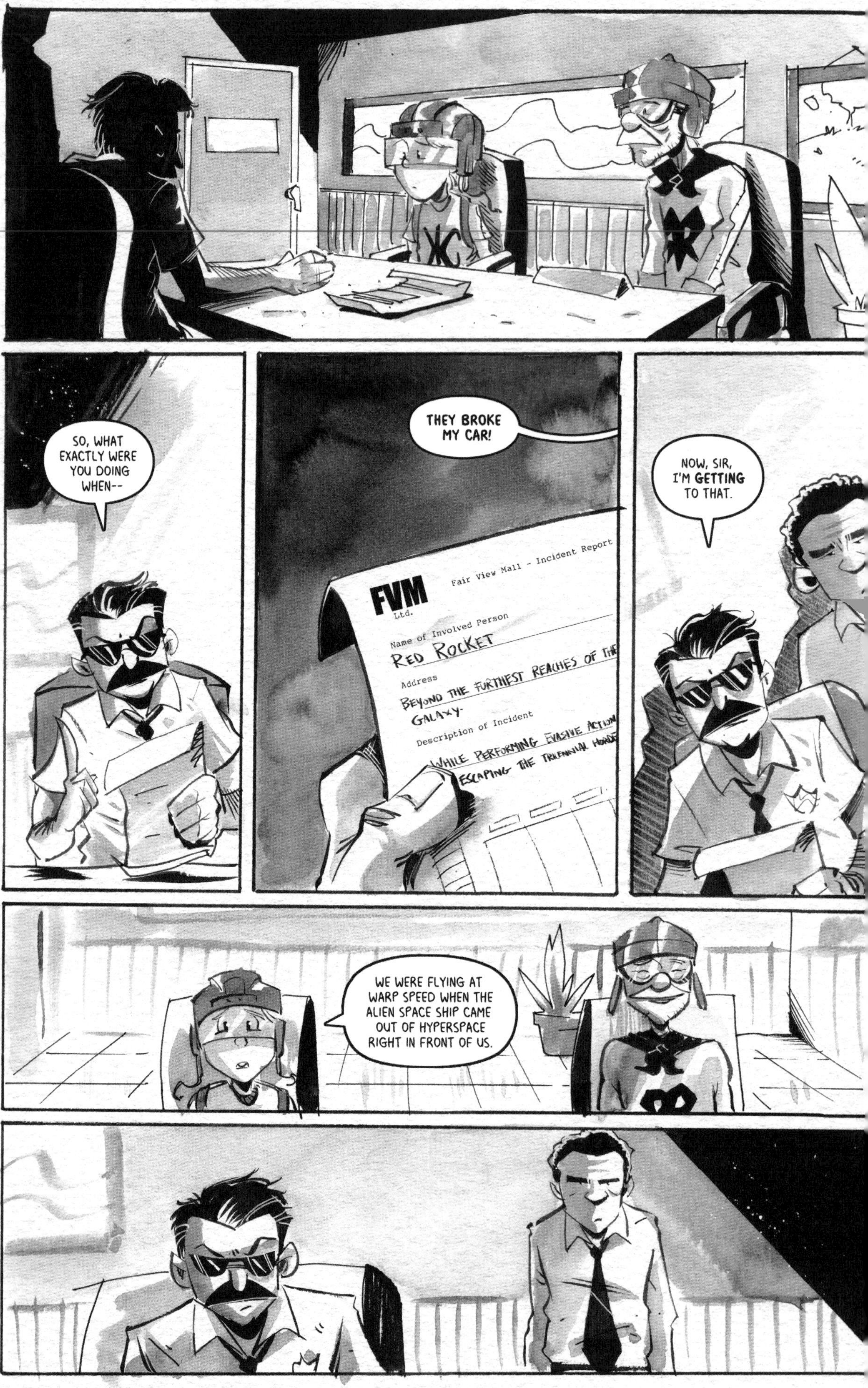

SO, WHAT EXACTLY WERE YOU DOING WHEN--
THEY BROKE MY CAR!
FVM Ltd.
Fair View Mall - Incident Report
Name of Involved Person
RED ROCKET
Address
BEYOND THE FURTHEST REACHES OF
GALAXY.
Description of Incident
WHILE PERFORMING EVASIVE
ESCAPING THE
NOW, SIR, I'M GETTING TO THAT.
WE WERE FLYING AT WARP SPEED WHEN THE ALIEN SPACE SHIP CAME OUT OF HYPERSPACE RIGHT IN FRONT OF US.

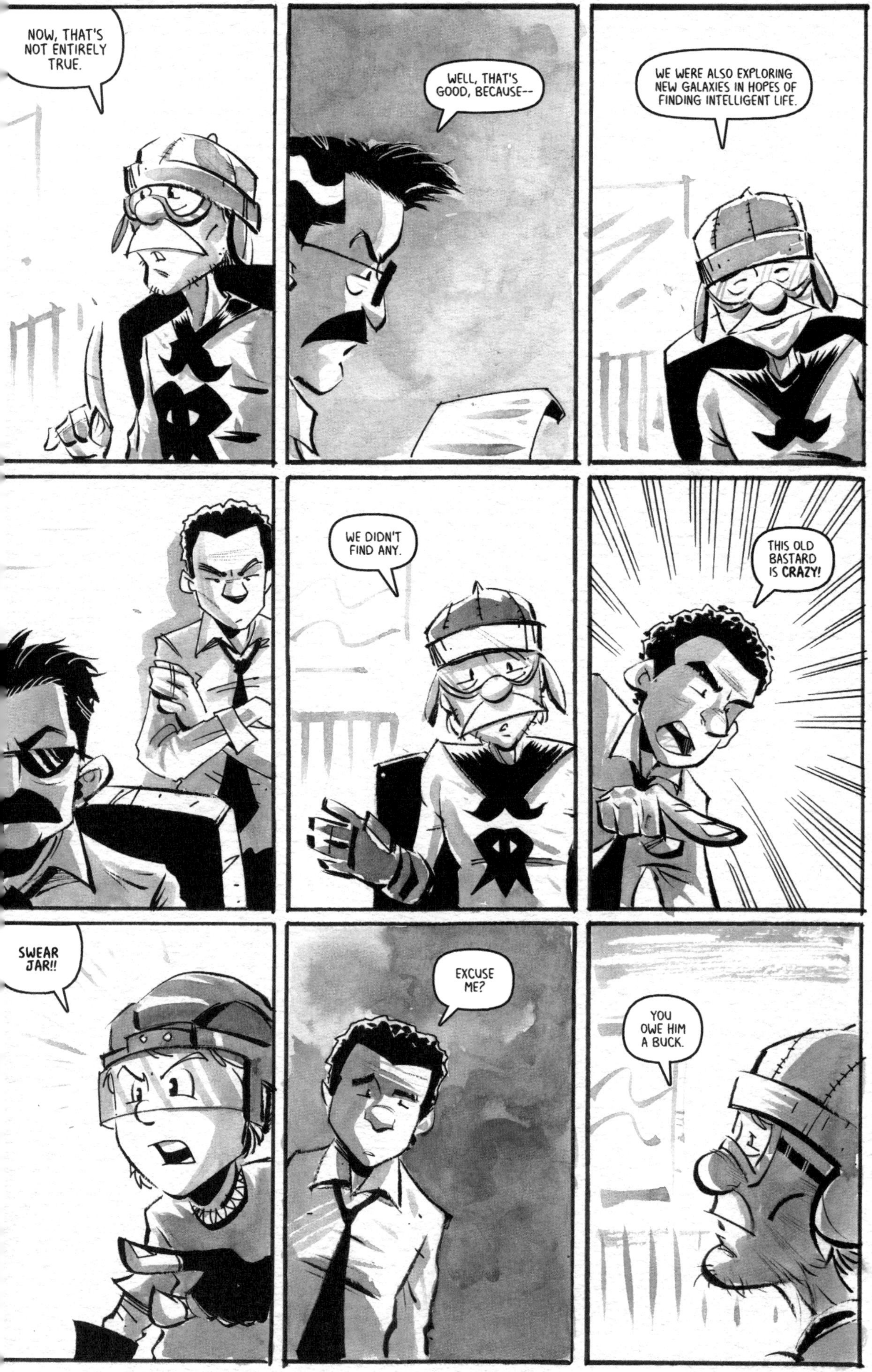
NOW, THAT'S NOT ENTIRELY TRUE.
WELL, THAT'S GOOD, BECAUSE--
WE WERE ALSO EXPLORING NEW GALAXIES IN HOPES OF FINDING INTELLIGENT LIFE.
WE DIDN'T FIND ANY.
THIS OLD BASTARD IS **CRAZY!**
SWEAR JAR!!
EXCUSE ME?
YOU OWE HIM A BUCK.

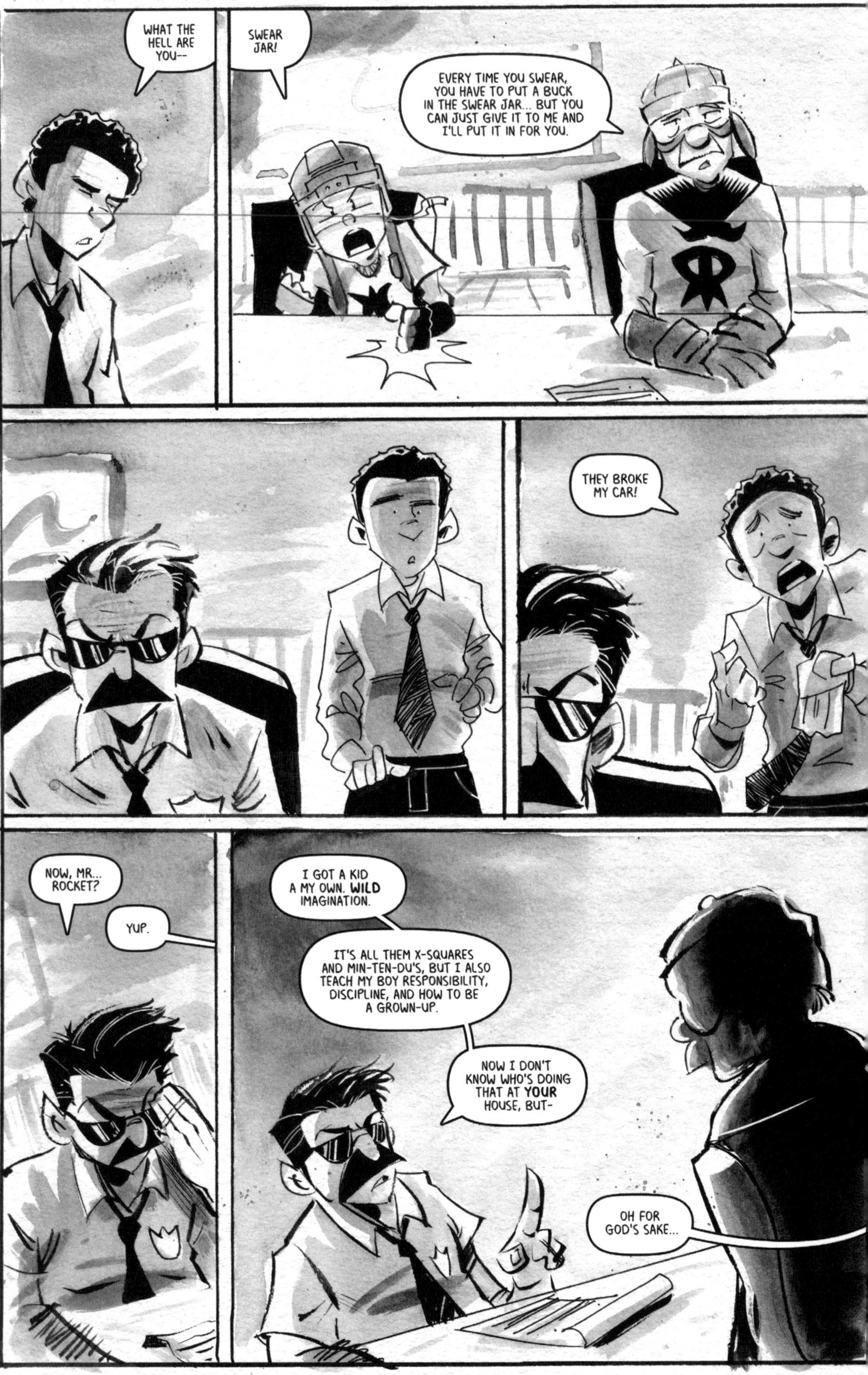
WHAT THE HELL ARE YOU--
SWEAR JAR!
EVERY TIME YOU SWEAR, YOU HAVE TO PUT A BUCK IN THE SWEAR JAR... BUT YOU CAN JUST GIVE IT TO ME AND I'LL PUT IT IN FOR YOU.
THEY BROKE MY CAR!
NOW, MR... ROCKET?
YUP.
I GOT A KID A MY OWN. WILD IMAGINATION.
IT'S ALL THEM X-SQUARES AND MIN-TEN-DU'S, BUT I ALSO TEACH MY BOY RESPONSIBILITY, DISCIPLINE, AND HOW TO BE A GROWN-UP.
NOW I DON'T KNOW WHO'S DOING THAT AT YOUR HOUSE, BUT-
OH FOR GOD'S SAKE...

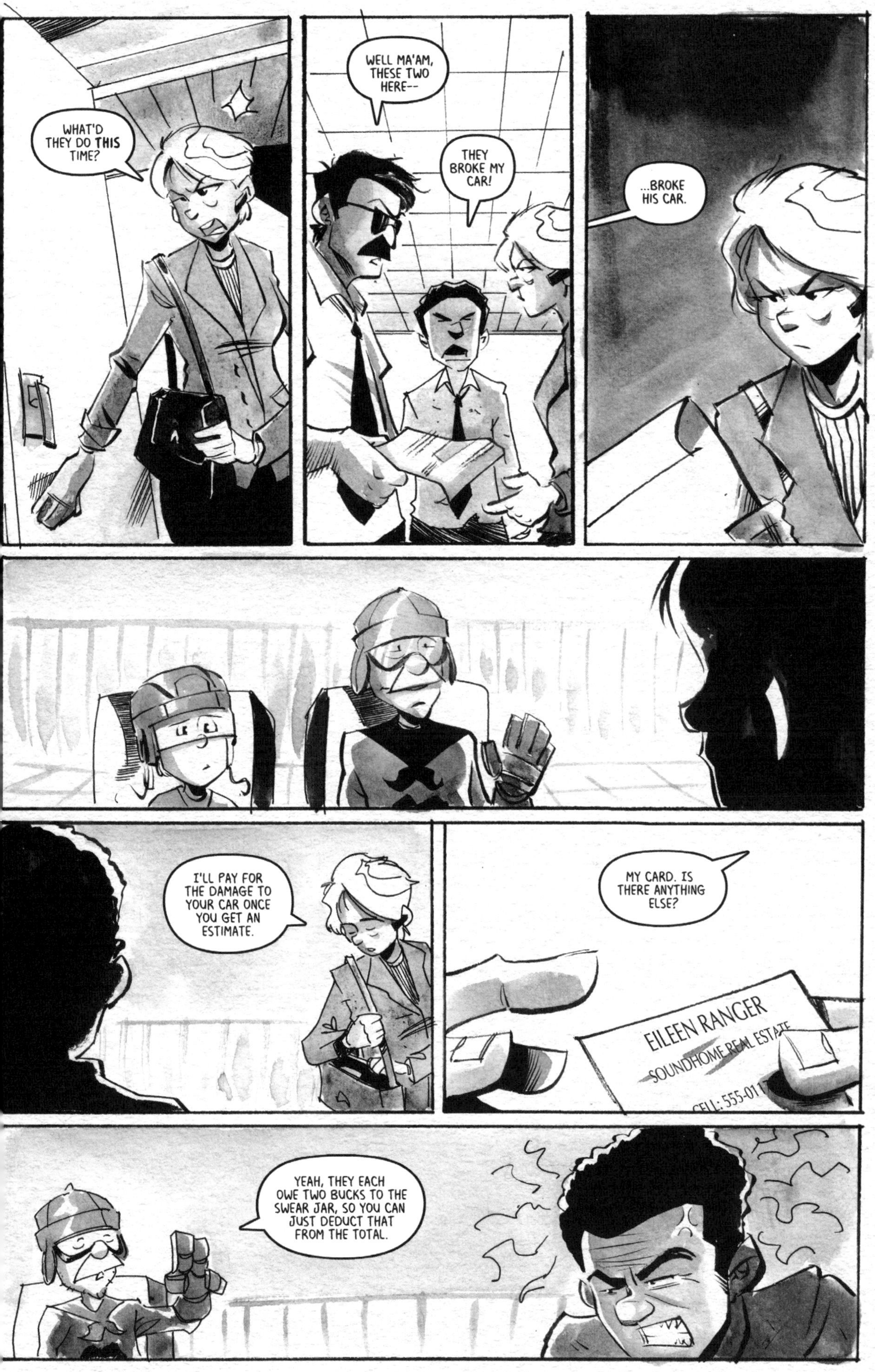
WHAT'D THEY DO **THIS** TIME?
WELL MA'AM, THESE TWO HERE--
THEY BROKE MY CAR!
...BROKE HIS CAR.
I'LL PAY FOR THE DAMAGE TO YOUR CAR ONCE YOU GET AN ESTIMATE.
MY CARD. IS THERE ANYTHING ELSE?
EILEEN RANGER
SOUNDHOME REAL ESTATE
YEAH, THEY EACH OWE TWO BUCKS TO THE SWEAR JAR, SO YOU CAN JUST DEDUCT THAT FROM THE TOTAL.

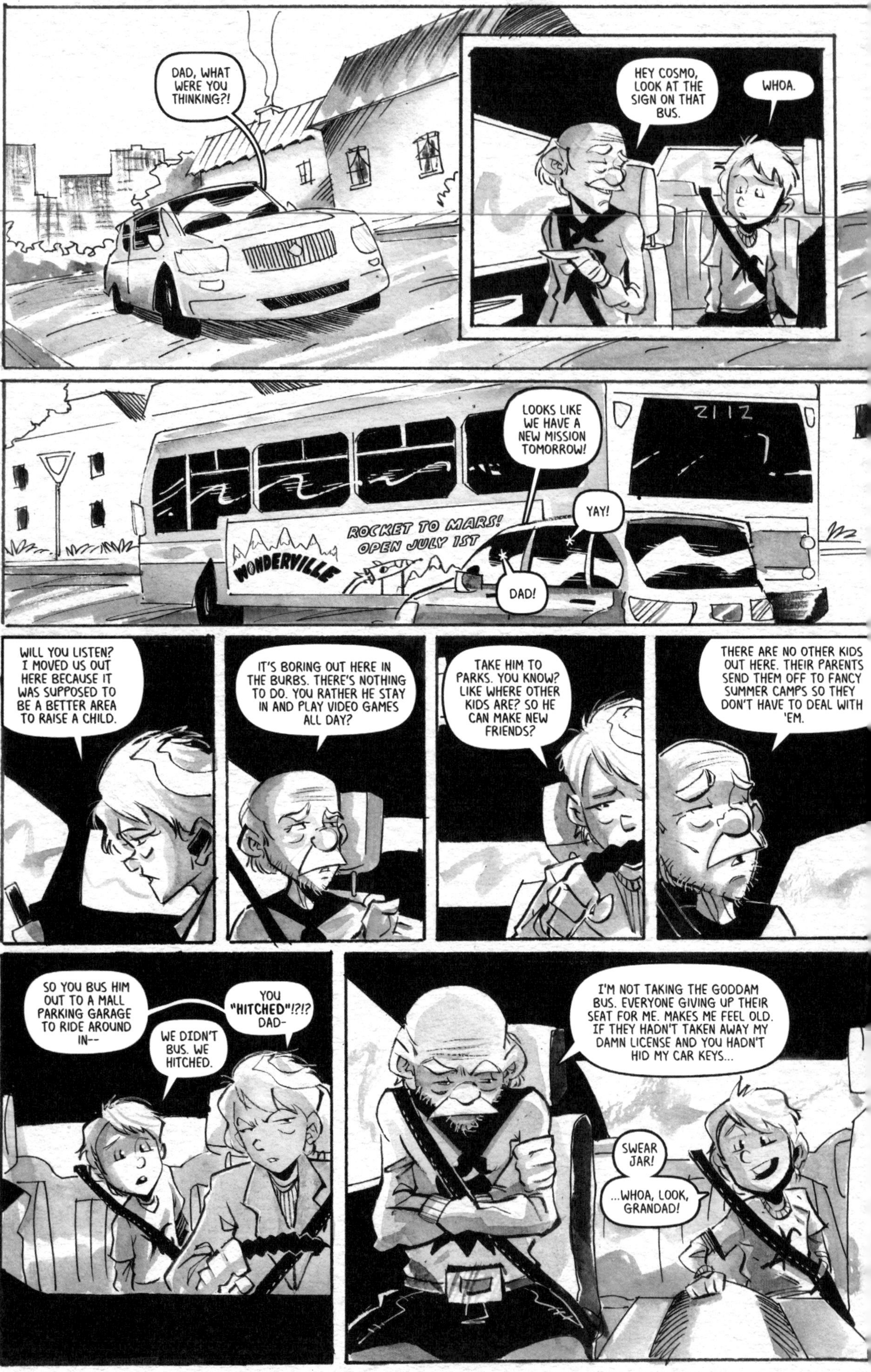
DAD, WHAT WERE YOU THINKING?!
HEY COSMO, LOOK AT THE SIGN ON THAT BUS.
WHOA.
LOOKS LIKE WE HAVE A NEW MISSION TOMORROW!
2112
ROCKET TO MARS! OPEN JULY 1ST
WONDERVILLE
YAY!
DAD!
WILL YOU LISTEN? I MOVED US OUT HERE BECAUSE IT WAS SUPPOSED TO BE A BETTER AREA TO RAISE A CHILD.
IT'S BORING OUT HERE IN THE BURBS. THERE'S NOTHING TO DO. YOU RATHER HE STAY IN AND PLAY VIDEO GAMES ALL DAY?
TAKE HIM TO PARKS. YOU KNOW? LIKE WHERE OTHER KIDS ARE? SO HE CAN MAKE NEW FRIENDS?
THERE ARE NO OTHER KIDS OUT HERE. THEIR PARENTS SEND THEM OFF TO FANCY SUMMER CAMPS SO THEY DON'T HAVE TO DEAL WITH 'EM.
SO YOU BUS HIM OUT TO A MALL PARKING GARAGE TO RIDE AROUND IN--
WE DIDN'T BUS. WE HITCHED.
YOU "HITCHED"!?!? DAD-
I'M NOT TAKING THE GODDAM BUS. EVERYONE GIVING UP THEIR SEAT FOR ME. MAKES ME FEEL OLD. IF THEY HADN'T TAKEN AWAY MY DAMN LICENSE AND YOU HADN'T HID MY CAR KEYS...
SWEAR JAR!
...WHOA, LOOK, GRANDAD!

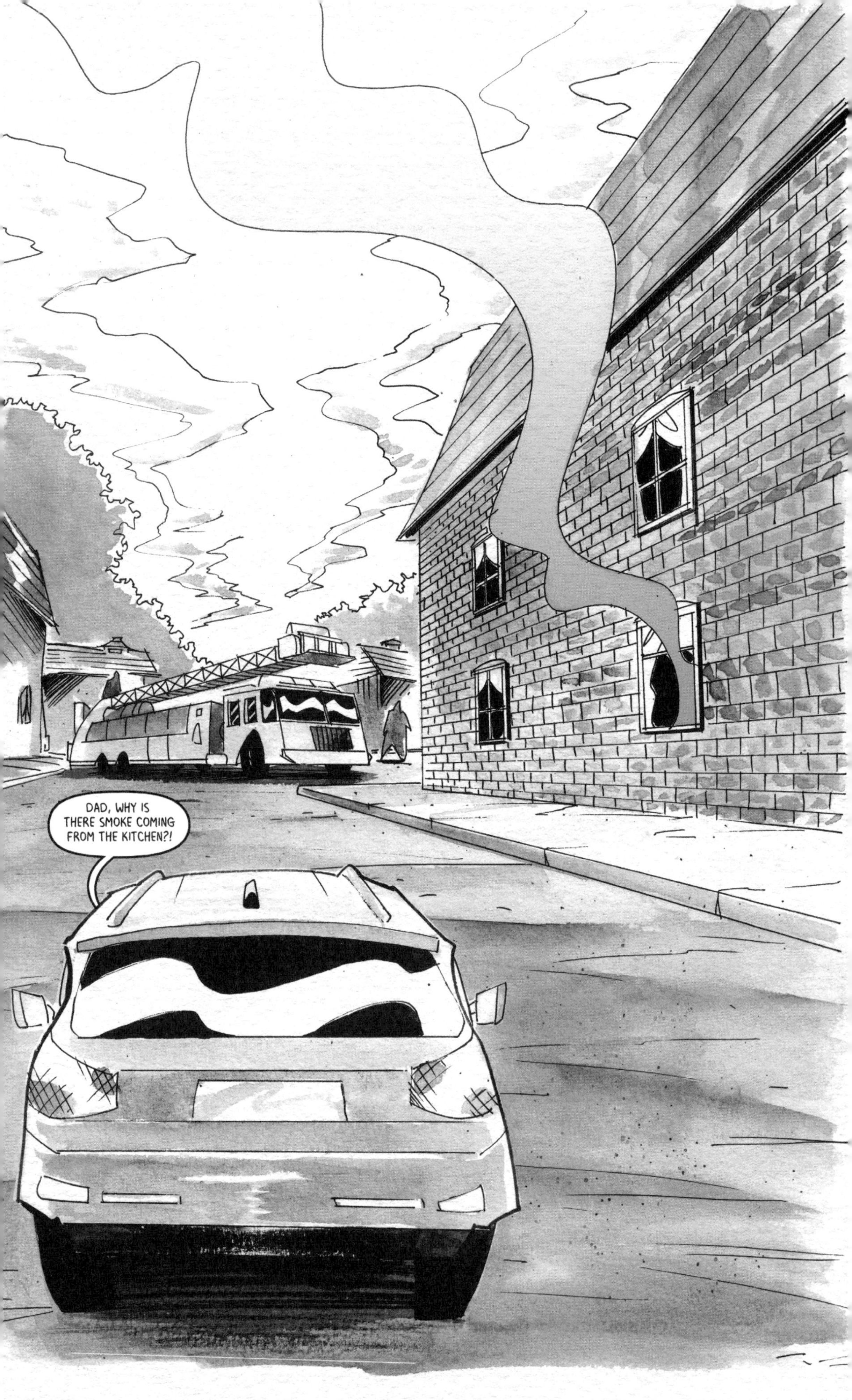
DAD, WHY IS THERE SMOKE COMING FROM THE KITCHEN?!

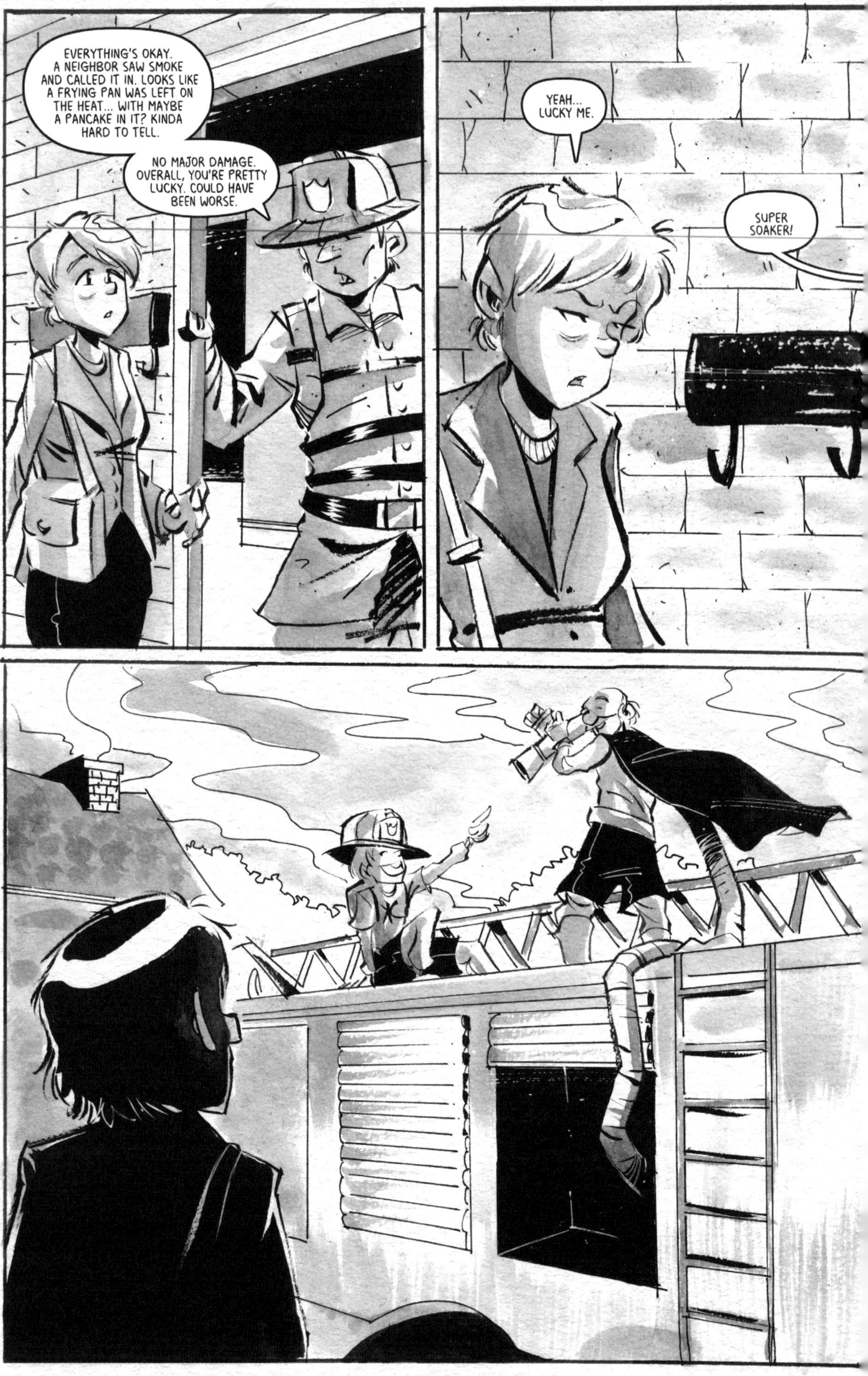
EVERYTHING'S OKAY. A NEIGHBOR SAW SMOKE AND CALLED IT IN. LOOKS LIKE A FRYING PAN WAS LEFT ON THE HEAT... WITH MAYBE A PANCAKE IN IT? KINDA HARD TO TELL.
NO MAJOR DAMAGE. OVERALL, YOU'RE PRETTY LUCKY. COULD HAVE BEEN WORSE.
YEAH... LUCKY ME.
SUPER SOAKER!

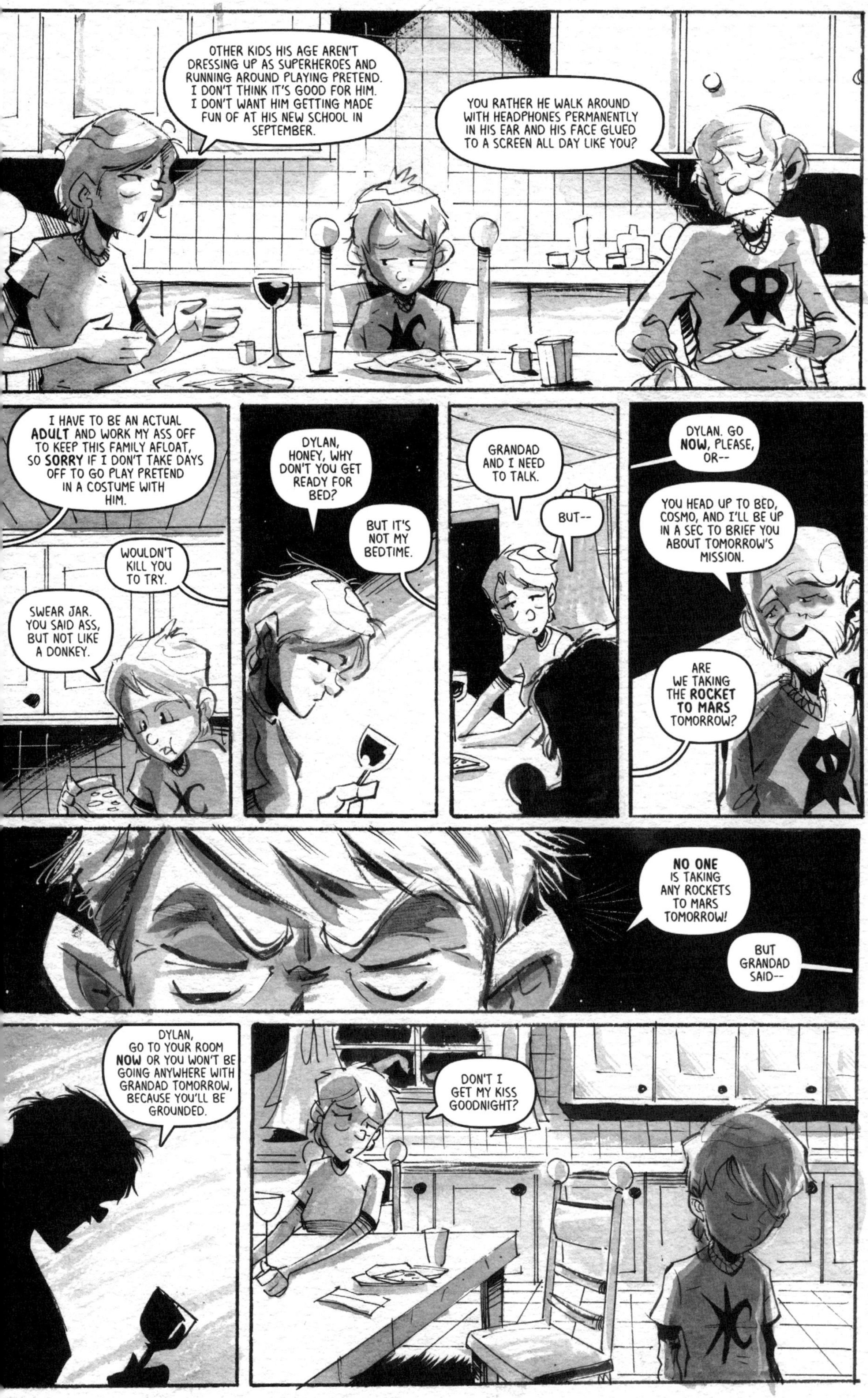
OTHER KIDS HIS AGE AREN'T DRESSING UP AS SUPERHEROES AND RUNNING AROUND PLAYING PRETEND. I DON'T THINK IT'S GOOD FOR HIM. I DON'T WANT HIM GETTING MADE FUN OF AT HIS NEW SCHOOL IN SEPTEMBER.
YOU RATHER HE WALK AROUND WITH HEADPHONES PERMANENTLY IN HIS EAR AND HIS FACE GLUED TO A SCREEN ALL DAY LIKE YOU?
I HAVE TO BE AN ACTUAL **ADULT** AND WORK MY ASS OFF TO KEEP THIS FAMILY AFLOAT, SO **SORRY** IF I DON'T TAKE DAYS OFF TO GO PLAY PRETEND IN A COSTUME WITH HIM.
WOULDN'T KILL YOU TO TRY.
SWEAR JAR. YOU SAID ASS, BUT NOT LIKE A DONKEY.
DYLAN, HONEY, WHY DON'T YOU GET READY FOR BED?
BUT IT'S NOT MY BEDTIME.
GRANDAD AND I NEED TO TALK.
BUT--
DYLAN. GO **NOW**, PLEASE, OR--
YOU HEAD UP TO BED, COSMO, AND I'LL BE UP IN A SEC TO BRIEF YOU ABOUT TOMORROW'S MISSION.
ARE WE TAKING THE **ROCKET TO MARS** TOMORROW?
NO ONE IS TAKING ANY ROCKETS TO MARS TOMORROW!
BUT GRANDAD SAID--
DYLAN, GO TO YOUR ROOM **NOW** OR YOU WON'T BE GOING ANYWHERE WITH GRANDAD TOMORROW, BECAUSE YOU'LL BE GROUNDED.
DON'T I GET MY KISS GOODNIGHT?

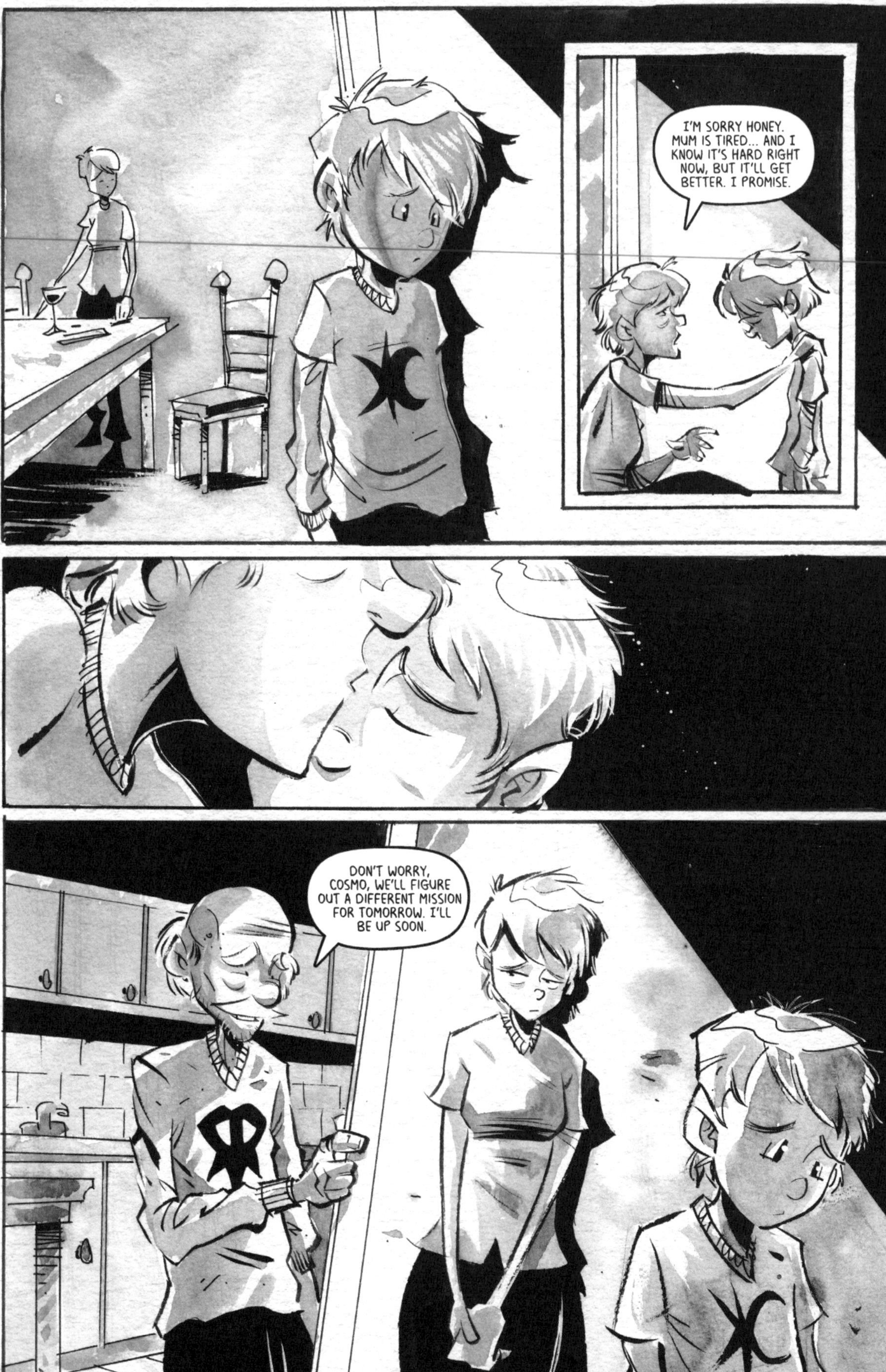
I'M SORRY HONEY. MUM IS TIRED... AND I KNOW IT'S HARD RIGHT NOW, BUT IT'LL GET BETTER. I PROMISE.
DON'T WORRY, COSMO, WE'LL FIGURE OUT A DIFFERENT MISSION FOR TOMORROW. I'LL BE UP SOON.

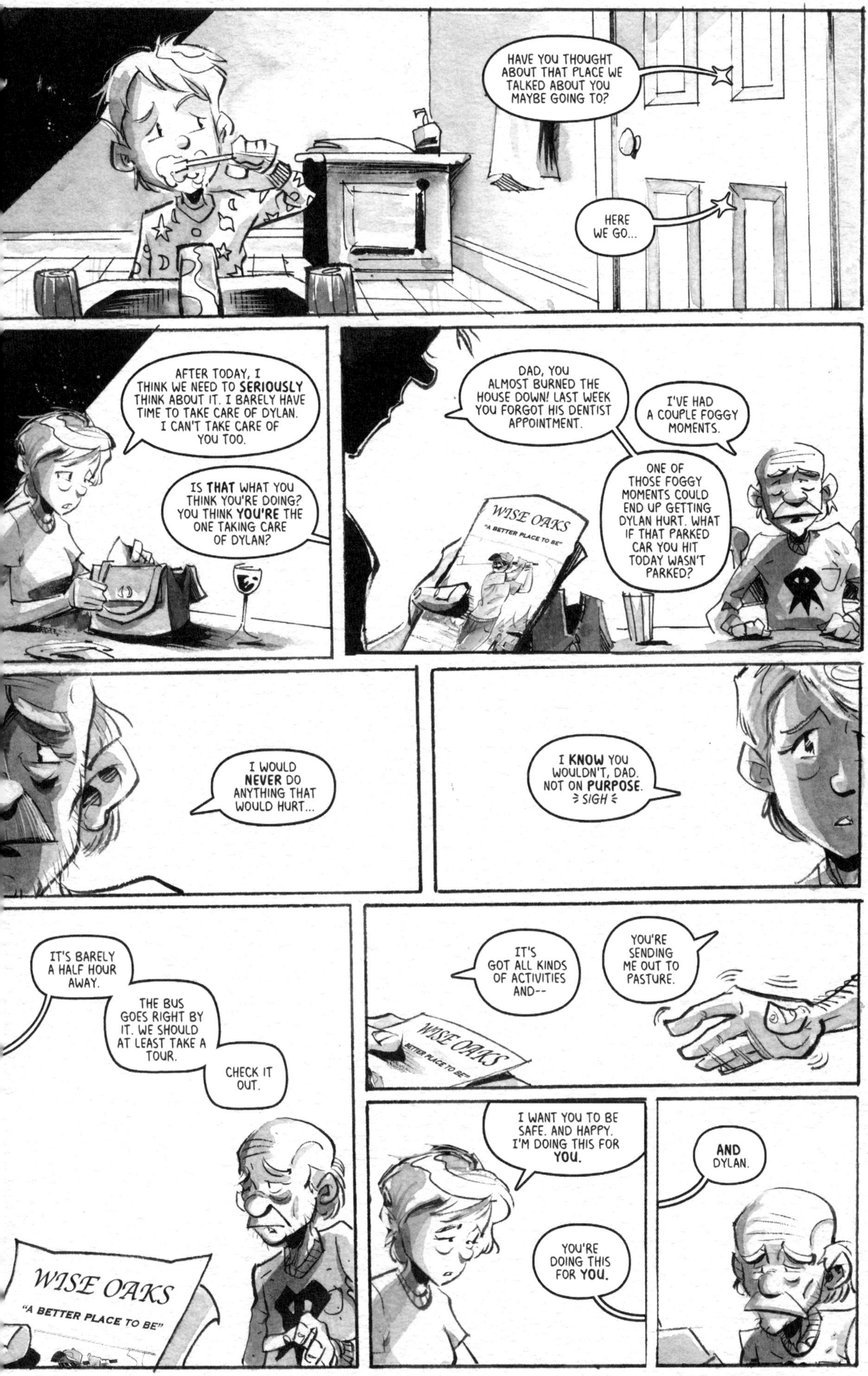

HAVE YOU THOUGHT ABOUT THAT PLACE WE TALKED ABOUT YOU MAYBE GOING TO?
HERE WE GO...
AFTER TODAY, I THINK WE NEED TO **SERIOUSLY** THINK ABOUT IT. I BARELY HAVE TIME TO TAKE CARE OF DYLAN. I CAN'T TAKE CARE OF YOU TOO.
IS **THAT** WHAT YOU THINK YOU'RE DOING? YOU THINK **YOU'RE** THE ONE TAKING CARE OF DYLAN?
DAD, YOU ALMOST BURNED THE HOUSE DOWN! LAST WEEK YOU FORGOT HIS DENTIST APPOINTMENT.
I'VE HAD A COUPLE FOGGY MOMENTS.
ONE OF THOSE FOGGY MOMENTS COULD END UP GETTING DYLAN HURT. WHAT IF THAT PARKED CAR YOU HIT TODAY WASN'T PARKED?
WISE OAKS
"A BETTER PLACE TO BE"
I WOULD **NEVER** DO ANYTHING THAT WOULD HURT...
I **KNOW** YOU WOULDN'T, DAD. NOT ON **PURPOSE**. *SIGH*
IT'S BARELY A HALF HOUR AWAY.
THE BUS GOES RIGHT BY IT. WE SHOULD AT LEAST TAKE A TOUR.
CHECK IT OUT.
WISE OAKS
"A BETTER PLACE TO BE"
IT'S GOT ALL KINDS OF ACTIVITIES AND--
YOU'RE SENDING ME OUT TO PASTURE.
WISE OAKS
BETTER PLACE TO BE"
I WANT YOU TO BE SAFE. AND HAPPY. I'M DOING THIS FOR **YOU.**
YOU'RE DOING THIS FOR **YOU.**
AND DYLAN.

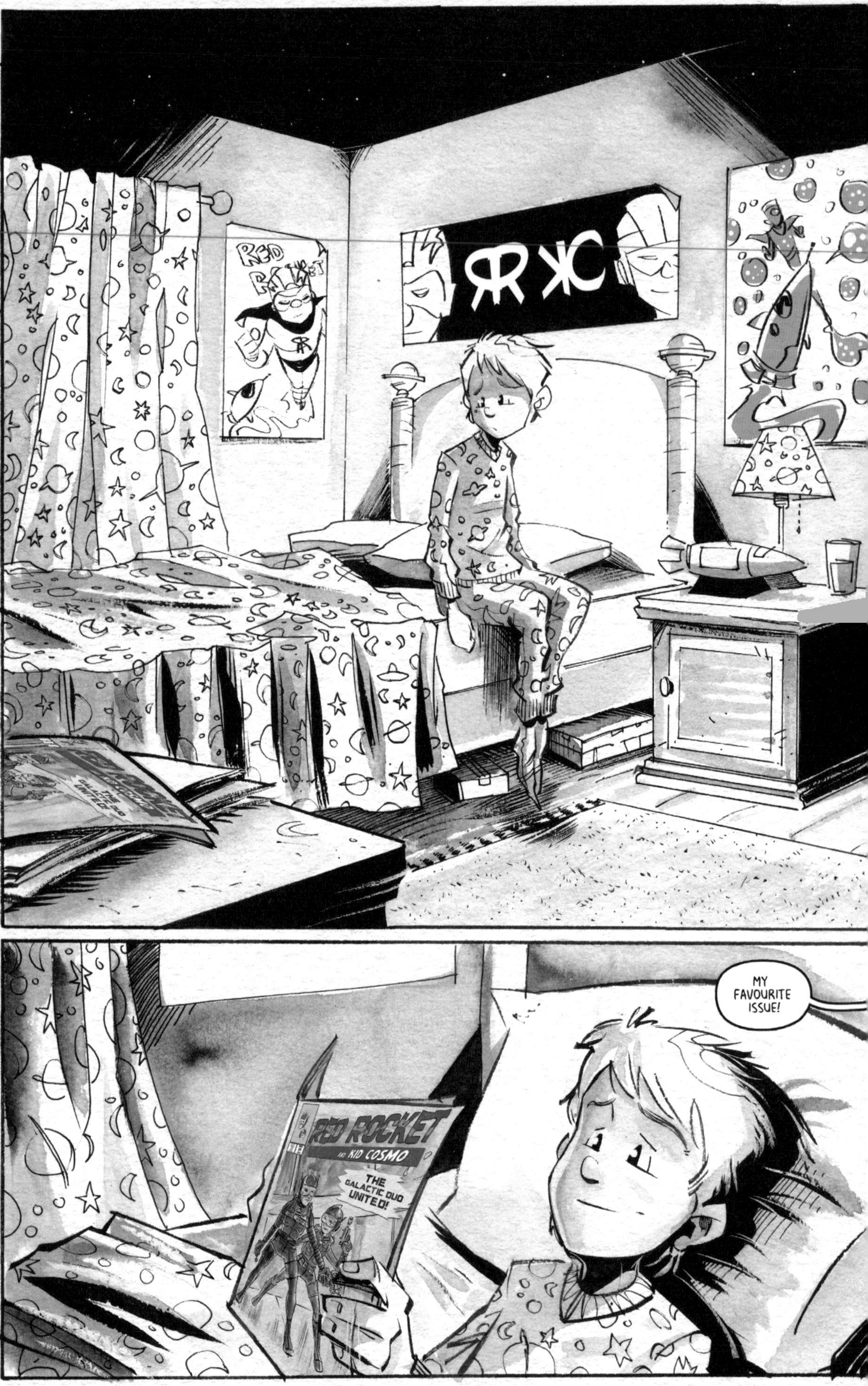
RED ROCKET
AND KID COSMO
THE GALACTIC DUO UNITED!
MY FAVOURITE ISSUE!

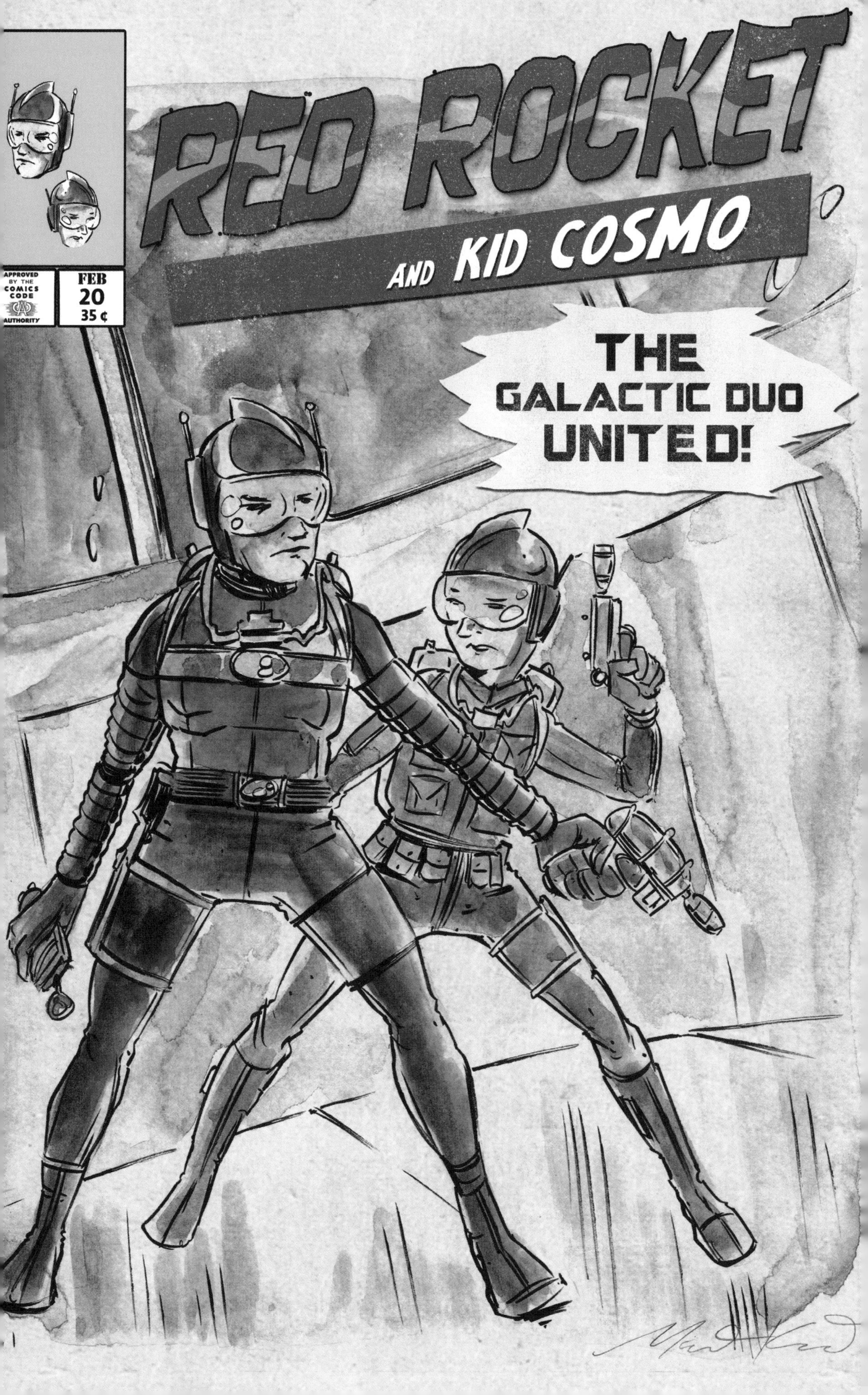

RED ROCKET
AND KID COSMO
APPROVED BY THE COMICS CODE AUTHORITY
FEB
20
35¢
THE GALACTIC DUO UNITED!

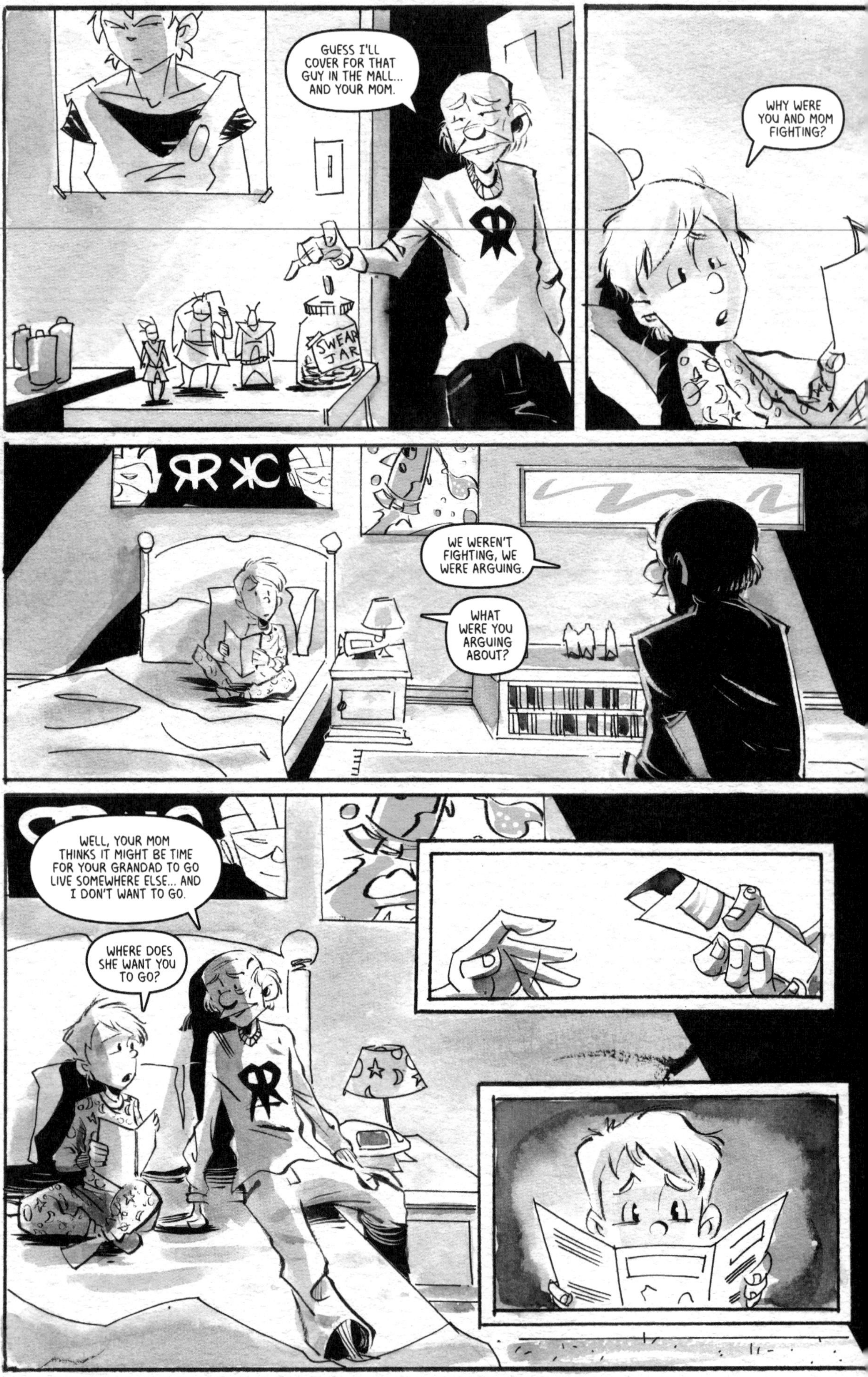
GUESS I'LL COVER FOR THAT GUY IN THE MALL... AND YOUR MOM.
SWEAR JAR
WHY WERE YOU AND MOM FIGHTING?
WE WEREN'T FIGHTING, WE WERE ARGUING.
WHAT WERE YOU ARGUING ABOUT?
WELL, YOUR MOM THINKS IT MIGHT BE TIME FOR YOUR GRANDAD TO GO LIVE SOMEWHERE ELSE... AND I DON'T WANT TO GO.
WHERE DOES SHE WANT YOU TO GO?

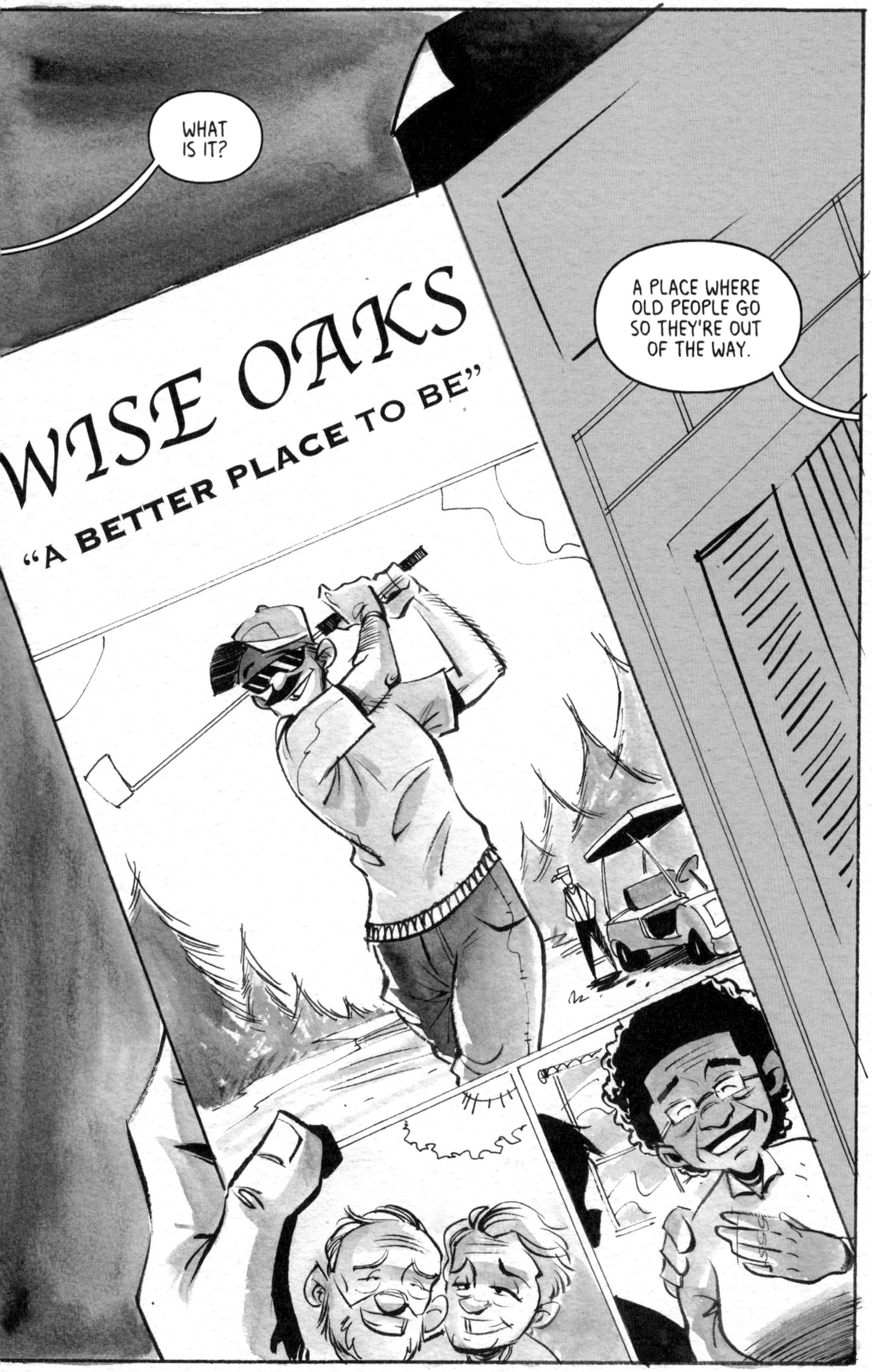
WHAT IS IT?
WISE OAKS
"A BETTER PLACE TO BE"
A PLACE WHERE OLD PEOPLE GO SO THEY'RE OUT OF THE WAY.

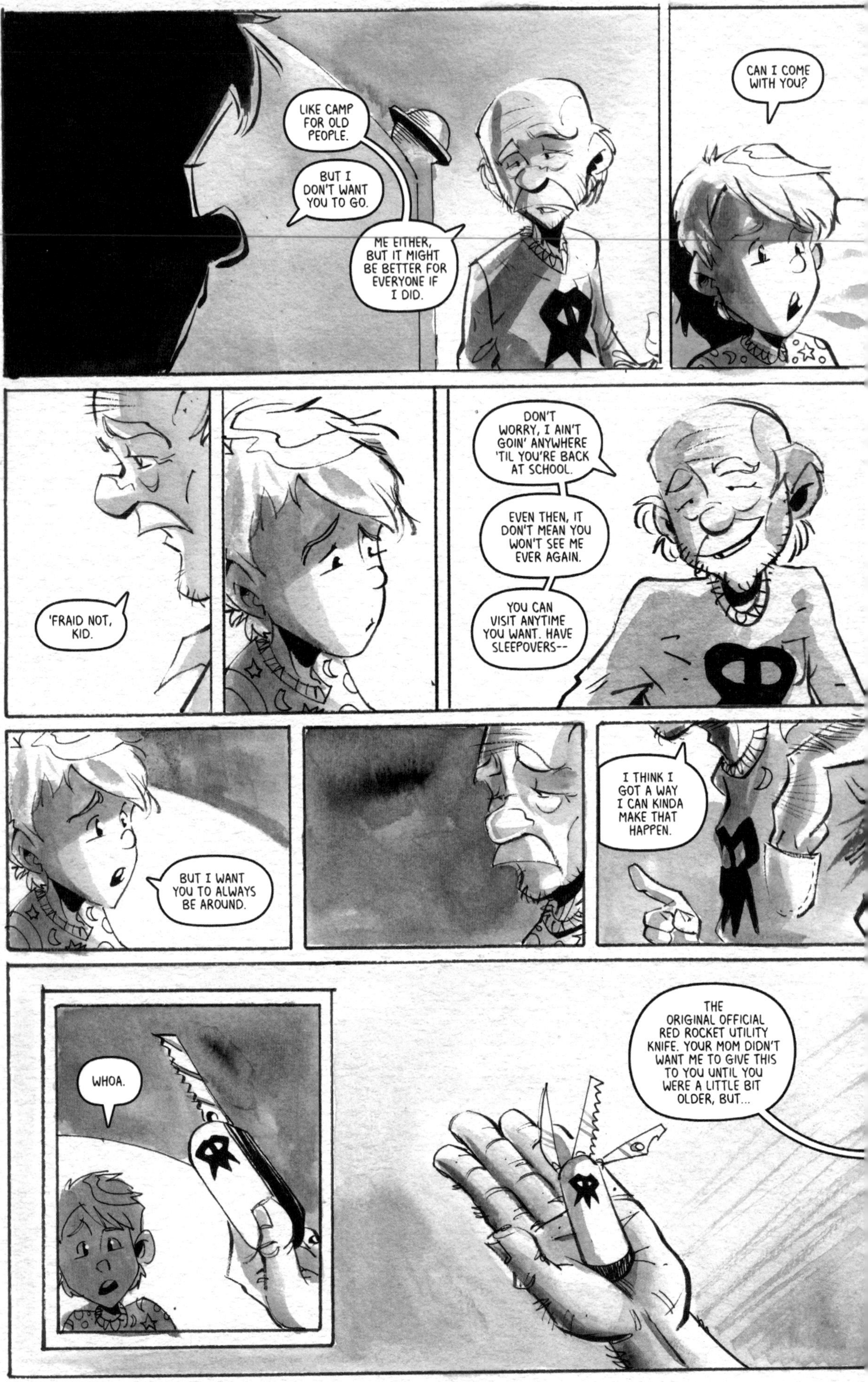

LIKE CAMP FOR OLD PEOPLE.
BUT I DON'T WANT YOU TO GO.
ME EITHER, BUT IT MIGHT BE BETTER FOR EVERYONE IF I DID.
CAN I COME WITH YOU?
'FRAID NOT, KID.
DON'T WORRY, I AIN'T GOIN' ANYWHERE 'TIL YOU'RE BACK AT SCHOOL.
EVEN THEN, IT DON'T MEAN YOU WON'T SEE ME EVER AGAIN.
YOU CAN VISIT ANYTIME YOU WANT. HAVE SLEEPOVERS--
BUT I WANT YOU TO ALWAYS BE AROUND.
I THINK I GOT A WAY I CAN KINDA MAKE THAT HAPPEN.
THE ORIGINAL OFFICIAL RED ROCKET UTILITY KNIFE. YOUR MOM DIDN'T WANT ME TO GIVE THIS TO YOU UNTIL YOU WERE A LITTLE BIT OLDER, BUT...
WHOA.

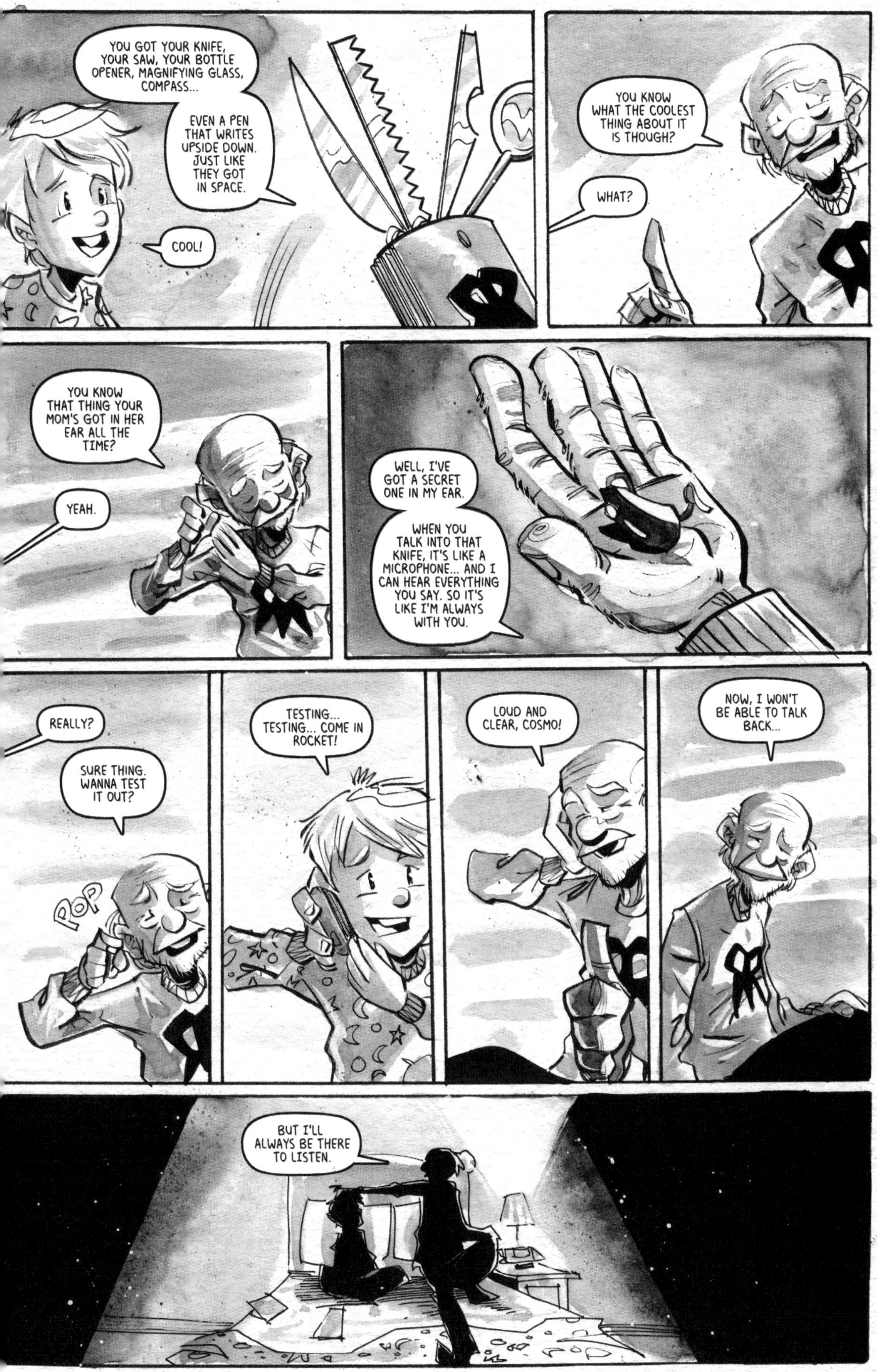
YOU GOT YOUR KNIFE, YOUR SAW, YOUR BOTTLE OPENER, MAGNIFYING GLASS, COMPASS...
EVEN A PEN THAT WRITES UPSIDE DOWN. JUST LIKE THEY GOT IN SPACE.
COOL!
YOU KNOW WHAT THE COOLEST THING ABOUT IT IS THOUGH?
WHAT?
YOU KNOW THAT THING YOUR MOM'S GOT IN HER EAR ALL THE TIME?
YEAH.
WELL, I'VE GOT A SECRET ONE IN MY EAR.
WHEN YOU TALK INTO THAT KNIFE, IT'S LIKE A MICROPHONE... AND I CAN HEAR EVERYTHING YOU SAY. SO IT'S LIKE I'M ALWAYS WITH YOU.
REALLY?
SURE THING. WANNA TEST IT OUT?
POP
TESTING... TESTING... COME IN ROCKET!
LOUD AND CLEAR, COSMO!
NOW, I WON'T BE ABLE TO TALK BACK...
BUT I'LL ALWAYS BE THERE TO LISTEN.

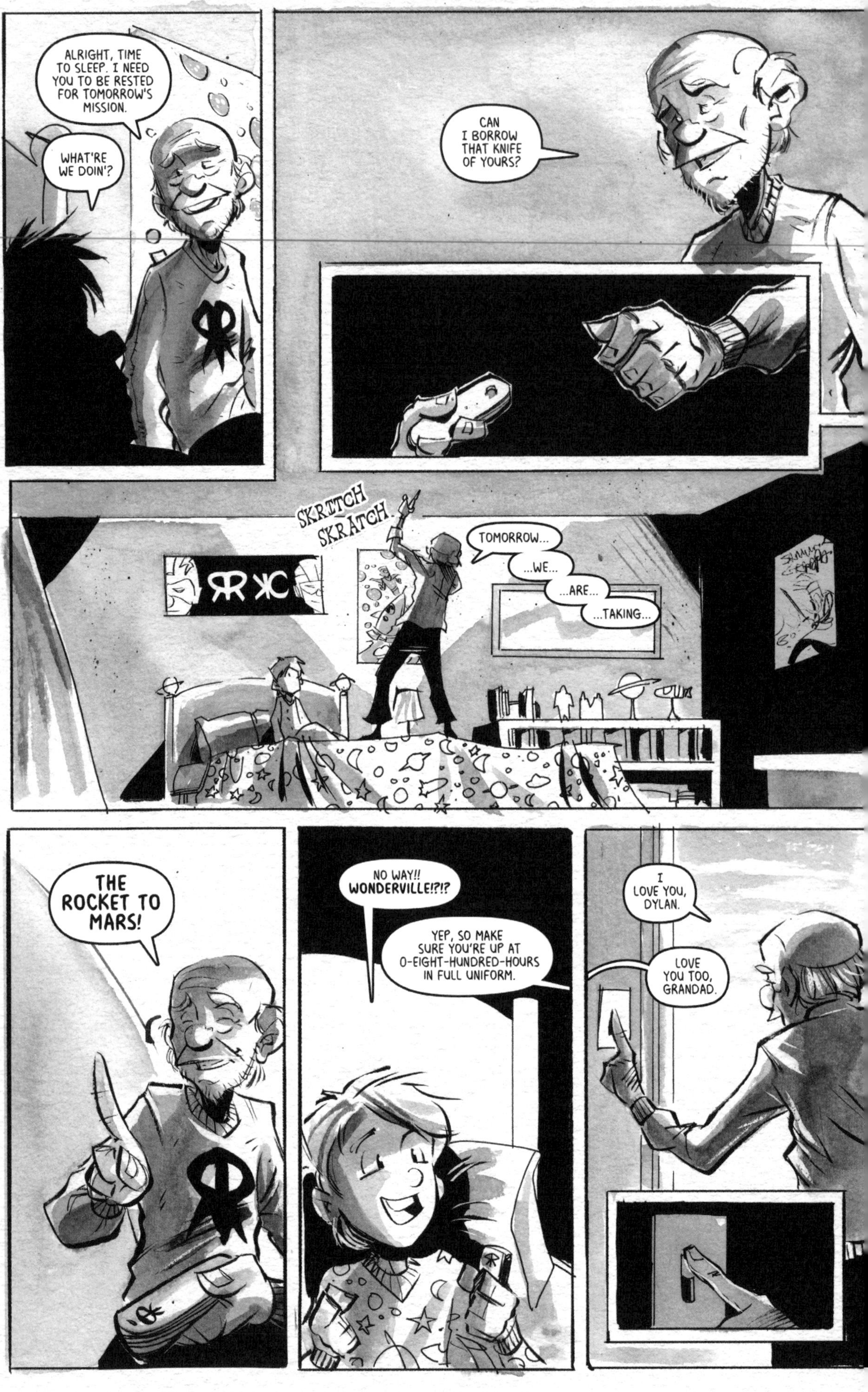

ALRIGHT, TIME TO SLEEP. I NEED YOU TO BE RESTED FOR TOMORROW'S MISSION.
WHAT'RE WE DOIN'?
CAN I BORROW THAT KNIFE OF YOURS?
SKRITCH SKRATCH
TOMORROW...
...WE...
...ARE...
...TAKING...
RR KC
THE ROCKET TO MARS!
NO WAY!! **WONDERVILLE!?!?**
YEP, SO MAKE SURE YOU'RE UP AT O-EIGHT-HUNDRED-HOURS IN FULL UNIFORM.
I LOVE YOU, DYLAN.
LOVE YOU TOO, GRANDAD.

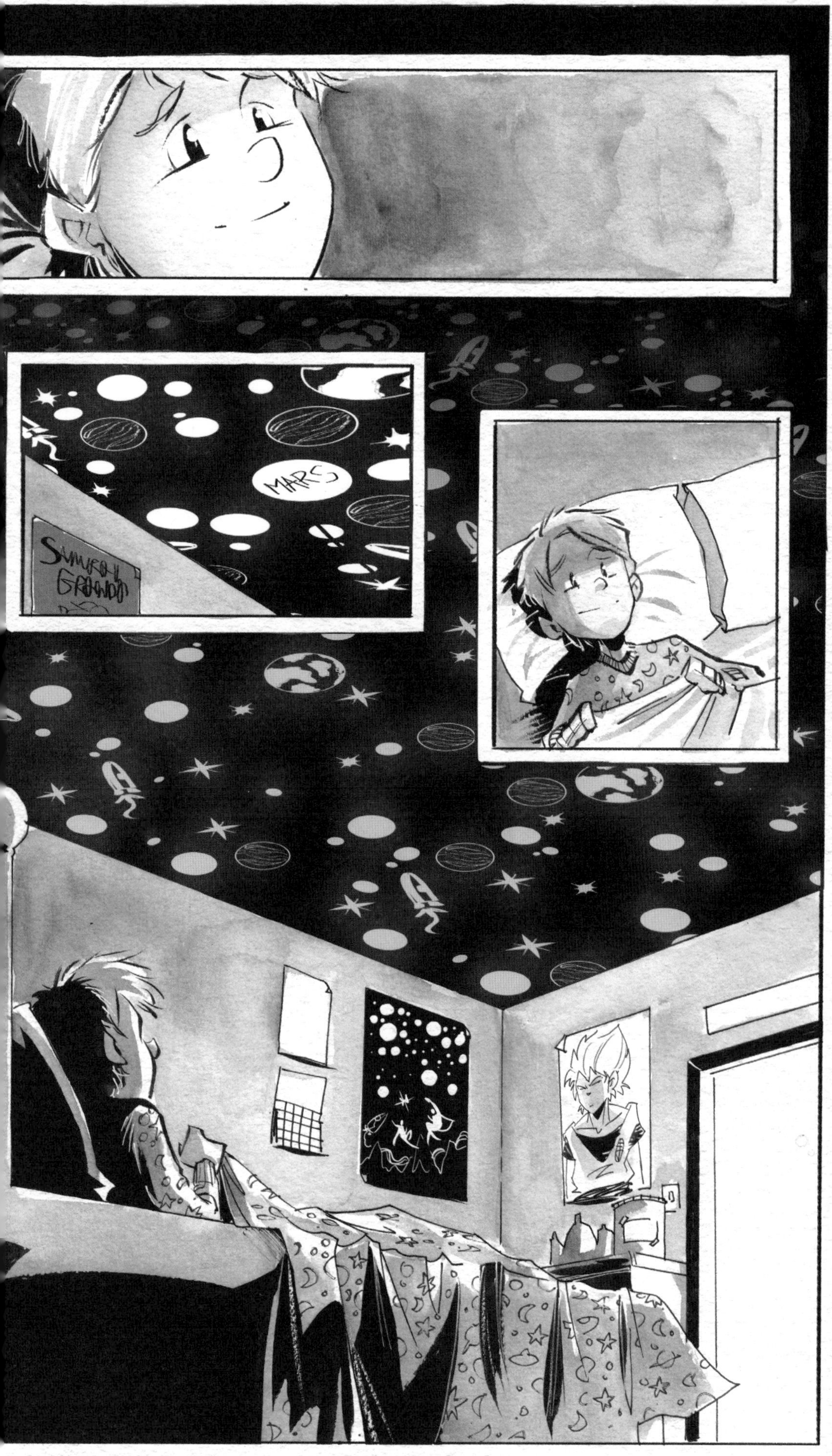
MARS

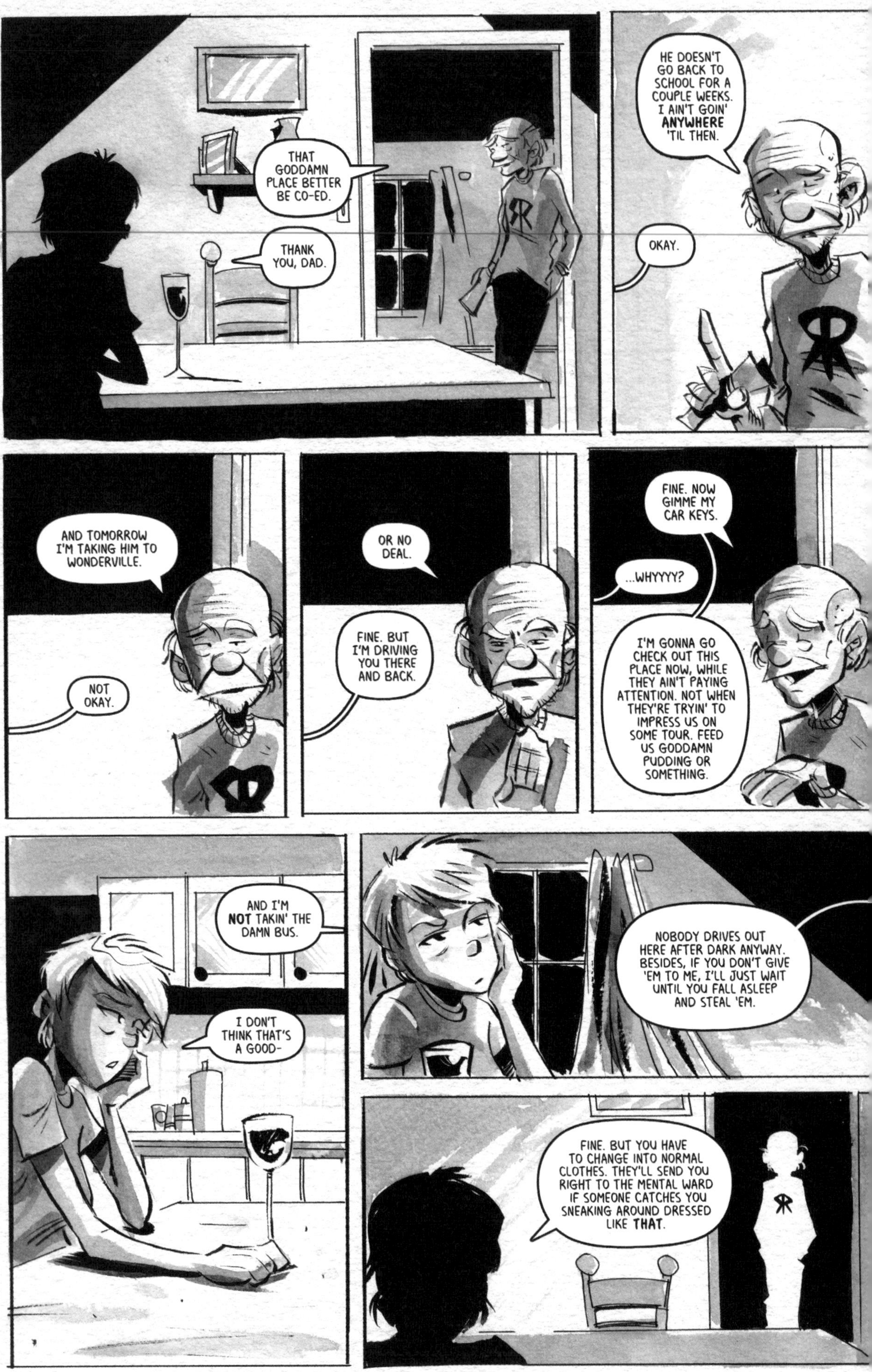
THAT GODDAMN PLACE BETTER BE CO-ED.
THANK YOU, DAD.
HE DOESN'T GO BACK TO SCHOOL FOR A COUPLE WEEKS. I AIN'T GOIN' **ANYWHERE** 'TIL THEN.
OKAY.
AND TOMORROW I'M TAKING HIM TO WONDERVILLE.
NOT OKAY.
OR NO DEAL.
FINE. BUT I'M DRIVING YOU THERE AND BACK.
FINE. NOW GIMME MY CAR KEYS.
...WHYYYY?
I'M GONNA GO CHECK OUT THIS PLACE NOW, WHILE THEY AIN'T PAYING ATTENTION. NOT WHEN THEY'RE TRYIN' TO IMPRESS US ON SOME TOUR. FEED US GODDAMN PUDDING OR SOMETHING.
AND I'M **NOT** TAKIN' THE DAMN BUS.
I DON'T THINK THAT'S A GOOD-
NOBODY DRIVES OUT HERE AFTER DARK ANYWAY. BESIDES, IF YOU DON'T GIVE 'EM TO ME, I'LL JUST WAIT UNTIL YOU FALL ASLEEP AND STEAL 'EM.
FINE. BUT YOU HAVE TO CHANGE INTO NORMAL CLOTHES. THEY'LL SEND YOU RIGHT TO THE MENTAL WARD IF SOMEONE CATCHES YOU SNEAKING AROUND DRESSED LIKE **THAT**.

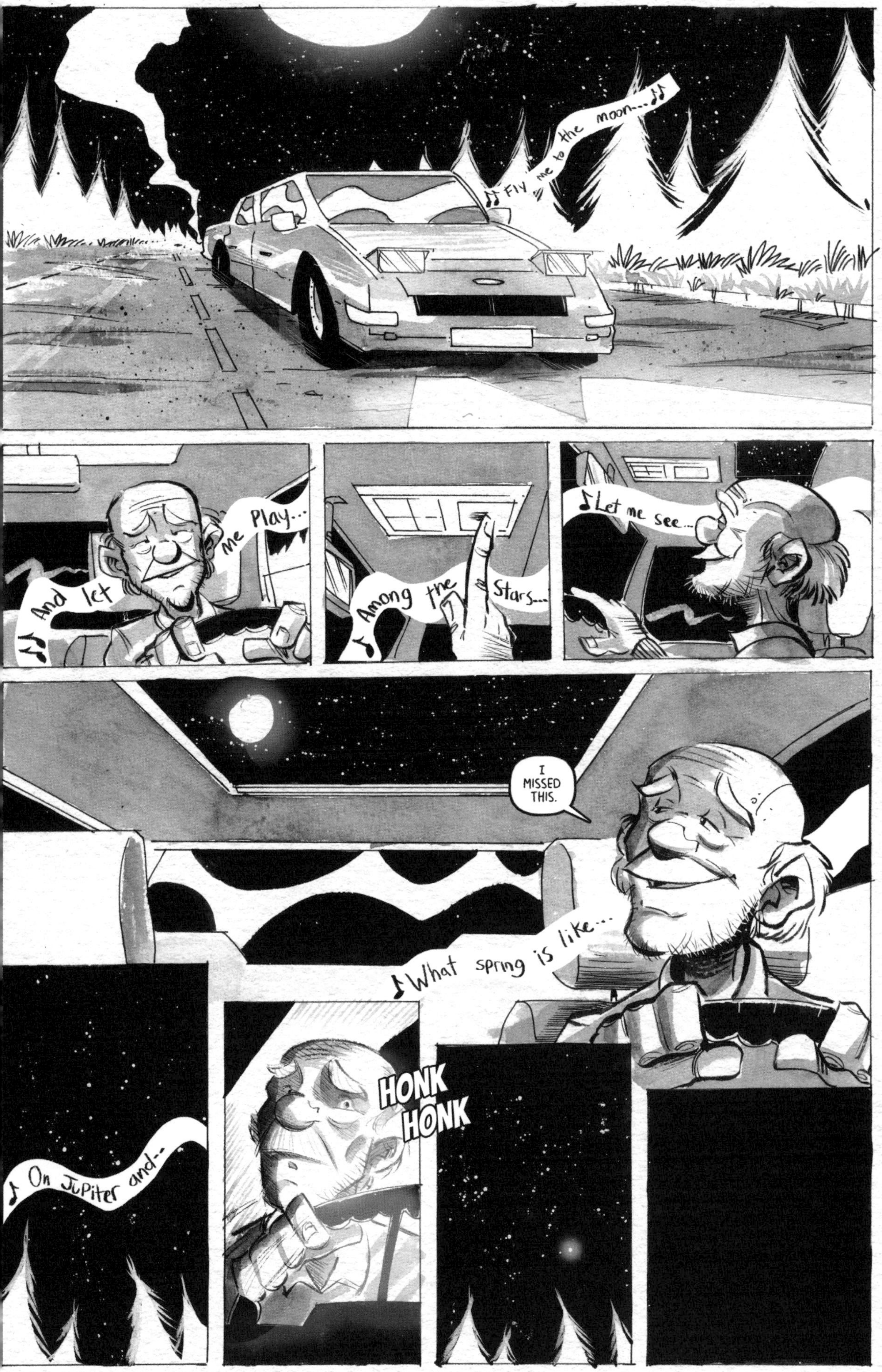
♫ Fly me to the moon... ♫
♫ And let me play...
♪ Among the stars...
♪ Let me see...
I MISSED THIS.
♪ What spring is like...
♪ On Jupiter and...
HONK HONK

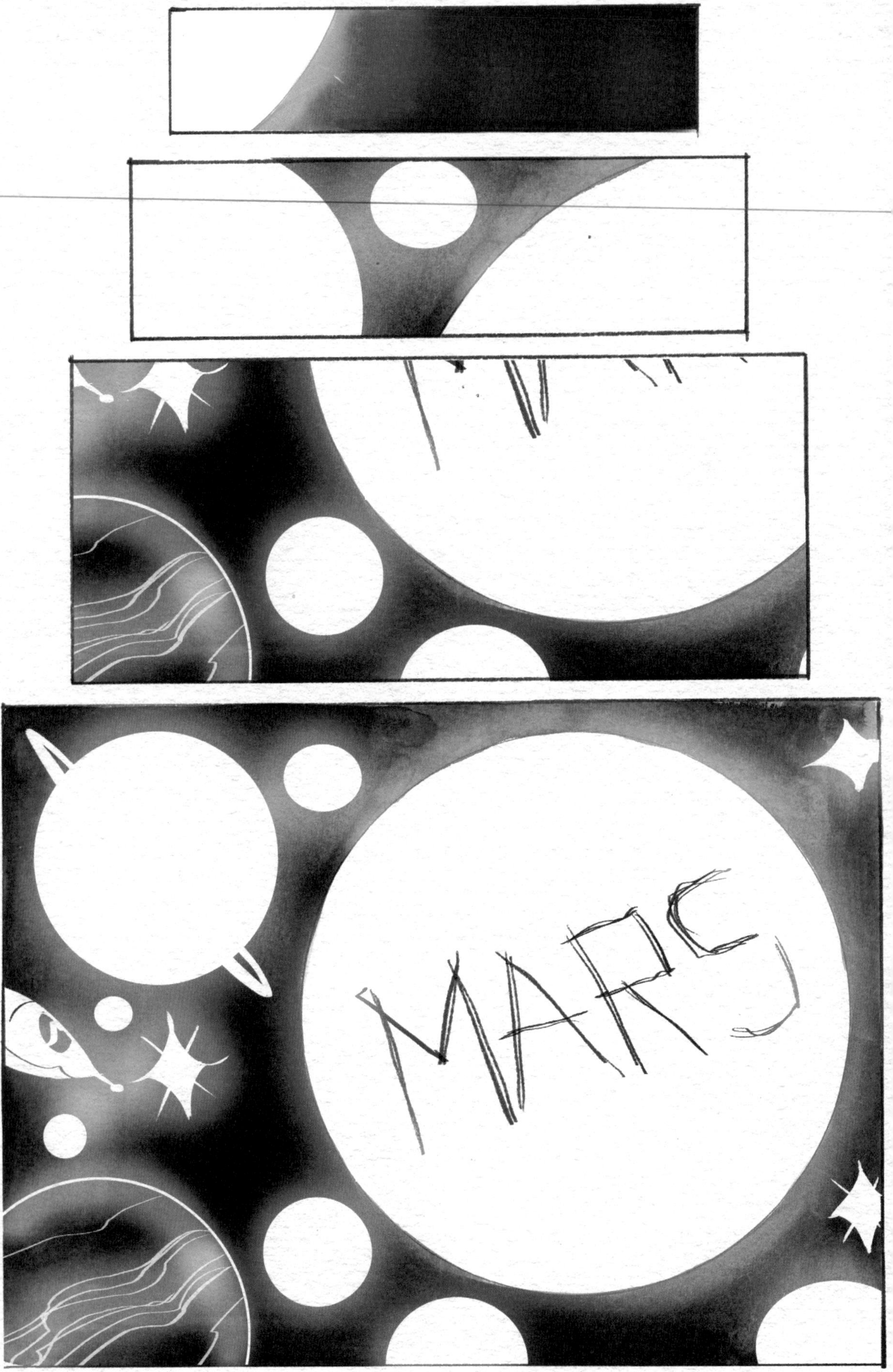
MARS

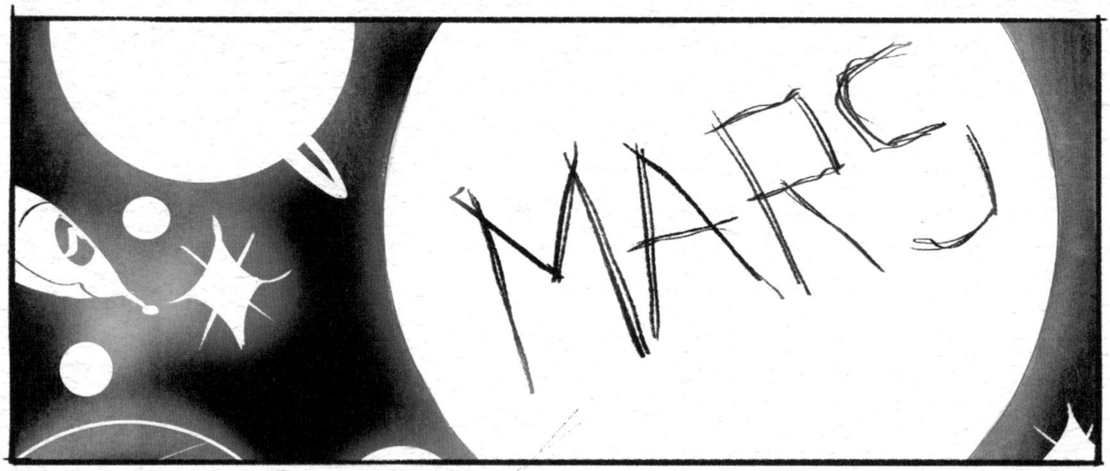
MARS
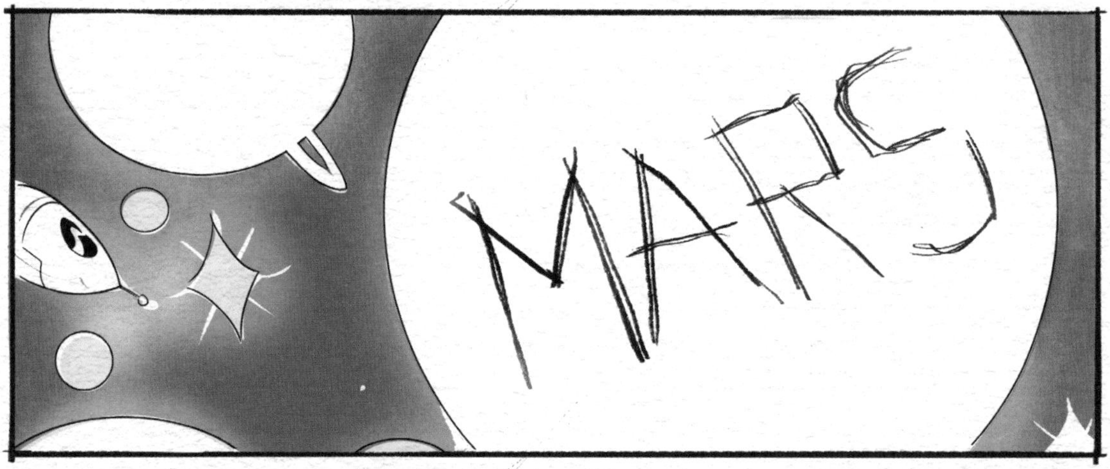
MARS
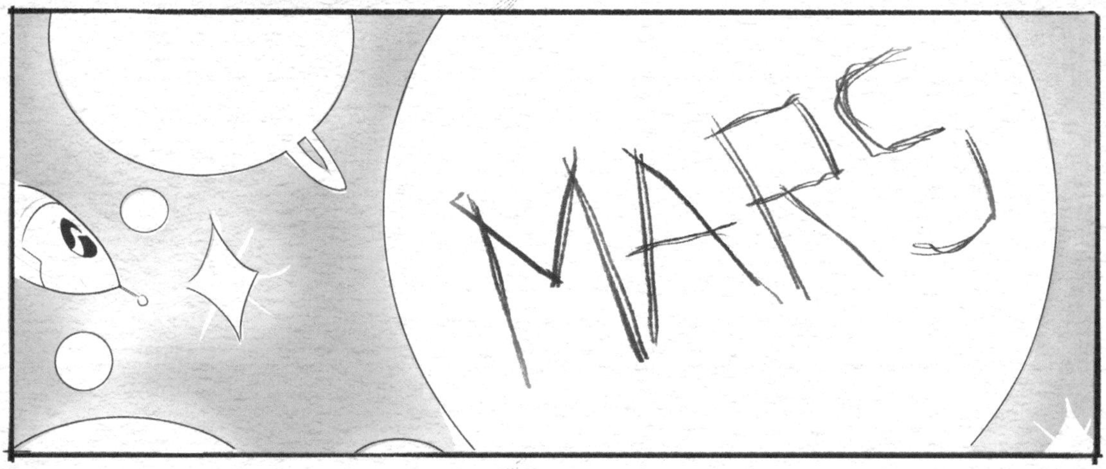
MARS
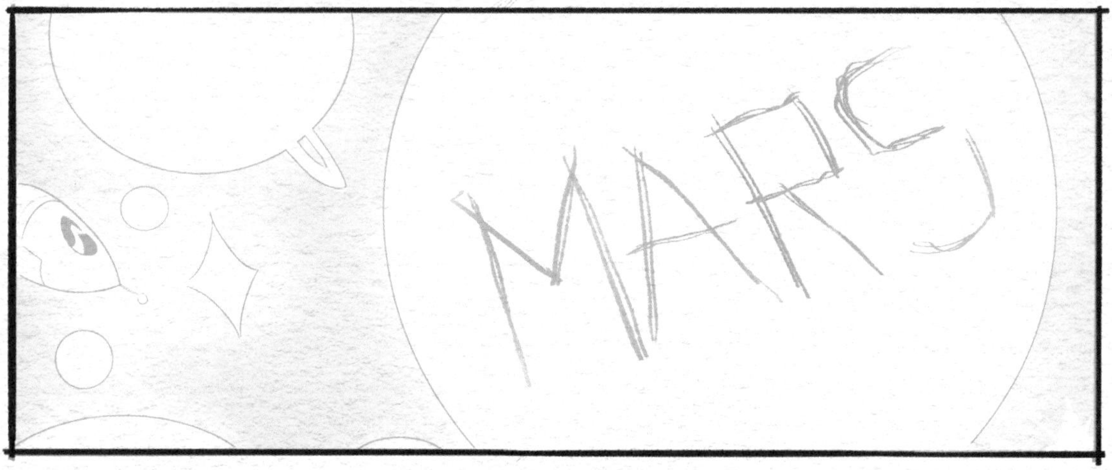
MARS

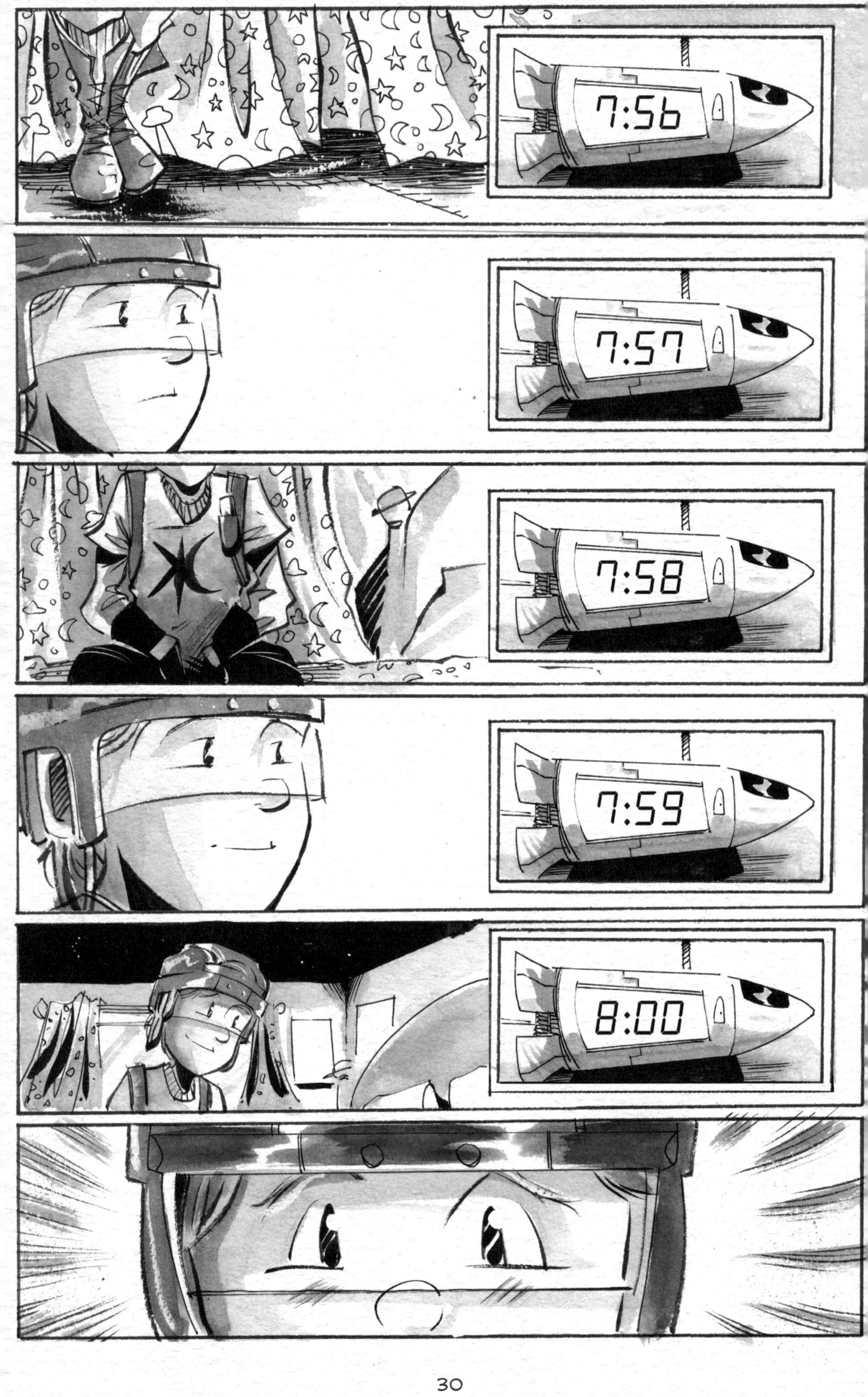
7:56
7:57
7:58
7:59
8:00

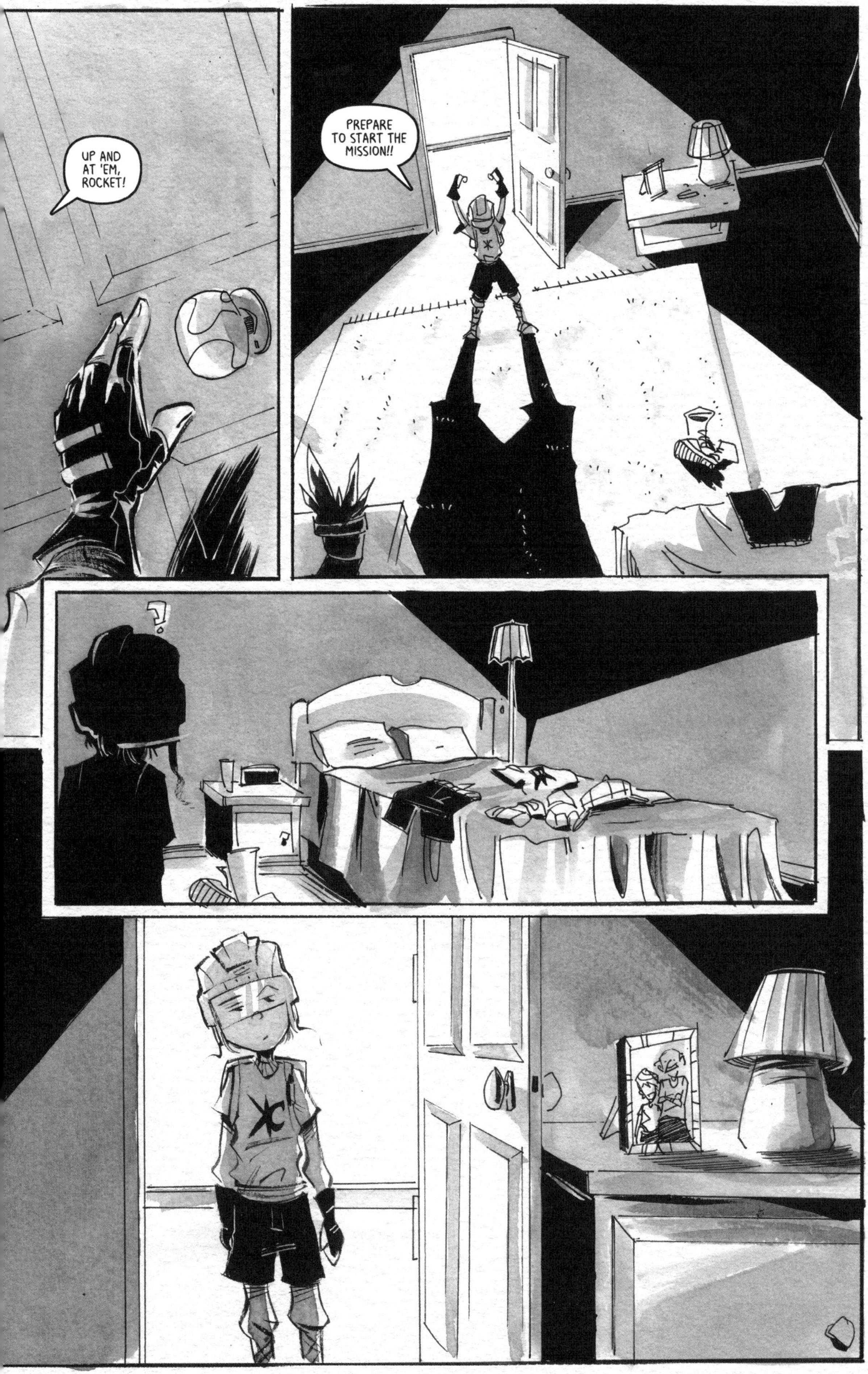
UP AND AT 'EM, ROCKET!
PREPARE TO START THE MISSION!!
?

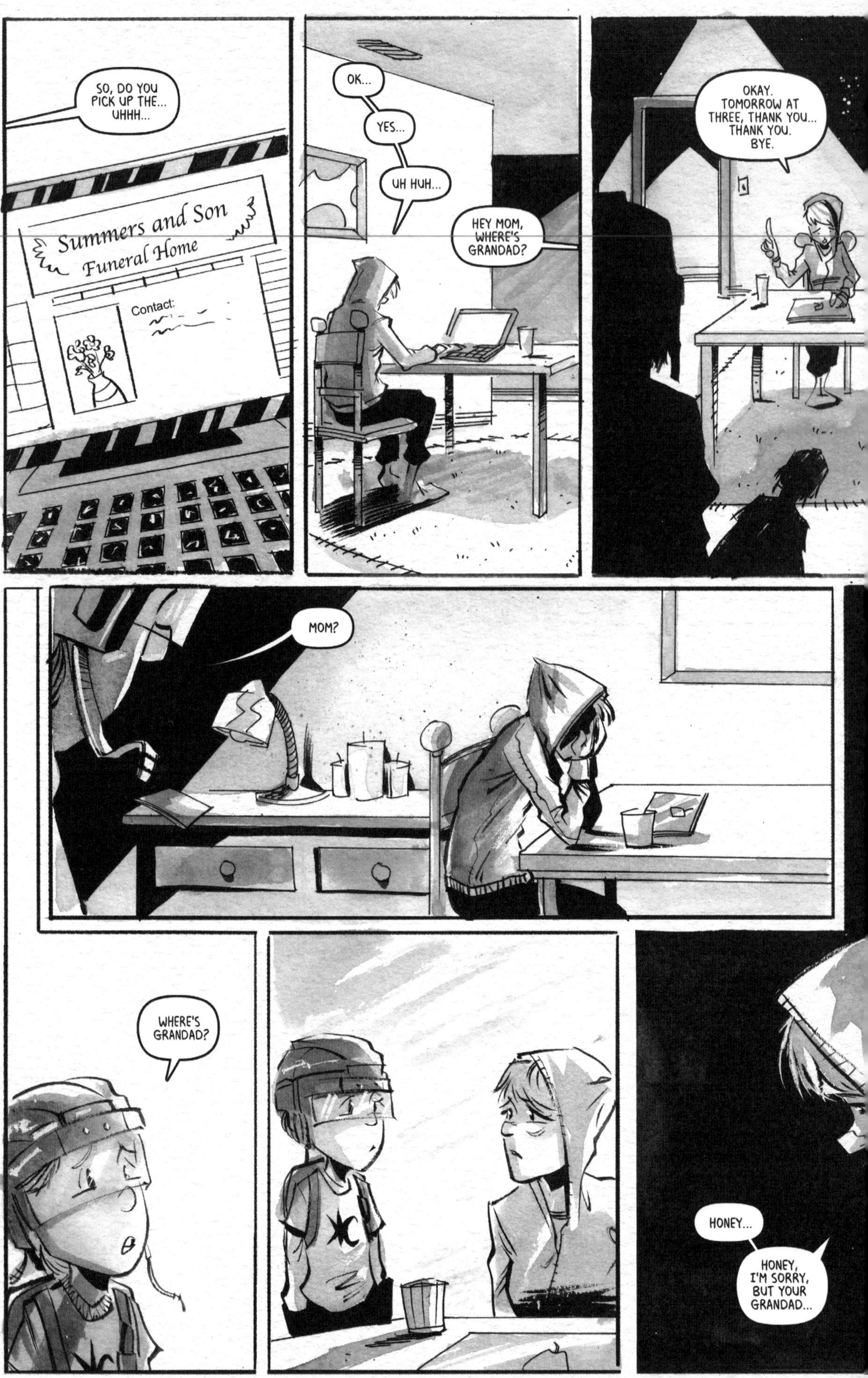
SO, DO YOU PICK UP THE... UHHH...
Summers and Son Funeral Home
Contact:
OK...
YES...
UH HUH...
HEY MOM, WHERE'S GRANDAD?
OKAY. TOMORROW AT THREE, THANK YOU... THANK YOU. BYE.
MOM?
WHERE'S GRANDAD?
HONEY...
HONEY, I'M SORRY, BUT YOUR GRANDAD...

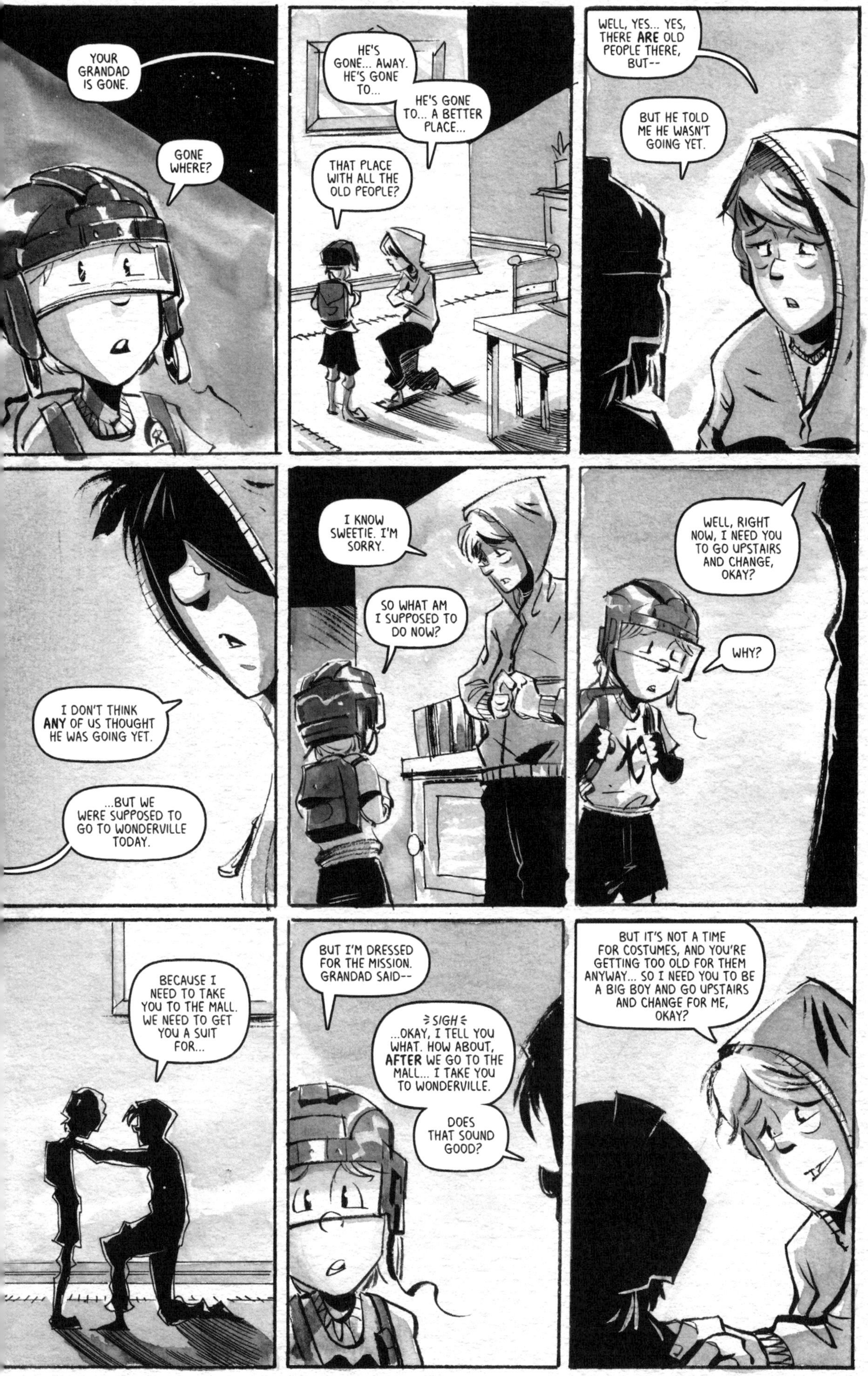
YOUR GRANDAD IS GONE.
GONE WHERE?
HE'S GONE... AWAY. HE'S GONE TO...
HE'S GONE TO... A BETTER PLACE...
THAT PLACE WITH ALL THE OLD PEOPLE?
WELL, YES... YES, THERE **ARE** OLD PEOPLE THERE, BUT--
BUT HE TOLD ME HE WASN'T GOING YET.
I DON'T THINK **ANY** OF US THOUGHT HE WAS GOING YET.
...BUT WE WERE SUPPOSED TO GO TO WONDERVILLE TODAY.
I KNOW SWEETIE. I'M SORRY.
SO WHAT AM I SUPPOSED TO DO NOW?
WELL, RIGHT NOW, I NEED YOU TO GO UPSTAIRS AND CHANGE, OKAY?
WHY?
BECAUSE I NEED TO TAKE YOU TO THE MALL. WE NEED TO GET YOU A SUIT FOR...
BUT I'M DRESSED FOR THE MISSION. GRANDAD SAID--
SIGH ...OKAY, I TELL YOU WHAT. HOW ABOUT, **AFTER** WE GO TO THE MALL... I TAKE YOU TO WONDERVILLE.
DOES THAT SOUND GOOD?
BUT IT'S NOT A TIME FOR COSTUMES, AND YOU'RE GETTING TOO OLD FOR THEM ANYWAY... SO I NEED YOU TO BE A BIG BOY AND GO UPSTAIRS AND CHANGE FOR ME, OKAY?

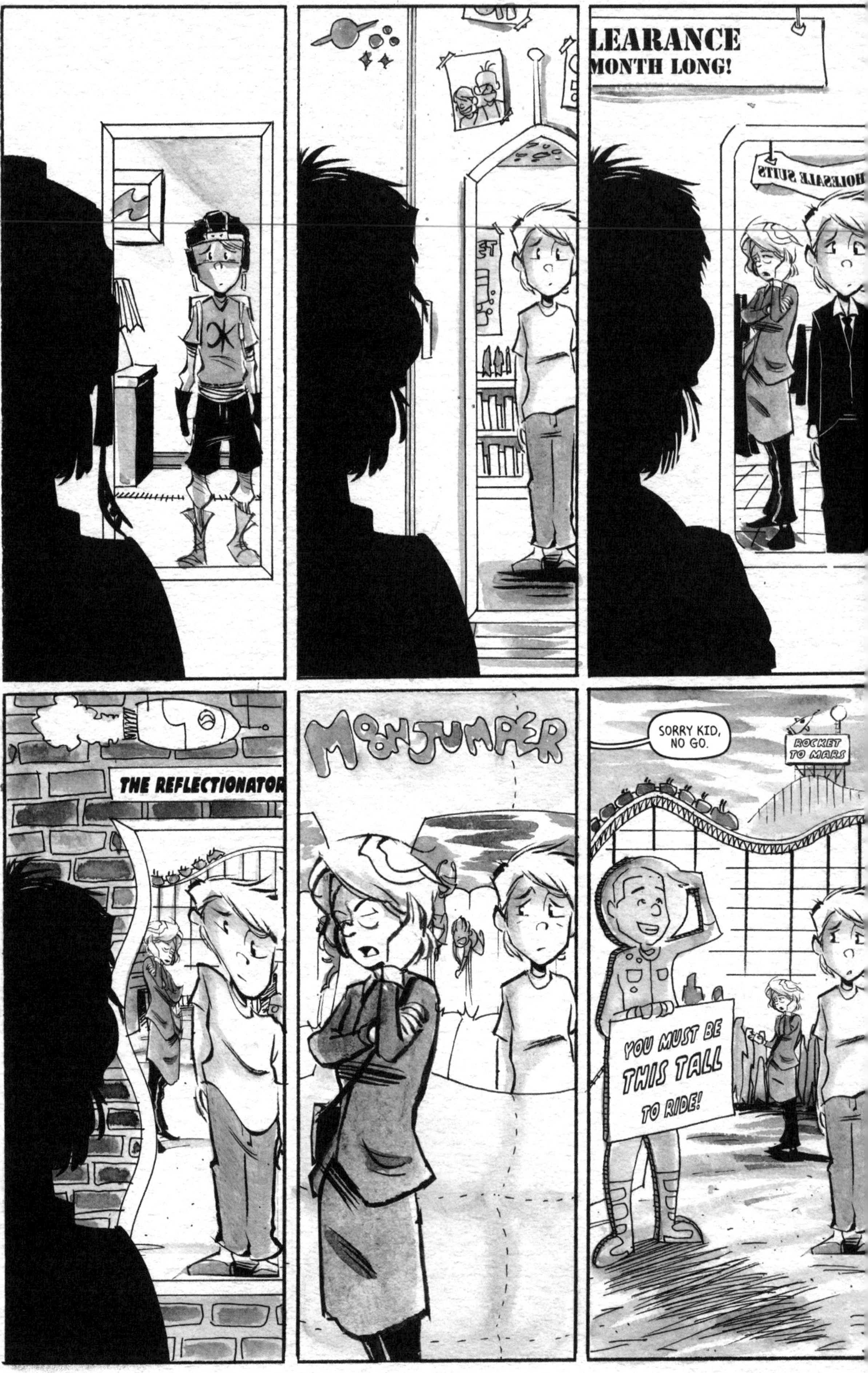
LEARANCE
MONTH LONG!
WHOLESALE SUITS
THE REFLECTIONATOR
MOONJUMPER
SORRY KID, NO GO.
ROCKET TO MARS
YOU MUST BE THIS TALL TO RIDE!

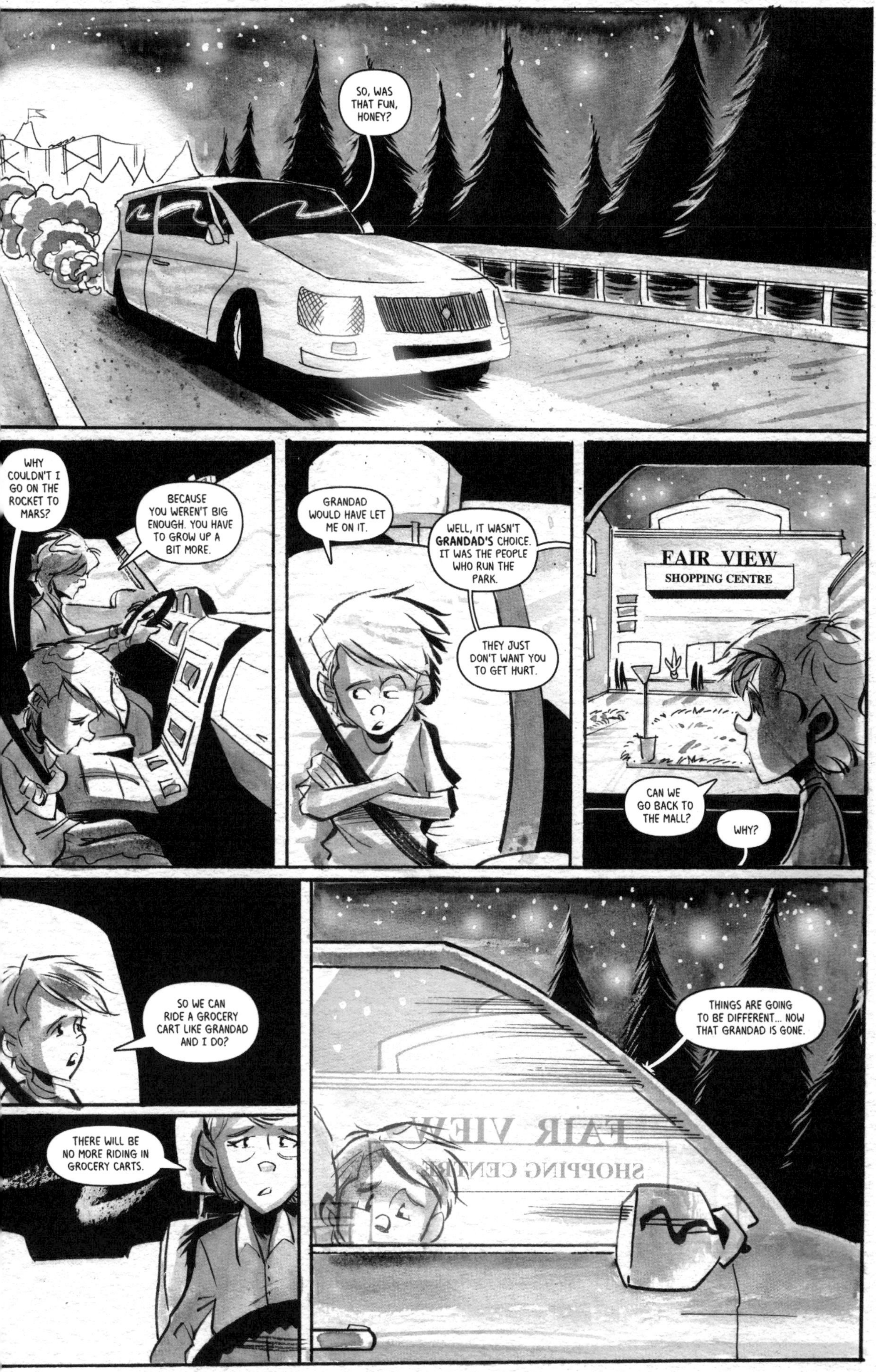
SO, WAS THAT FUN, HONEY?
WHY COULDN'T I GO ON THE ROCKET TO MARS?
BECAUSE YOU WEREN'T BIG ENOUGH. YOU HAVE TO GROW UP A BIT MORE.
GRANDAD WOULD HAVE LET ME ON IT.
WELL, IT WASN'T GRANDAD'S CHOICE. IT WAS THE PEOPLE WHO RUN THE PARK.
THEY JUST DON'T WANT YOU TO GET HURT.
FAIR VIEW
SHOPPING CENTRE
CAN WE GO BACK TO THE MALL?
WHY?
SO WE CAN RIDE A GROCERY CART LIKE GRANDAD AND I DO?
THERE WILL BE NO MORE RIDING IN GROCERY CARTS.
THINGS ARE GOING TO BE DIFFERENT... NOW THAT GRANDAD IS GONE.

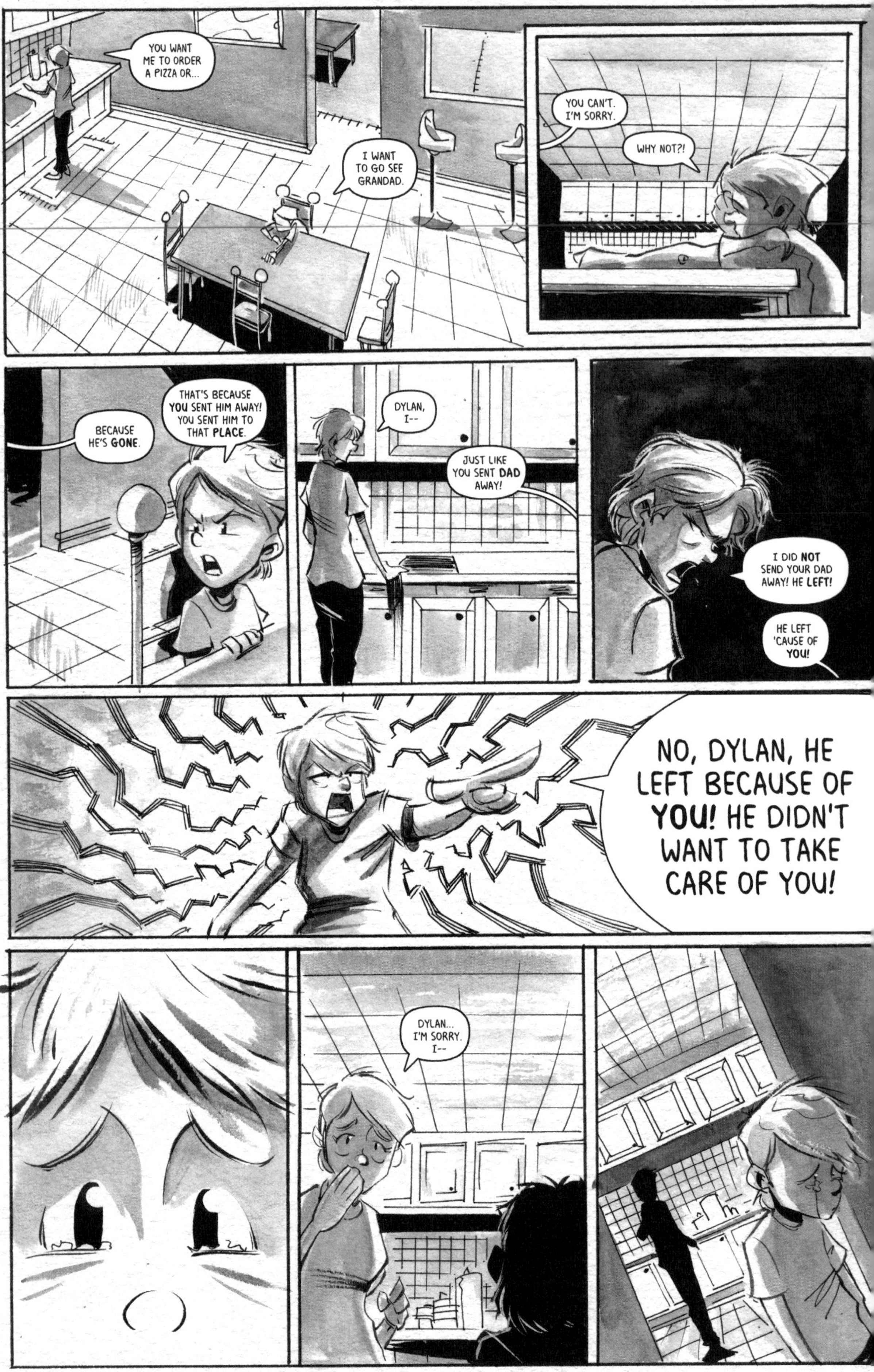
YOU WANT ME TO ORDER A PIZZA OR...
I WANT TO GO SEE GRANDAD.
YOU CAN'T. I'M SORRY.
WHY NOT?!
BECAUSE HE'S GONE.
THAT'S BECAUSE YOU SENT HIM AWAY! YOU SENT HIM TO THAT PLACE.
DYLAN, I--
JUST LIKE YOU SENT DAD AWAY!
I DID NOT SEND YOUR DAD AWAY! HE LEFT!
HE LEFT 'CAUSE OF YOU!
NO, DYLAN, HE LEFT BECAUSE OF YOU! HE DIDN'T WANT TO TAKE CARE OF YOU!
DYLAN... I'M SORRY. I--

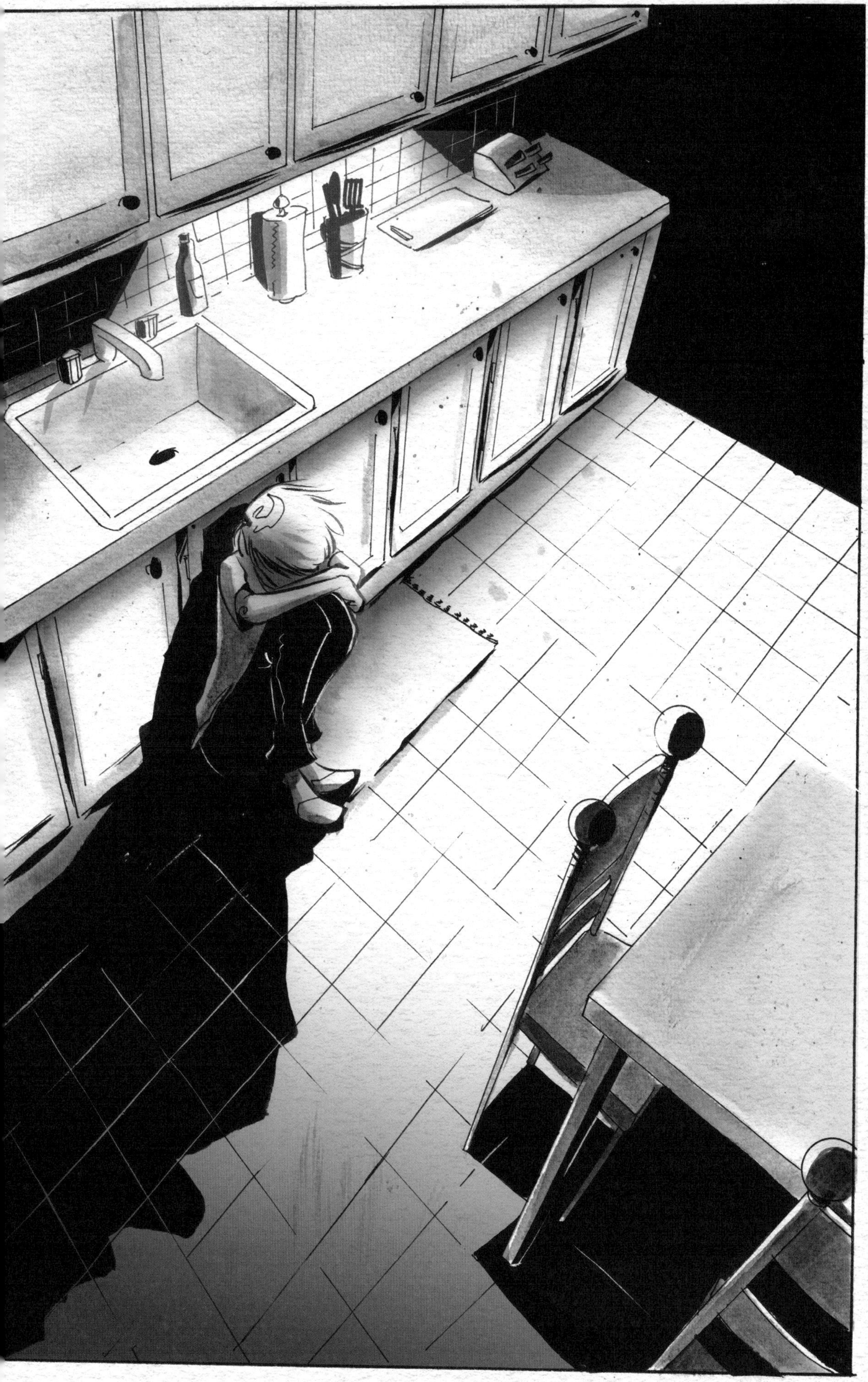

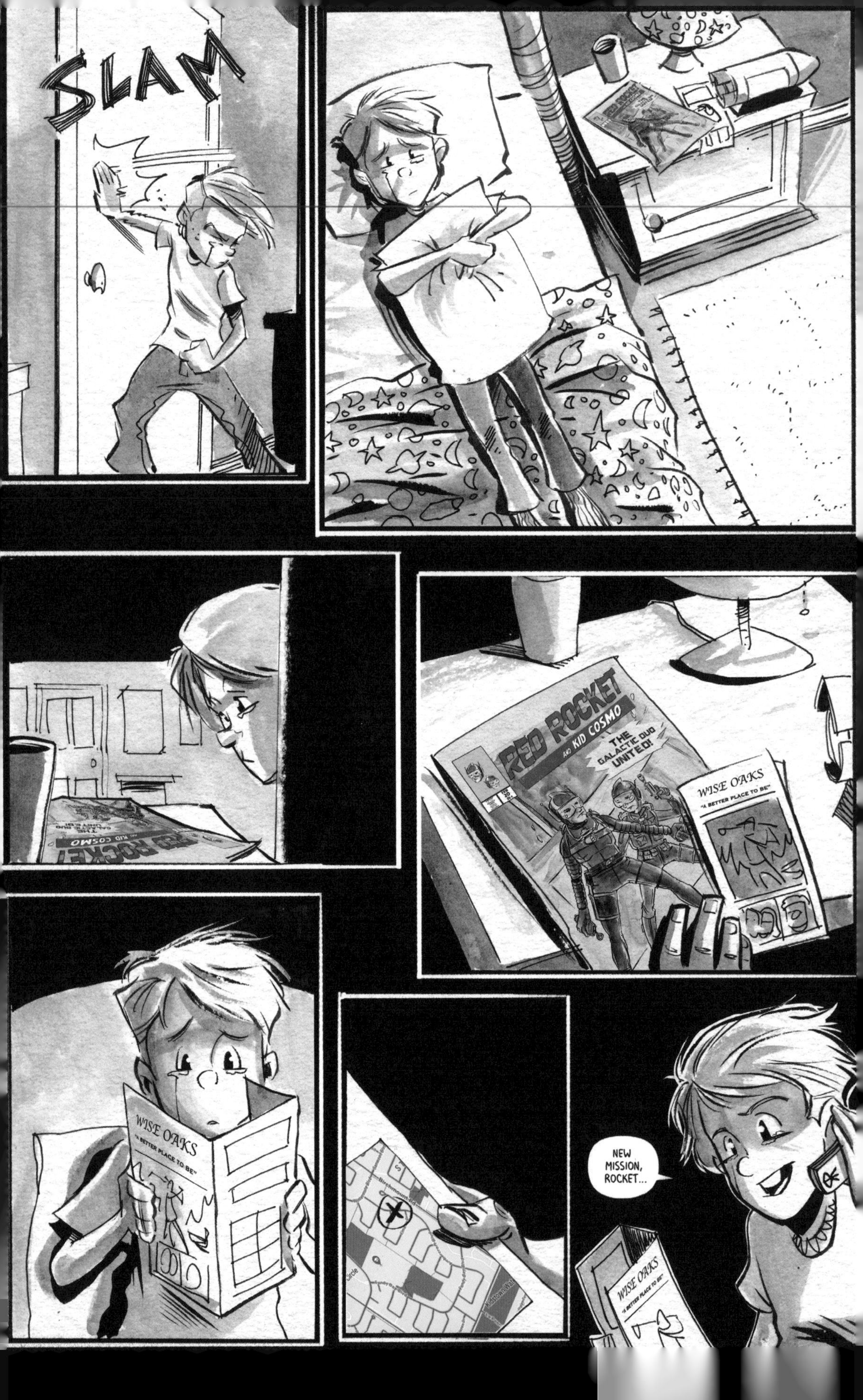

SLAM
RED ROCKET
AND KID COSMO
THE GALACTIC DUO UNITED!
WISE OAKS
"A BETTER PLACE TO BE"
WISE OAKS
"A BETTER PLACE TO BE"
NEW MISSION, ROCKET...
WISE OAKS
"A BETTER PLACE TO BE"

"I'M COMING
TO BE WITH YOU."

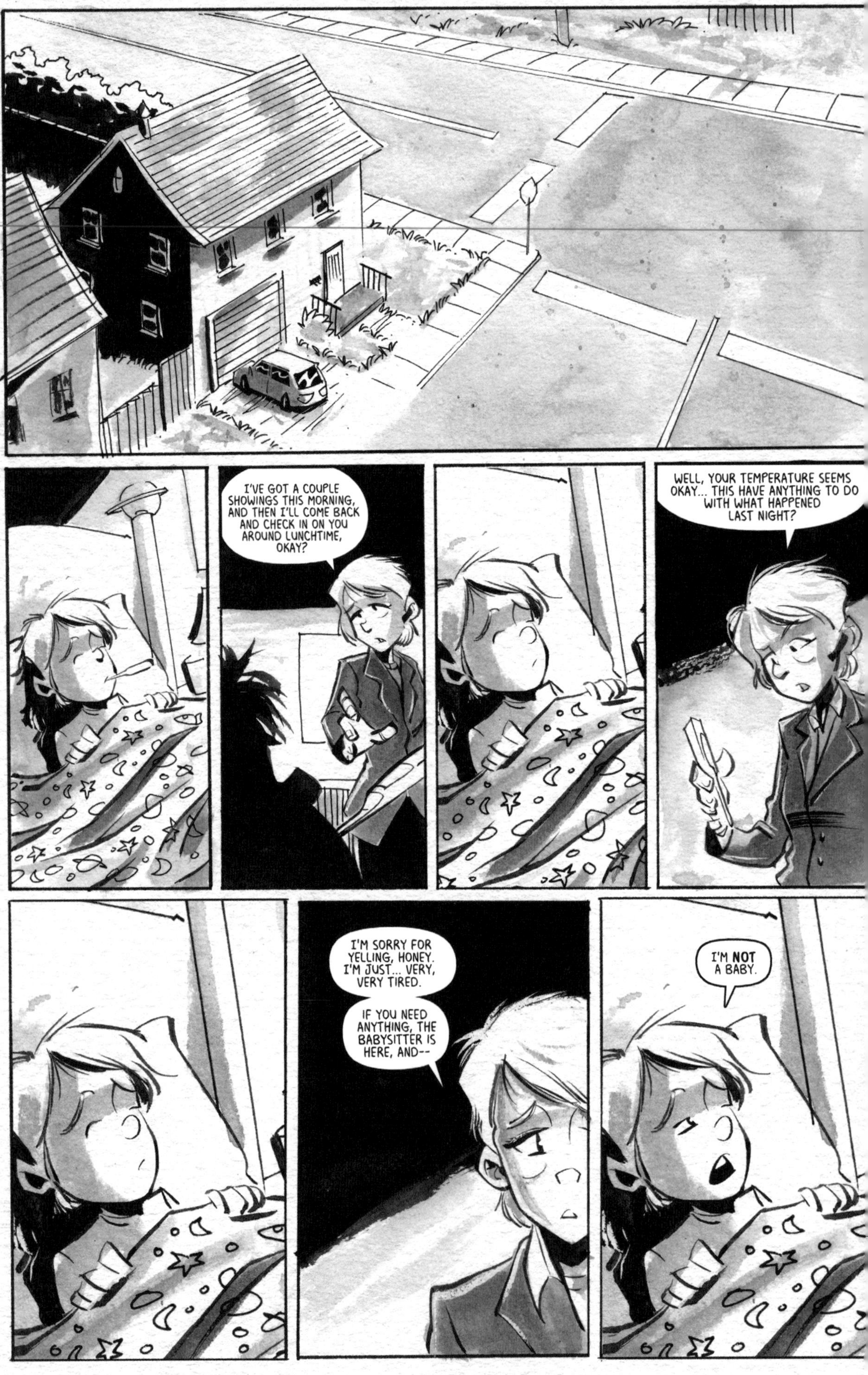

I'VE GOT A COUPLE SHOWINGS THIS MORNING, AND THEN I'LL COME BACK AND CHECK IN ON YOU AROUND LUNCHTIME, OKAY?
WELL, YOUR TEMPERATURE SEEMS OKAY... THIS HAVE ANYTHING TO DO WITH WHAT HAPPENED LAST NIGHT?
I'M SORRY FOR YELLING, HONEY. I'M JUST... VERY, VERY TIRED.
IF YOU NEED ANYTHING, THE BABYSITTER IS HERE, AND--
I'M **NOT** A BABY.

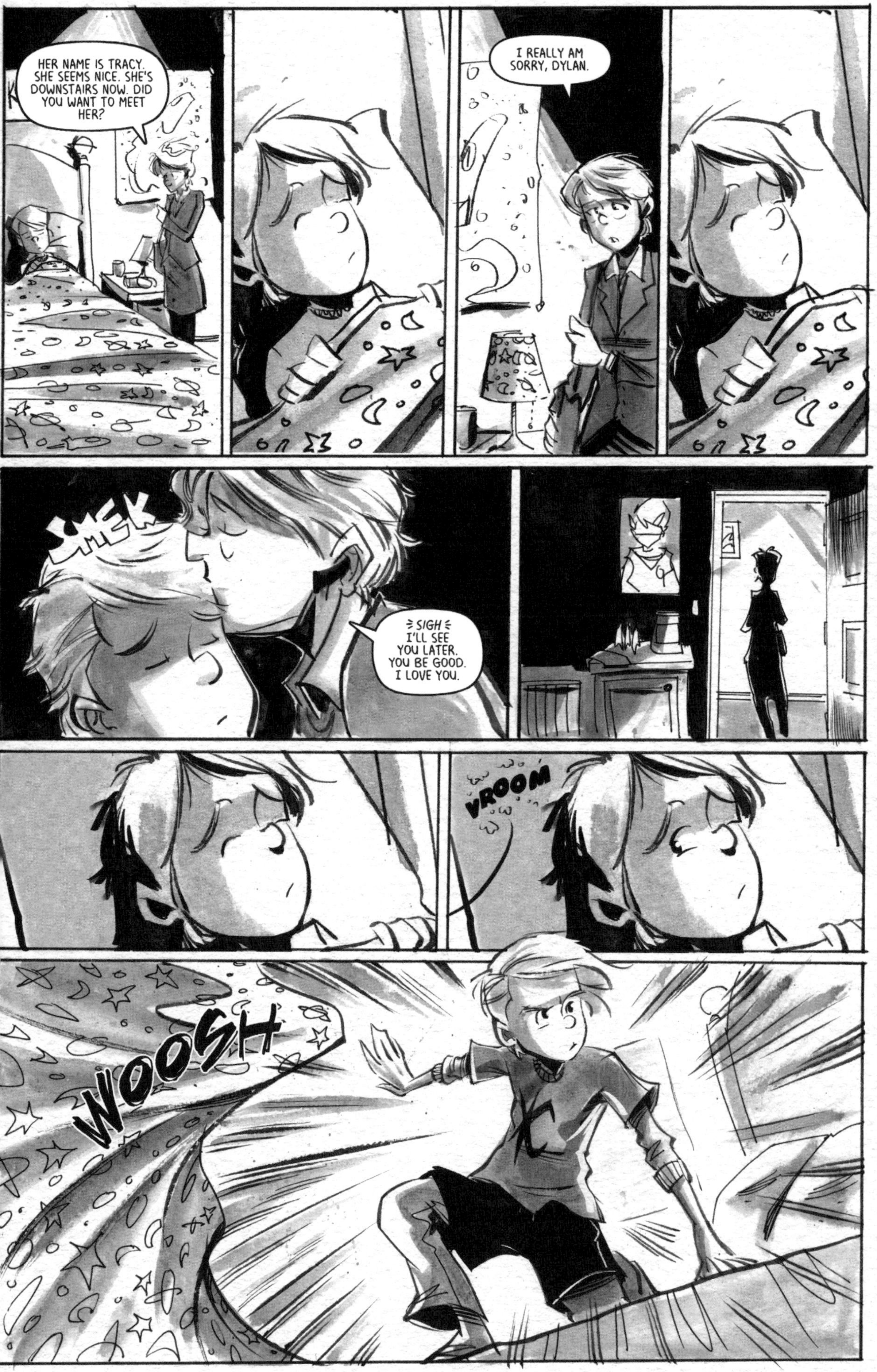

HER NAME IS TRACY. SHE SEEMS NICE. SHE'S DOWNSTAIRS NOW. DID YOU WANT TO MEET HER?
I REALLY AM SORRY, DYLAN.
SMEK
SIGH I'LL SEE YOU LATER. YOU BE GOOD. I LOVE YOU.
VROOM
WOOSH

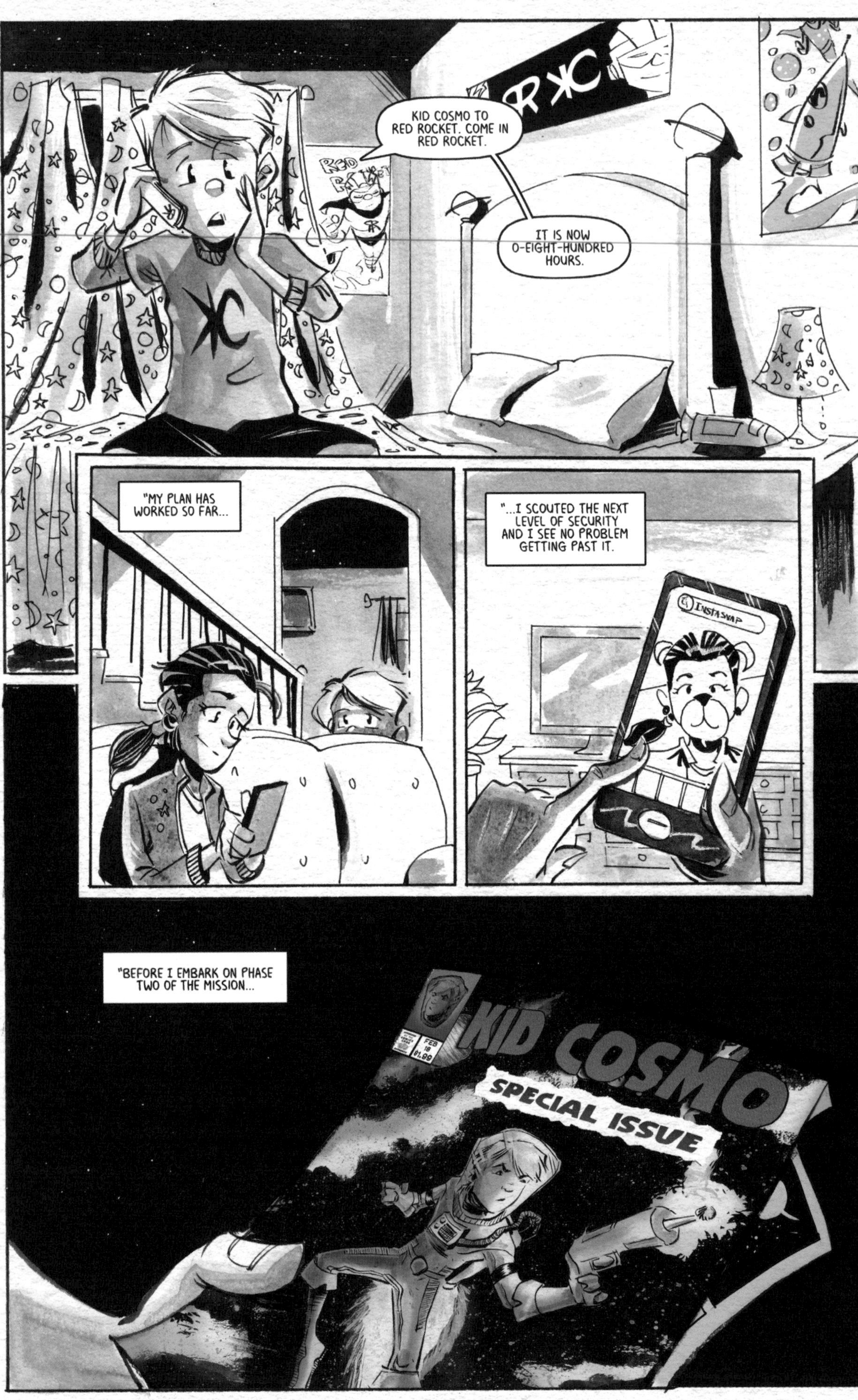

KID COSMO TO RED ROCKET. COME IN RED ROCKET.
IT IS NOW 0-EIGHT-HUNDRED HOURS.
"MY PLAN HAS WORKED SO FAR...
"...I SCOUTED THE NEXT LEVEL OF SECURITY AND I SEE NO PROBLEM GETTING PAST IT.
INSTASNAP
"BEFORE I EMBARK ON PHASE TWO OF THE MISSION...
KID COSMO
SPECIAL ISSUE
FEB 18
$1.99

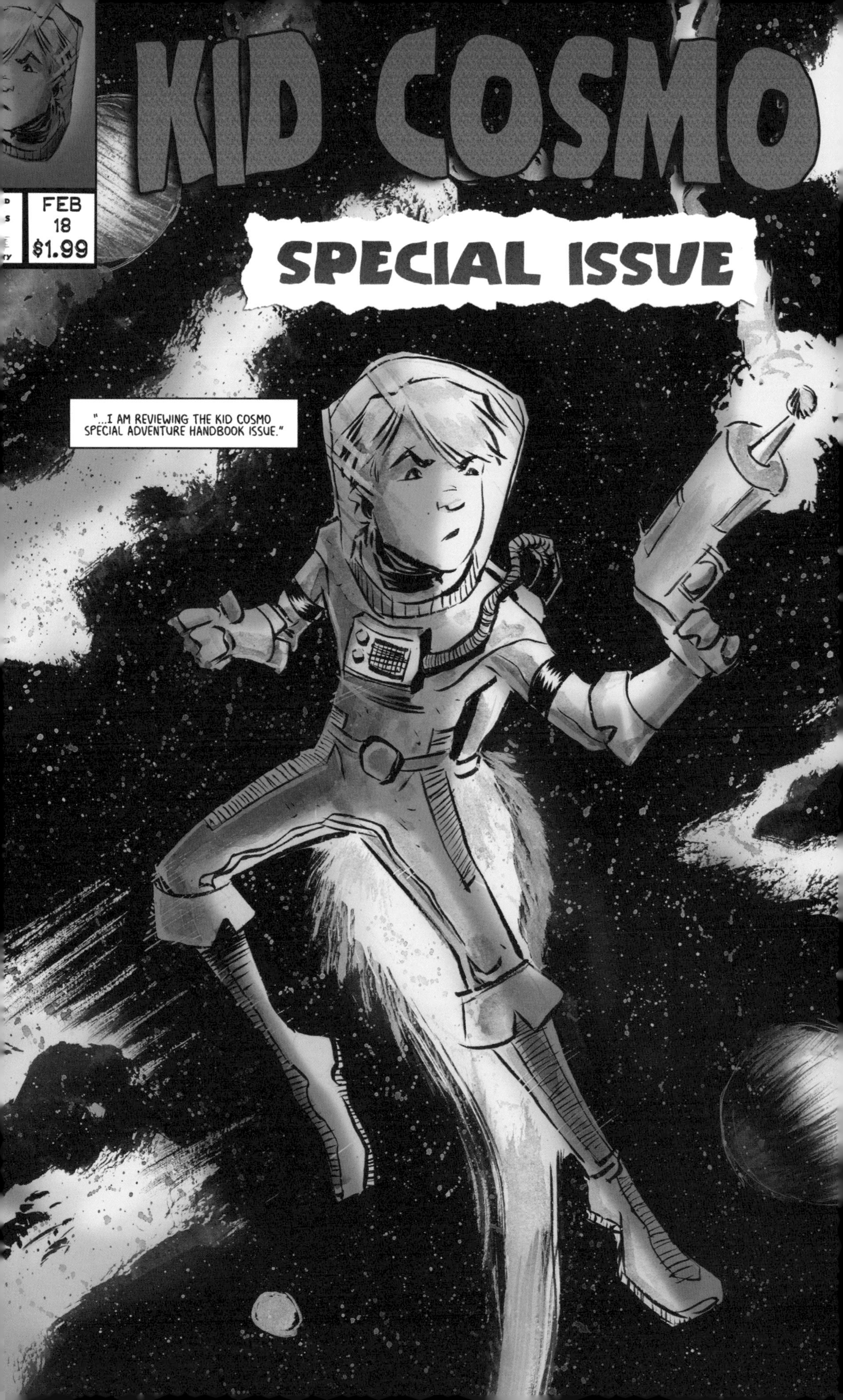
KID COSMO
FEB
18
$1.99
SPECIAL ISSUE
"...I AM REVIEWING THE KID COSMO SPECIAL ADVENTURE HANDBOOK ISSUE."

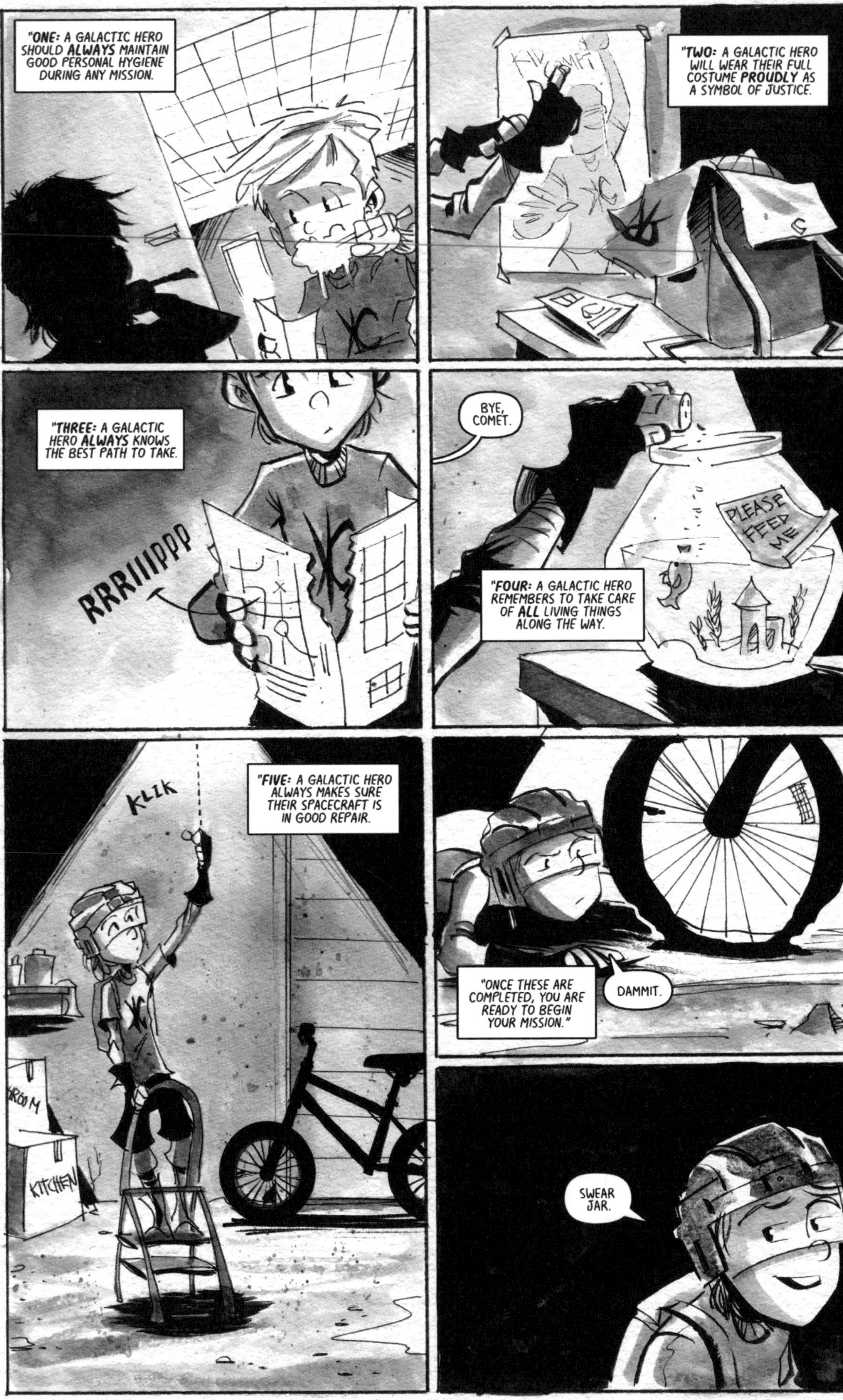
"ONE: A GALACTIC HERO SHOULD ALWAYS MAINTAIN GOOD PERSONAL HYGIENE DURING ANY MISSION.
"TWO: A GALACTIC HERO WILL WEAR THEIR FULL COSTUME PROUDLY AS A SYMBOL OF JUSTICE.
"THREE: A GALACTIC HERO ALWAYS KNOWS THE BEST PATH TO TAKE.
RRRIIIPPP
BYE, COMET.
PLEASE FEED ME
"FOUR: A GALACTIC HERO REMEMBERS TO TAKE CARE OF ALL LIVING THINGS ALONG THE WAY.
KLIK
"FIVE: A GALACTIC HERO ALWAYS MAKES SURE THEIR SPACECRAFT IS IN GOOD REPAIR.
KITCHEN
"ONCE THESE ARE COMPLETED, YOU ARE READY TO BEGIN YOUR MISSION."
DAMMIT.
SWEAR JAR.

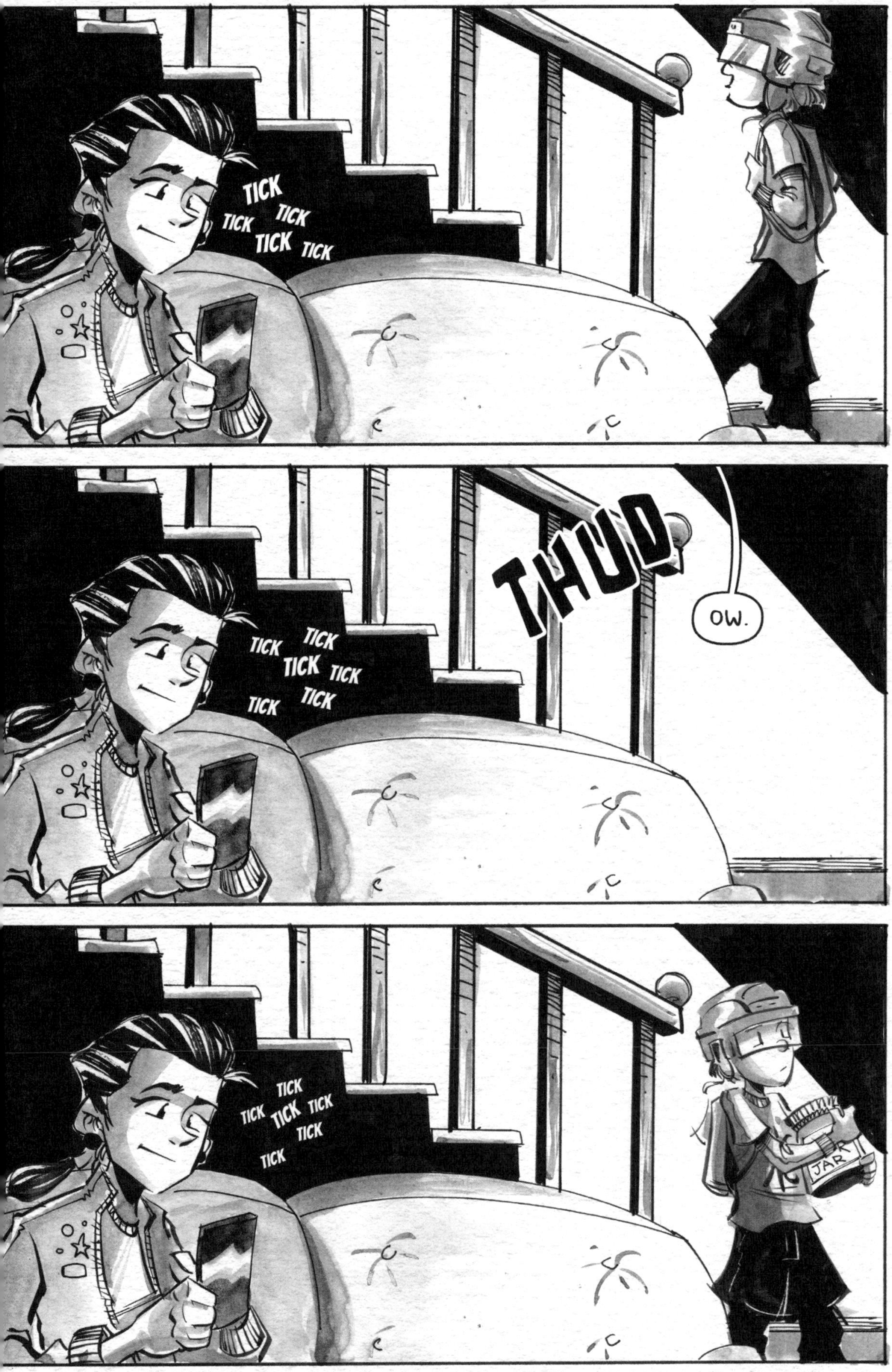
TICK TICK TICK TICK TICK
TICK TICK TICK TICK TICK TICK
THUD
OW.
TICK TICK TICK TICK TICK TICK
JAR

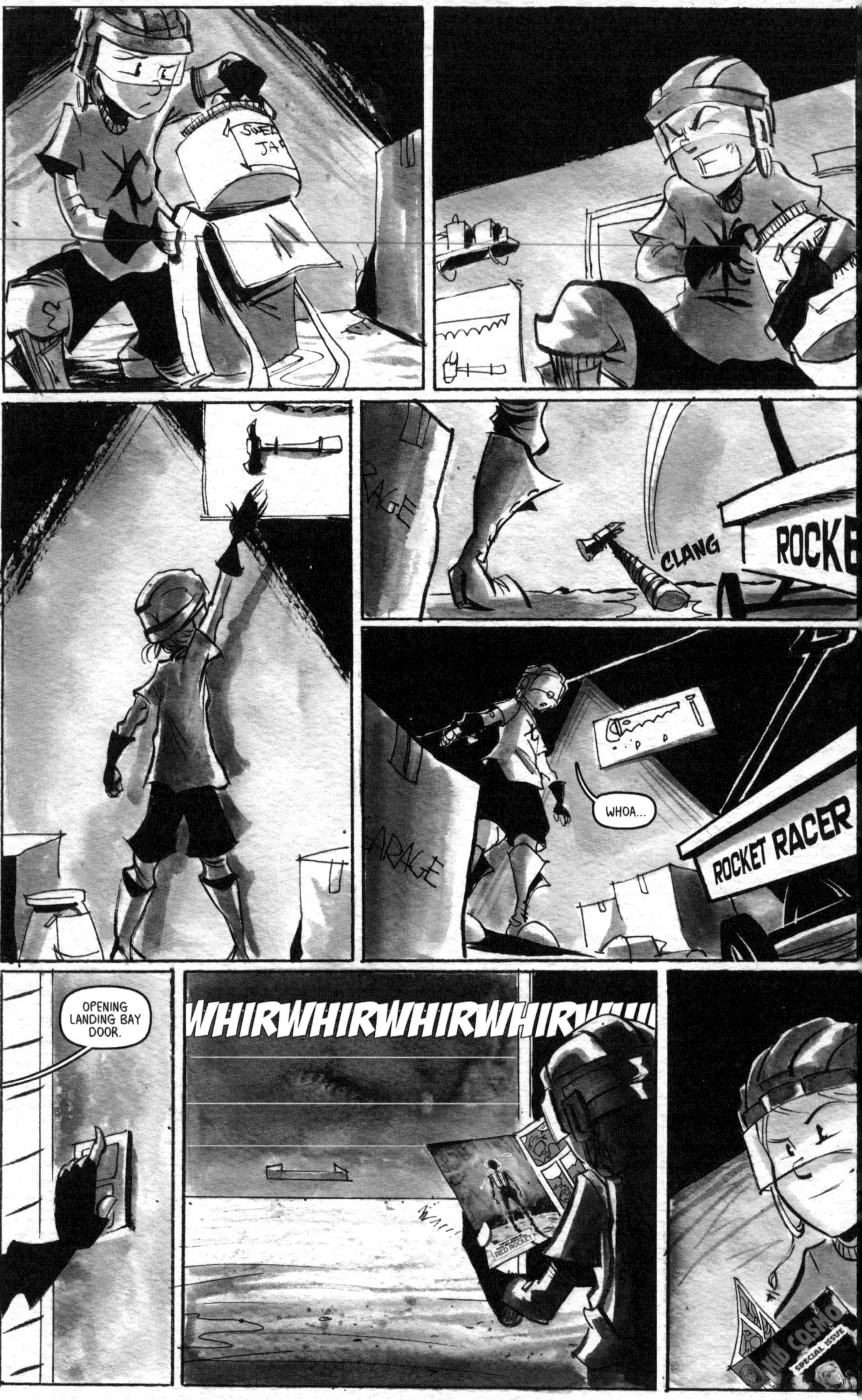
SWEAR JAR
CLANG
ROCKE
WHOA...
ROCKET RACER
OPENING LANDING BAY DOOR.
WHIRWHIRWHIRWHIR
RED ROCKET
KID COSMO
SPECIAL ISSUE

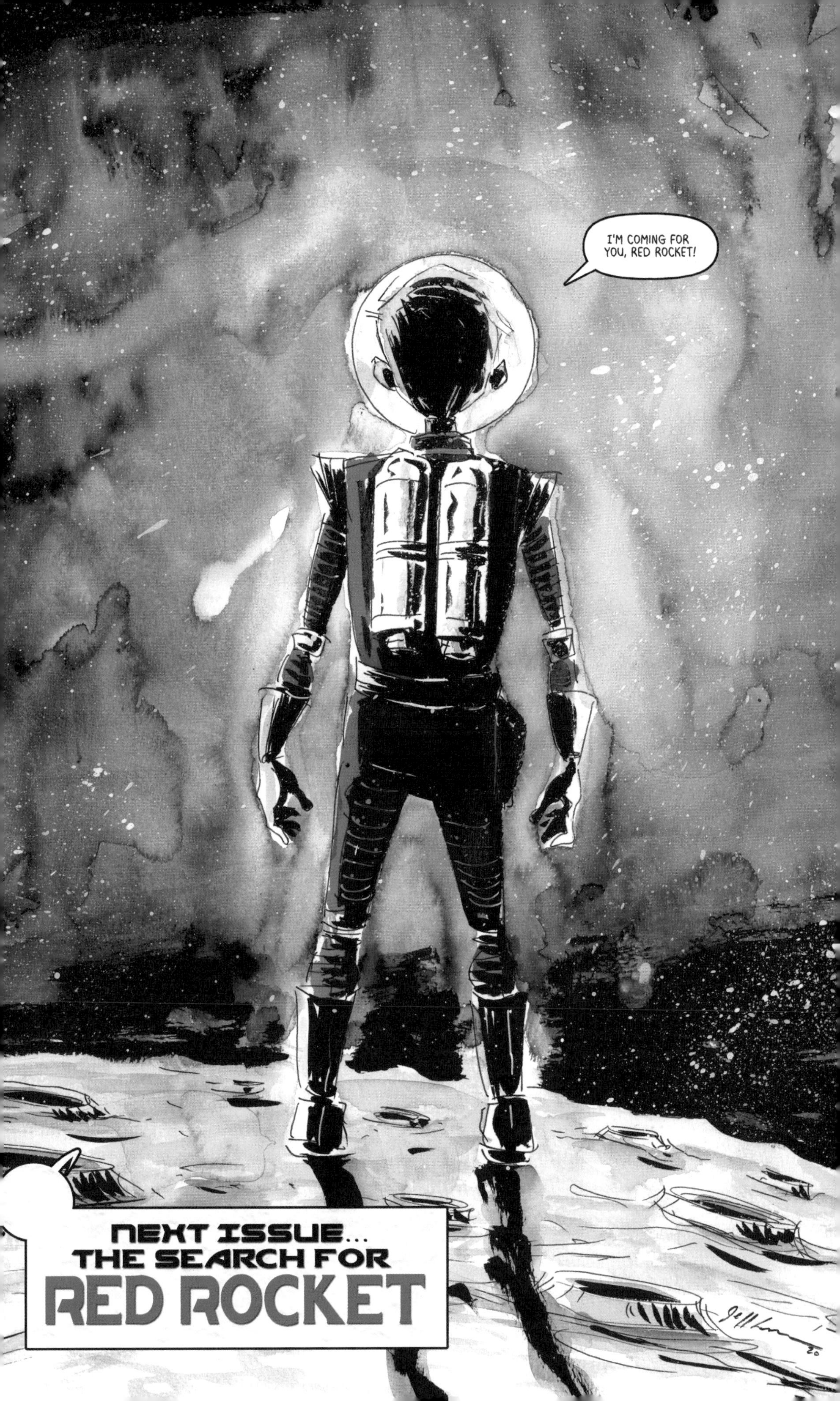
I'M COMING FOR YOU, RED ROCKET!
NEXT ISSUE... THE SEARCH FOR RED ROCKET

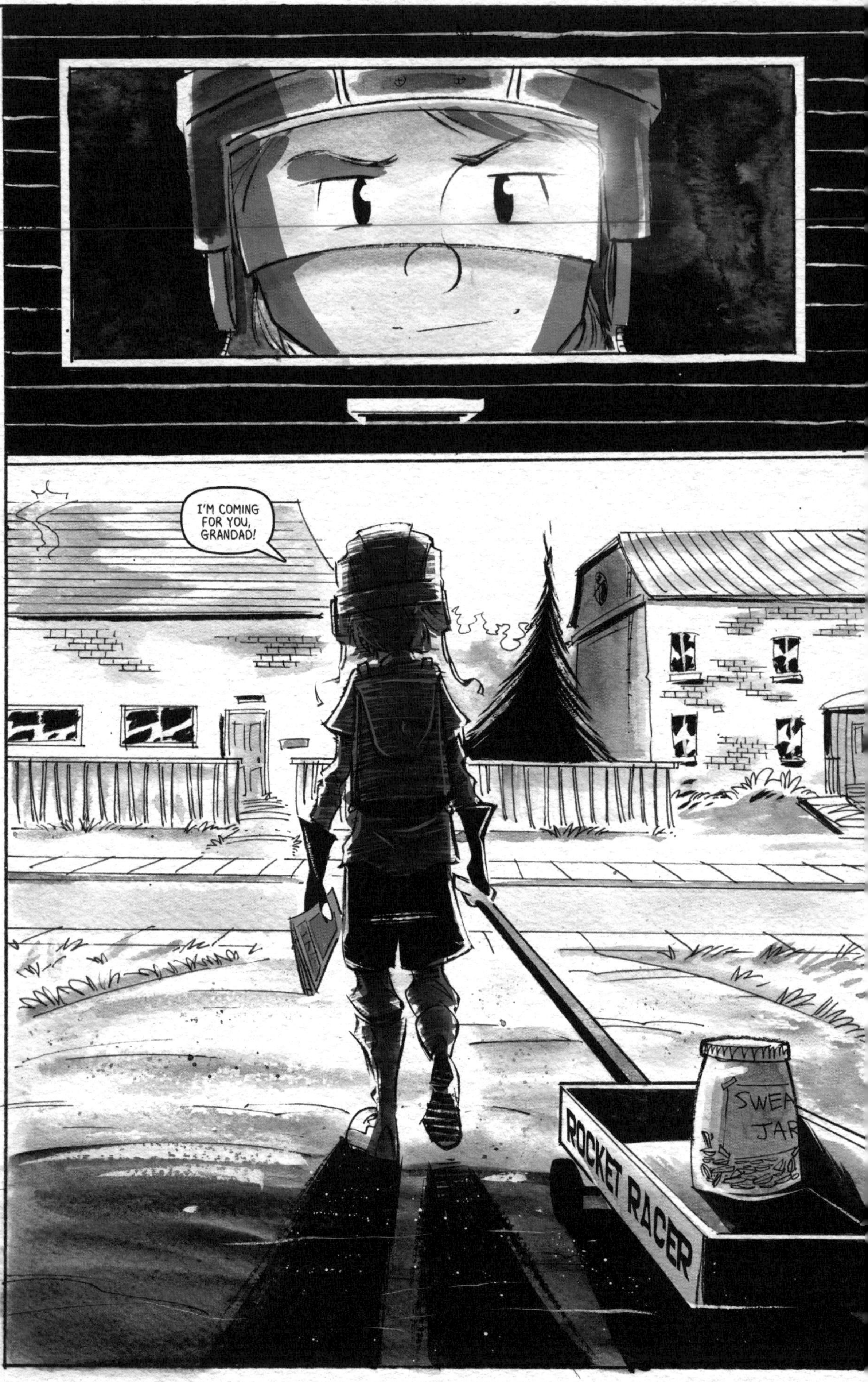
I'M COMING FOR YOU, GRANDAD!
ROCKET RACER
SWEAR JAR

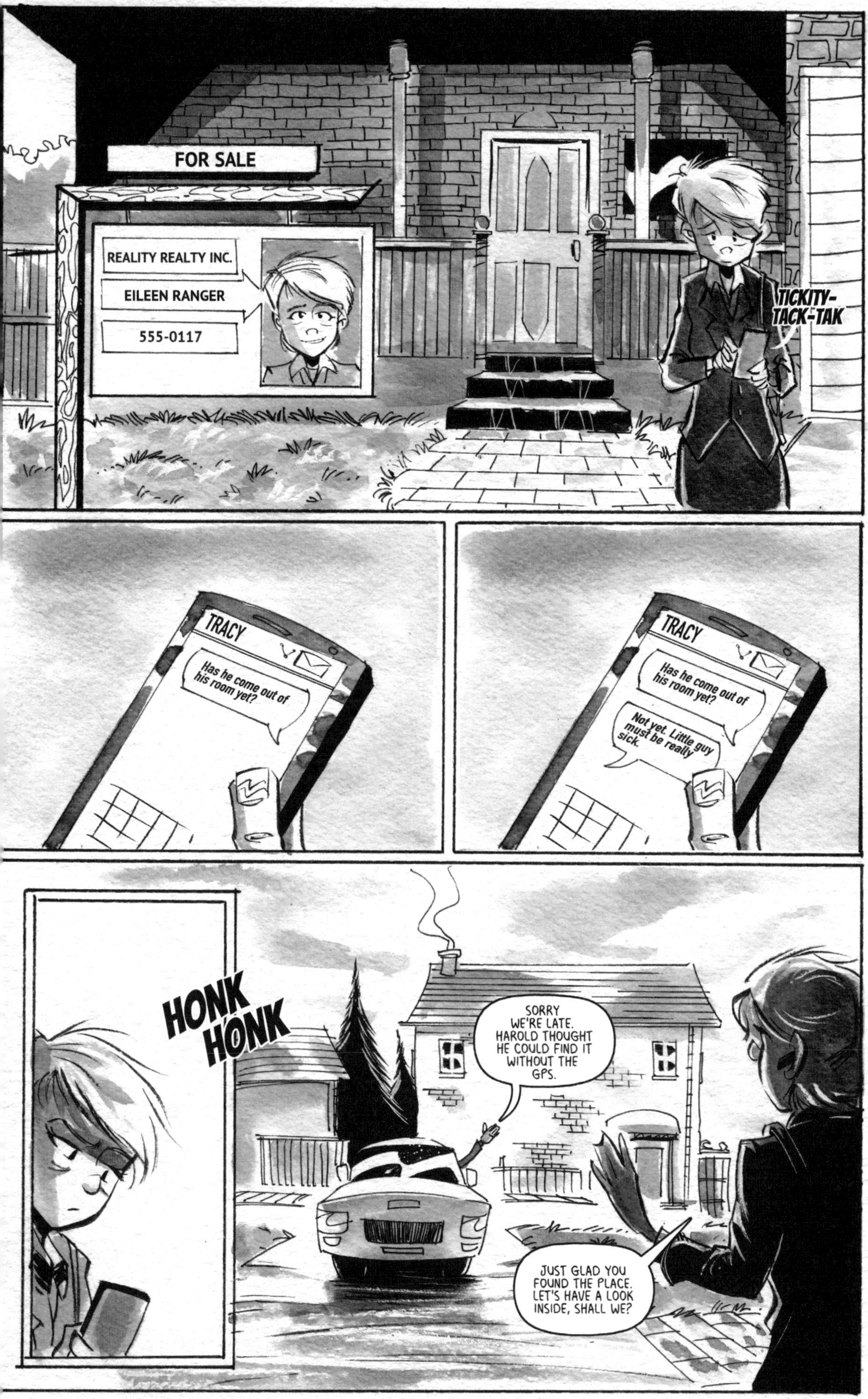
FOR SALE
REALITY REALTY INC.
EILEEN RANGER
555-0117
TICKITY-TACK-TAK
TRACY
Has he come out of his room yet?
TRACY
Has he come out of his room yet?
Not yet. Little guy must be really sick.
HONK HONK
SORRY WE'RE LATE. HAROLD THOUGHT HE COULD FIND IT WITHOUT THE GPS.
JUST GLAD YOU FOUND THE PLACE. LET'S HAVE A LOOK INSIDE, SHALL WE?

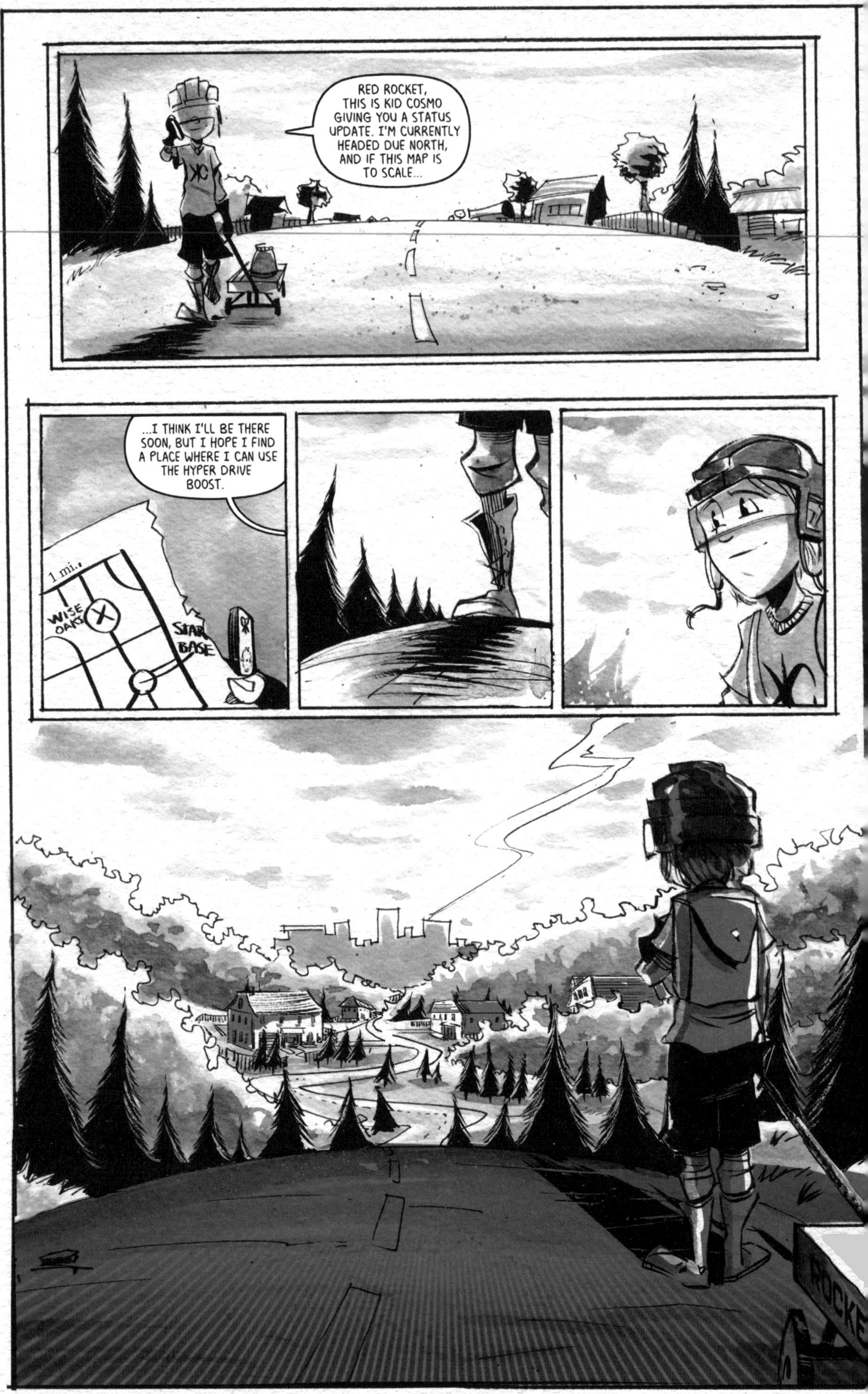
RED ROCKET, THIS IS KID COSMO GIVING YOU A STATUS UPDATE. I'M CURRENTLY HEADED DUE NORTH, AND IF THIS MAP IS TO SCALE...
...I THINK I'LL BE THERE SOON, BUT I HOPE I FIND A PLACE WHERE I CAN USE THE HYPER DRIVE BOOST.
1 mi.
WISE OAK
STAR BASE
ROCKE

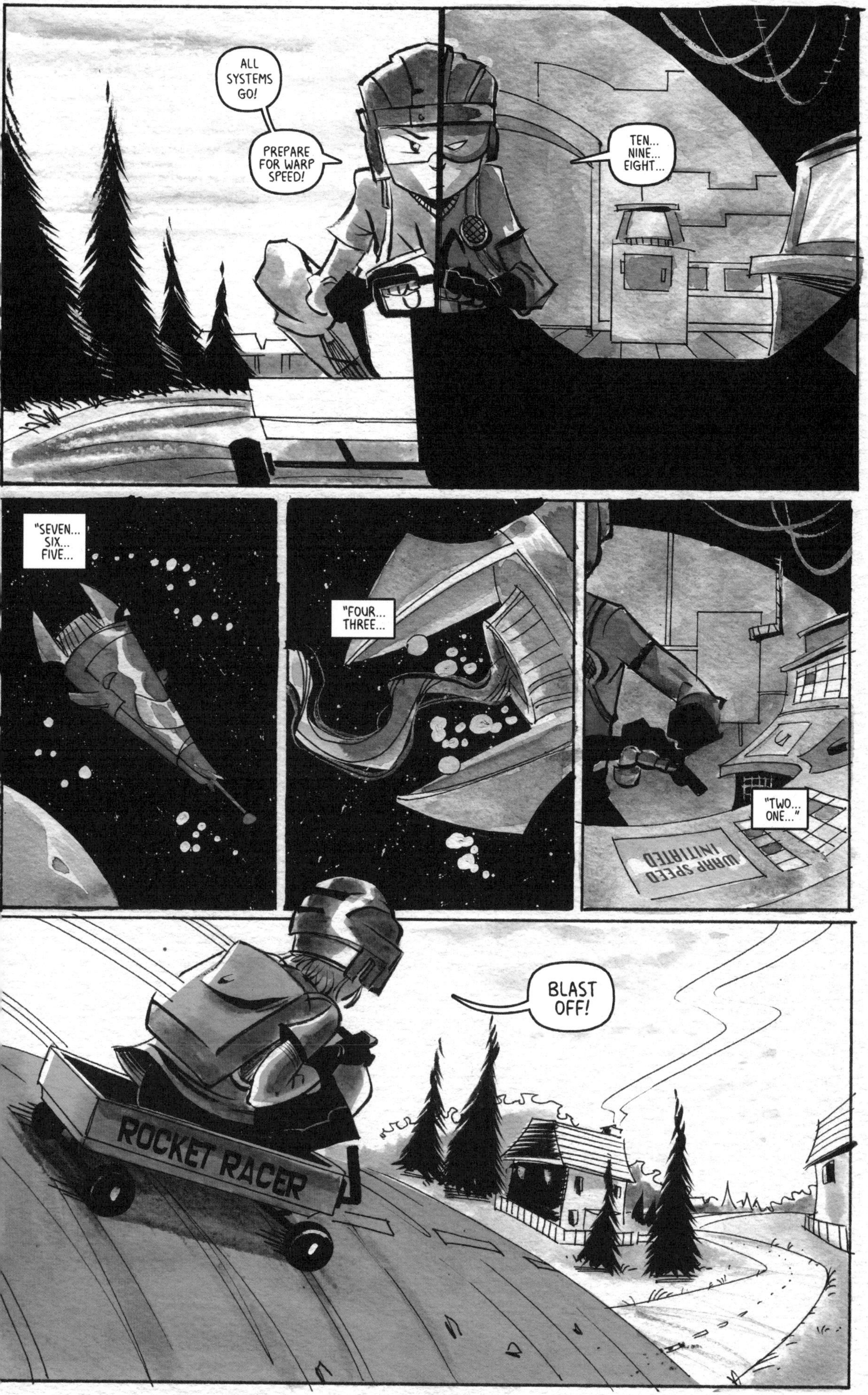
ALL SYSTEMS GO!
PREPARE FOR WARP SPEED!
TEN... NINE... EIGHT...
"SEVEN... SIX... FIVE...
"FOUR... THREE...
"TWO... ONE..."
WARP SPEED INITIATED
ROCKET RACER
BLAST OFF!

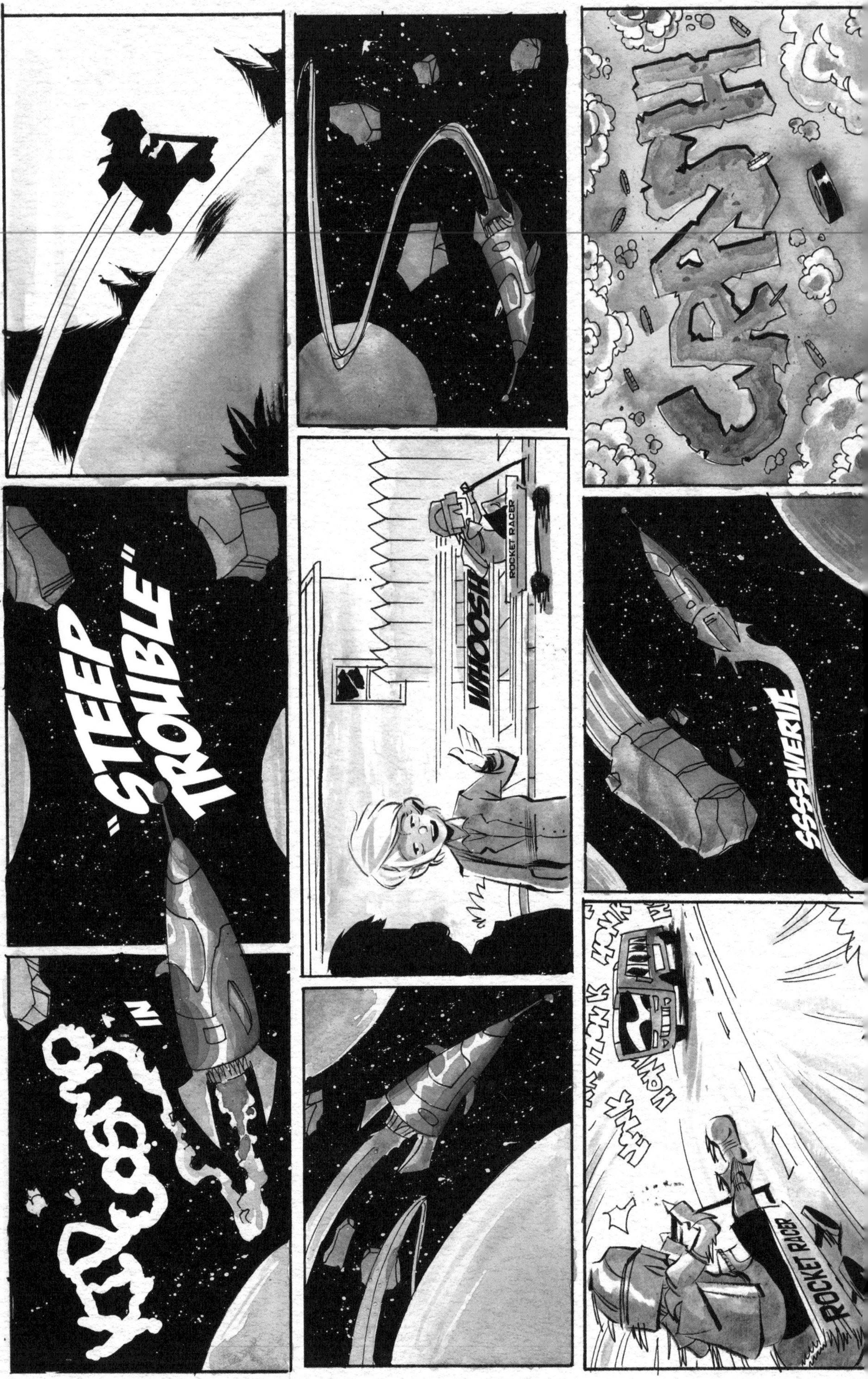

VROOM
"IN"
"STEEP TROUBLE"
WHOOSH
ROCKET RACER
SSSSWERVE
CRASH
HONK HONK
ROCKET RACER

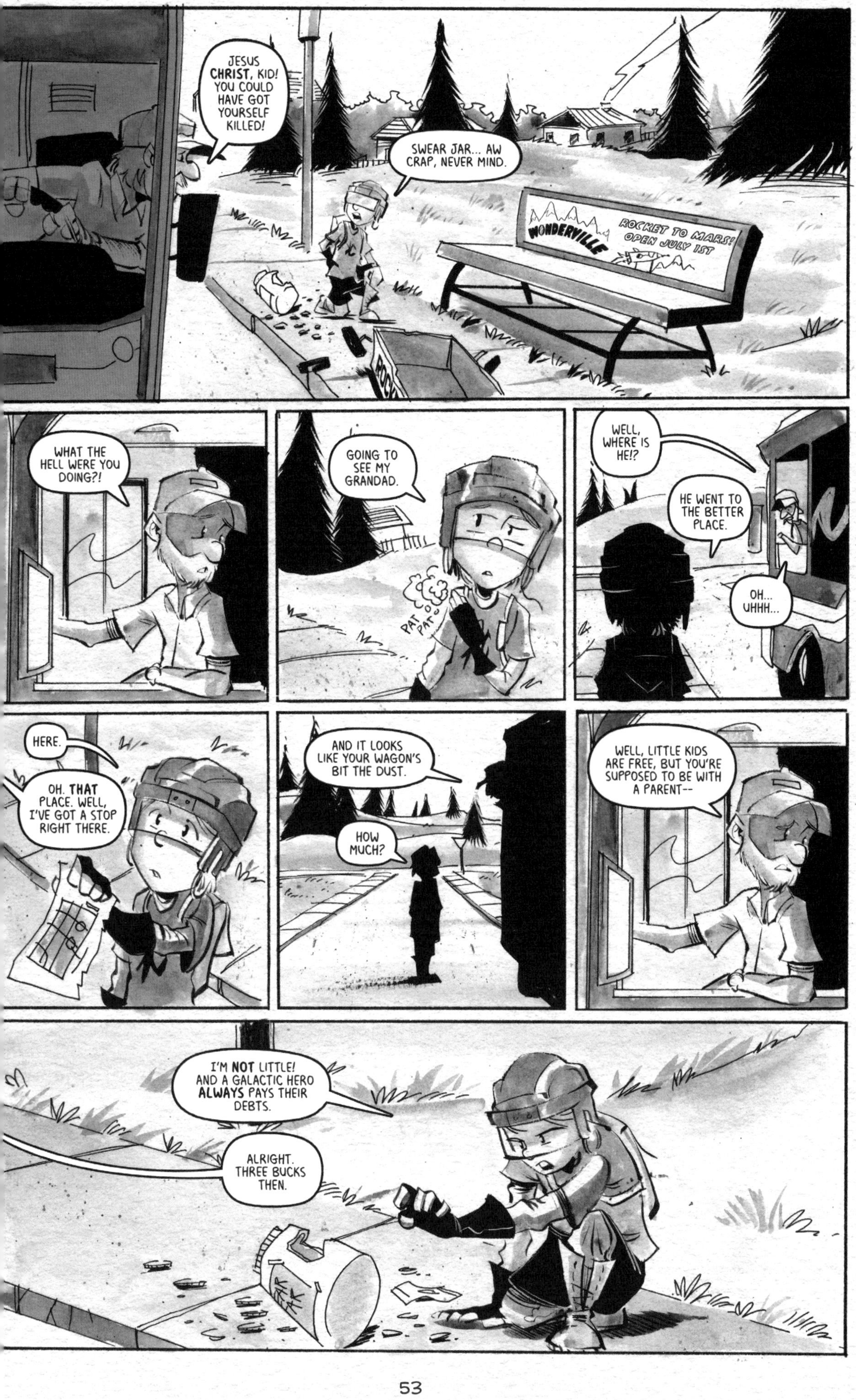
JESUS CHRIST, KID! YOU COULD HAVE GOT YOURSELF KILLED!
SWEAR JAR... AW CRAP, NEVER MIND.
WONDERVILLE
ROCKET TO MARS! OPEN JULY 1ST
WHAT THE HELL WERE YOU DOING?!
GOING TO SEE MY GRANDAD.
PAT PAT
WELL, WHERE IS HE!?
HE WENT TO THE BETTER PLACE.
OH... UHHH...
HERE.
OH. THAT PLACE. WELL, I'VE GOT A STOP RIGHT THERE.
AND IT LOOKS LIKE YOUR WAGON'S BIT THE DUST.
HOW MUCH?
WELL, LITTLE KIDS ARE FREE, BUT YOU'RE SUPPOSED TO BE WITH A PARENT--
I'M NOT LITTLE! AND A GALACTIC HERO ALWAYS PAYS THEIR DEBTS.
ALRIGHT. THREE BUCKS THEN.

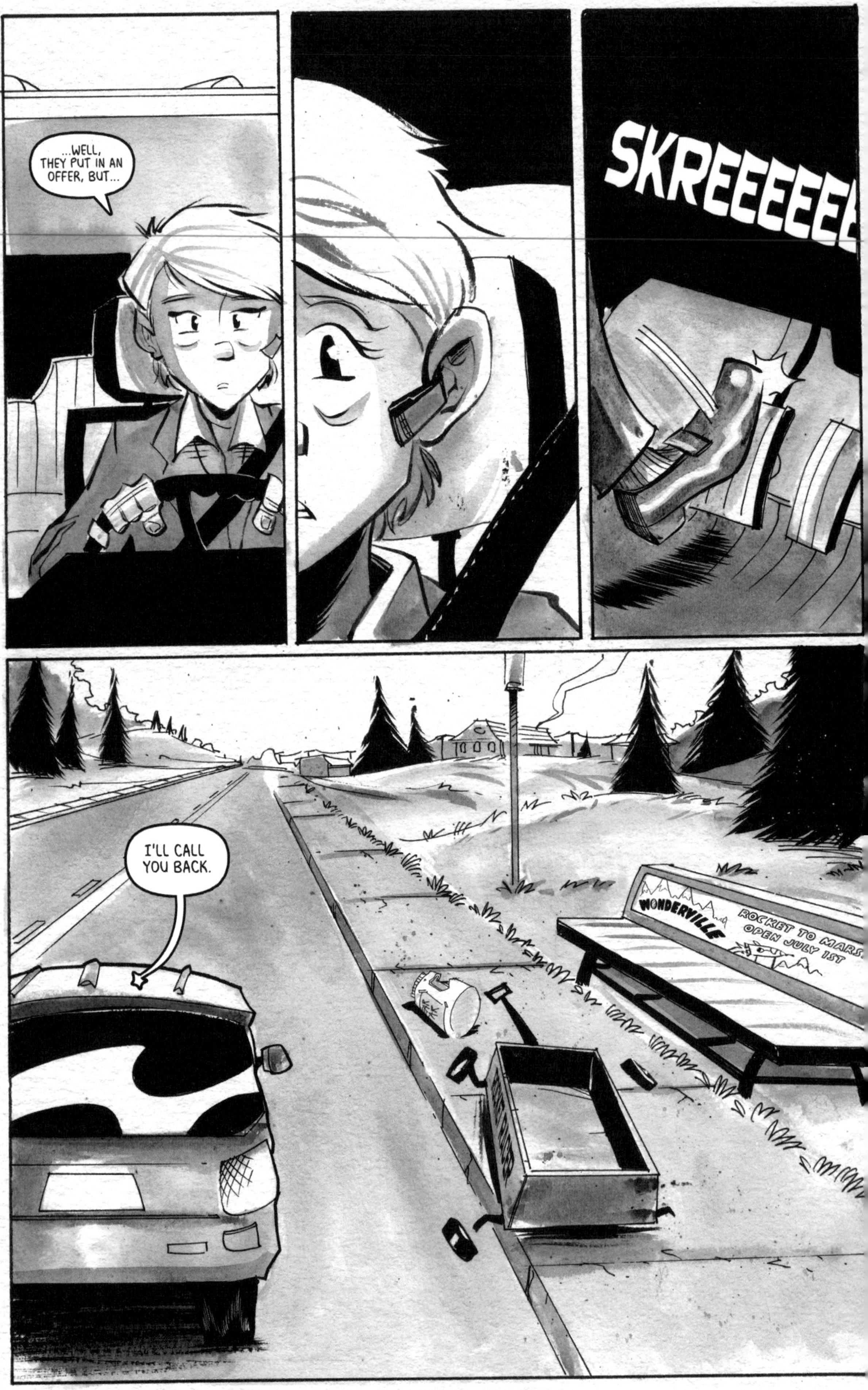
...WELL, THEY PUT IN AN OFFER, BUT...
SKREEEEEE
I'LL CALL YOU BACK.
WONDERVILLE
ROCKET TO MARS
OPEN JULY 1ST

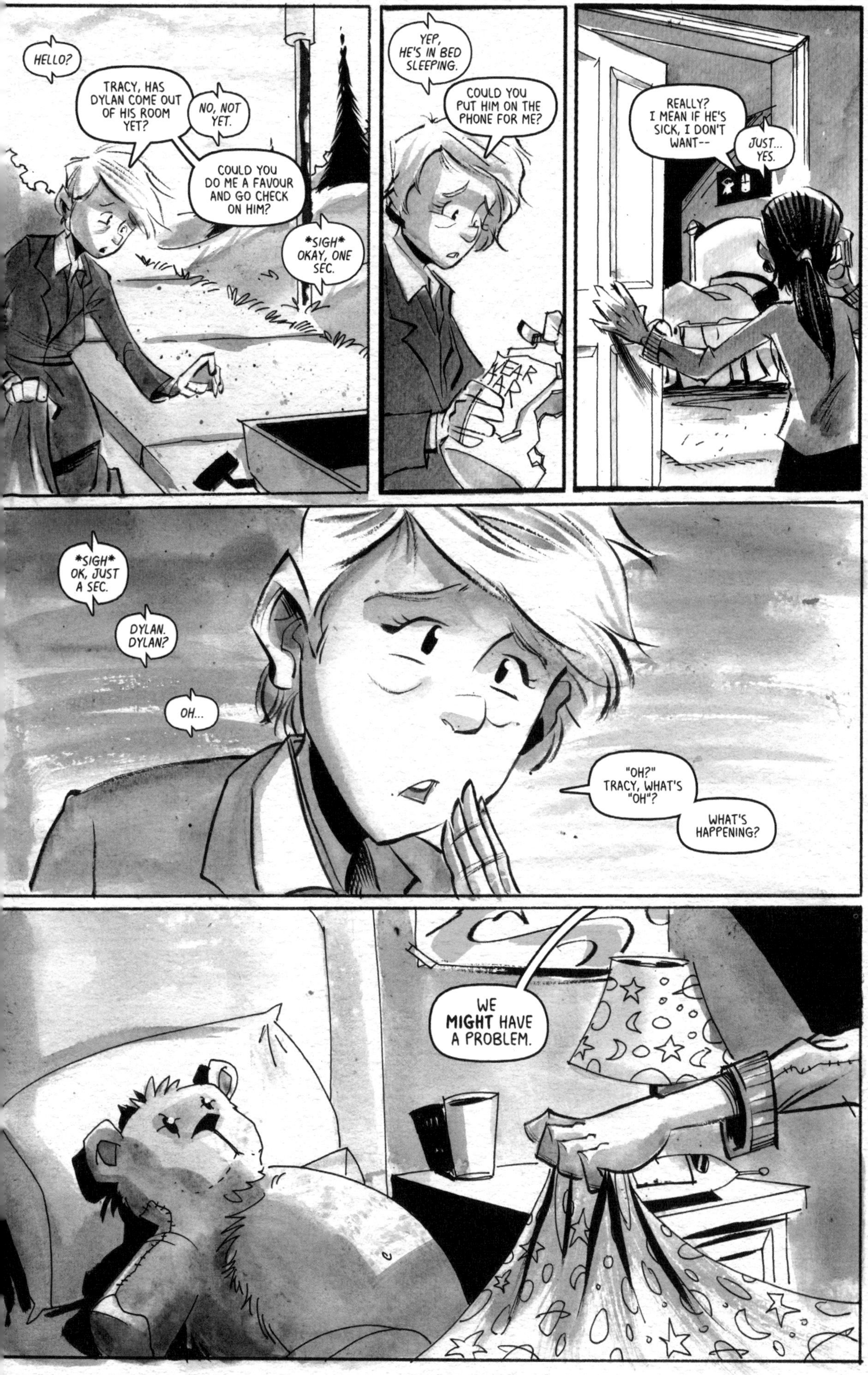
HELLO?
TRACY, HAS DYLAN COME OUT OF HIS ROOM YET?
NO, NOT YET.
COULD YOU DO ME A FAVOUR AND GO CHECK ON HIM?
SIGH OKAY, ONE SEC.
YEP, HE'S IN BED SLEEPING.
COULD YOU PUT HIM ON THE PHONE FOR ME?
REALLY? I MEAN IF HE'S SICK, I DON'T WANT--
JUST... YES.
SIGH OK, JUST A SEC.
DYLAN. DYLAN?
OH...
"OH?" TRACY, WHAT'S "OH"?
WHAT'S HAPPENING?
WE MIGHT HAVE A PROBLEM.

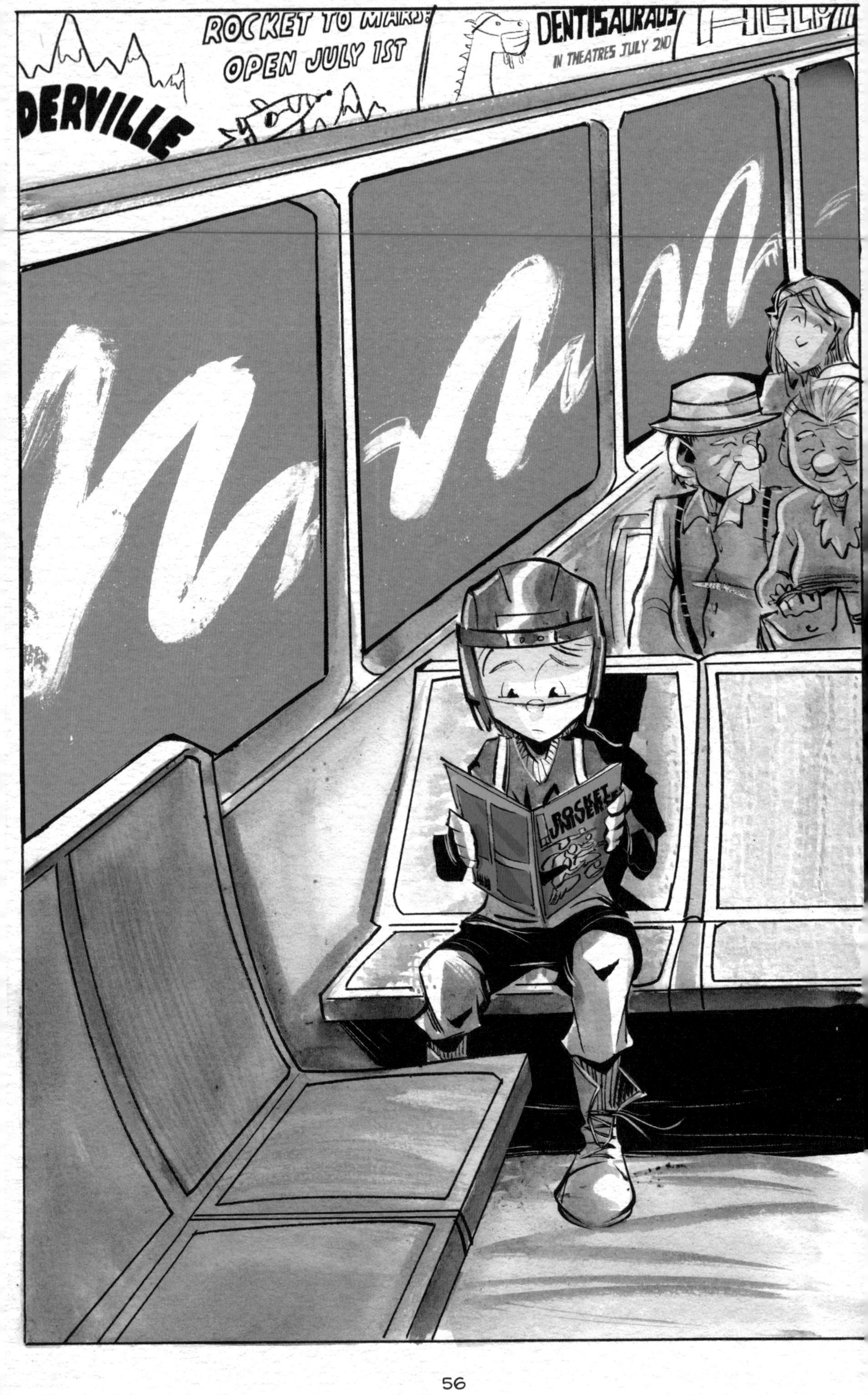
DERVILLE
ROCKET TO MARS!
OPEN JULY 1ST
DENTISAURAUS
IN THEATRES JULY 2ND
ROCKET

ROBOT RED

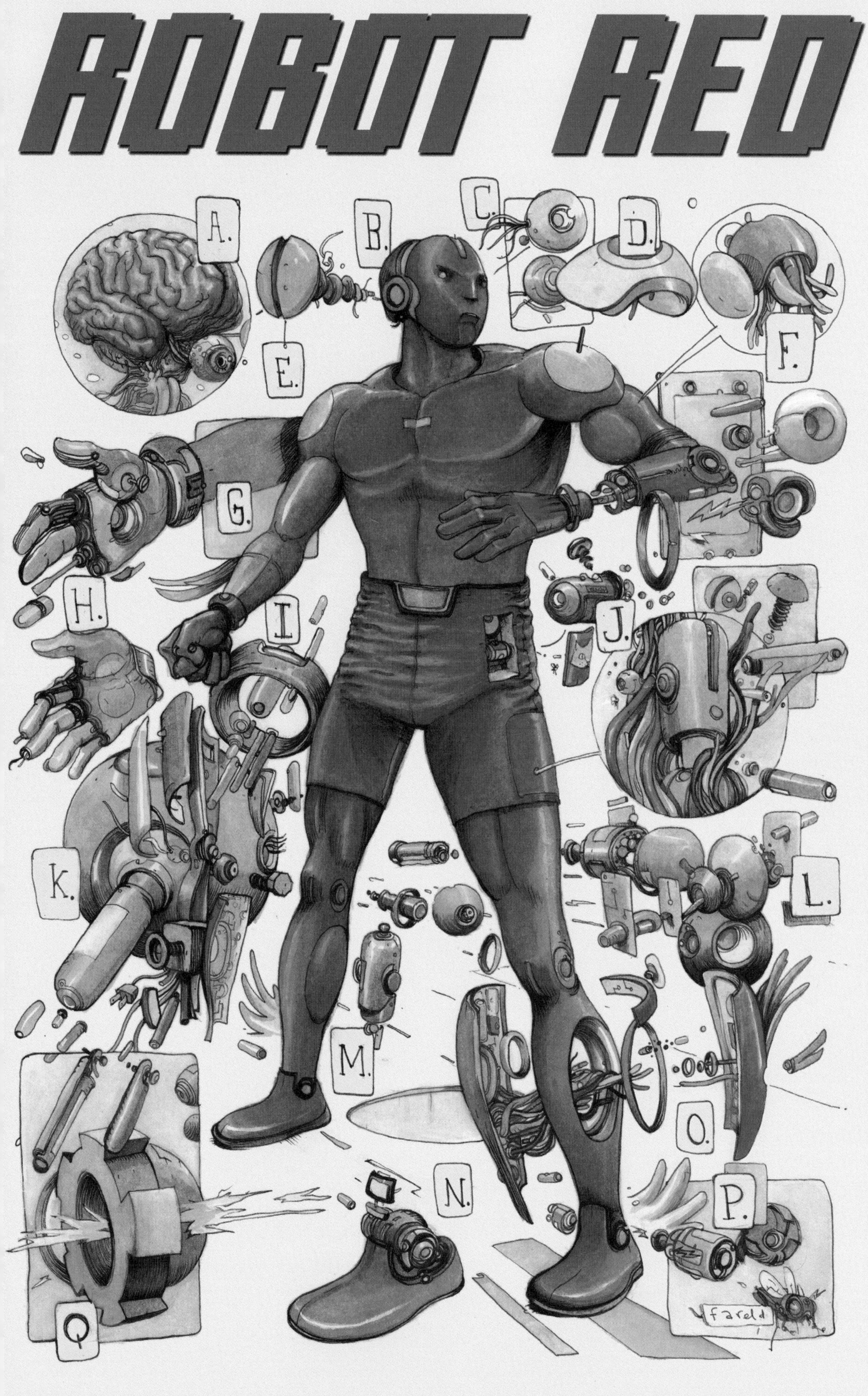
A.
B.
C.
D.
E.
F.
G.
H.
I.
J.
K.
L.
M.
N.
O.
P.
Q

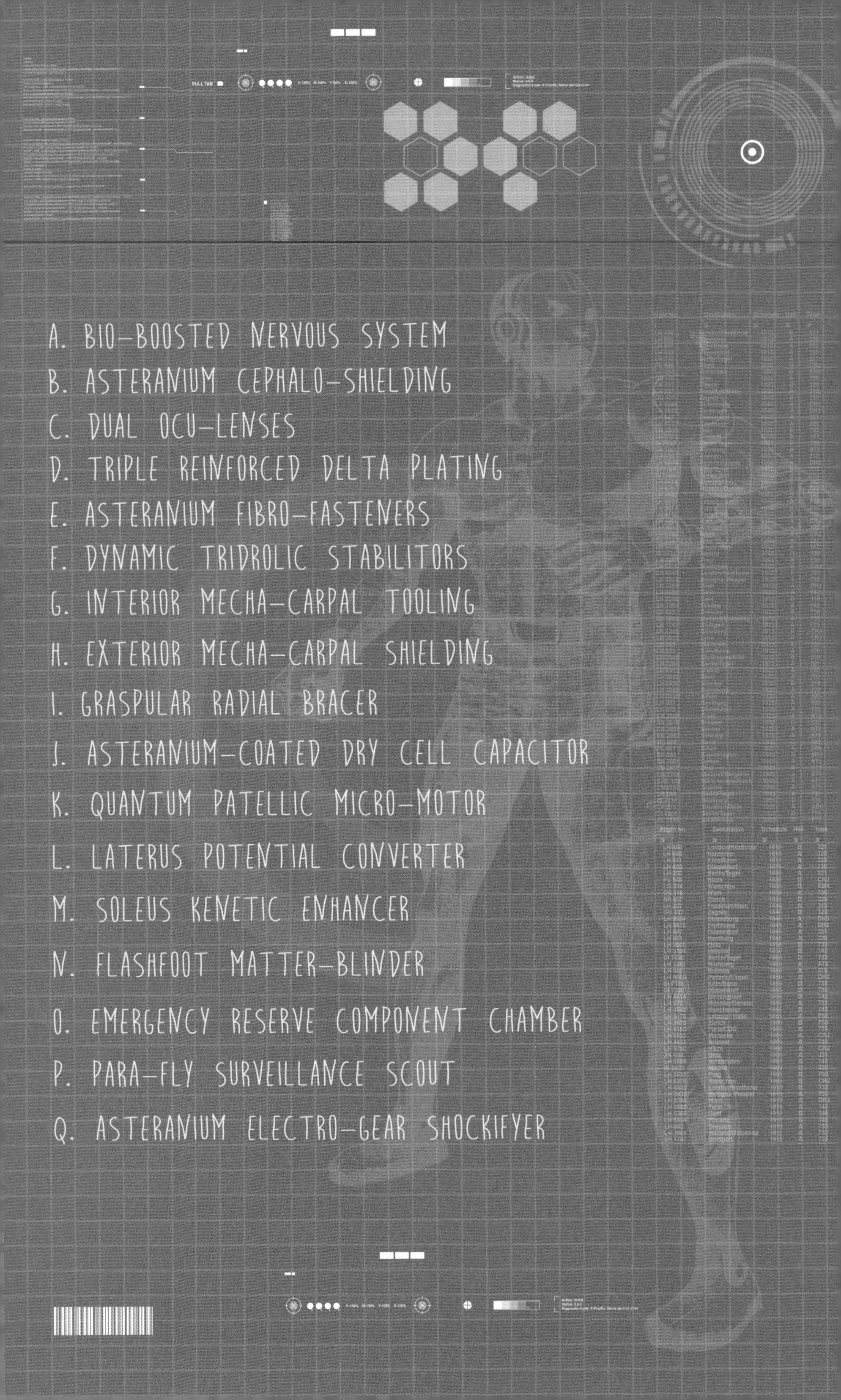
A. BIO-BOOSTED NERVOUS SYSTEM
B. ASTERANIUM CEPHALO-SHIELDING
C. DUAL OCU-LENSES
D. TRIPLE REINFORCED DELTA PLATING
E. ASTERANIUM FIBRO-FASTENERS
F. DYNAMIC TRIDROLIC STABILITORS
G. INTERIOR MECHA-CARPAL TOOLING
H. EXTERIOR MECHA-CARPAL SHIELDING
I. GRASPULAR RADIAL BRACER
J. ASTERANIUM-COATED DRY CELL CAPACITOR
K. QUANTUM PATELLIC MICRO-MOTOR
L. LATERUS POTENTIAL CONVERTER
M. SOLEUS KENETIC ENHANCER
N. FLASHFOOT MATTER-BLINDER
O. EMERGENCY RESERVE COMPONENT CHAMBER
P. PARA-FLY SURVEILLANCE SCOUT
Q. ASTERANIUM ELECTRO-GEAR SHOCKIFYER

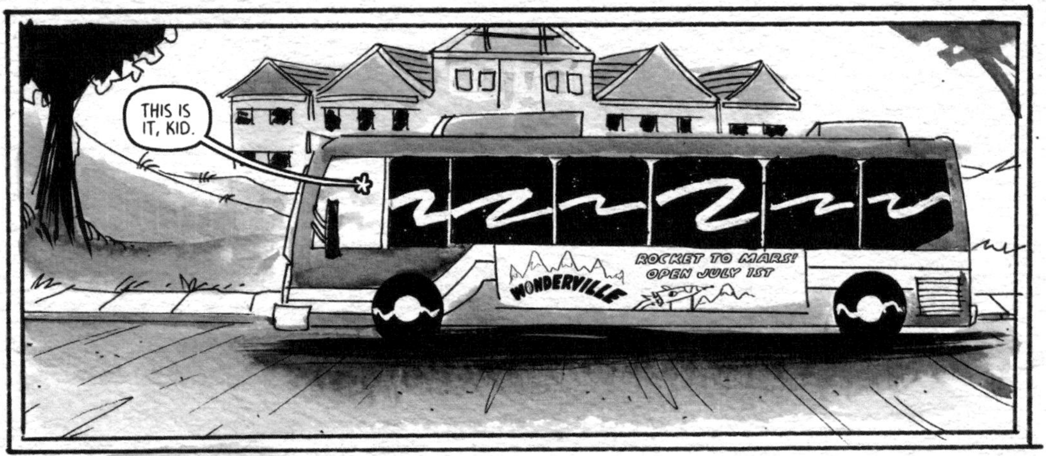
THIS IS IT, KID.
ROCKET TO MARS! OPEN JULY 1ST
WONDERVILLE

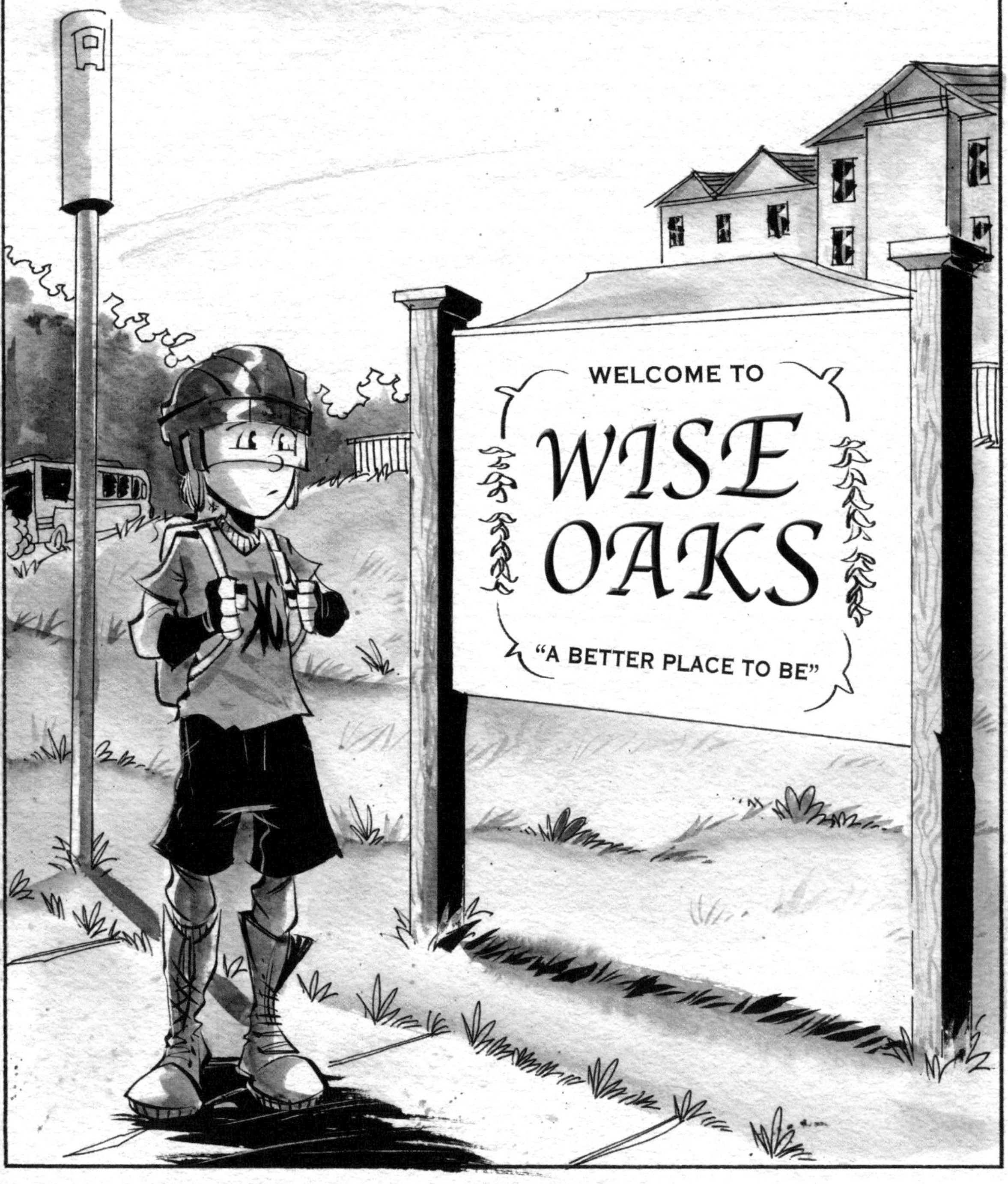
WELCOME TO
WISE OAKS
"A BETTER PLACE TO BE"

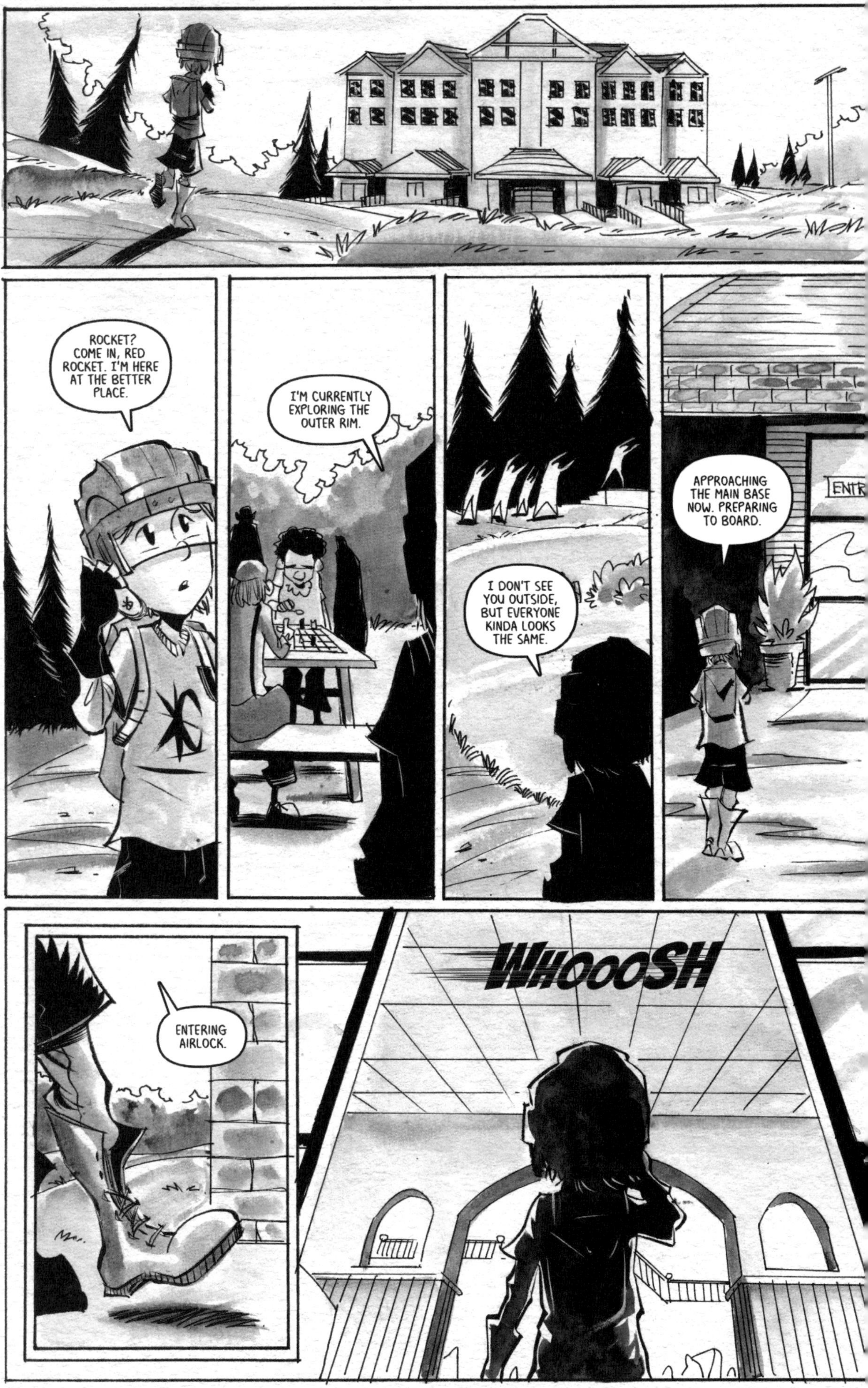
ROCKET? COME IN, RED ROCKET. I'M HERE AT THE BETTER PLACE.
I'M CURRENTLY EXPLORING THE OUTER RIM.
I DON'T SEE YOU OUTSIDE, BUT EVERYONE KINDA LOOKS THE SAME.
APPROACHING THE MAIN BASE NOW. PREPARING TO BOARD.
ENTERING AIRLOCK.
WHOOOSH

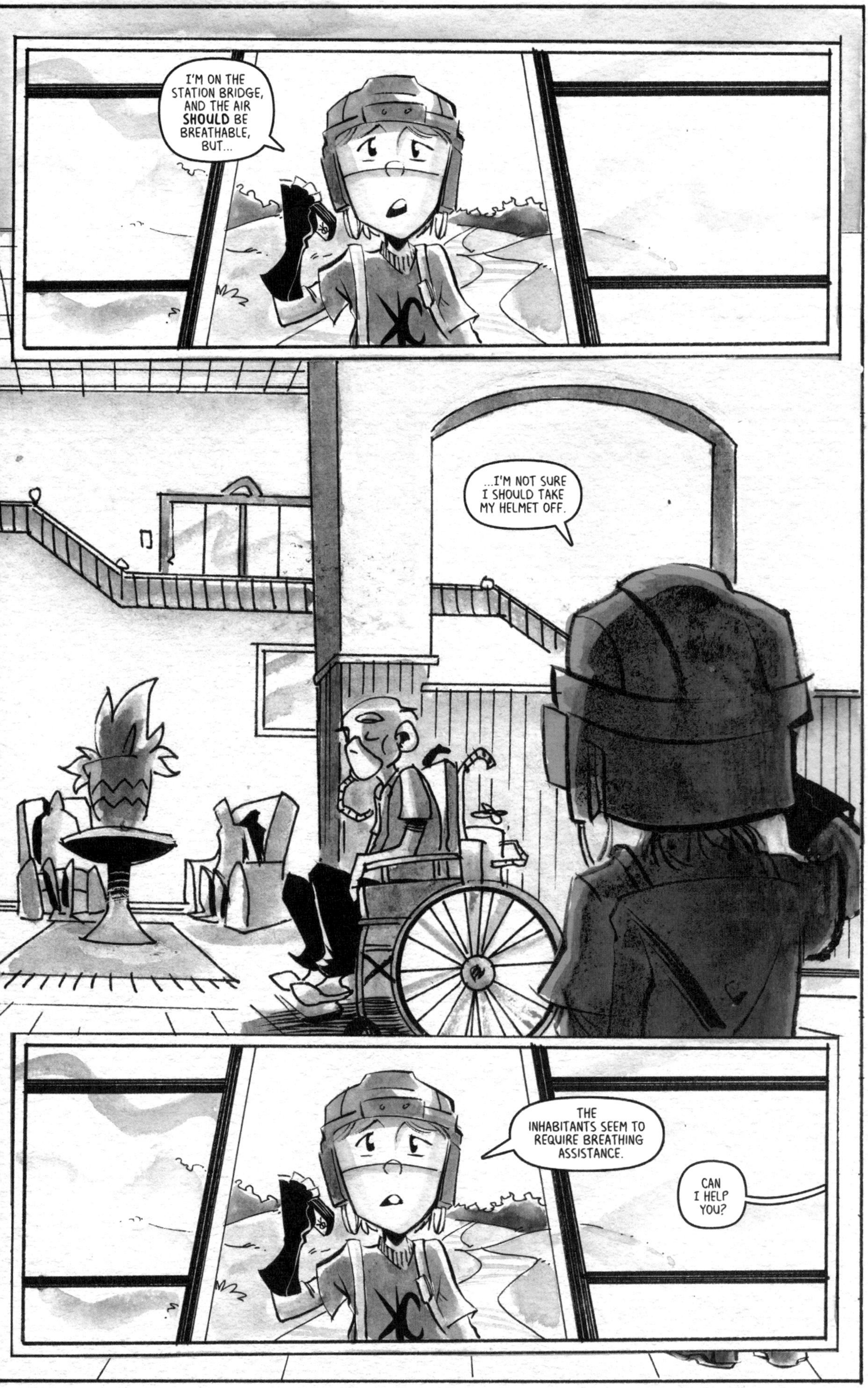
I'M ON THE STATION BRIDGE, AND THE AIR **SHOULD** BE BREATHABLE, BUT...
...I'M NOT SURE I SHOULD TAKE MY HELMET OFF.
THE INHABITANTS SEEM TO REQUIRE BREATHING ASSISTANCE.
CAN I HELP YOU?

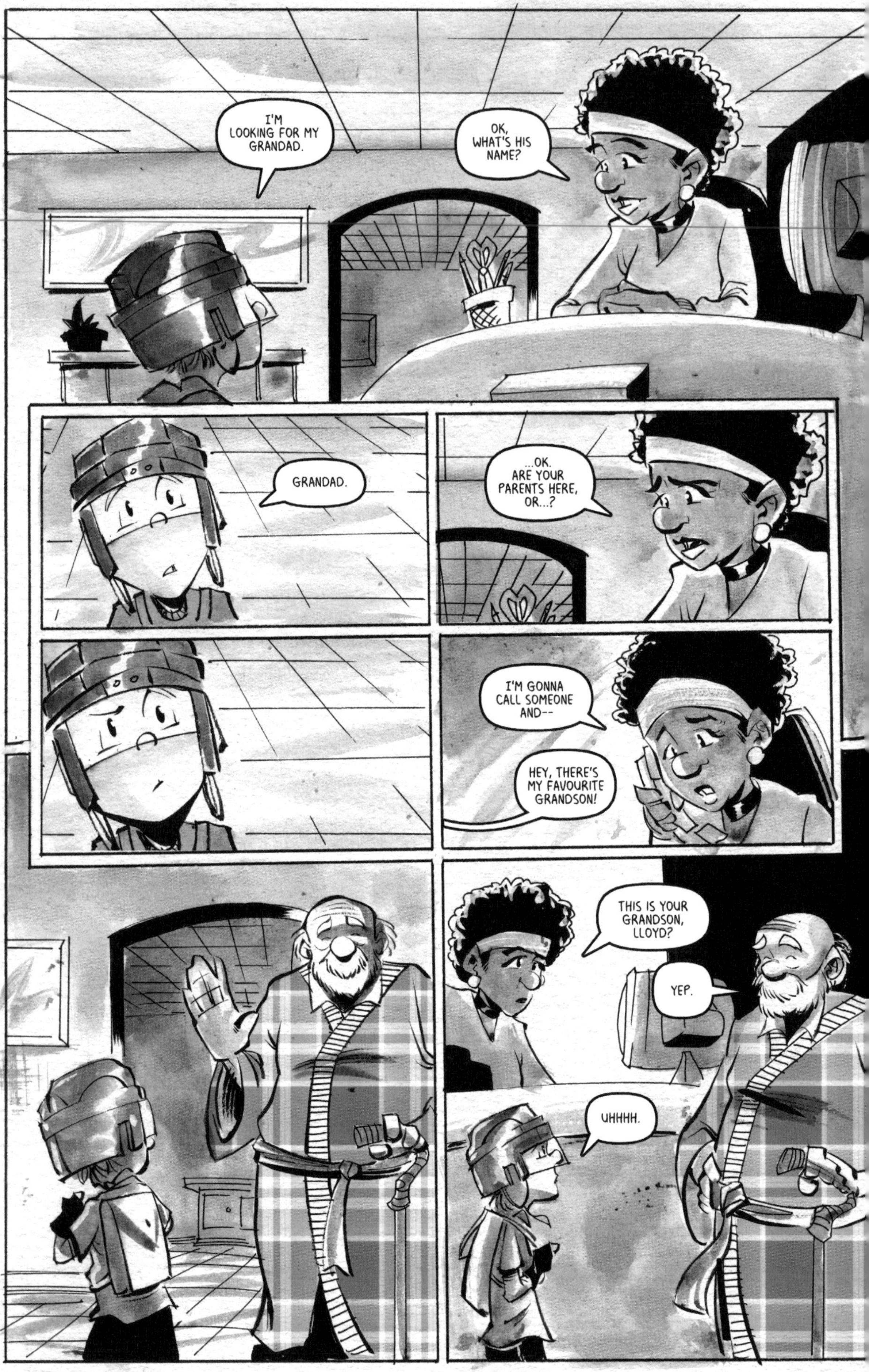
I'M LOOKING FOR MY GRANDAD.
OK, WHAT'S HIS NAME?
GRANDAD.
...OK. ARE YOUR PARENTS HERE, OR...?
I'M GONNA CALL SOMEONE AND--
HEY, THERE'S MY FAVOURITE GRANDSON!
THIS IS YOUR GRANDSON, LLOYD?
YEP.
UHHHH.

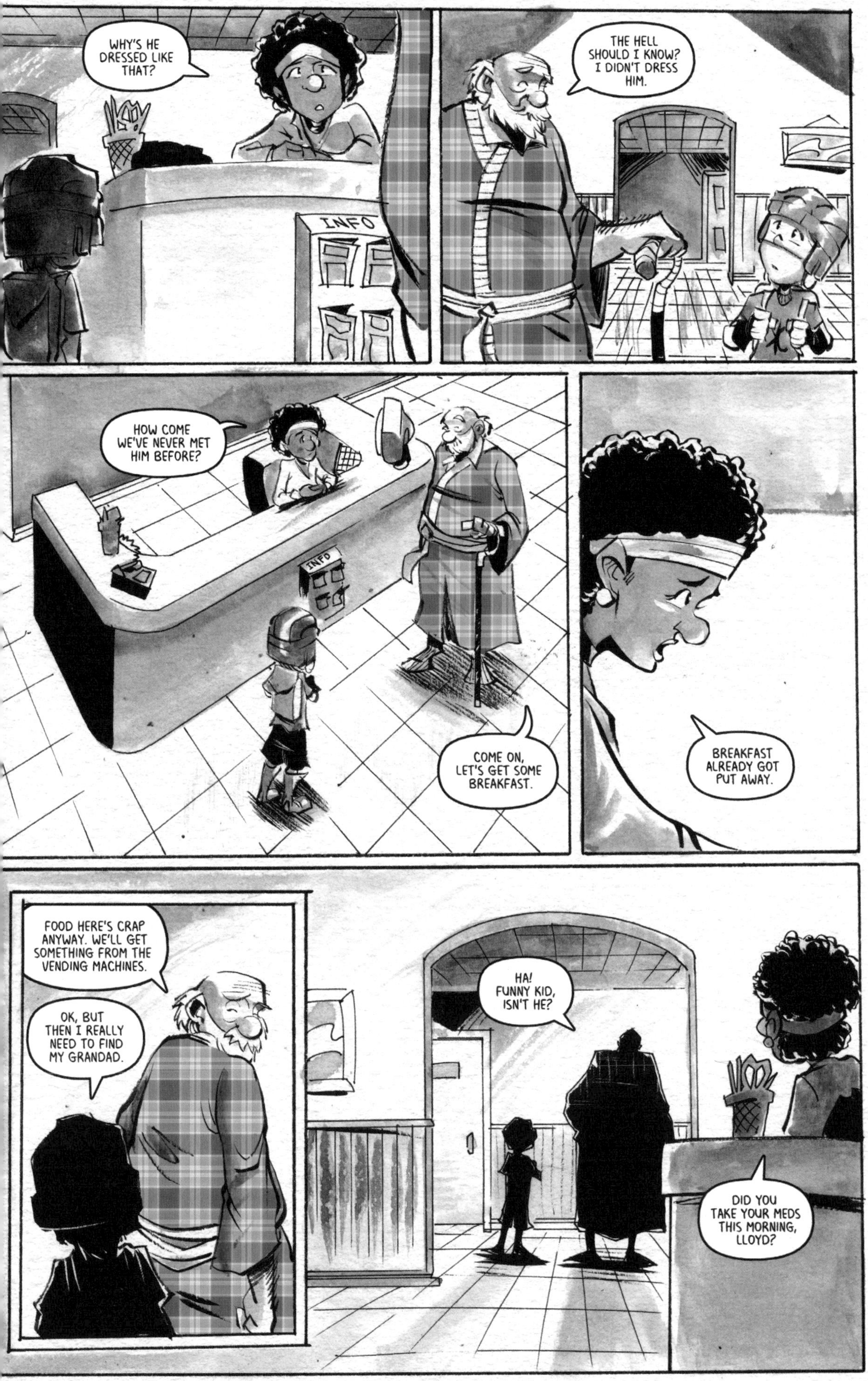
WHY'S HE DRESSED LIKE THAT?
THE HELL SHOULD I KNOW? I DIDN'T DRESS HIM.
INFO
HOW COME WE'VE NEVER MET HIM BEFORE?
INFO
COME ON, LET'S GET SOME BREAKFAST.
BREAKFAST ALREADY GOT PUT AWAY.
FOOD HERE'S CRAP ANYWAY. WE'LL GET SOMETHING FROM THE VENDING MACHINES.
OK, BUT THEN I REALLY NEED TO FIND MY GRANDAD.
HA! FUNNY KID, ISN'T HE?
DID YOU TAKE YOUR MEDS THIS MORNING, LLOYD?

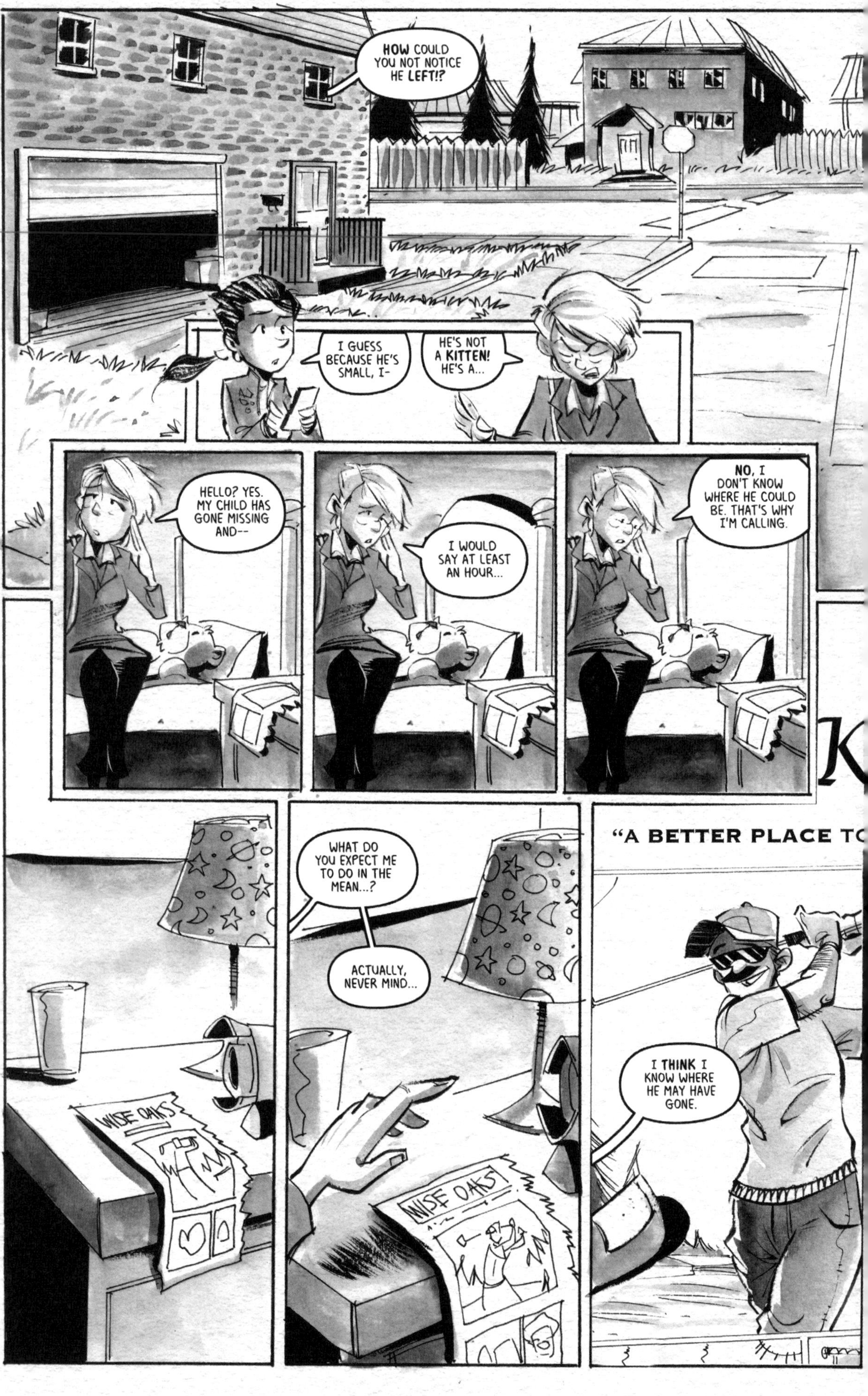
HOW COULD YOU NOT NOTICE HE LEFT!?
I GUESS BECAUSE HE'S SMALL, I-
HE'S NOT A KITTEN! HE'S A...
HELLO? YES. MY CHILD HAS GONE MISSING AND--
I WOULD SAY AT LEAST AN HOUR...
NO, I DON'T KNOW WHERE HE COULD BE. THAT'S WHY I'M CALLING.
WISE OAKS
WHAT DO YOU EXPECT ME TO DO IN THE MEAN...?
ACTUALLY, NEVER MIND...
WISE OAKS
"A BETTER PLACE T
I THINK I KNOW WHERE HE MAY HAVE GONE.

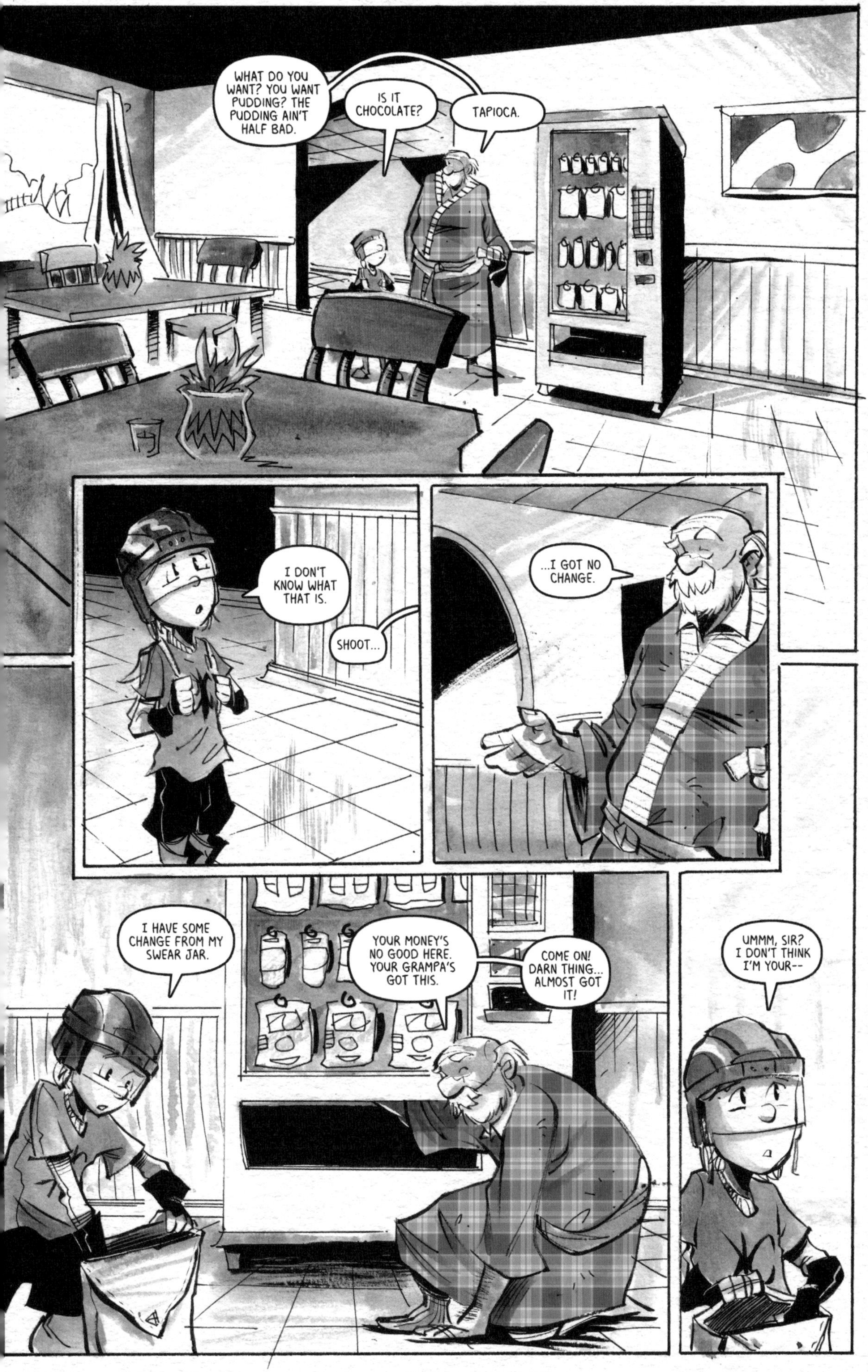
WHAT DO YOU WANT? YOU WANT PUDDING? THE PUDDING AIN'T HALF BAD.
IS IT CHOCOLATE?
TAPIOCA.
I DON'T KNOW WHAT THAT IS.
SHOOT...
...I GOT NO CHANGE.
I HAVE SOME CHANGE FROM MY SWEAR JAR.
YOUR MONEY'S NO GOOD HERE. YOUR GRAMPA'S GOT THIS.
COME ON! DARN THING... ALMOST GOT IT!
UMMM, SIR? I DON'T THINK I'M YOUR--

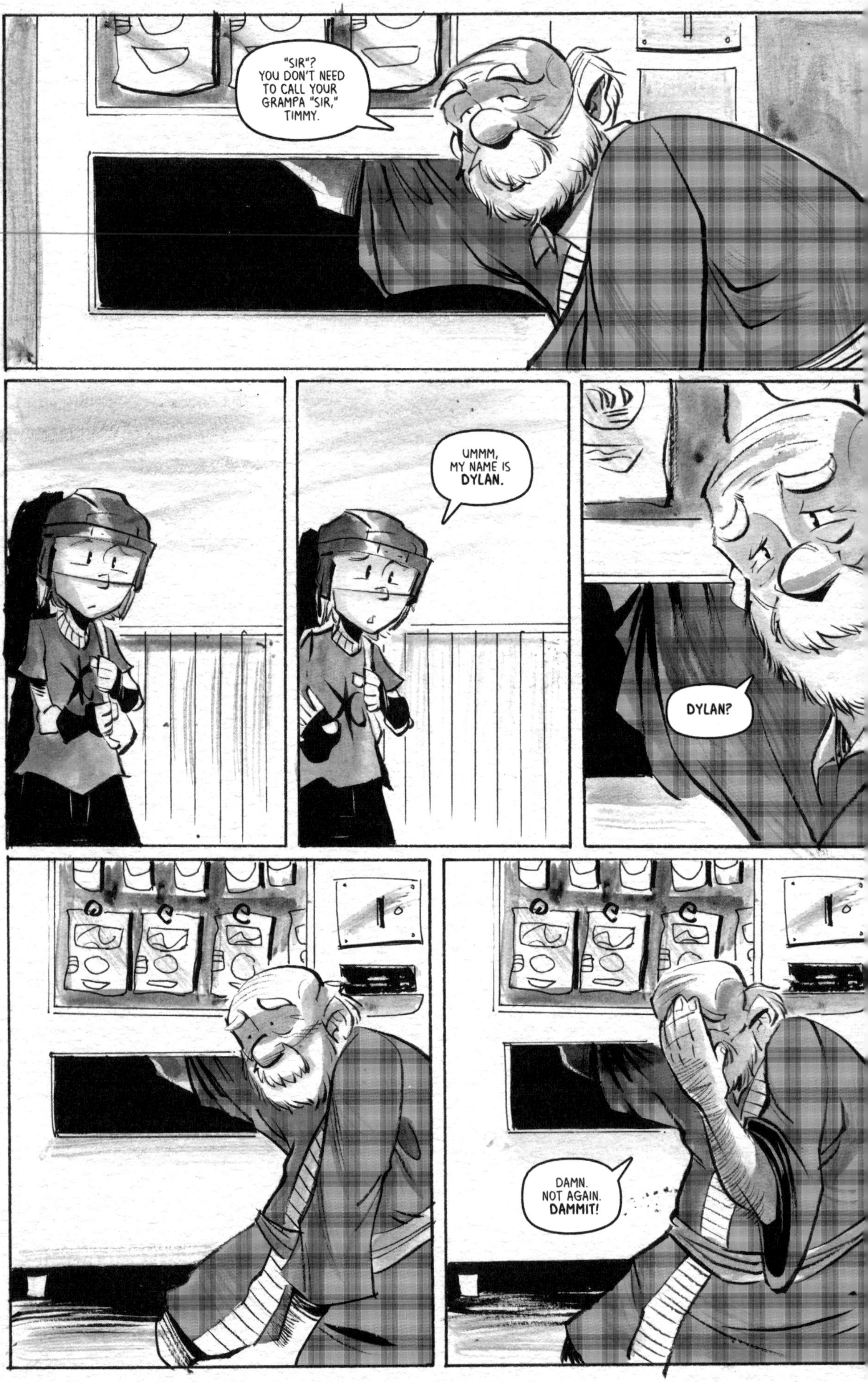

"SIR"? YOU DON'T NEED TO CALL YOUR GRAMPA "SIR," TIMMY.
UMMM, MY NAME IS **DYLAN.**
DYLAN?
DAMN. NOT AGAIN. **DAMMIT!**

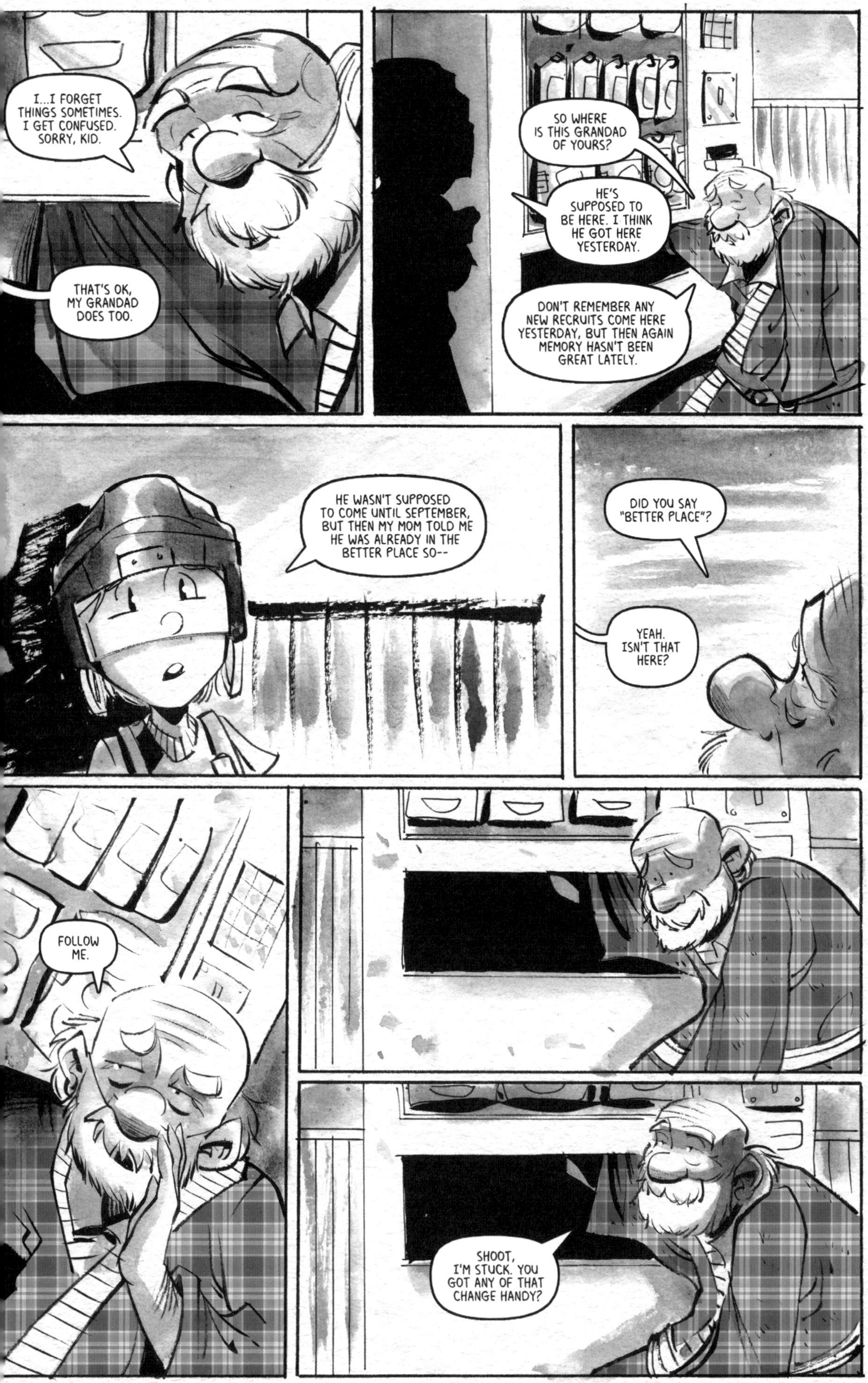
I...I FORGET THINGS SOMETIMES. I GET CONFUSED. SORRY, KID.
THAT'S OK, MY GRANDAD DOES TOO.
SO WHERE IS THIS GRANDAD OF YOURS?
HE'S SUPPOSED TO BE HERE. I THINK HE GOT HERE YESTERDAY.
DON'T REMEMBER ANY NEW RECRUITS COME HERE YESTERDAY, BUT THEN AGAIN MEMORY HASN'T BEEN GREAT LATELY.
HE WASN'T SUPPOSED TO COME UNTIL SEPTEMBER, BUT THEN MY MOM TOLD ME HE WAS ALREADY IN THE BETTER PLACE SO--
DID YOU SAY "BETTER PLACE"?
YEAH. ISN'T THAT HERE?
FOLLOW ME.
SHOOT, I'M STUCK. YOU GOT ANY OF THAT CHANGE HANDY?

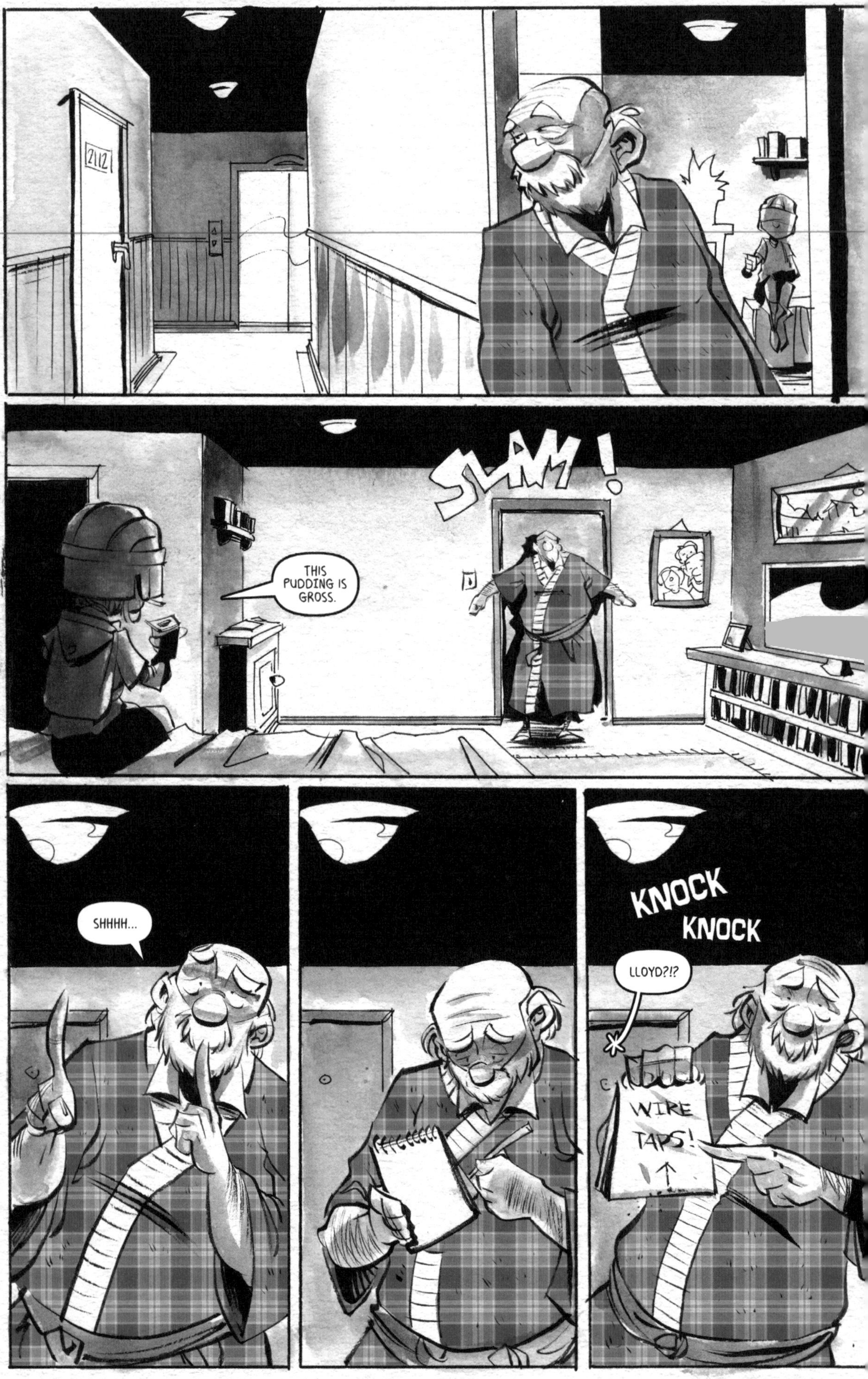
2112
SLAM!
THIS PUDDING IS GROSS.
SHHHH...
KNOCK
KNOCK
LLOYD?!?
WIRE TAPS!

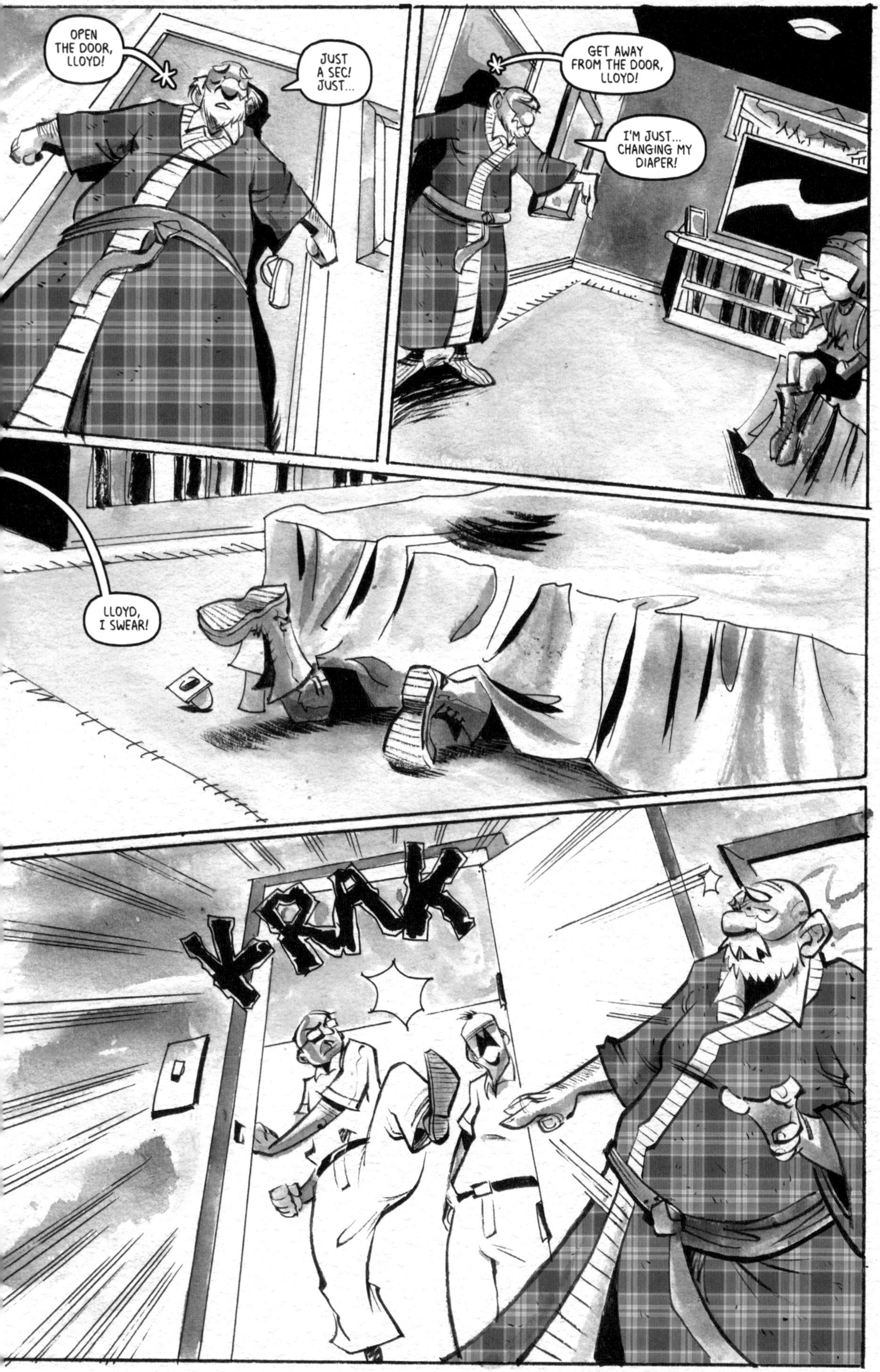
OPEN THE DOOR, LLOYD!
JUST A SEC! JUST...
GET AWAY FROM THE DOOR, LLOYD!
I'M JUST... CHANGING MY DIAPER!
LLOYD, I SWEAR!
KRAK

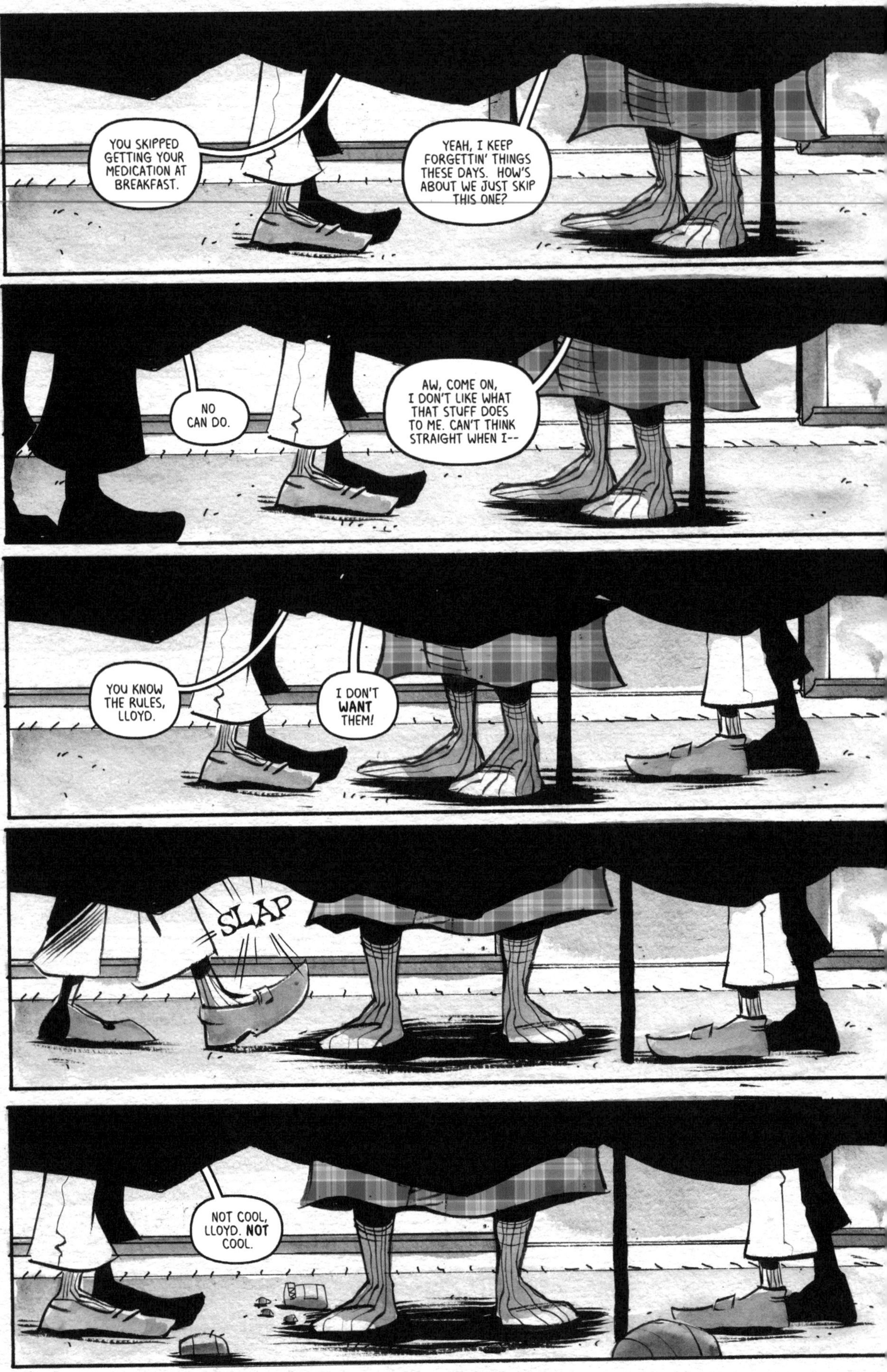
YOU SKIPPED GETTING YOUR MEDICATION AT BREAKFAST.
YEAH, I KEEP FORGETTIN' THINGS THESE DAYS. HOW'S ABOUT WE JUST SKIP THIS ONE?
NO CAN DO.
AW, COME ON, I DON'T LIKE WHAT THAT STUFF DOES TO ME. CAN'T THINK STRAIGHT WHEN I--
YOU KNOW THE RULES, LLOYD.
I DON'T **WANT** THEM!
SLAP
NOT COOL, LLOYD. **NOT** COOL.

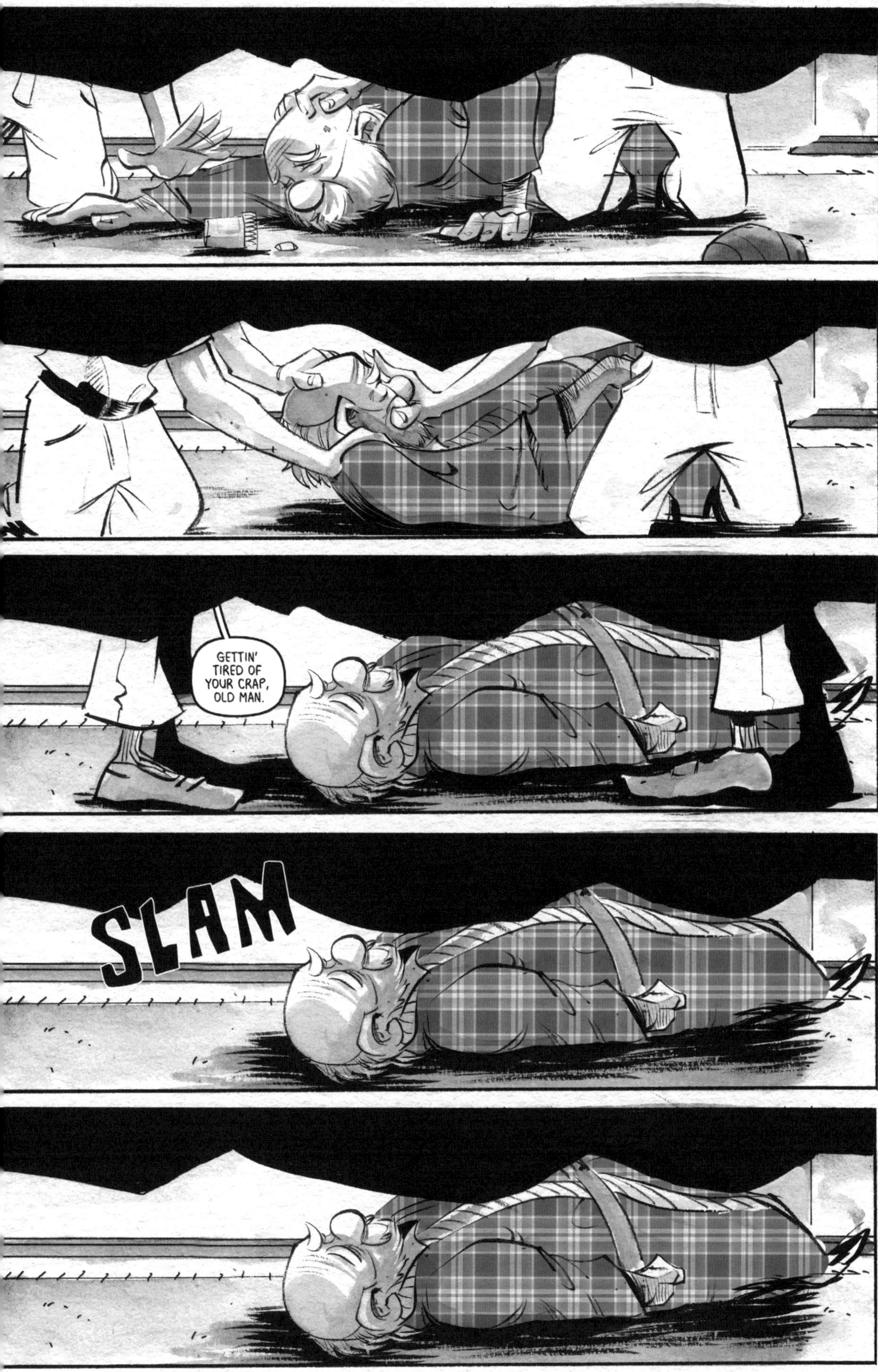
GETTIN' TIRED OF YOUR CRAP, OLD MAN.
SLAM

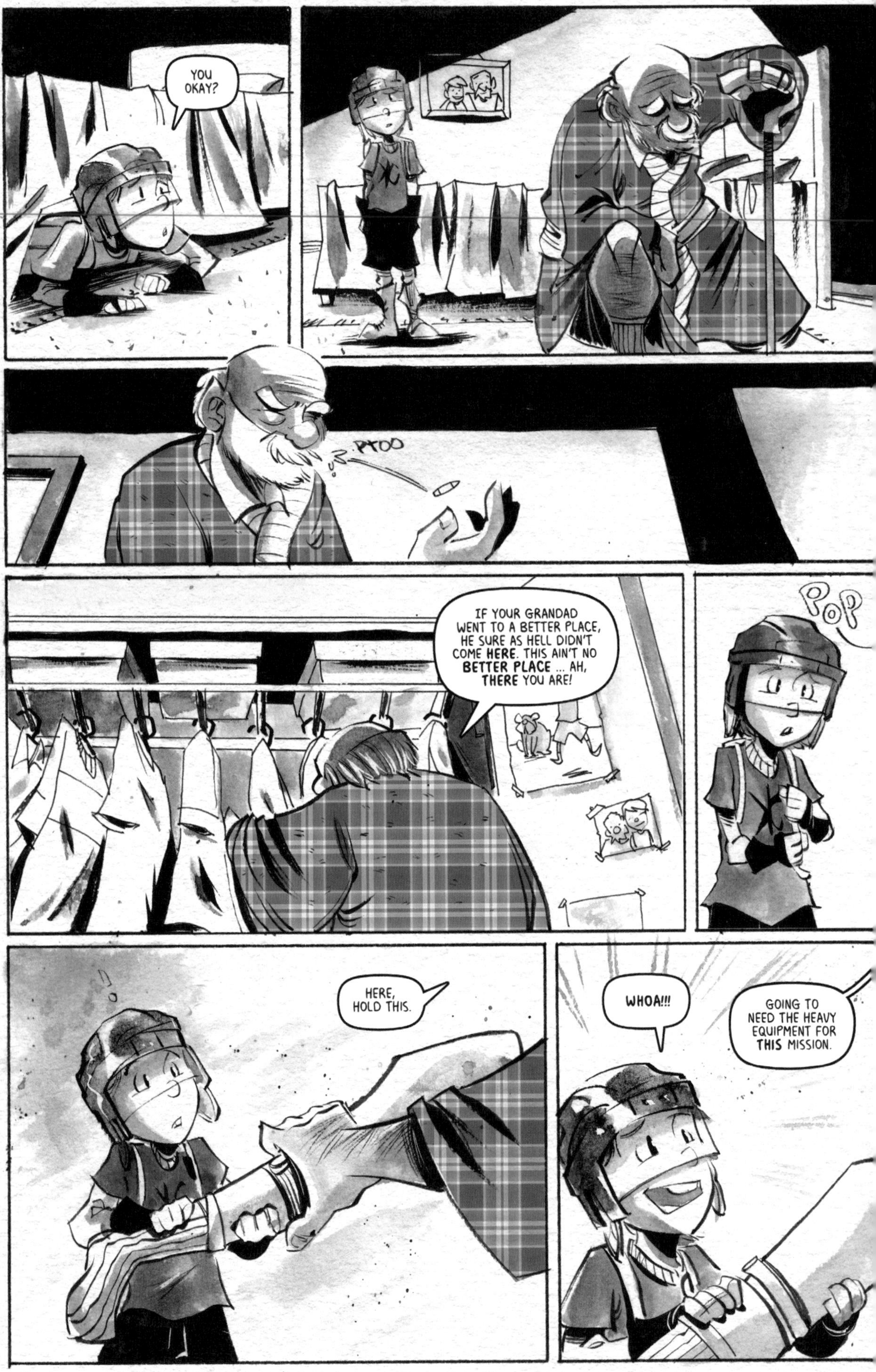
YOU OKAY?
PTOO
IF YOUR GRANDAD WENT TO A BETTER PLACE, HE SURE AS HELL DIDN'T COME **HERE**. THIS AIN'T NO **BETTER PLACE** ... AH, **THERE** YOU ARE!
POP
HERE, HOLD THIS.
WHOA!!!
GOING TO NEED THE HEAVY EQUIPMENT FOR **THIS** MISSION.

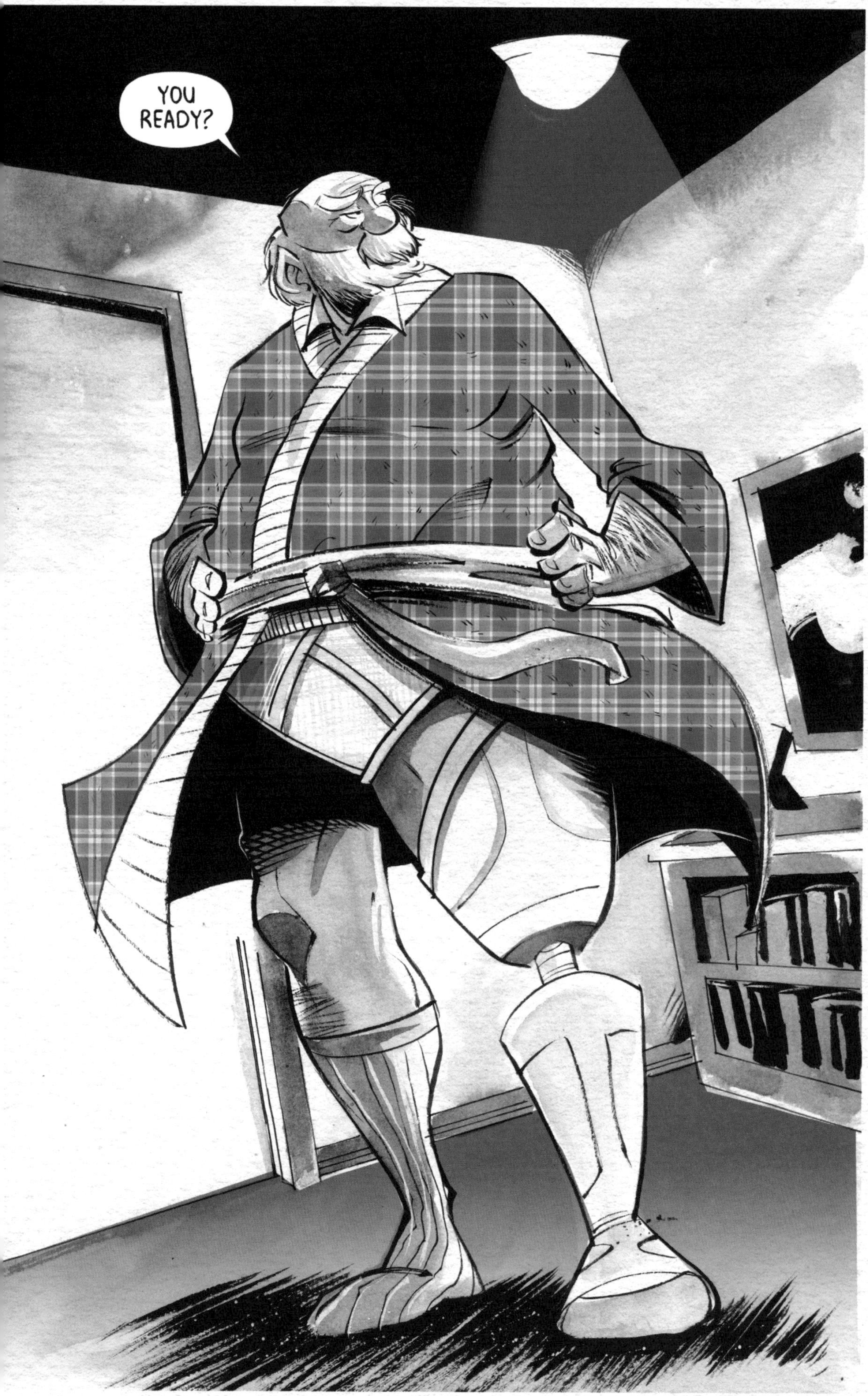
YOU READY?

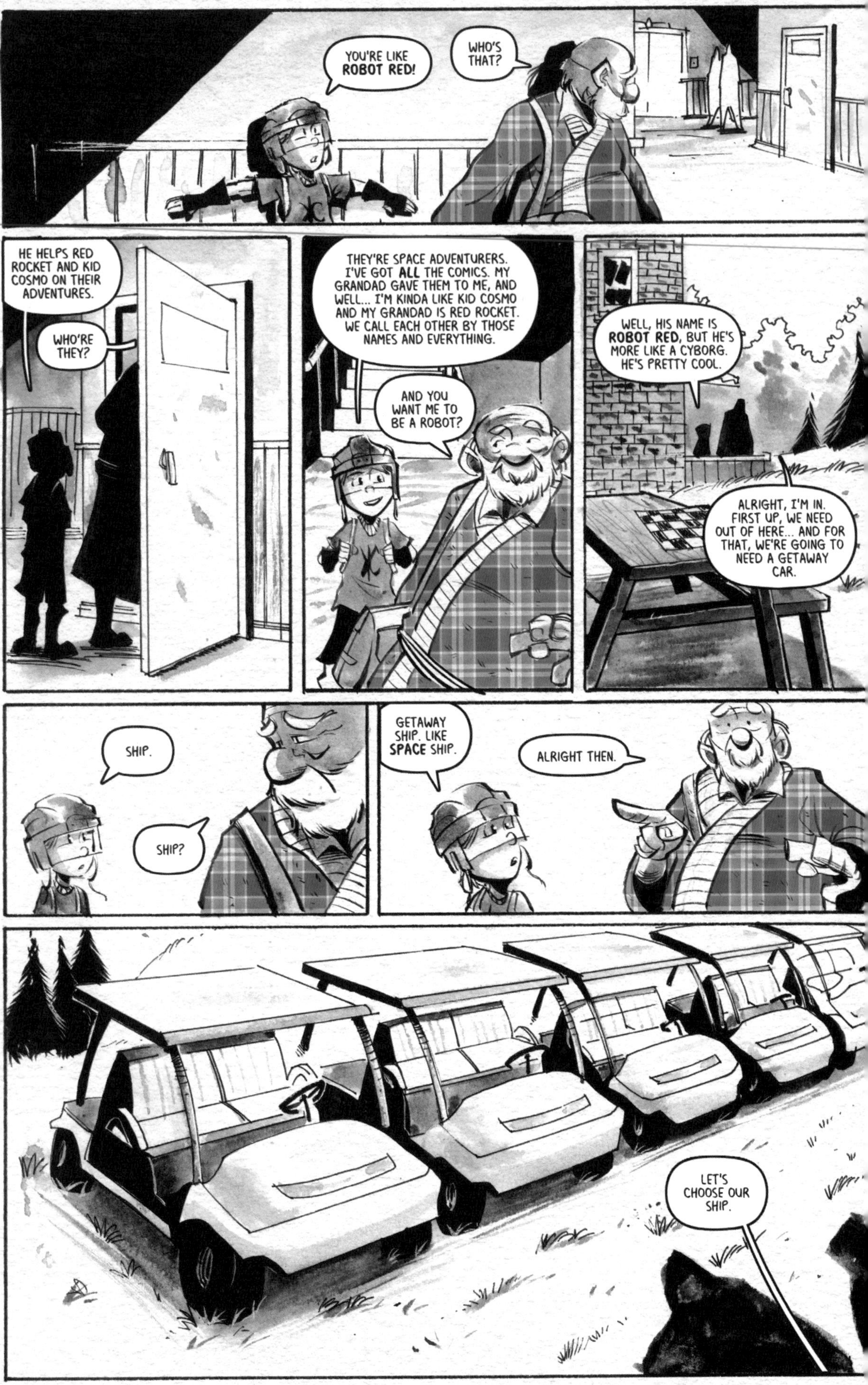
YOU'RE LIKE ROBOT RED!
WHO'S THAT?
HE HELPS RED ROCKET AND KID COSMO ON THEIR ADVENTURES.
WHO'RE THEY?
THEY'RE SPACE ADVENTURERS. I'VE GOT ALL THE COMICS. MY GRANDAD GAVE THEM TO ME, AND WELL... I'M KINDA LIKE KID COSMO AND MY GRANDAD IS RED ROCKET. WE CALL EACH OTHER BY THOSE NAMES AND EVERYTHING.
AND YOU WANT ME TO BE A ROBOT?
WELL, HIS NAME IS ROBOT RED, BUT HE'S MORE LIKE A CYBORG. HE'S PRETTY COOL.
ALRIGHT, I'M IN. FIRST UP, WE NEED OUT OF HERE... AND FOR THAT, WE'RE GOING TO NEED A GETAWAY CAR.
SHIP.
SHIP?
GETAWAY SHIP. LIKE SPACE SHIP.
ALRIGHT THEN.
LET'S CHOOSE OUR SHIP.

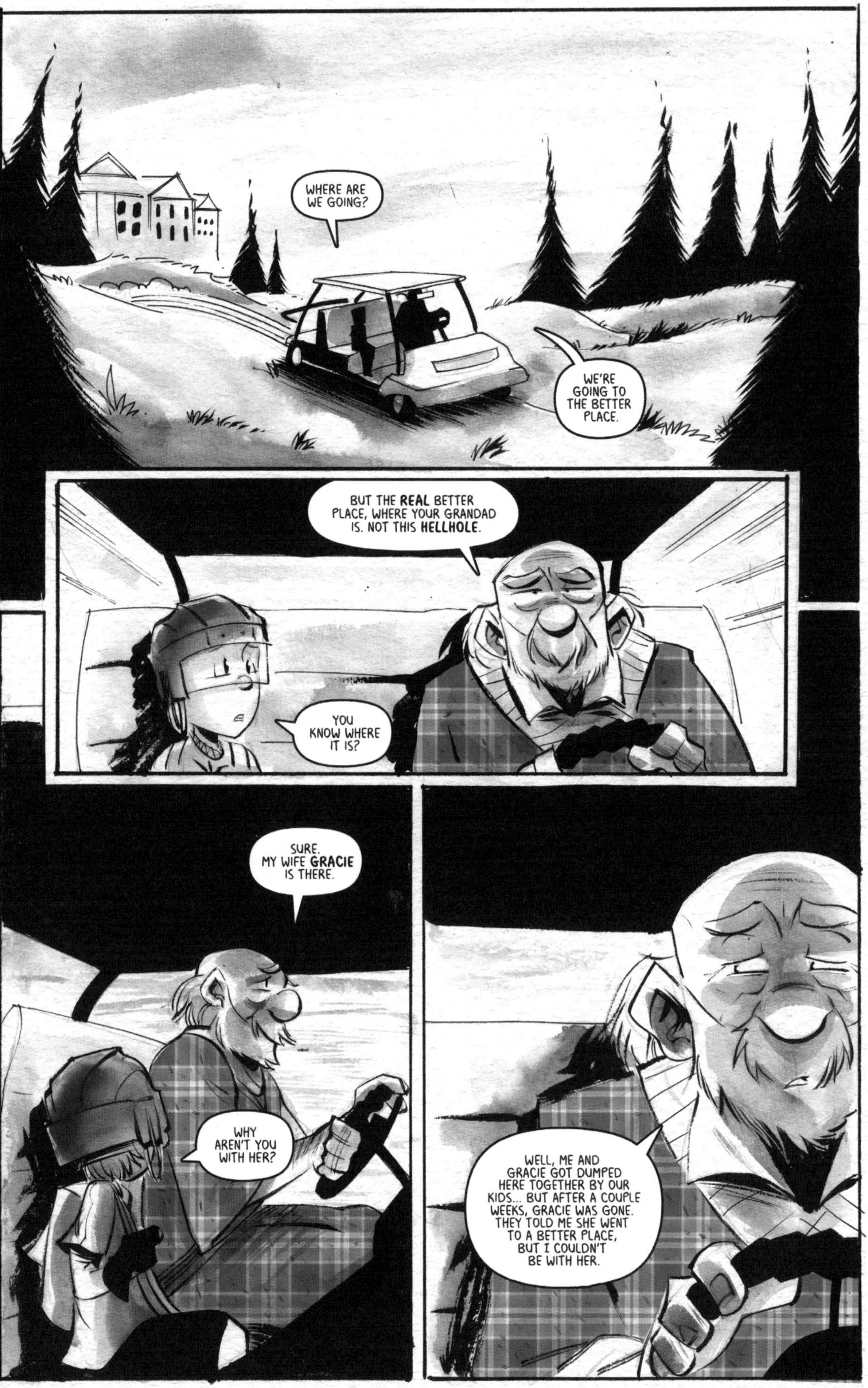
WHERE ARE WE GOING?
WE'RE GOING TO THE BETTER PLACE.
BUT THE **REAL** BETTER PLACE, WHERE YOUR GRANDAD IS. NOT THIS **HELLHOLE**.
YOU KNOW WHERE IT IS?
SURE. MY WIFE **GRACIE** IS THERE.
WHY AREN'T YOU WITH HER?
WELL, ME AND GRACIE GOT DUMPED HERE TOGETHER BY OUR KIDS... BUT AFTER A COUPLE WEEKS, GRACIE WAS GONE. THEY TOLD ME SHE WENT TO A BETTER PLACE, BUT I COULDN'T BE WITH HER.

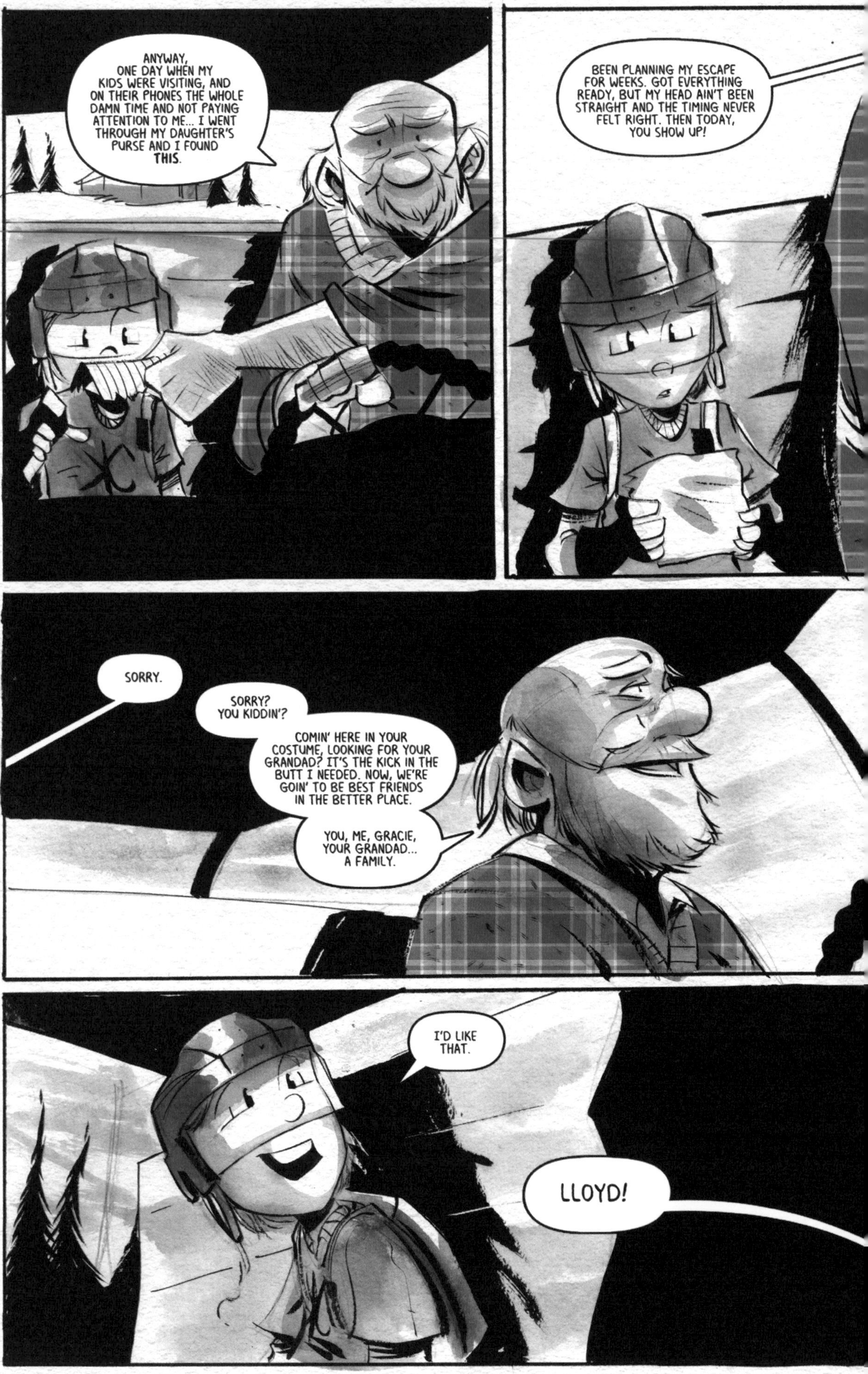
ANYWAY, ONE DAY WHEN MY KIDS WERE VISITING, AND ON THEIR PHONES THE WHOLE DAMN TIME AND NOT PAYING ATTENTION TO ME... I WENT THROUGH MY DAUGHTER'S PURSE AND I FOUND **THIS**.
BEEN PLANNING MY ESCAPE FOR WEEKS. GOT EVERYTHING READY, BUT MY HEAD AIN'T BEEN STRAIGHT AND THE TIMING NEVER FELT RIGHT. THEN TODAY, YOU SHOW UP!
SORRY.
SORRY? YOU KIDDIN'?
COMIN' HERE IN YOUR COSTUME, LOOKING FOR YOUR GRANDAD? IT'S THE KICK IN THE BUTT I NEEDED. NOW, WE'RE GOIN' TO BE BEST FRIENDS IN THE BETTER PLACE.
YOU, ME, GRACIE, YOUR GRANDAD... A FAMILY.
I'D LIKE THAT.
LLOYD!

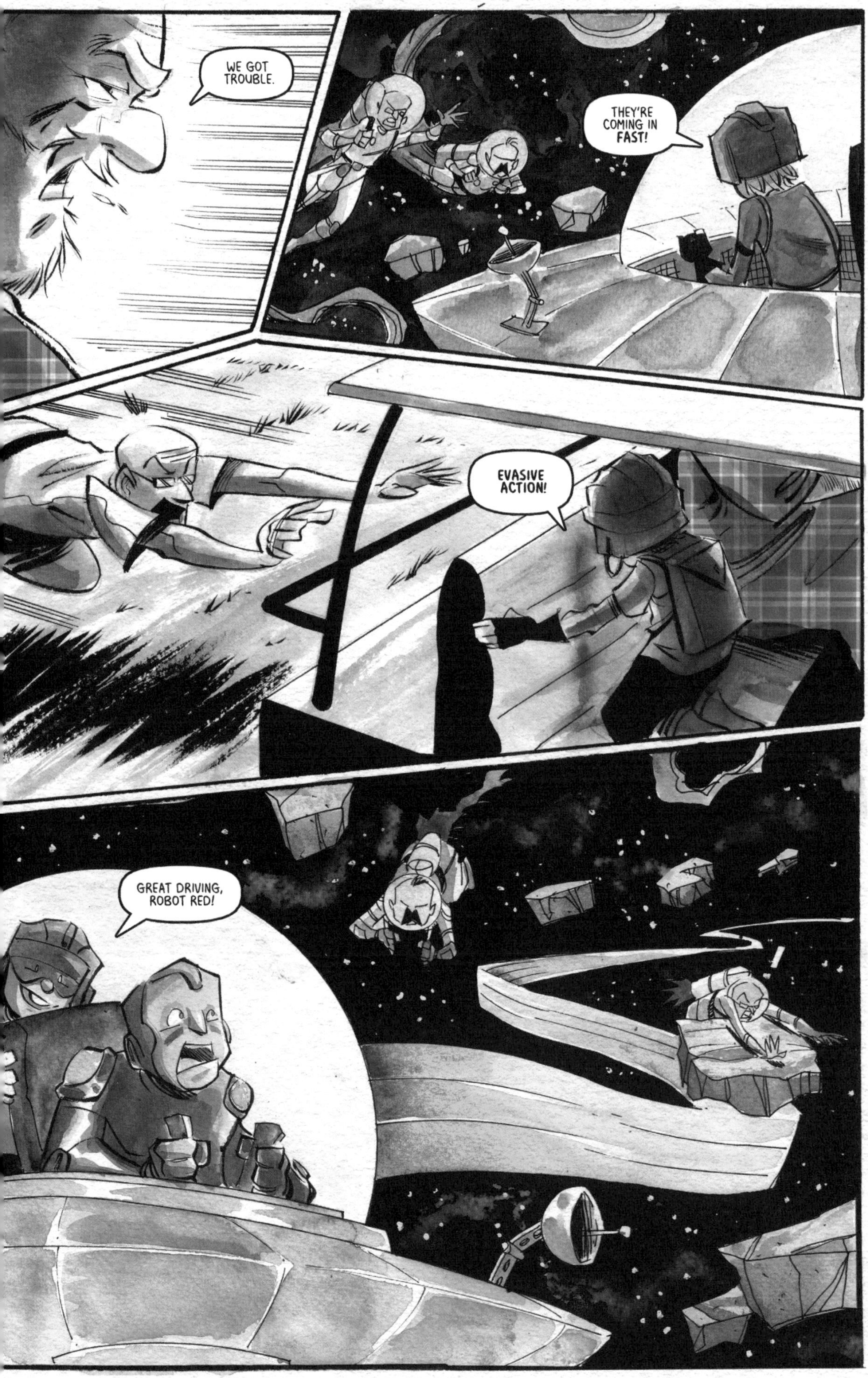
WE GOT TROUBLE.
THEY'RE COMING IN FAST!
EVASIVE ACTION!
GREAT DRIVING, ROBOT RED!

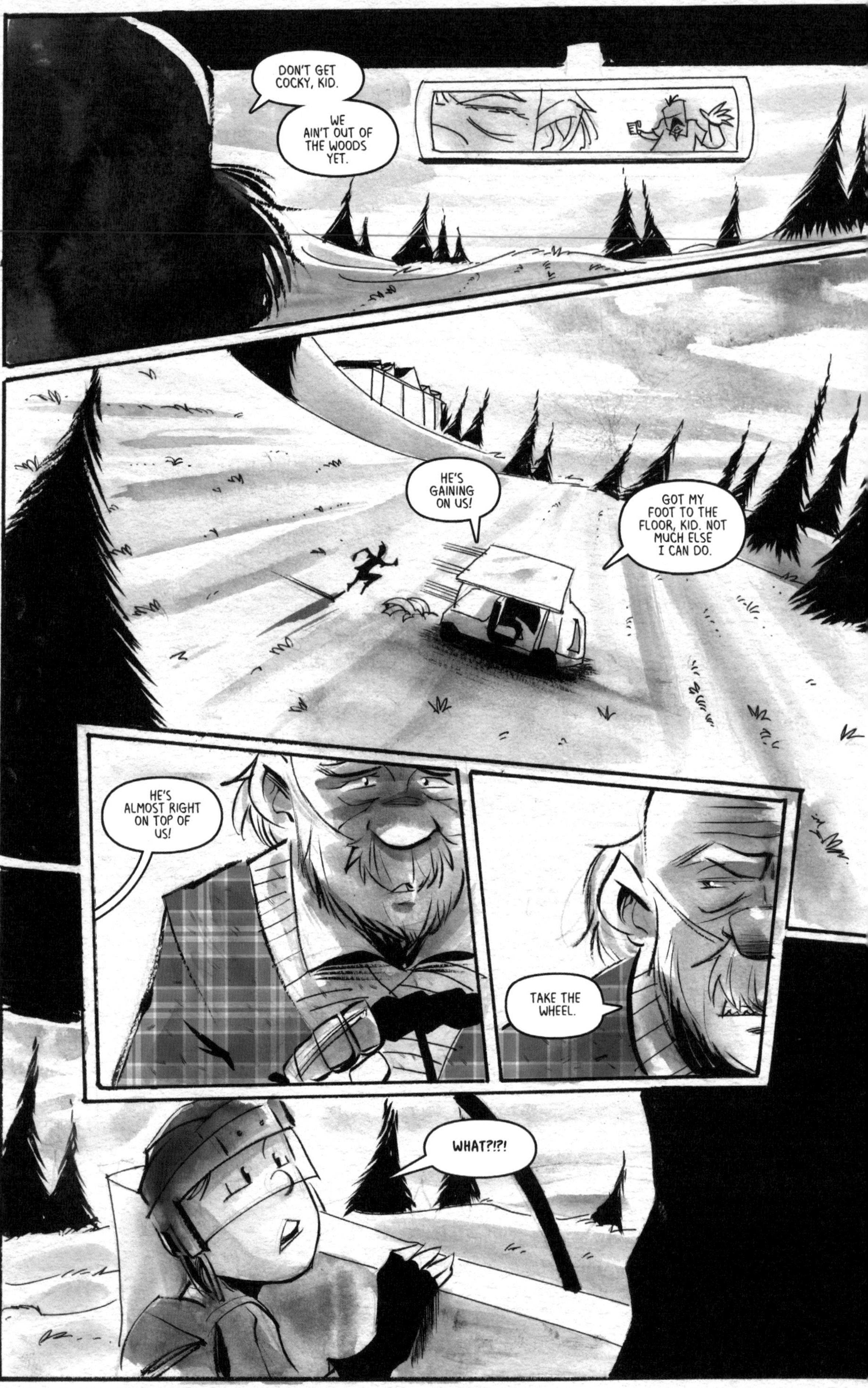
DON'T GET COCKY, KID.
WE AIN'T OUT OF THE WOODS YET.
HE'S GAINING ON US!
GOT MY FOOT TO THE FLOOR, KID. NOT MUCH ELSE I CAN DO.
HE'S ALMOST RIGHT ON TOP OF US!
TAKE THE WHEEL.
WHAT?!?!

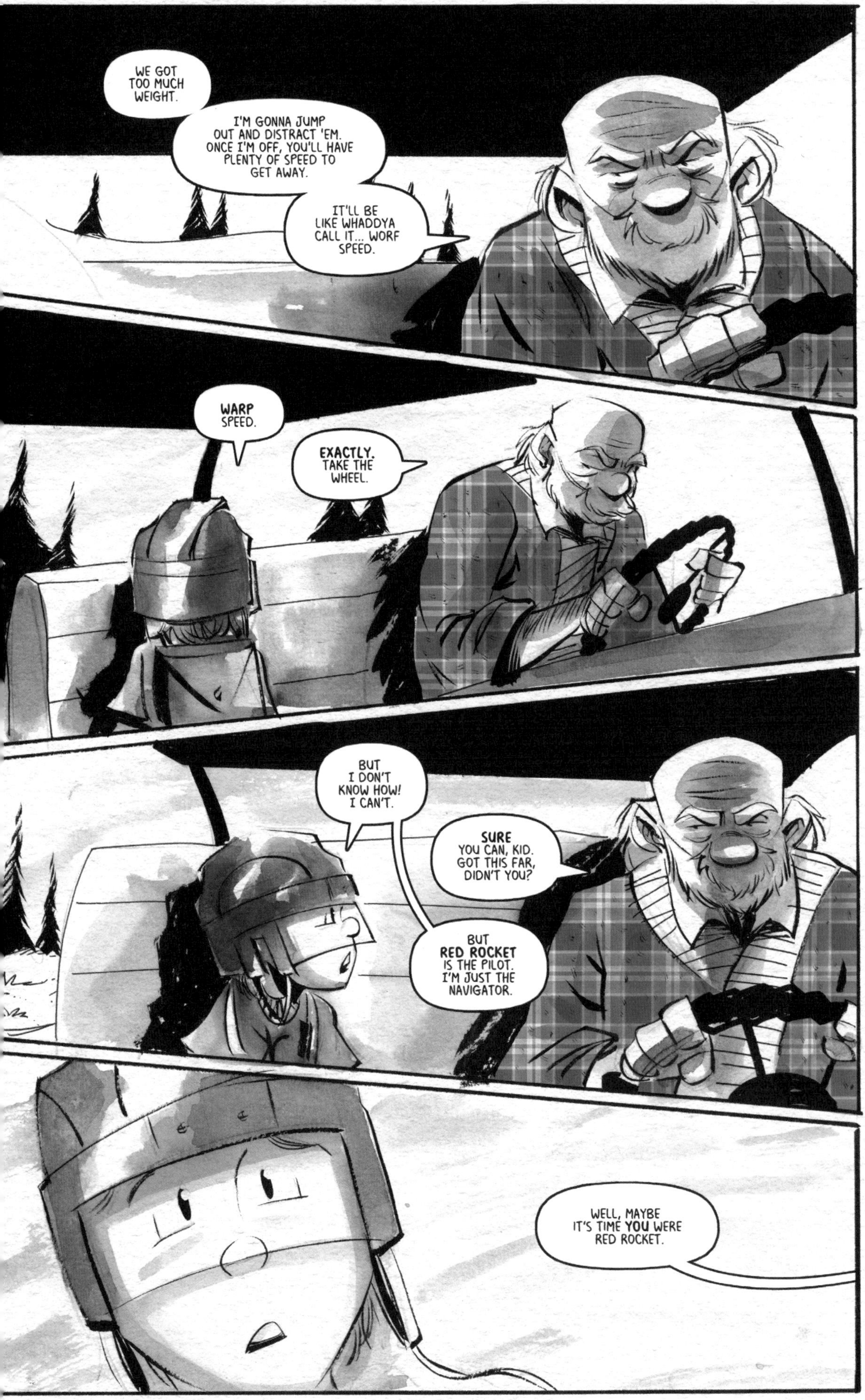
WE GOT TOO MUCH WEIGHT.
I'M GONNA JUMP OUT AND DISTRACT 'EM. ONCE I'M OFF, YOU'LL HAVE PLENTY OF SPEED TO GET AWAY.
IT'LL BE LIKE WHADDYA CALL IT... WORF SPEED.
WARP SPEED.
EXACTLY. TAKE THE WHEEL.
BUT I DON'T KNOW HOW! I CAN'T.
SURE YOU CAN, KID. GOT THIS FAR, DIDN'T YOU?
BUT **RED ROCKET** IS THE PILOT. I'M JUST THE NAVIGATOR.
WELL, MAYBE IT'S TIME **YOU** WERE RED ROCKET.

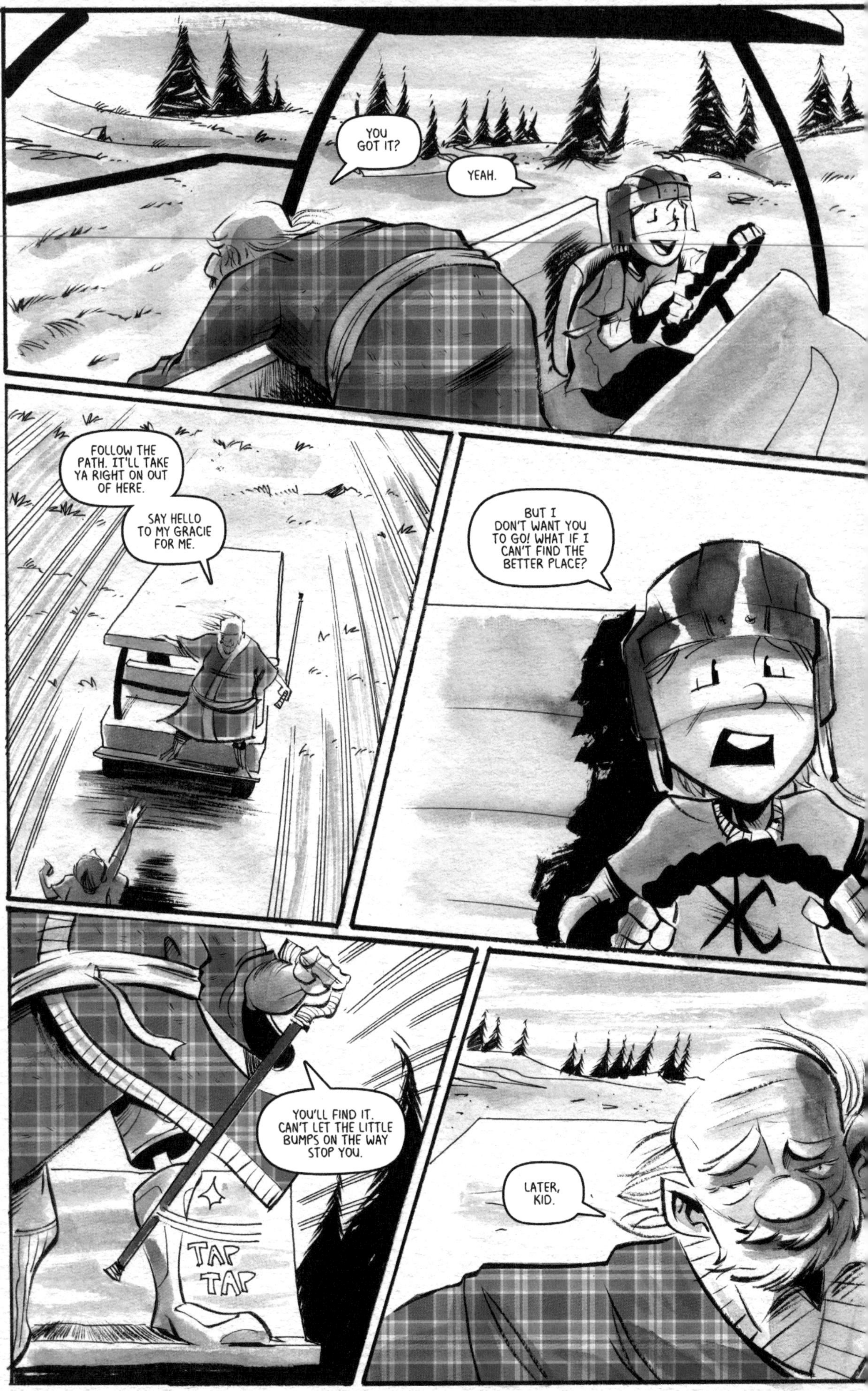

YOU GOT IT?
YEAH.
FOLLOW THE PATH. IT'LL TAKE YA RIGHT ON OUT OF HERE.
SAY HELLO TO MY GRACIE FOR ME.
BUT I DON'T WANT YOU TO GO! WHAT IF I CAN'T FIND THE BETTER PLACE?
YOU'LL FIND IT. CAN'T LET THE LITTLE BUMPS ON THE WAY STOP YOU.
TAP TAP
LATER, KID.

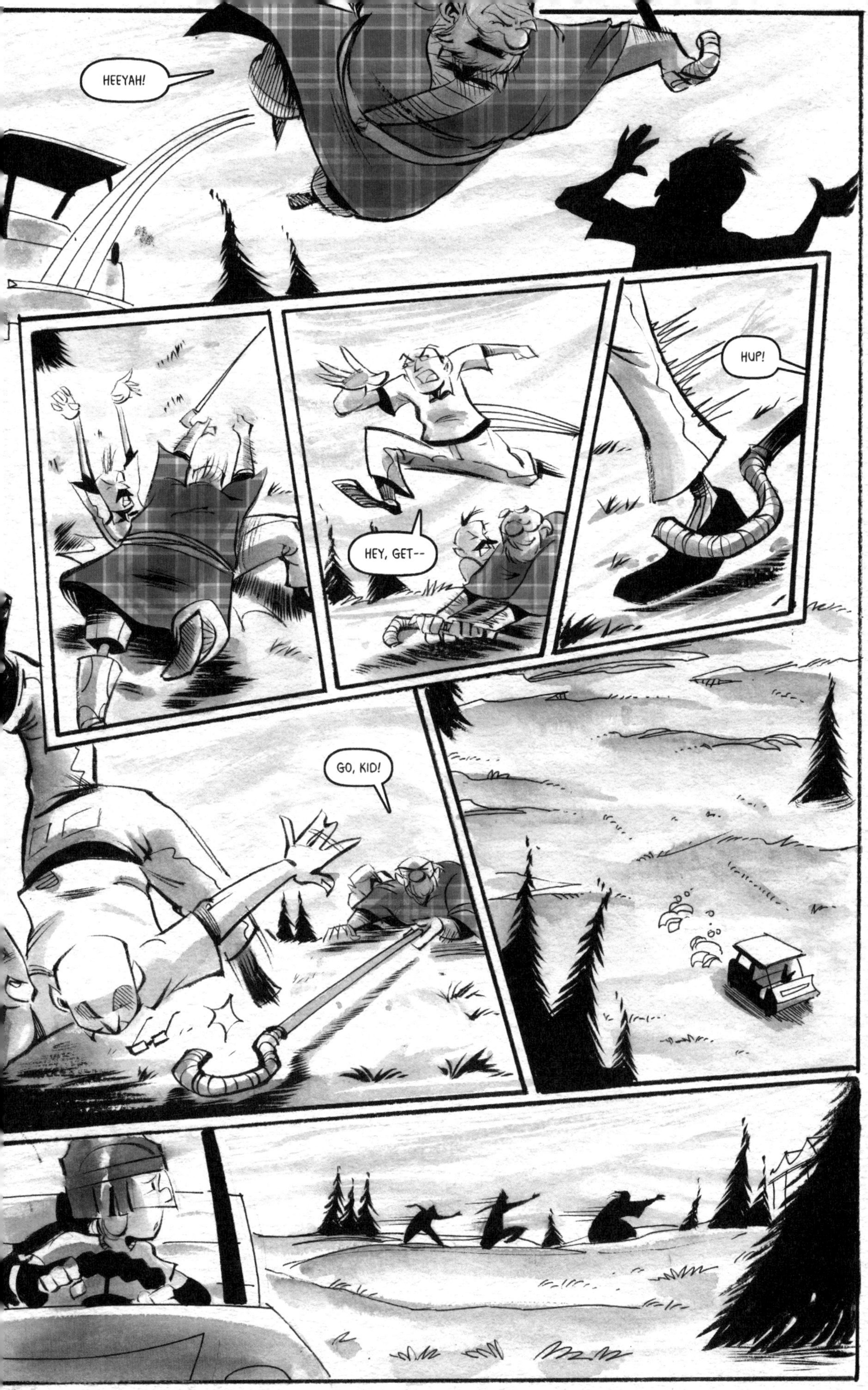
HEEYAH!
HEY, GET--
HUP!
GO, KID!

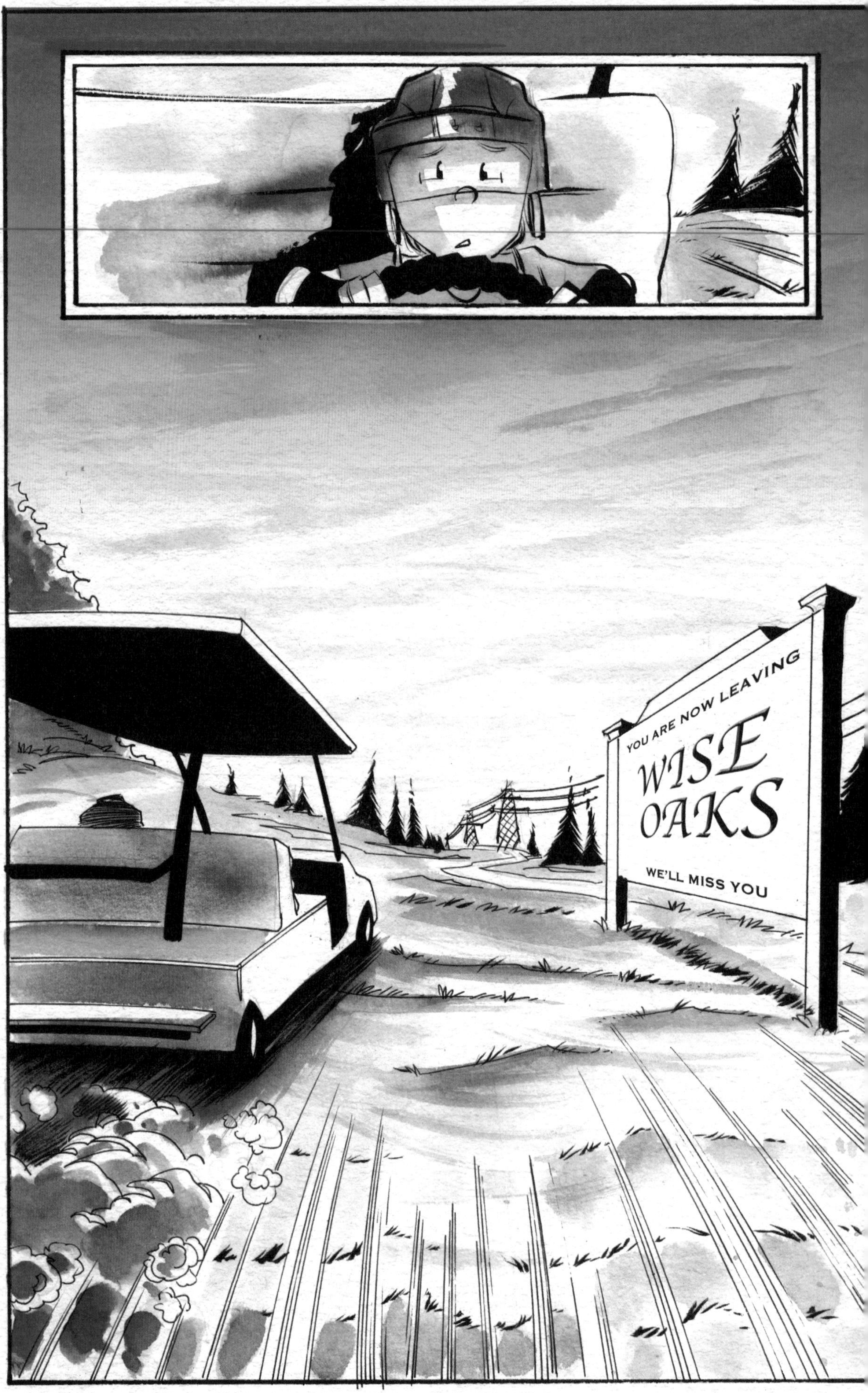
YOU ARE NOW LEAVING
WISE OAKS
WE'LL MISS YOU

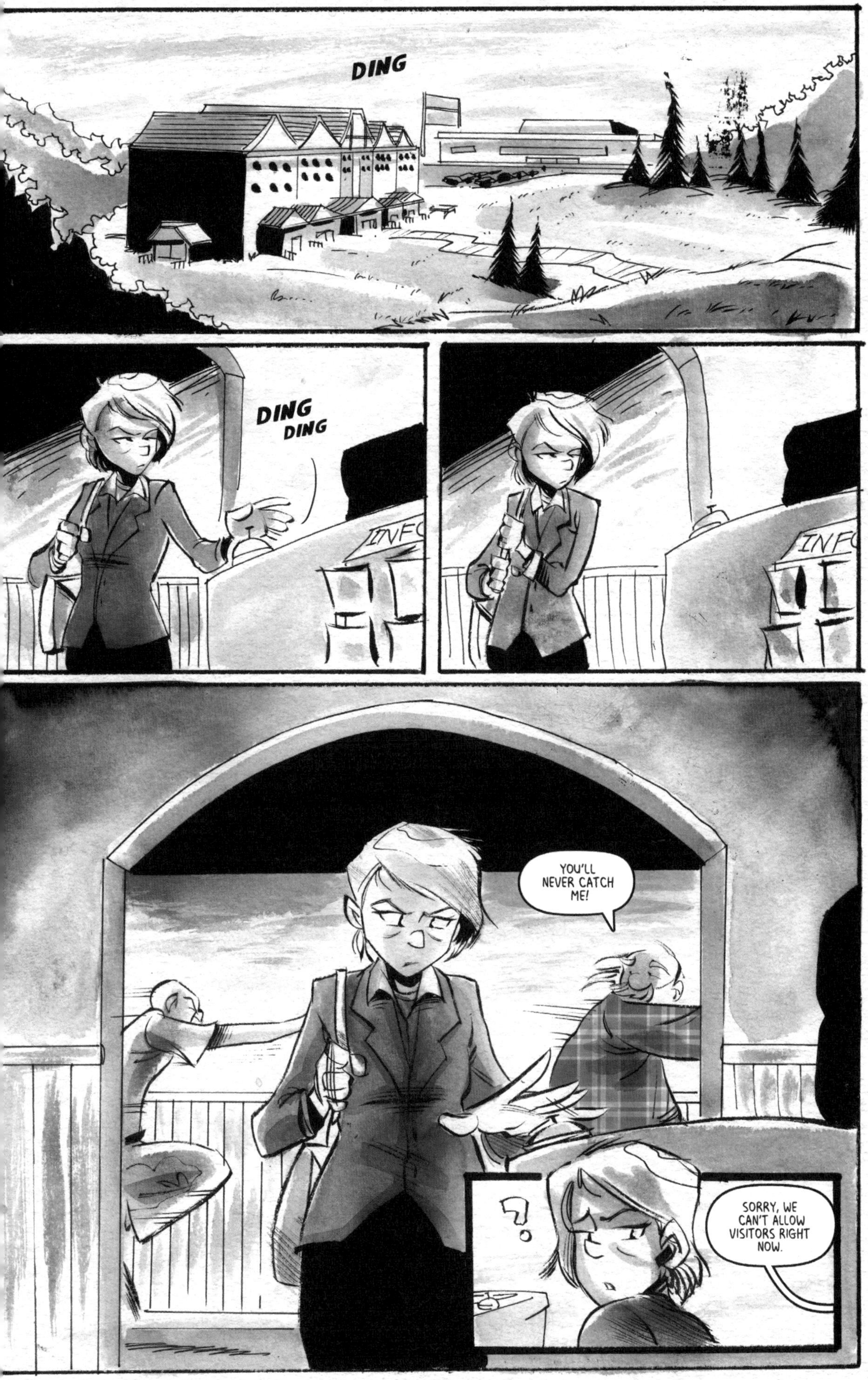
DING
DING
DING
YOU'LL NEVER CATCH ME!
?
SORRY, WE CAN'T ALLOW VISITORS RIGHT NOW.

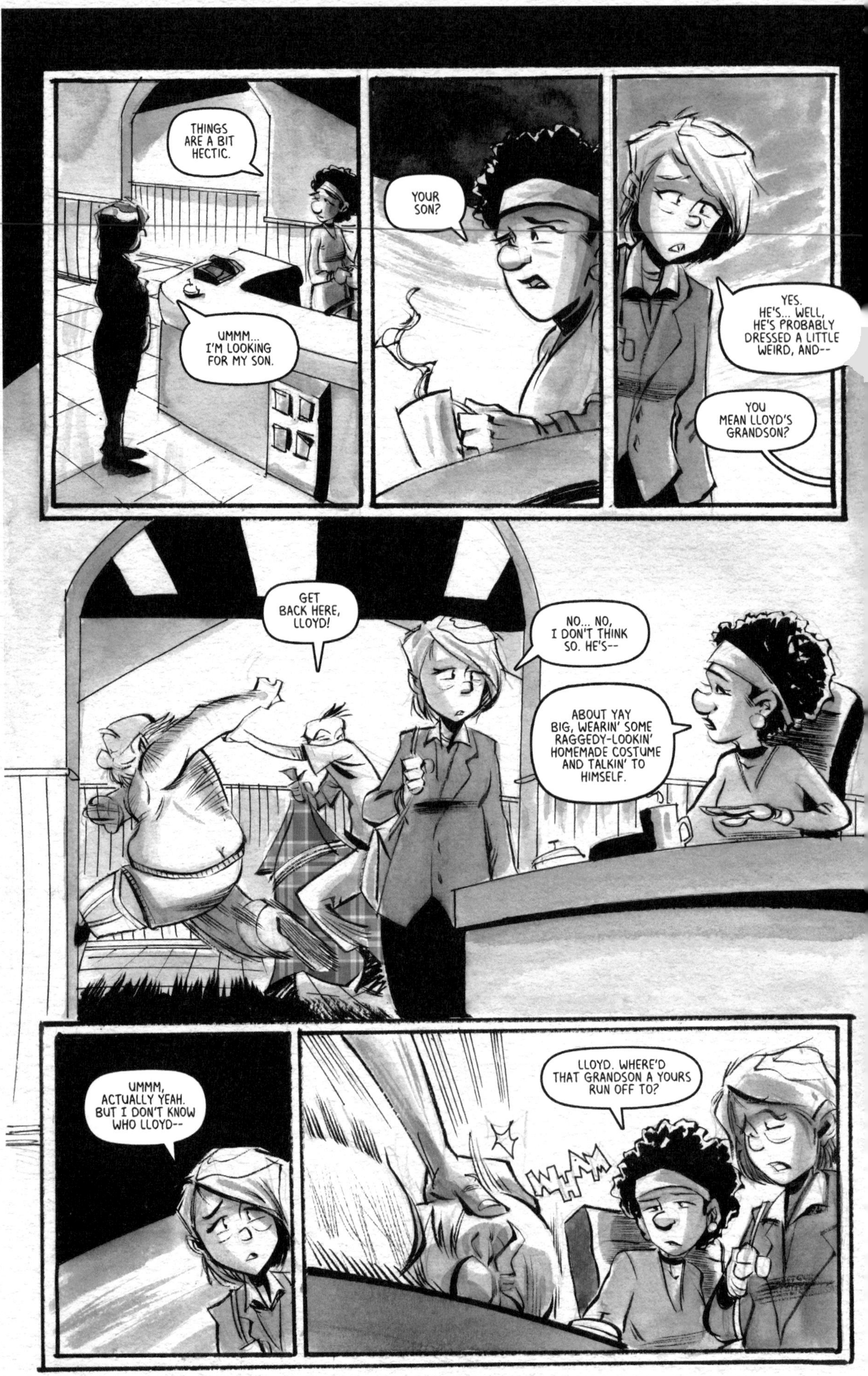

THINGS ARE A BIT HECTIC.
UMMM... I'M LOOKING FOR MY SON.
YOUR SON?
YES. HE'S... WELL, HE'S PROBABLY DRESSED A LITTLE WEIRD, AND--
YOU MEAN LLOYD'S GRANDSON?
GET BACK HERE, LLOYD!
NO... NO, I DON'T THINK SO. HE'S--
ABOUT YAY BIG, WEARIN' SOME RAGGEDY-LOOKIN' HOMEMADE COSTUME AND TALKIN' TO HIMSELF.
UMMM, ACTUALLY YEAH. BUT I DON'T KNOW WHO LLOYD--
LLOYD. WHERE'D THAT GRANDSON A YOURS RUN OFF TO?
WHAM

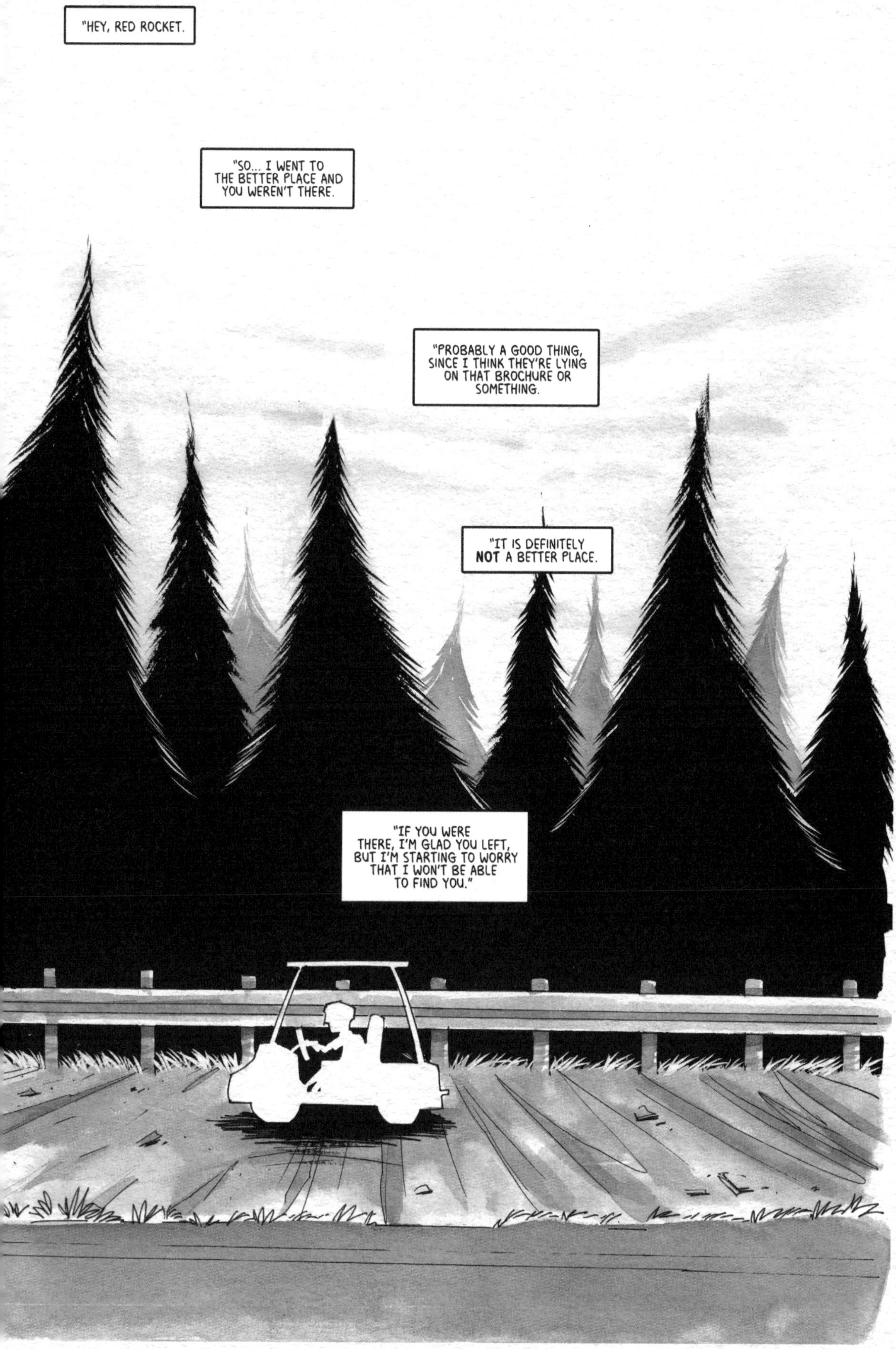
"HEY, RED ROCKET.
"SO... I WENT TO THE BETTER PLACE AND YOU WEREN'T THERE.
"PROBABLY A GOOD THING, SINCE I THINK THEY'RE LYING ON THAT BROCHURE OR SOMETHING.
"IT IS DEFINITELY **NOT** A BETTER PLACE.
"IF YOU WERE THERE, I'M GLAD YOU LEFT, BUT I'M STARTING TO WORRY THAT I WON'T BE ABLE TO FIND YOU."

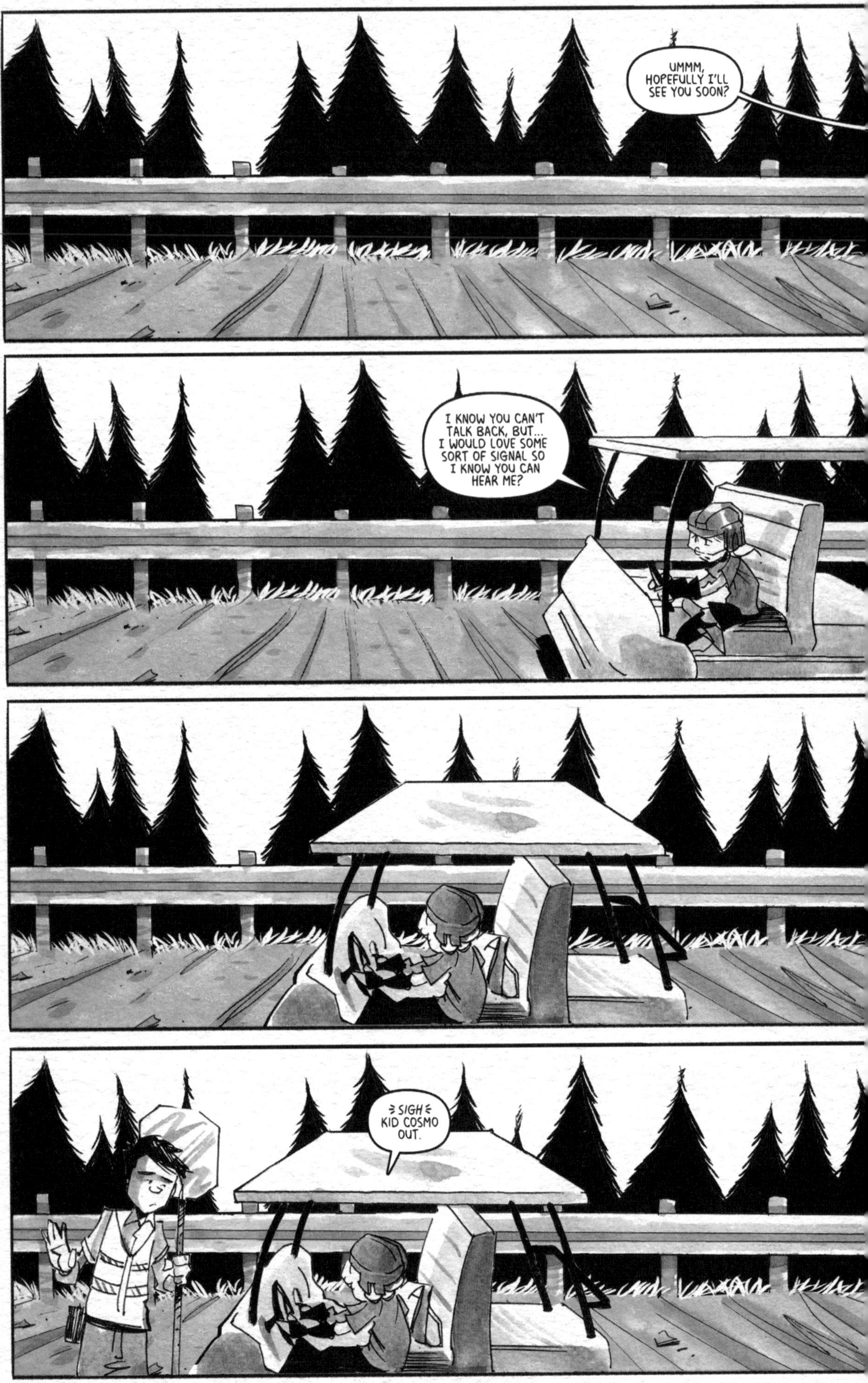
UMMM, HOPEFULLY I'LL SEE YOU SOON?
I KNOW YOU CAN'T TALK BACK, BUT... I WOULD LOVE SOME SORT OF SIGNAL SO I KNOW YOU CAN HEAR ME?
SIGH
KID COSMO OUT.

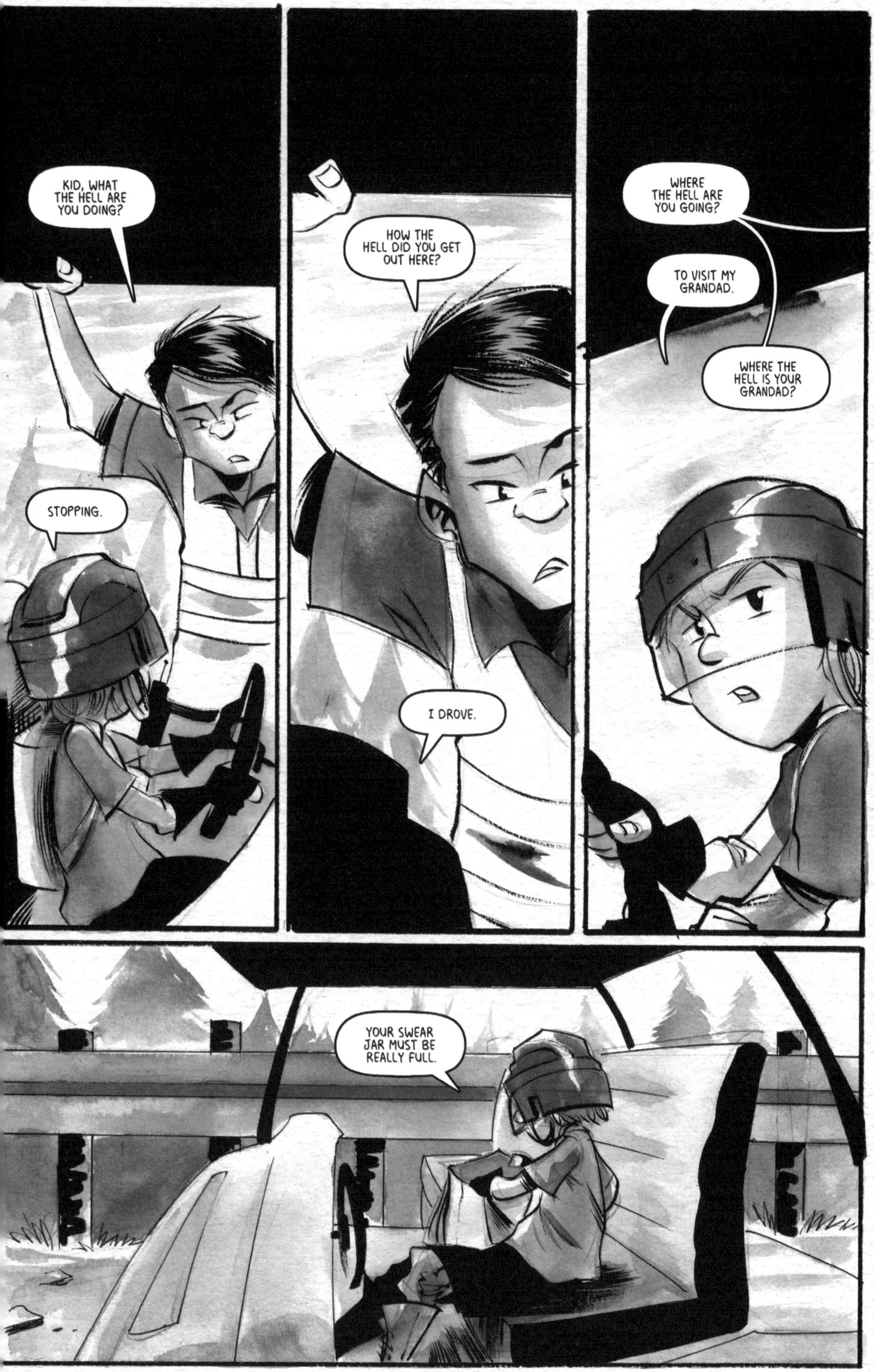
KID, WHAT THE HELL ARE YOU DOING?
STOPPING.
HOW THE HELL DID YOU GET OUT HERE?
I DROVE.
WHERE THE HELL ARE YOU GOING?
TO VISIT MY GRANDAD.
WHERE THE HELL IS YOUR GRANDAD?
YOUR SWEAR JAR MUST BE REALLY FULL.

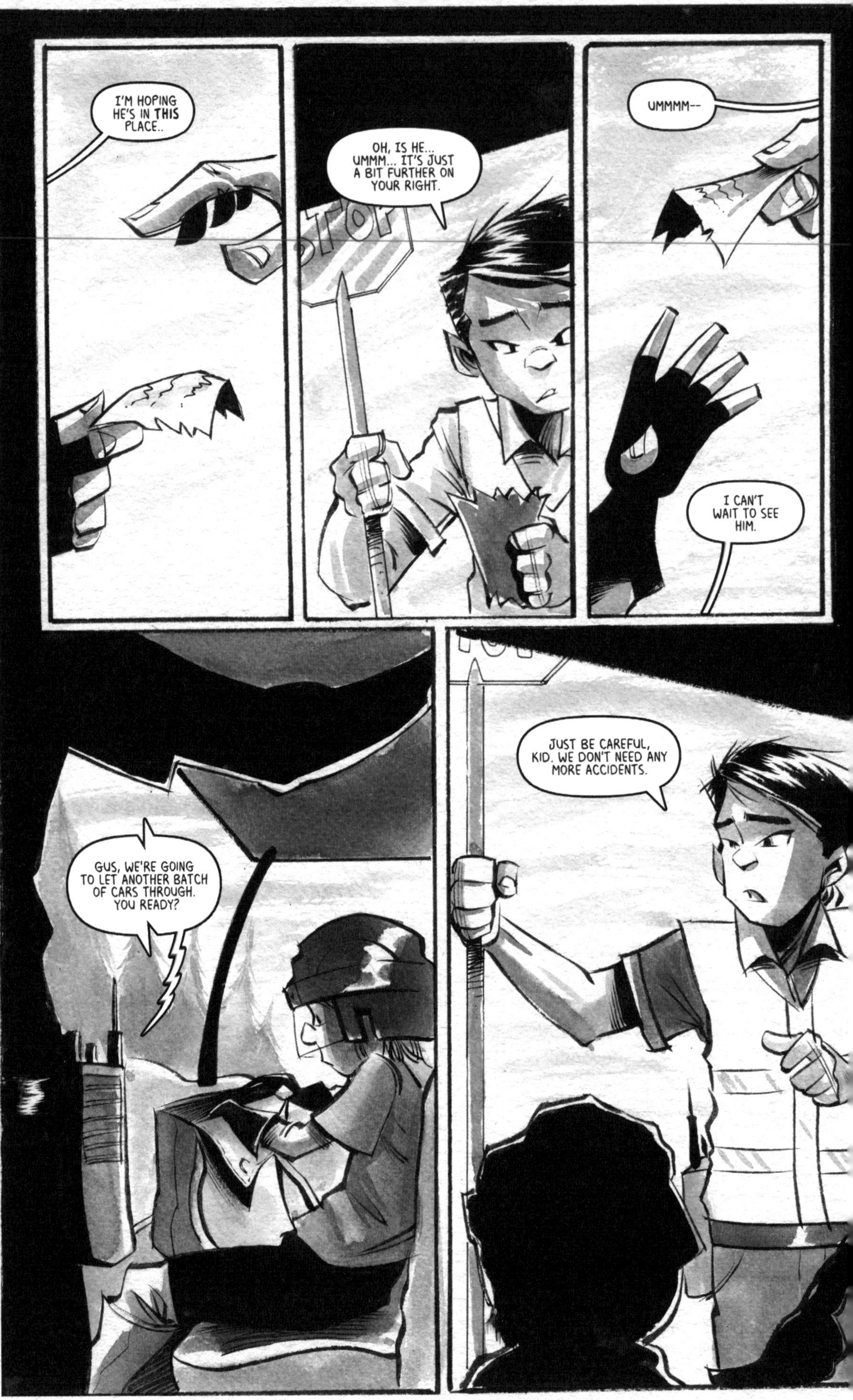
I'M HOPING HE'S IN **THIS** PLACE..
OH, IS HE... UMMM... IT'S JUST A BIT FURTHER ON YOUR RIGHT.
STOP
UMMMM--
I CAN'T WAIT TO SEE HIM.
GUS, WE'RE GOING TO LET ANOTHER BATCH OF CARS THROUGH. YOU READY?
JUST BE CAREFUL, KID. WE DON'T NEED ANY MORE ACCIDENTS.

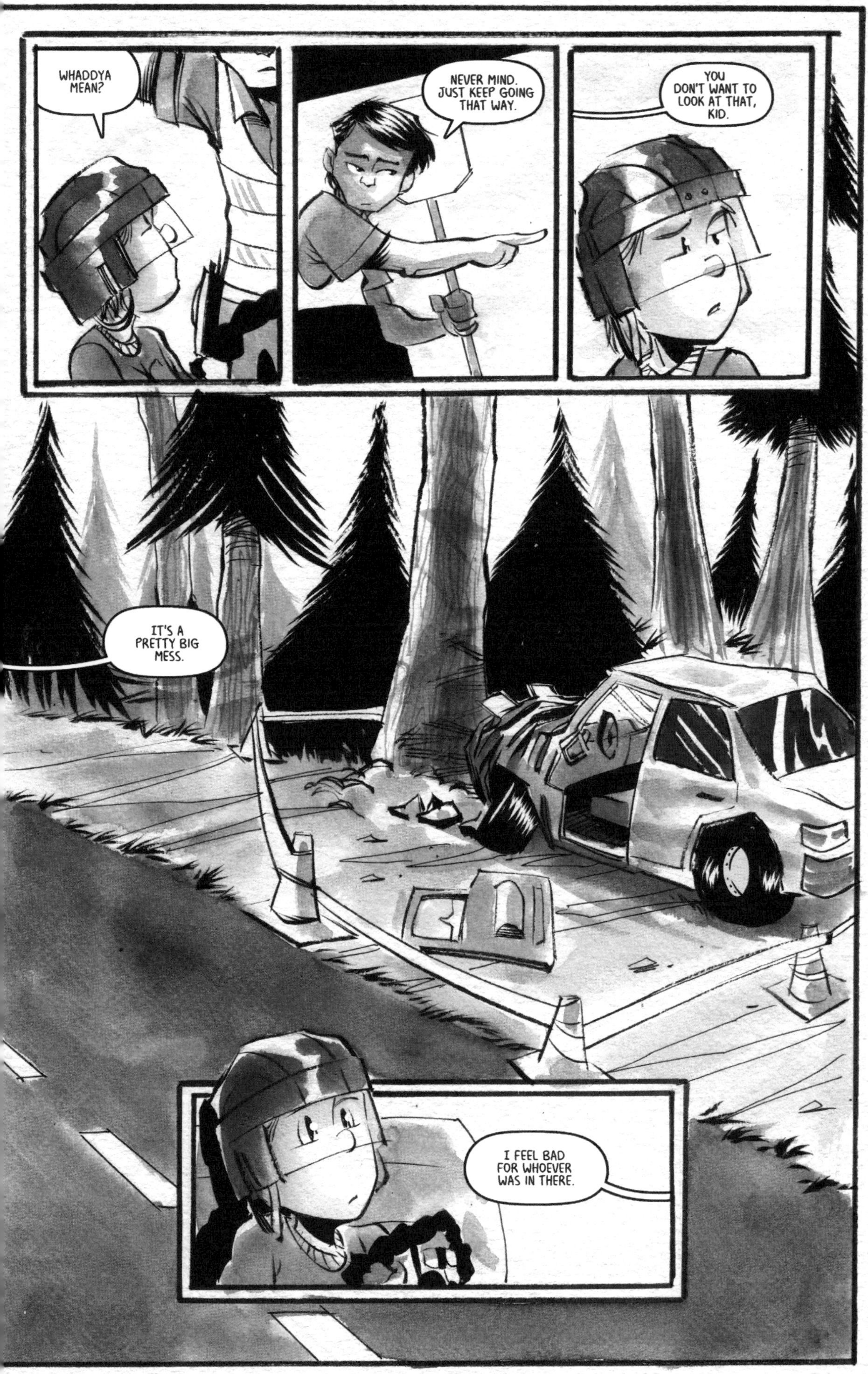
WHADDYA MEAN?
NEVER MIND. JUST KEEP GOING THAT WAY.
YOU DON'T WANT TO LOOK AT THAT, KID.
IT'S A PRETTY BIG MESS.
I FEEL BAD FOR WHOEVER WAS IN THERE.

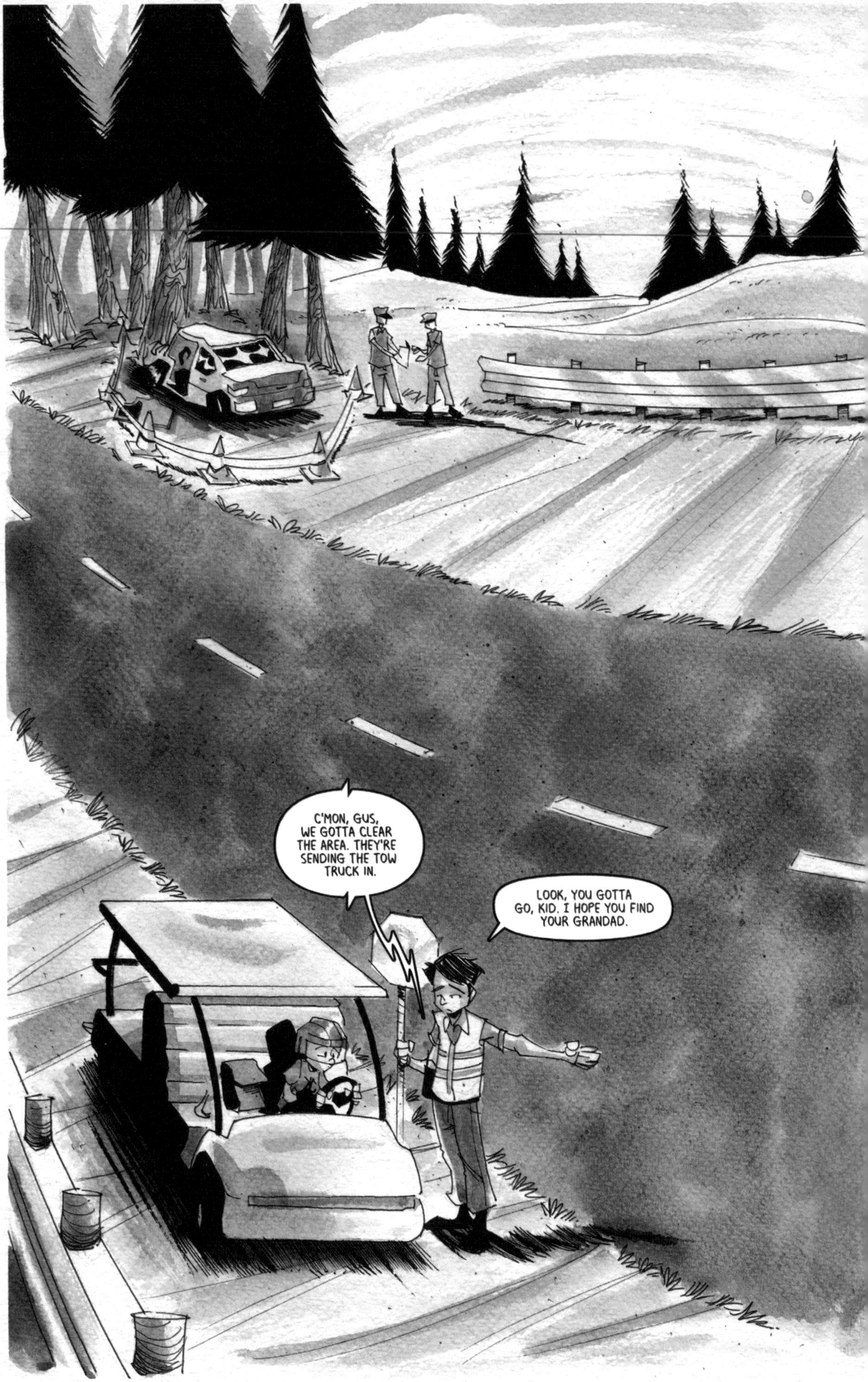
C'MON, GUS, WE GOTTA CLEAR THE AREA. THEY'RE SENDING THE TOW TRUCK IN.
LOOK, YOU GOTTA GO, KID. I HOPE YOU FIND YOUR GRANDAD.

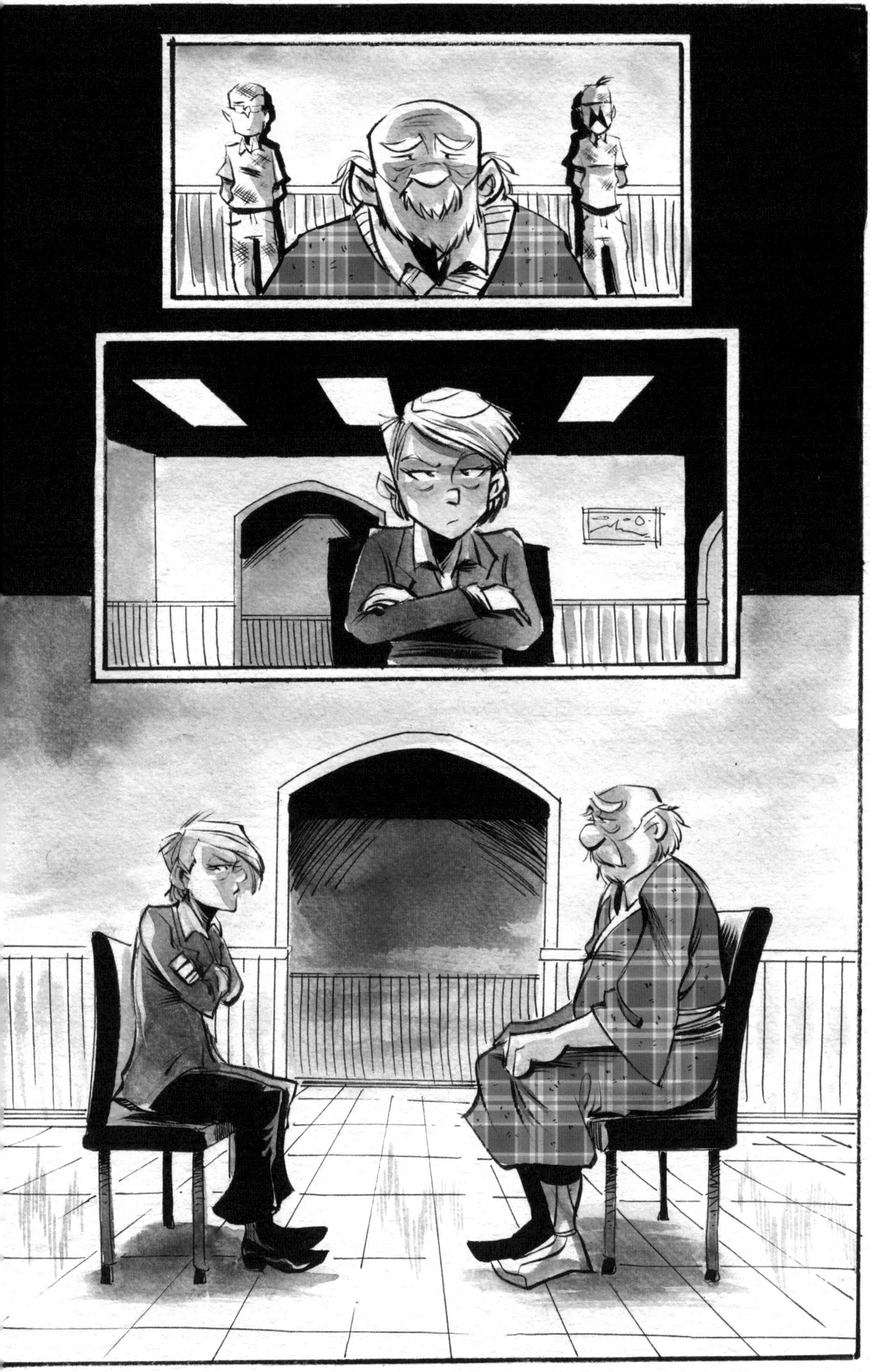

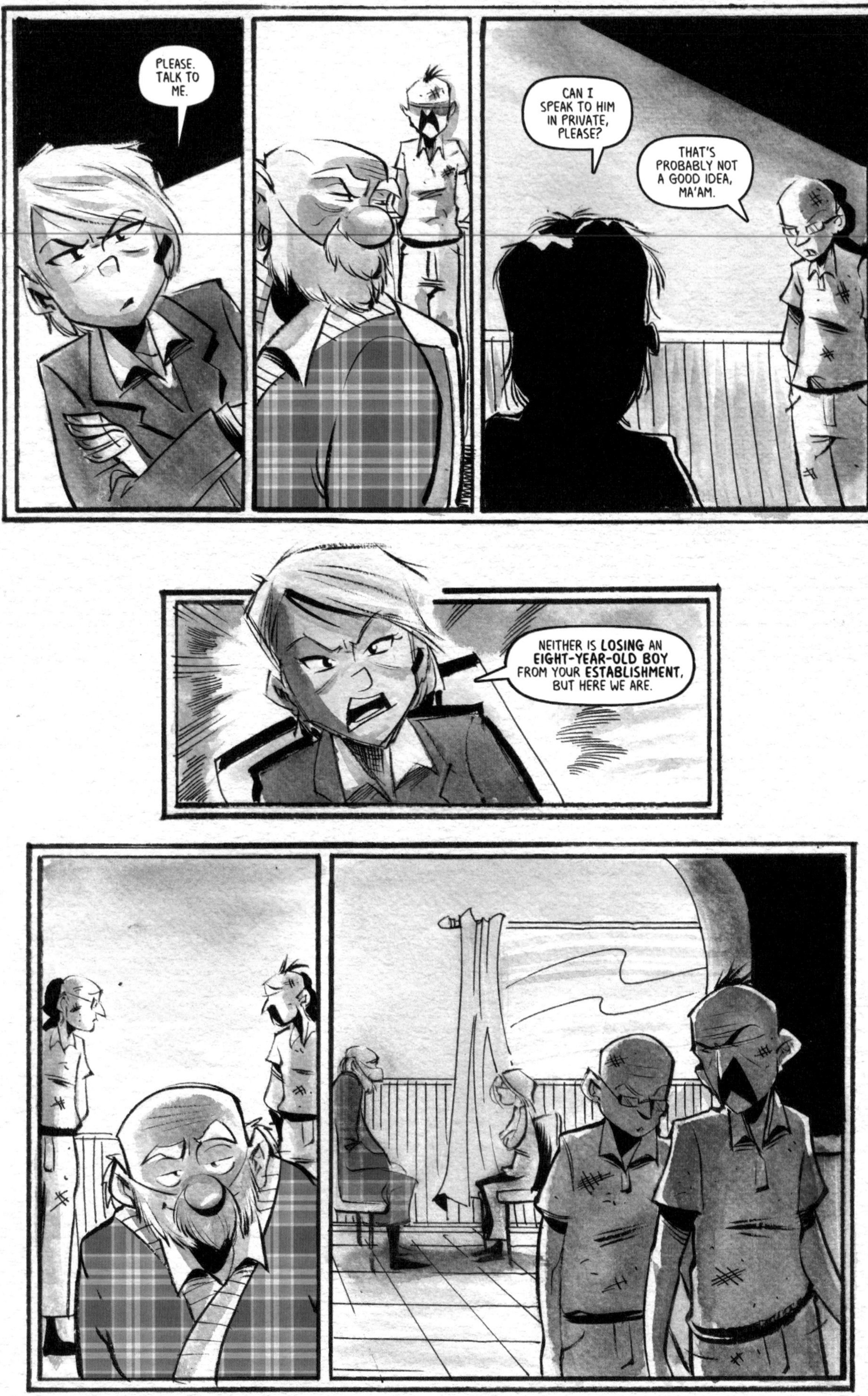
PLEASE. TALK TO ME.
CAN I SPEAK TO HIM IN PRIVATE, PLEASE?
THAT'S PROBABLY NOT A GOOD IDEA, MA'AM.
NEITHER IS **LOSING** AN **EIGHT-YEAR-OLD BOY** FROM YOUR **ESTABLISHMENT**, BUT HERE WE ARE.

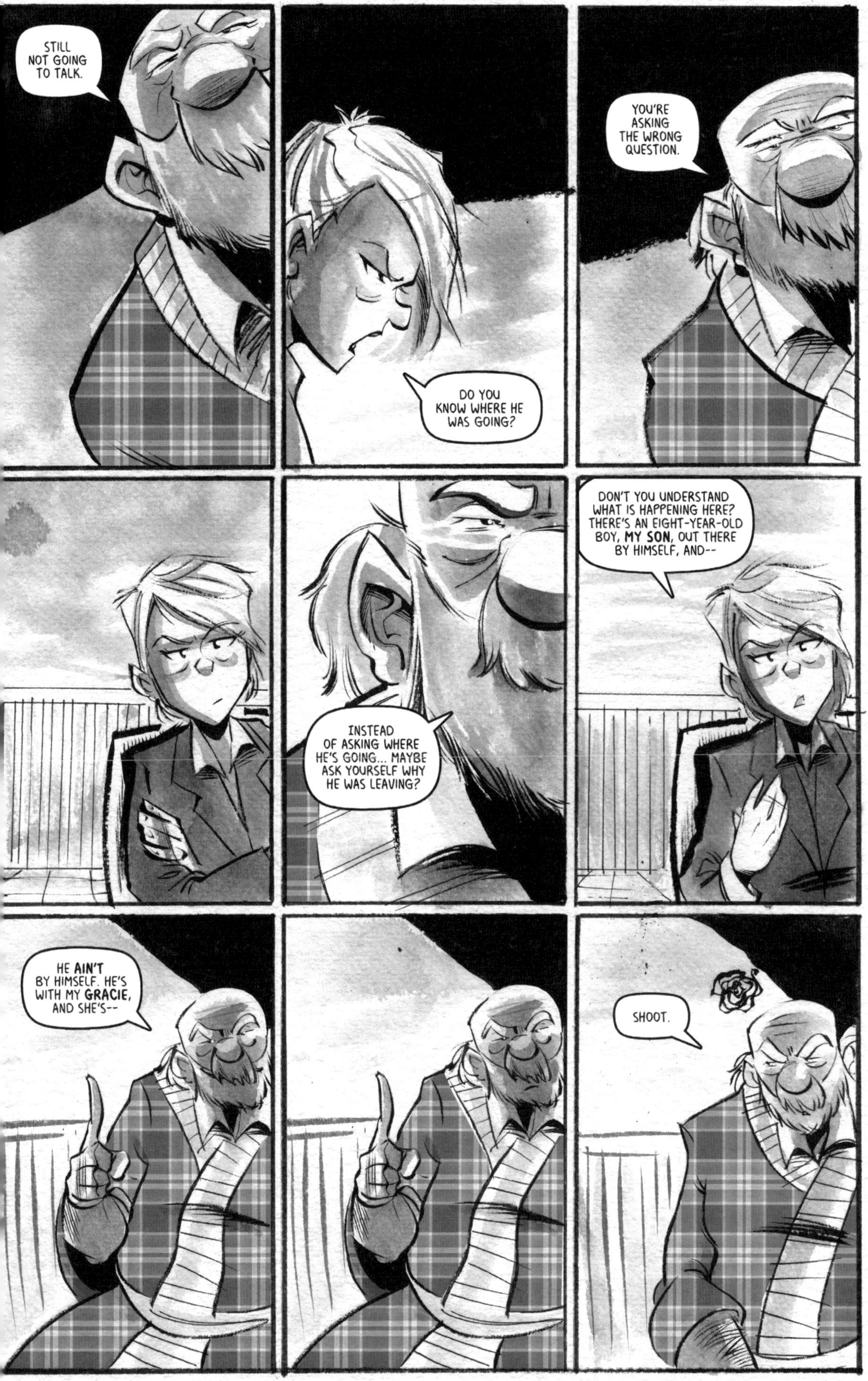
STILL NOT GOING TO TALK.
DO YOU KNOW WHERE HE WAS GOING?
YOU'RE ASKING THE WRONG QUESTION.
INSTEAD OF ASKING WHERE HE'S GOING... MAYBE ASK YOURSELF WHY HE WAS LEAVING?
DON'T YOU UNDERSTAND WHAT IS HAPPENING HERE? THERE'S AN EIGHT-YEAR-OLD BOY, **MY SON**, OUT THERE BY HIMSELF, AND--
HE **AIN'T** BY HIMSELF. HE'S WITH MY **GRACIE**, AND SHE'S--
SHOOT.

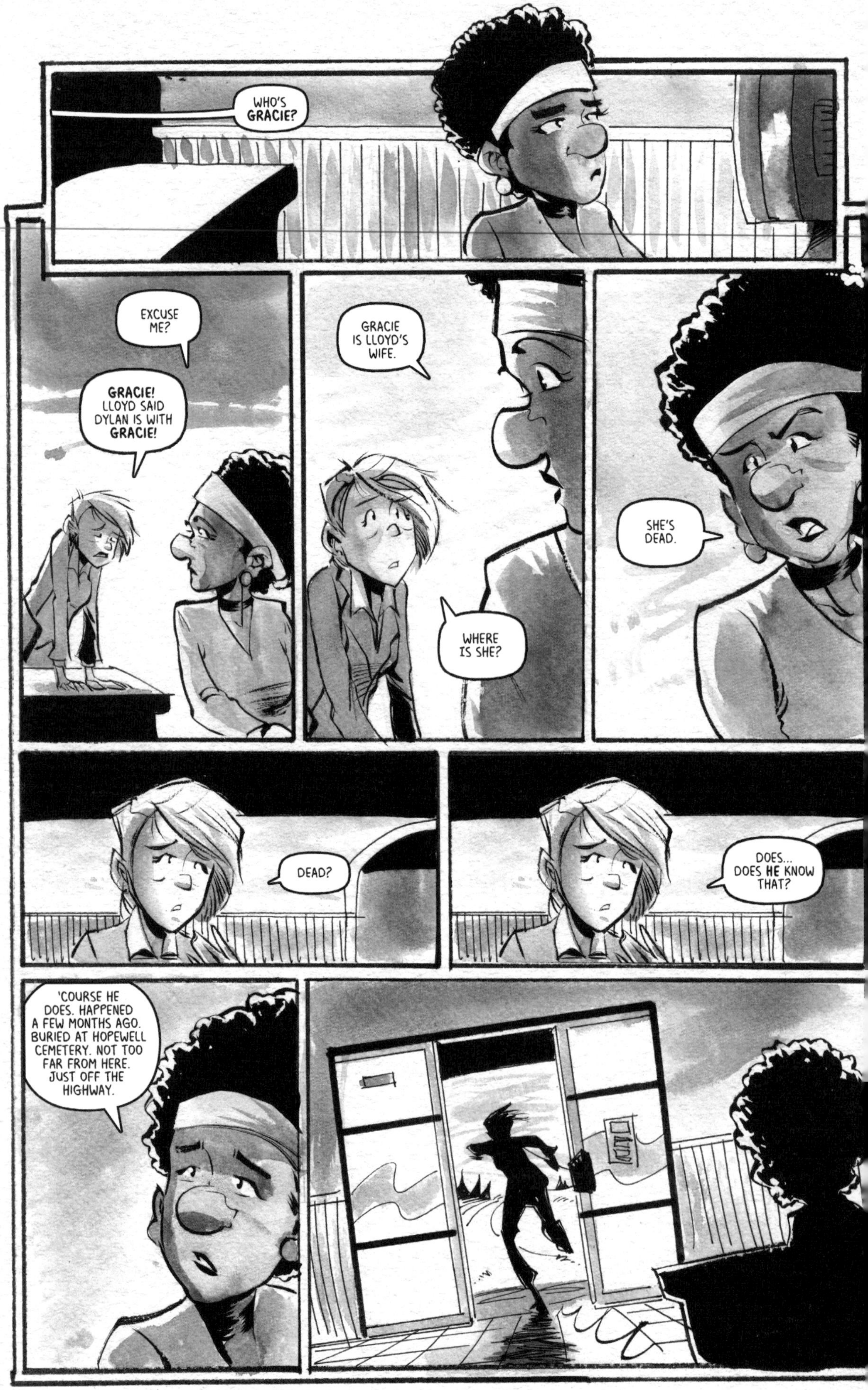
WHO'S GRACIE?
EXCUSE ME?
GRACIE! LLOYD SAID DYLAN IS WITH GRACIE!
GRACIE IS LLOYD'S WIFE.
WHERE IS SHE?
SHE'S DEAD.
DEAD?
DOES... DOES HE KNOW THAT?
'COURSE HE DOES. HAPPENED A FEW MONTHS AGO. BURIED AT HOPEWELL CEMETERY. NOT TOO FAR FROM HERE. JUST OFF THE HIGHWAY.

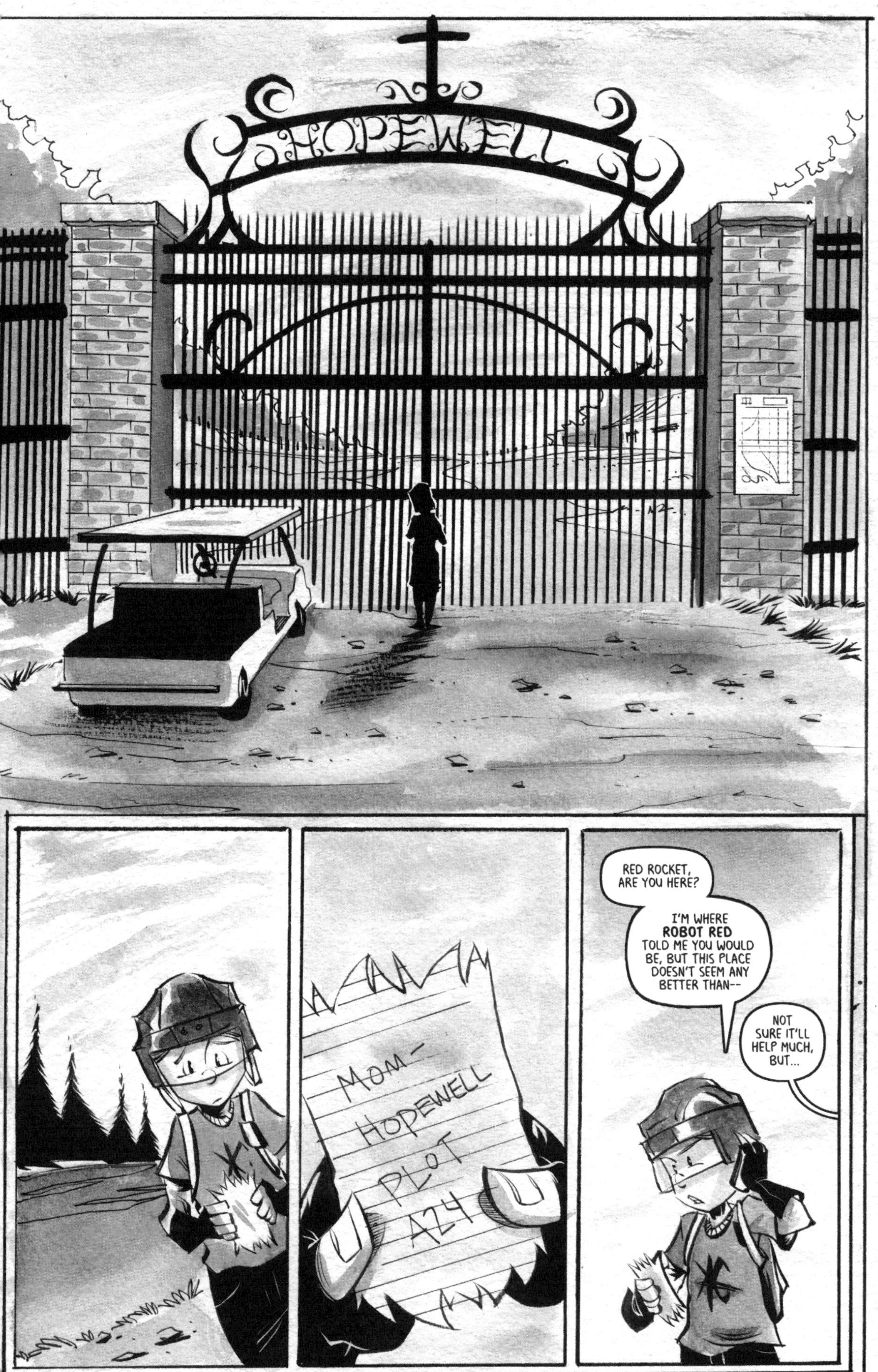
HOPEWELL
MOM-
HOPEWELL
PLOT
A24
RED ROCKET, ARE YOU HERE?
I'M WHERE **ROBOT RED** TOLD ME YOU WOULD BE, BUT THIS PLACE DOESN'T SEEM ANY BETTER THAN--
NOT SURE IT'LL HELP MUCH, BUT...

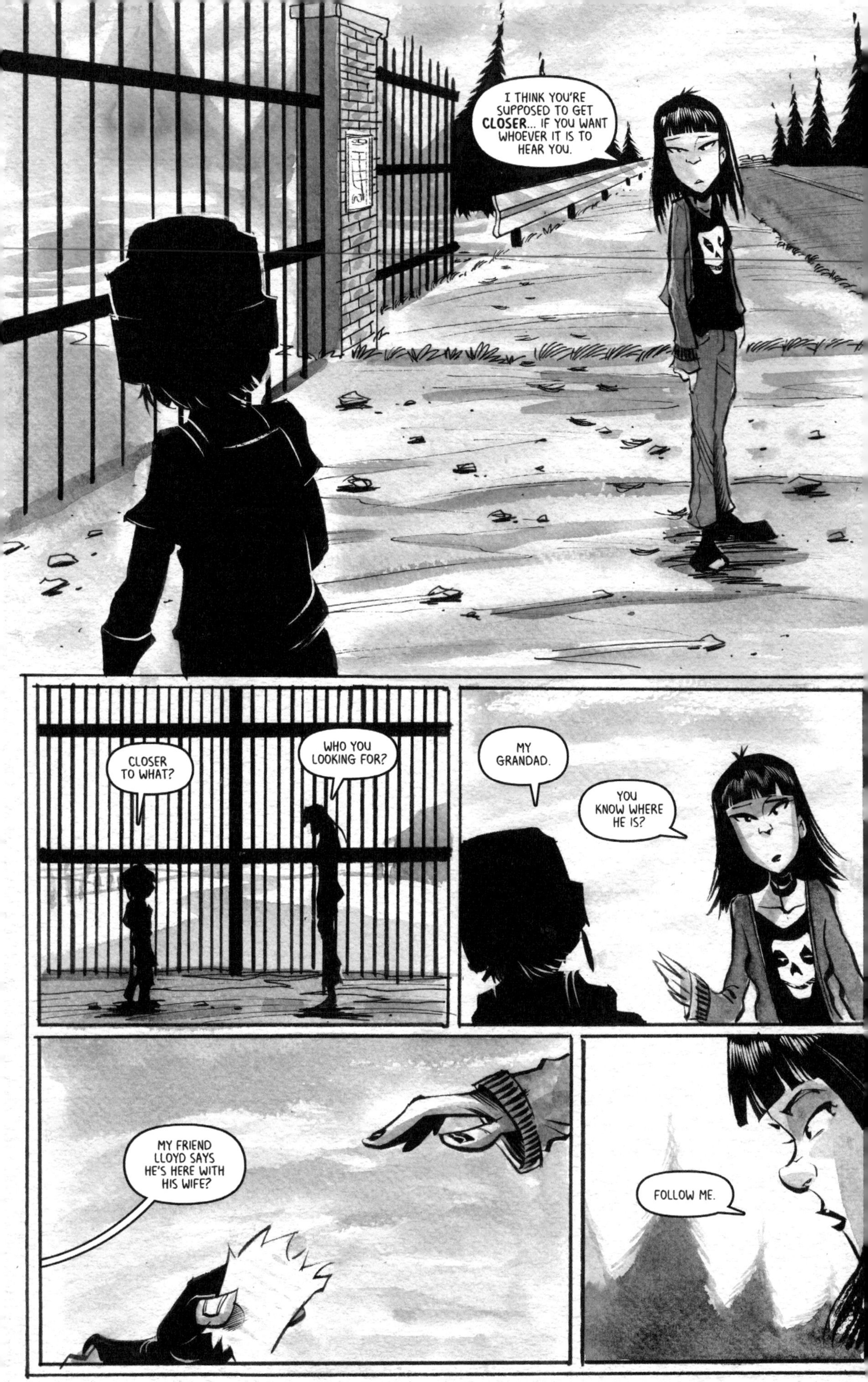

I THINK YOU'RE SUPPOSED TO GET CLOSER... IF YOU WANT WHOEVER IT IS TO HEAR YOU.
CLOSER TO WHAT?
WHO YOU LOOKING FOR?
MY GRANDAD.
YOU KNOW WHERE HE IS?
MY FRIEND LLOYD SAYS HE'S HERE WITH HIS WIFE?
FOLLOW ME.

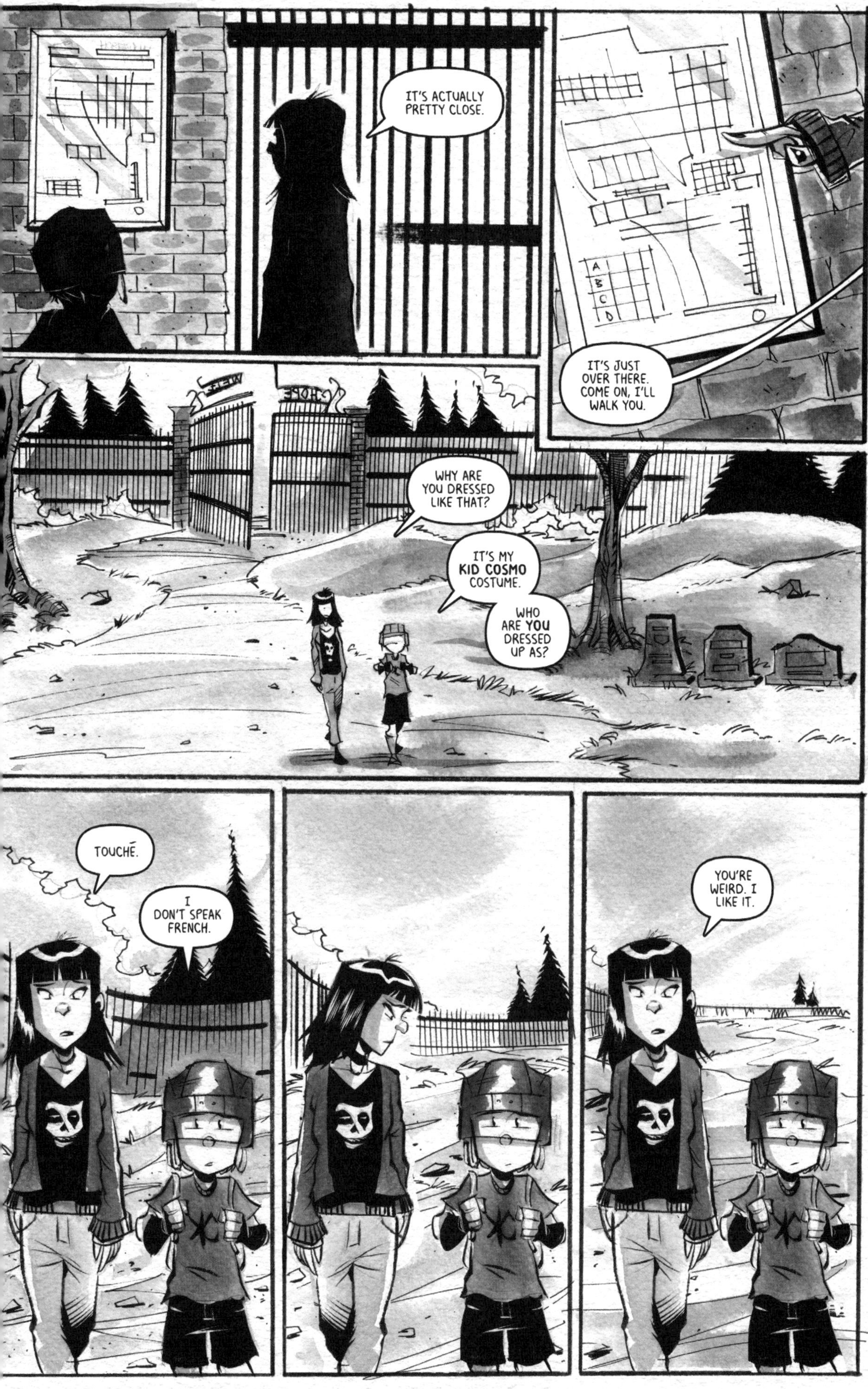
IT'S ACTUALLY PRETTY CLOSE.
IT'S JUST OVER THERE. COME ON, I'LL WALK YOU.
WHY ARE YOU DRESSED LIKE THAT?
IT'S MY **KID COSMO** COSTUME.
WHO ARE **YOU** DRESSED UP AS?
TOUCHÉ.
I DON'T SPEAK FRENCH.
YOU'RE WEIRD. I LIKE IT.

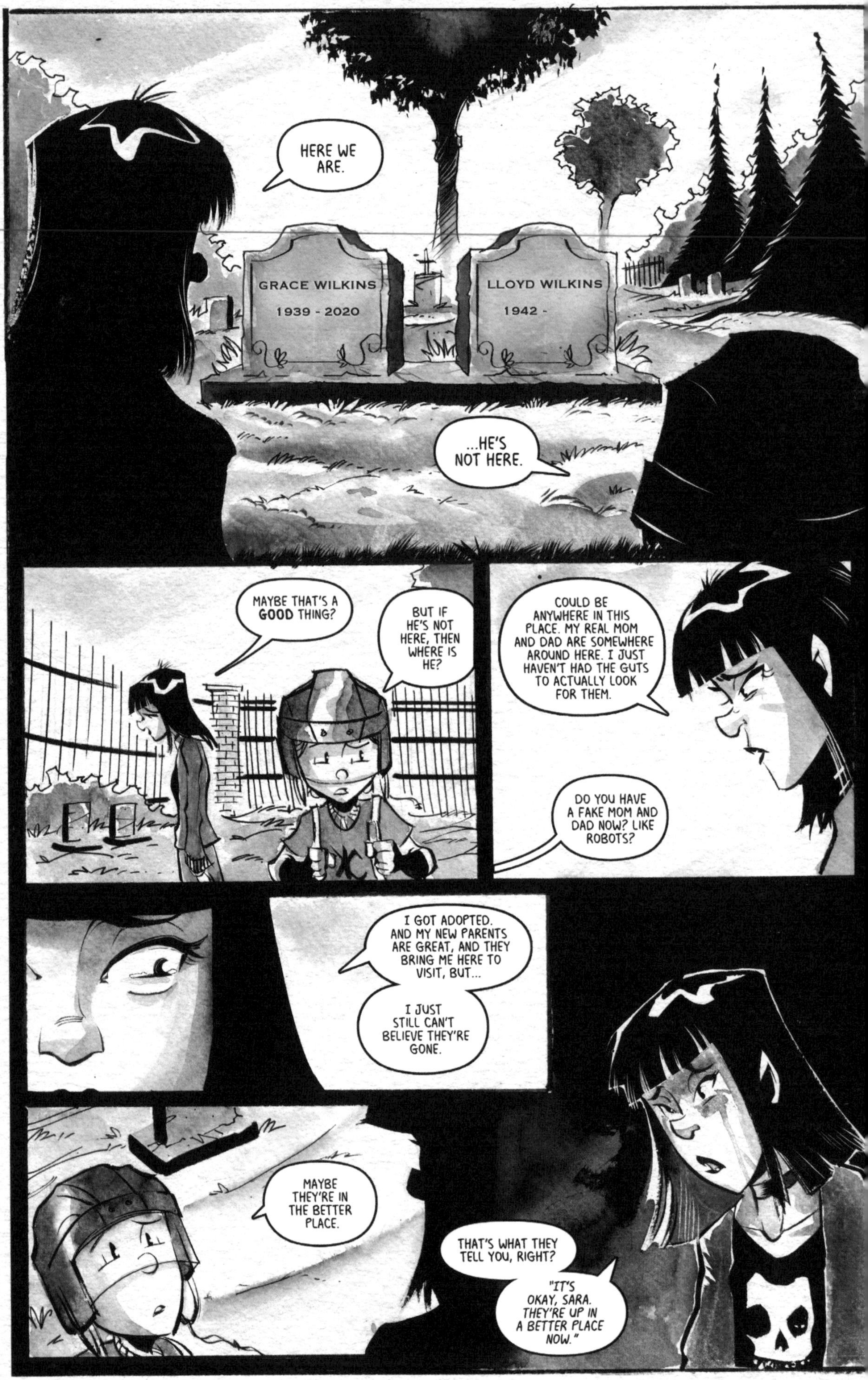
HERE WE ARE.
GRACE WILKINS
1939 - 2020
LLOYD WILKINS
1942 -
...HE'S NOT HERE.
MAYBE THAT'S A **GOOD** THING?
BUT IF HE'S NOT HERE, THEN WHERE IS HE?
COULD BE ANYWHERE IN THIS PLACE. MY REAL MOM AND DAD ARE SOMEWHERE AROUND HERE. I JUST HAVEN'T HAD THE GUTS TO ACTUALLY LOOK FOR THEM.
DO YOU HAVE A FAKE MOM AND DAD NOW? LIKE ROBOTS?
I GOT ADOPTED. AND MY NEW PARENTS ARE GREAT, AND THEY BRING ME HERE TO VISIT, BUT...
I JUST STILL CAN'T BELIEVE THEY'RE GONE.
MAYBE THEY'RE IN THE BETTER PLACE.
THAT'S WHAT THEY TELL YOU, RIGHT?
"IT'S OKAY, SARA. THEY'RE UP IN A BETTER PLACE NOW."

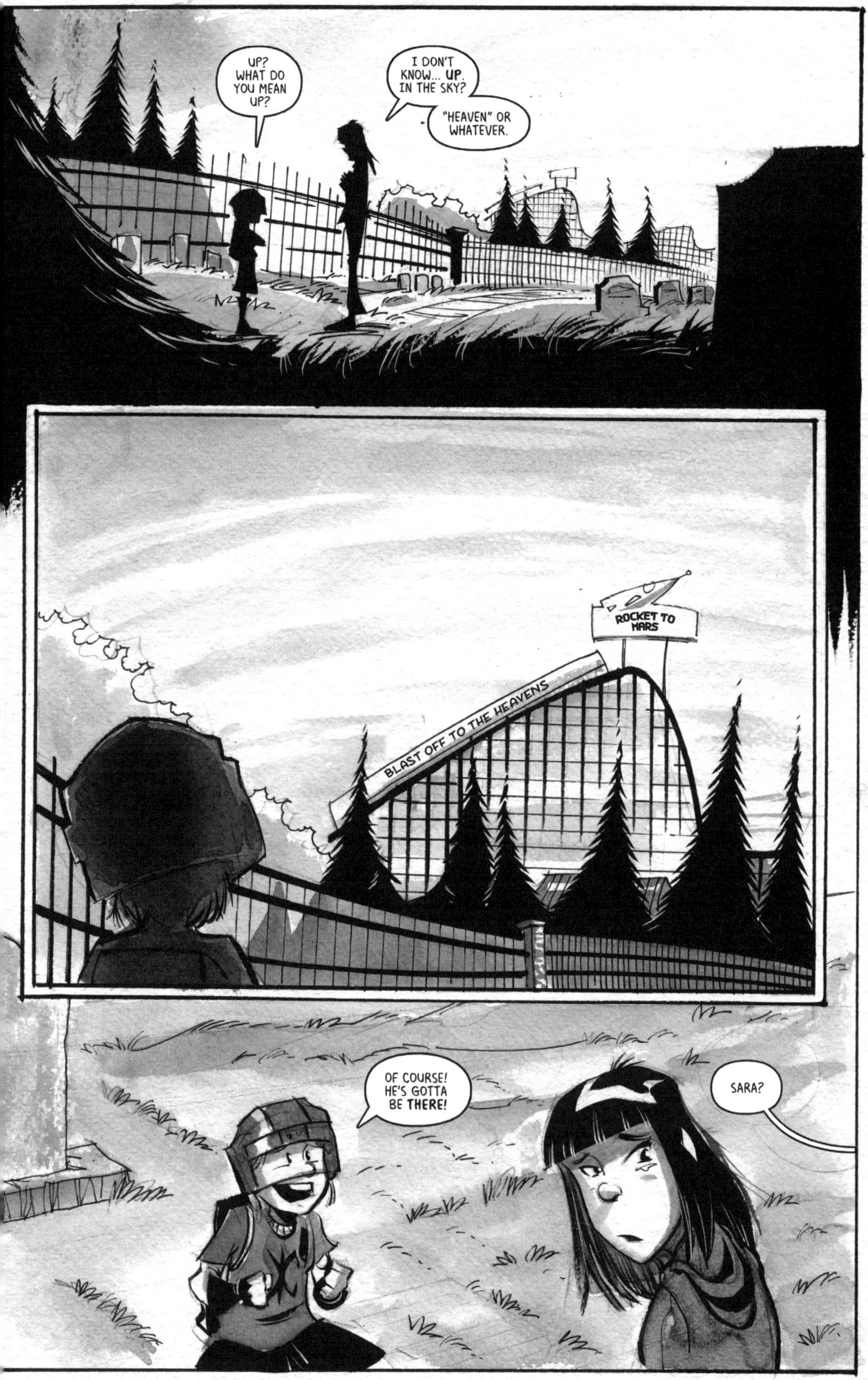
UP? WHAT DO YOU MEAN UP?
I DON'T KNOW... **UP**. IN THE SKY?
"HEAVEN" OR WHATEVER.
ROCKET TO MARS
BLAST OFF TO THE HEAVENS
OF COURSE! HE'S GOTTA BE **THERE**!
SARA?

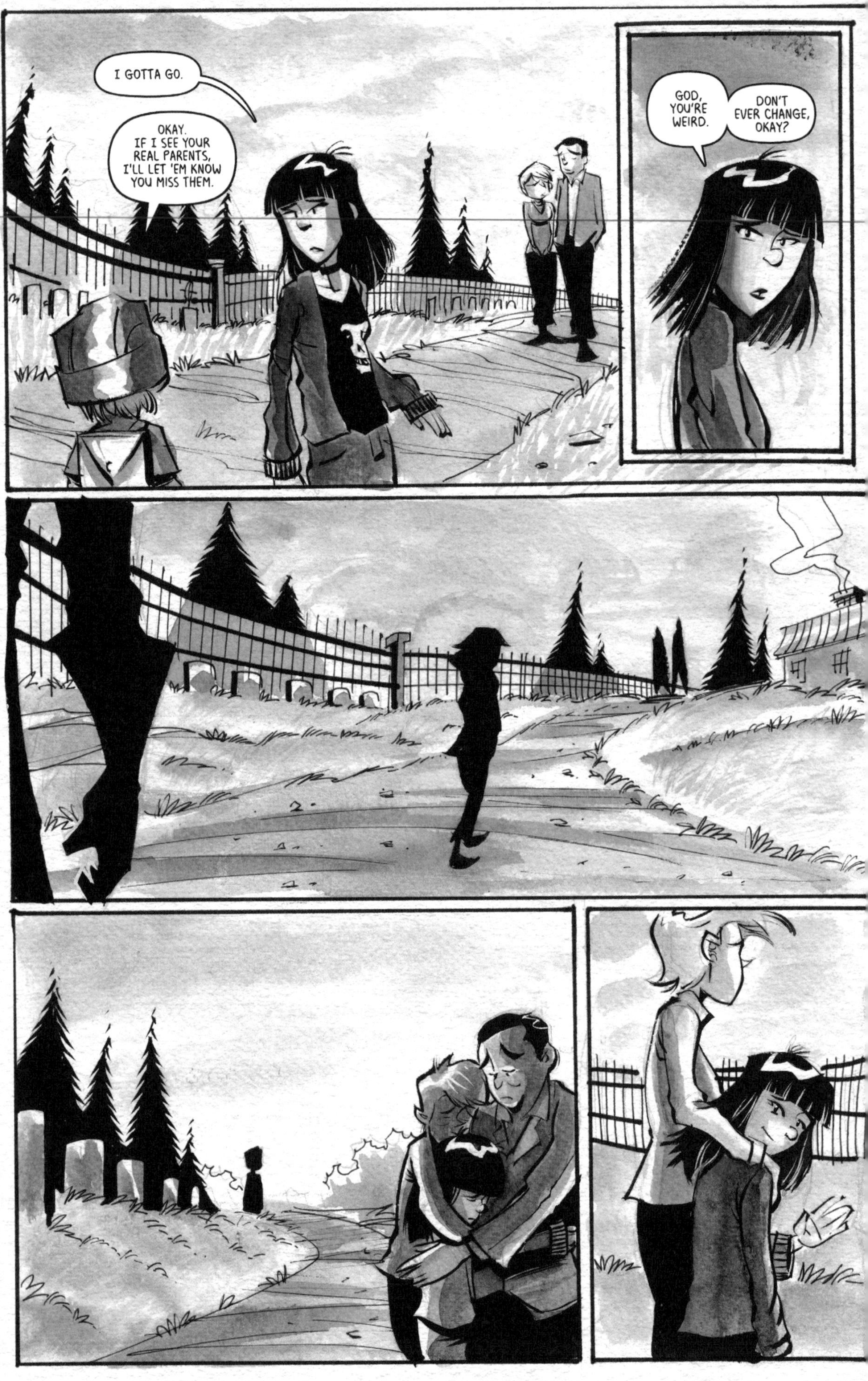
I GOTTA GO.
OKAY. IF I SEE YOUR REAL PARENTS, I'LL LET 'EM KNOW YOU MISS THEM.
GOD, YOU'RE WEIRD.
DON'T EVER CHANGE, OKAY?

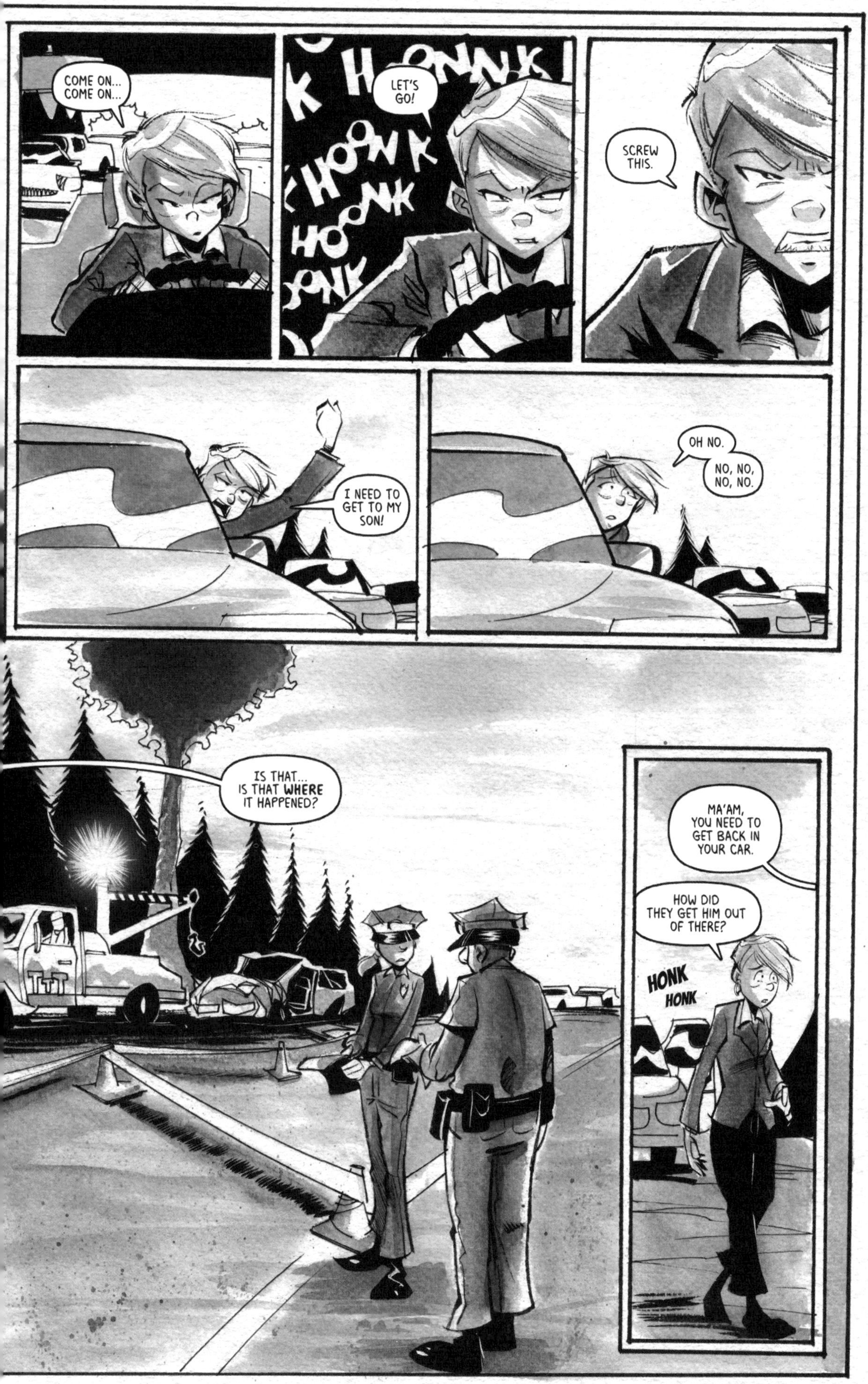
COME ON...
COME ON...
HONNK! HONK
LET'S GO!
HOONK HOONK HOONK HONK
SCREW THIS.
I NEED TO GET TO MY SON!
OH NO.
NO, NO, NO, NO.
IS THAT... IS THAT WHERE IT HAPPENED?
MA'AM, YOU NEED TO GET BACK IN YOUR CAR.
HOW DID THEY GET HIM OUT OF THERE?
HONK
HONK

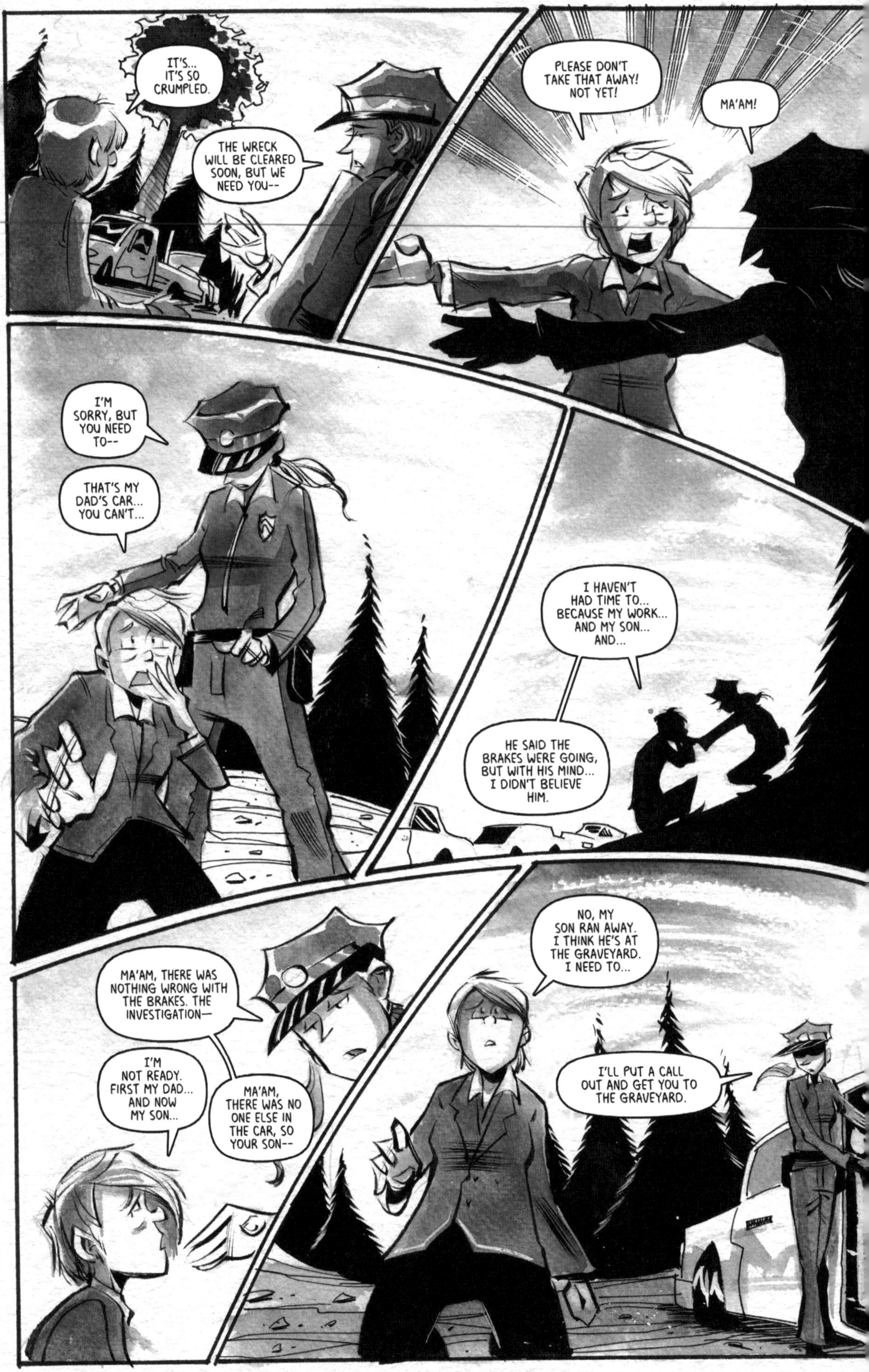
IT'S... IT'S SO CRUMPLED.
THE WRECK WILL BE CLEARED SOON, BUT WE NEED YOU--
PLEASE DON'T TAKE THAT AWAY! NOT YET!
MA'AM!
I'M SORRY, BUT YOU NEED TO--
THAT'S MY DAD'S CAR... YOU CAN'T...
I HAVEN'T HAD TIME TO... BECAUSE MY WORK... AND MY SON... AND...
HE SAID THE BRAKES WERE GOING, BUT WITH HIS MIND... I DIDN'T BELIEVE HIM.
MA'AM, THERE WAS NOTHING WRONG WITH THE BRAKES. THE INVESTIGATION—
I'M NOT READY. FIRST MY DAD... AND NOW MY SON...
MA'AM, THERE WAS NO ONE ELSE IN THE CAR, SO YOUR SON--
NO, MY SON RAN AWAY. I THINK HE'S AT THE GRAVEYARD. I NEED TO...
I'LL PUT A CALL OUT AND GET YOU TO THE GRAVEYARD.

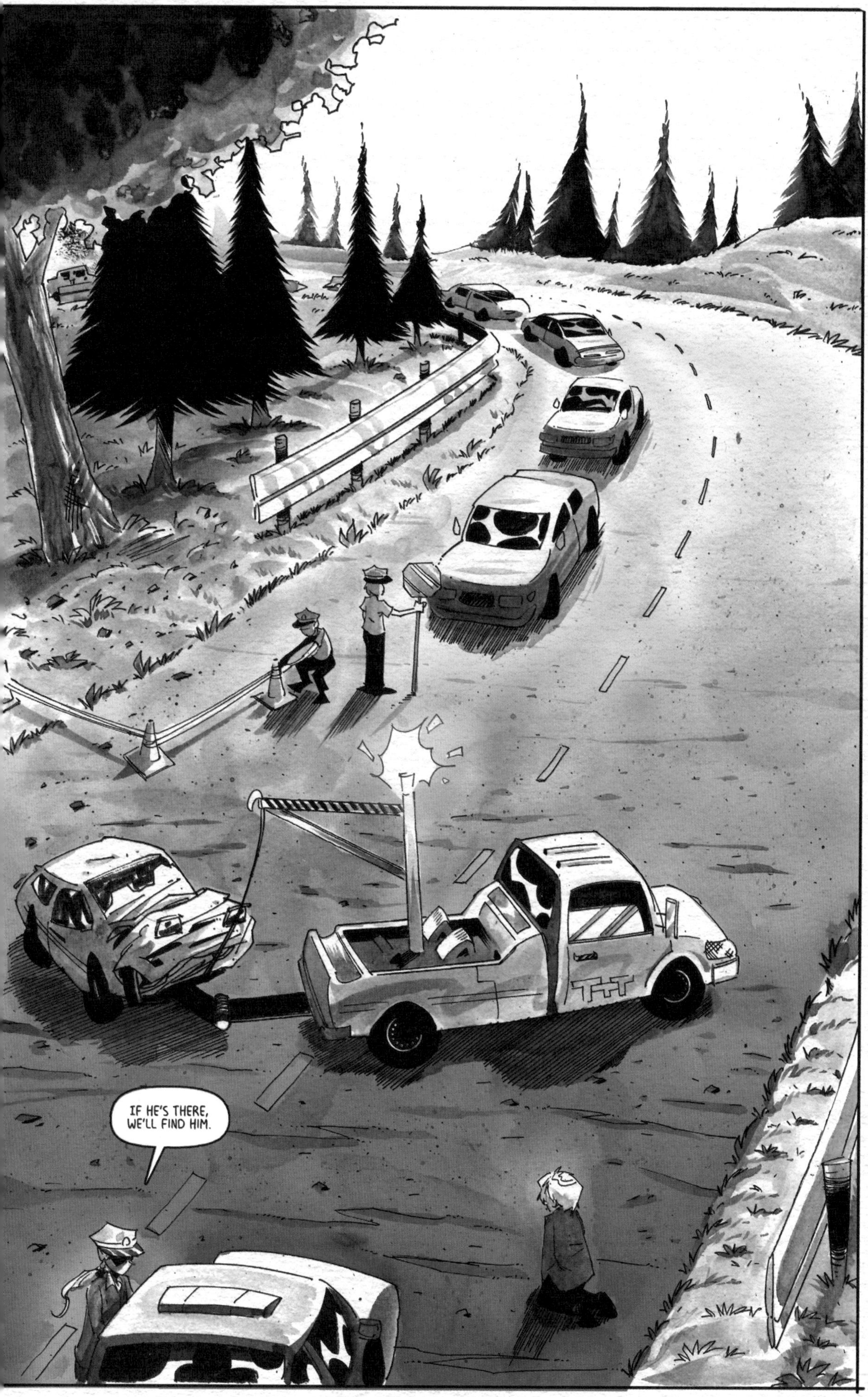
IF HE'S THERE, WE'LL FIND HIM.

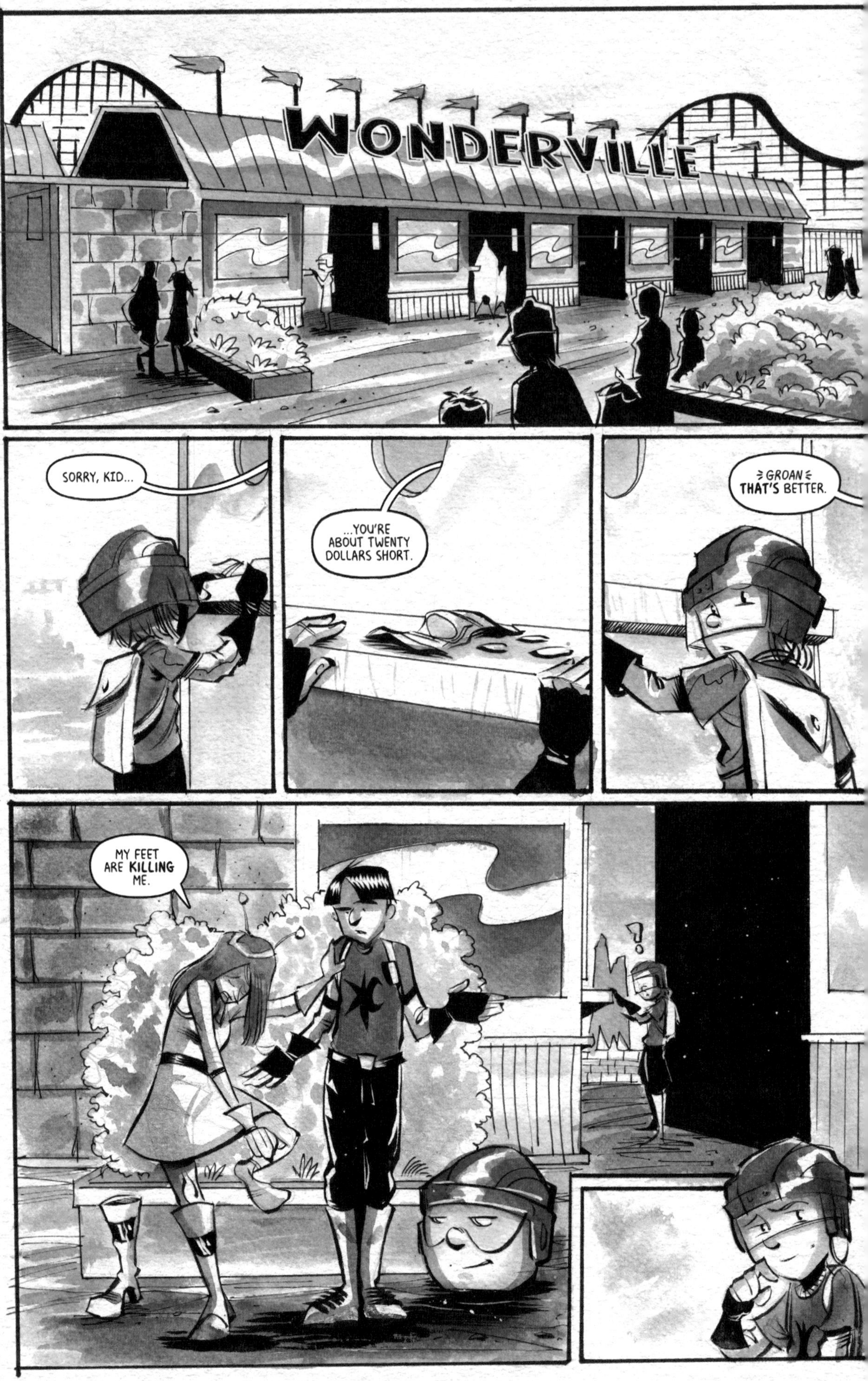
WONDERVILLE
SORRY, KID...
...YOU'RE ABOUT TWENTY DOLLARS SHORT.
GROAN
THAT'S BETTER.
MY FEET ARE KILLING ME.
!

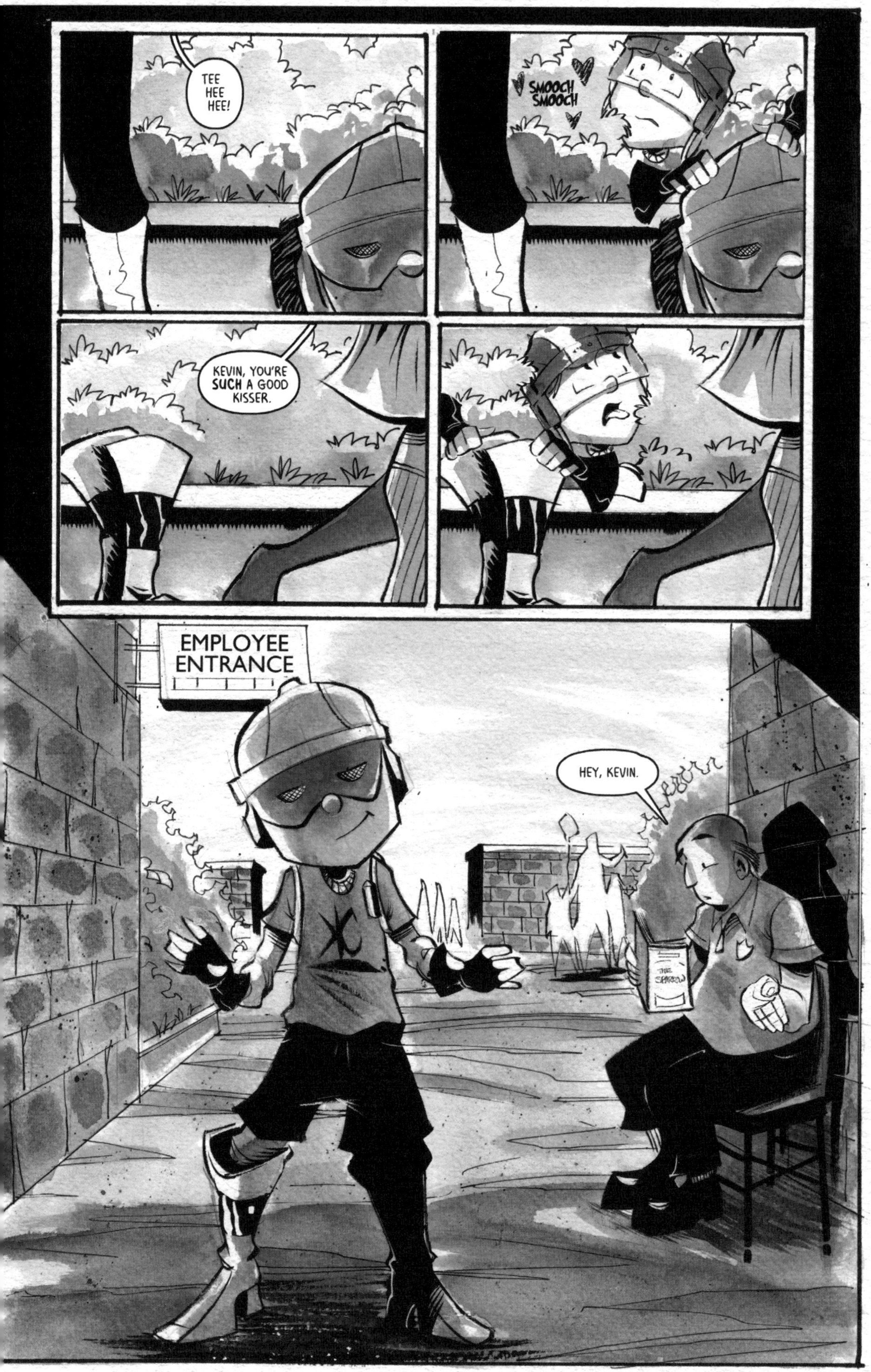
TEE HEE HEE!
SMOOCH SMOOCH
KEVIN, YOU'RE SUCH A GOOD KISSER.
EMPLOYEE ENTRANCE
HEY, KEVIN.

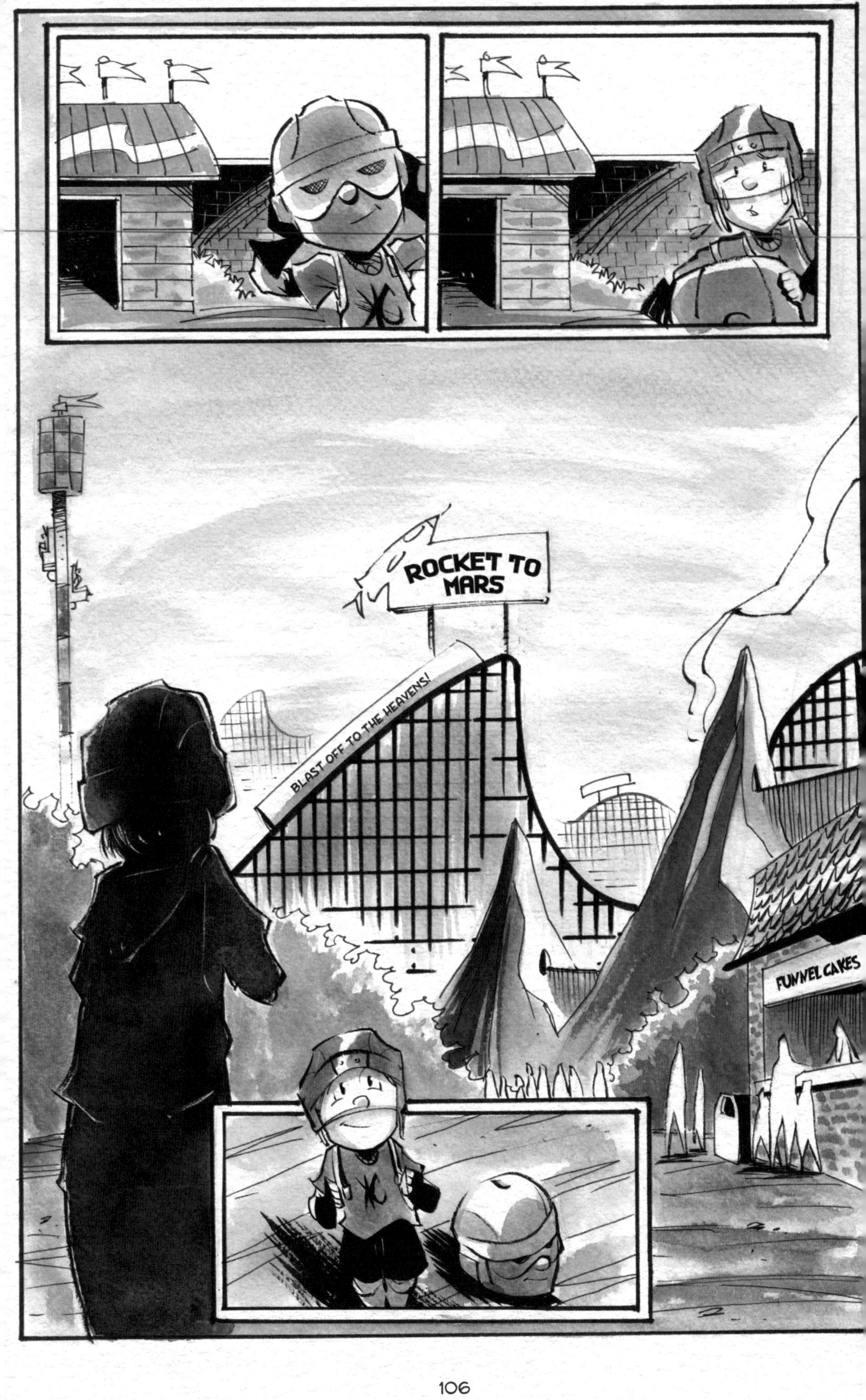
ROCKET TO MARS
BLAST OFF TO THE HEAVENS!
FUNNEL CAKES

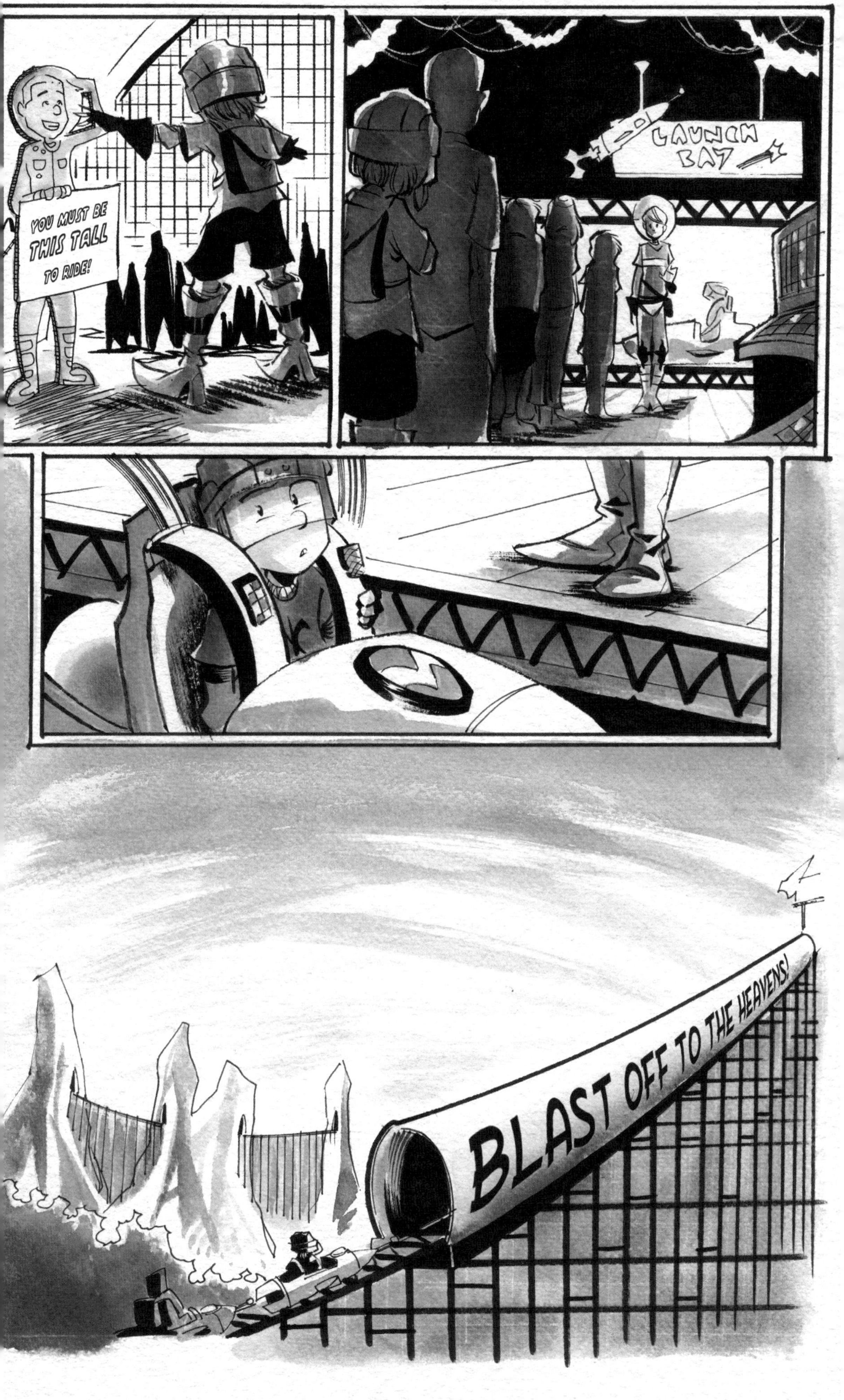
YOU MUST BE THIS TALL TO RIDE!
LAUNCH BAY
BLAST OFF TO THE HEAVENS!

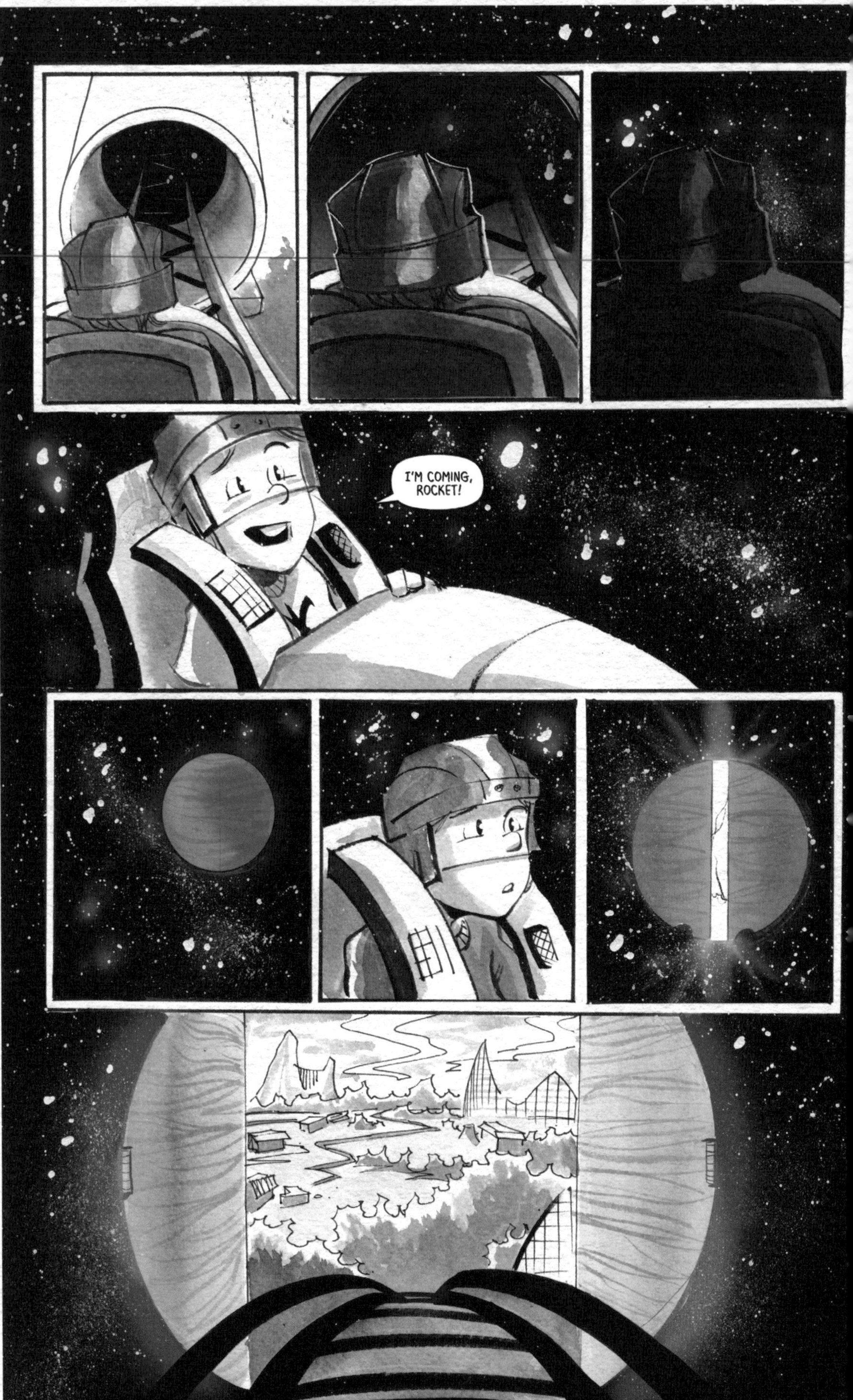
I'M COMING, ROCKET!

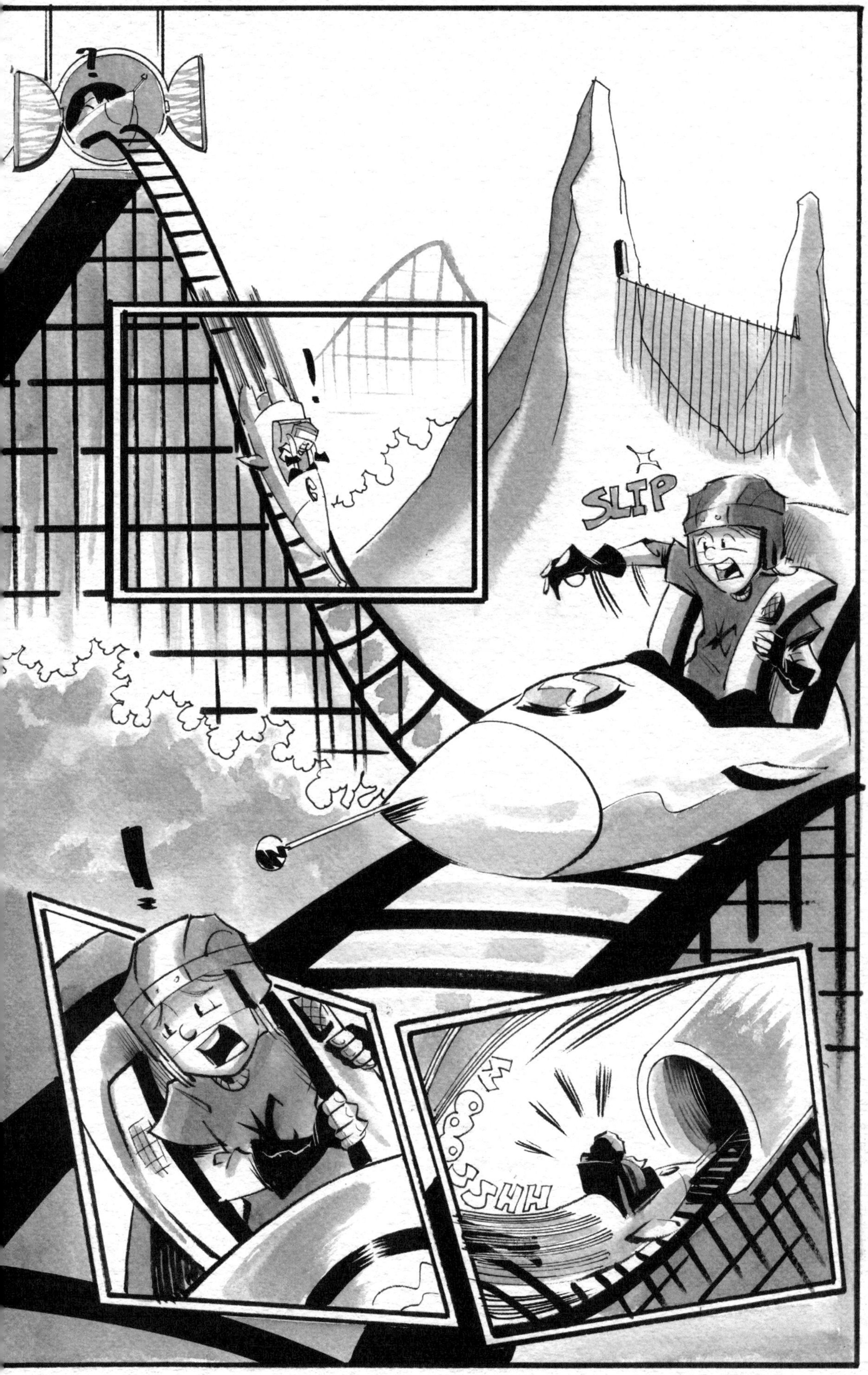
SLIP
WOOSSHH

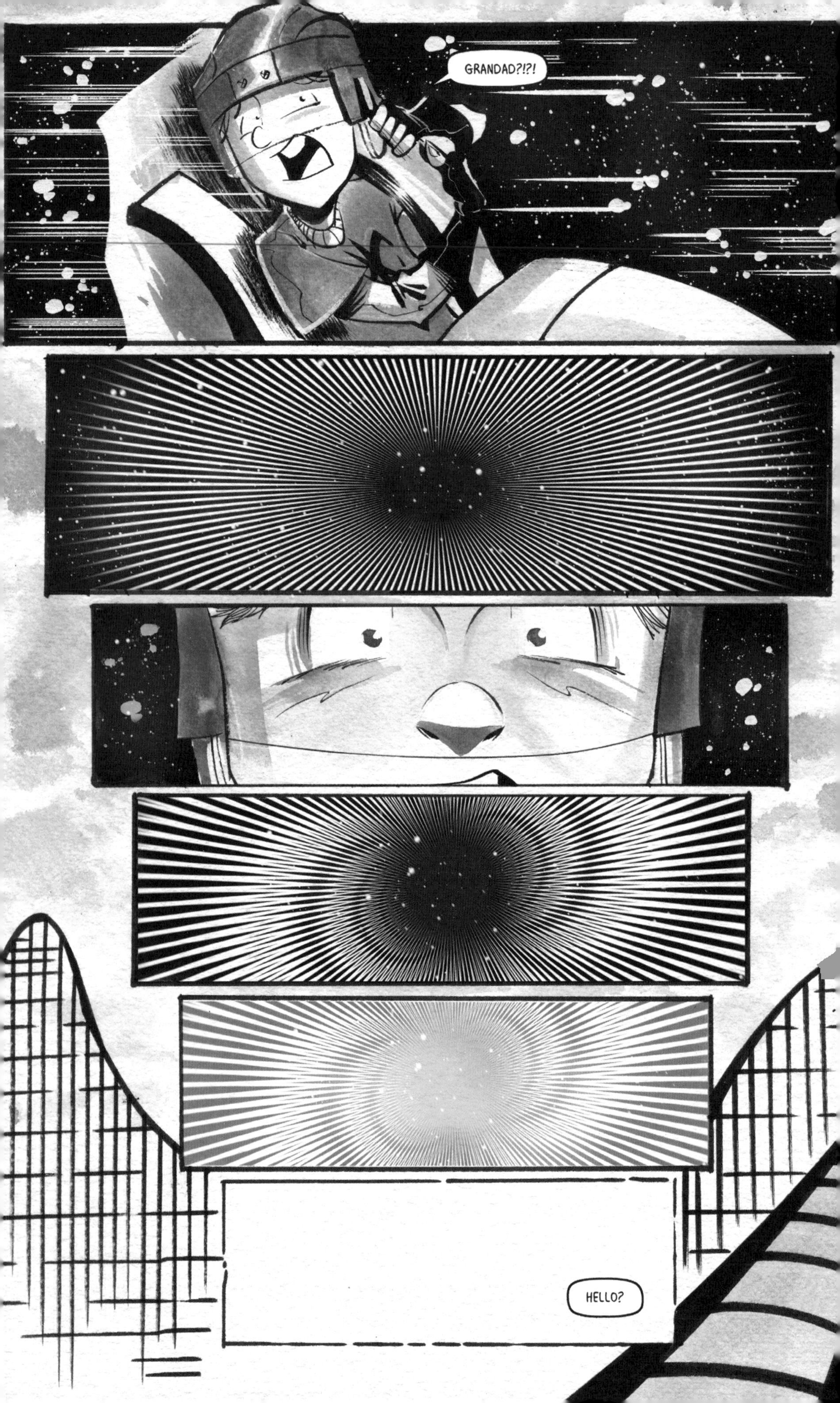
GRANDAD?!?!
HELLO?

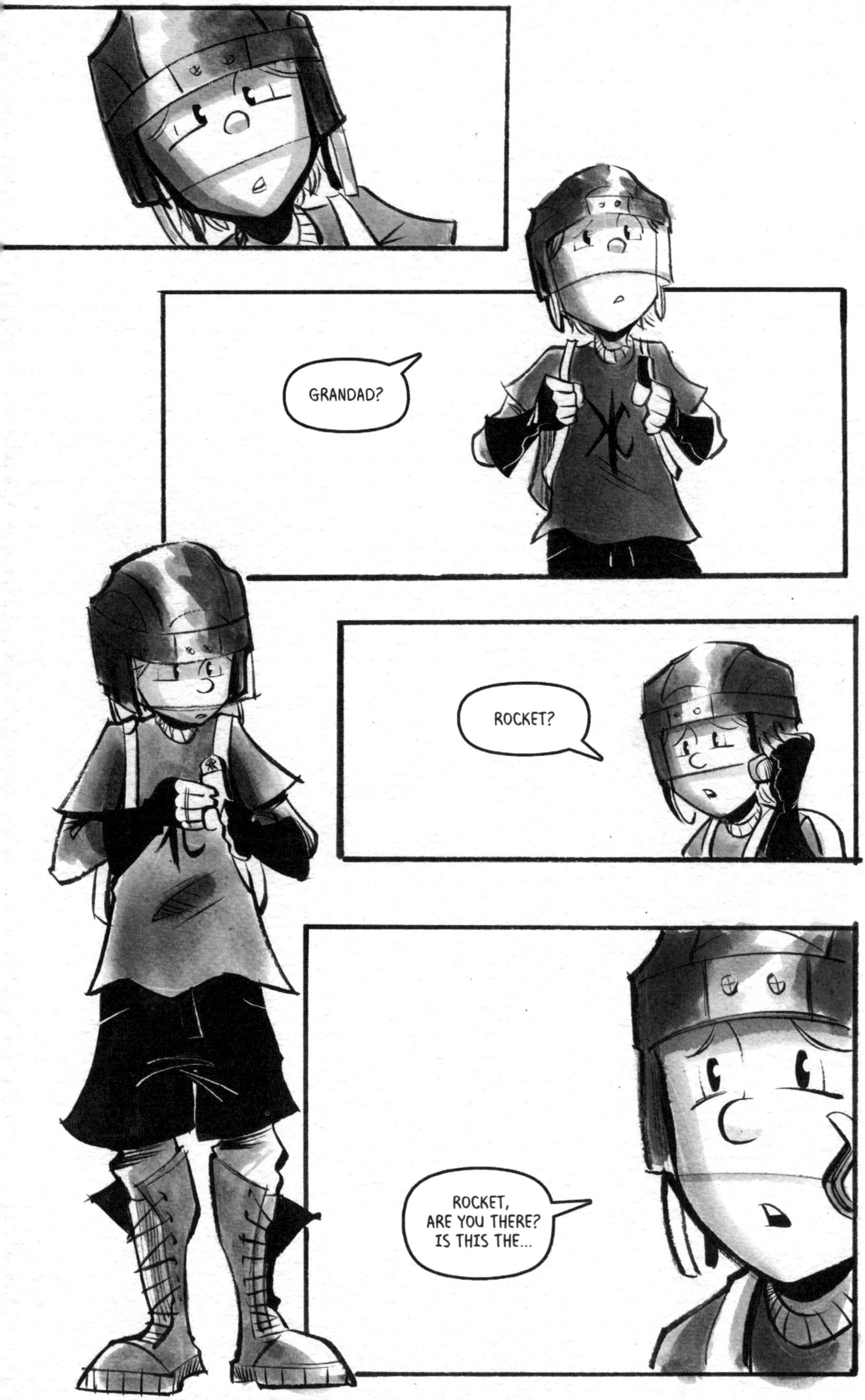
GRANDAD?
ROCKET?
ROCKET,
ARE YOU THERE?
IS THIS THE...

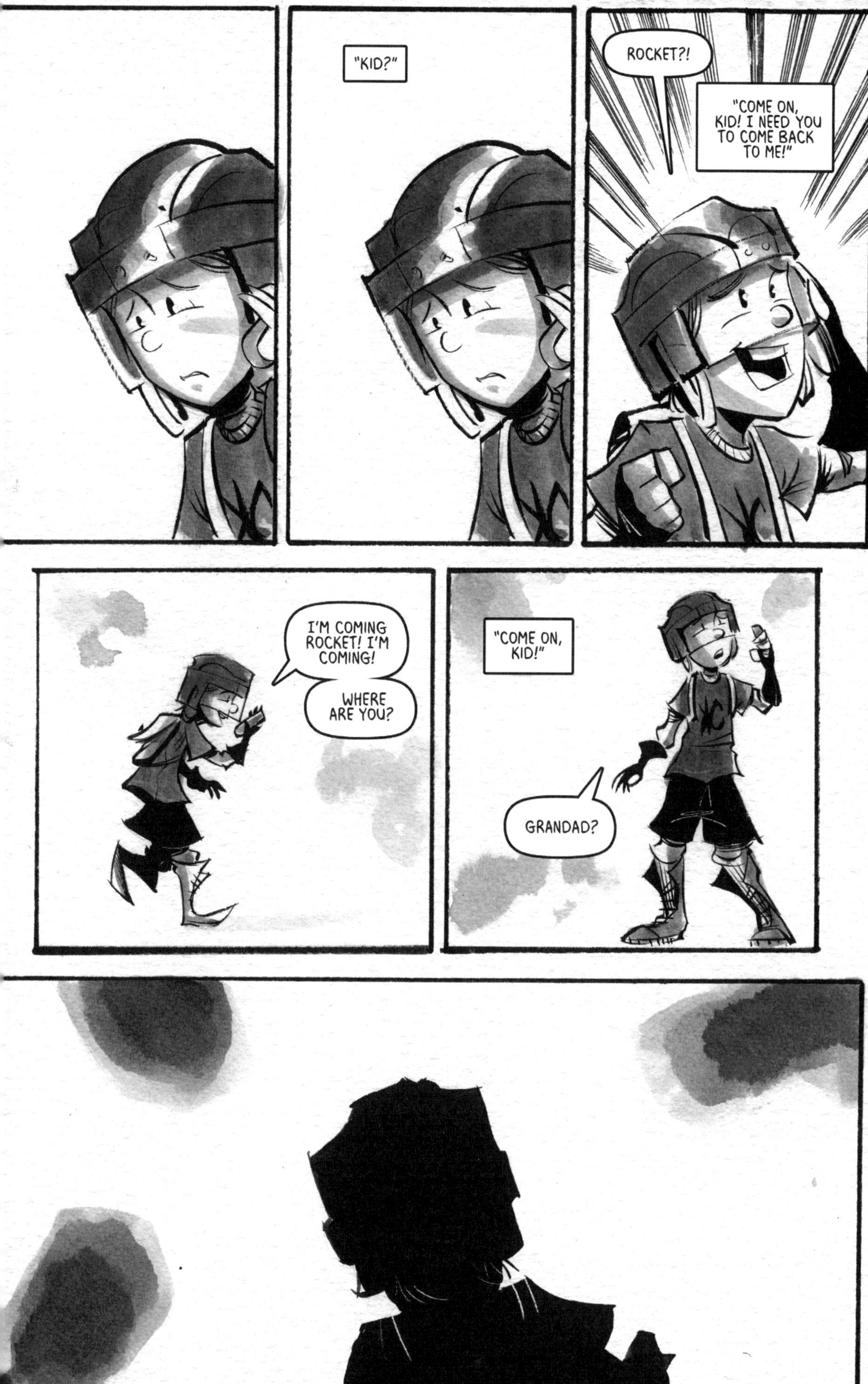
"KID?"
ROCKET?!
"COME ON, KID! I NEED YOU TO COME BACK TO ME!"
I'M COMING ROCKET! I'M COMING!
WHERE ARE YOU?
"COME ON, KID!"
GRANDAD?

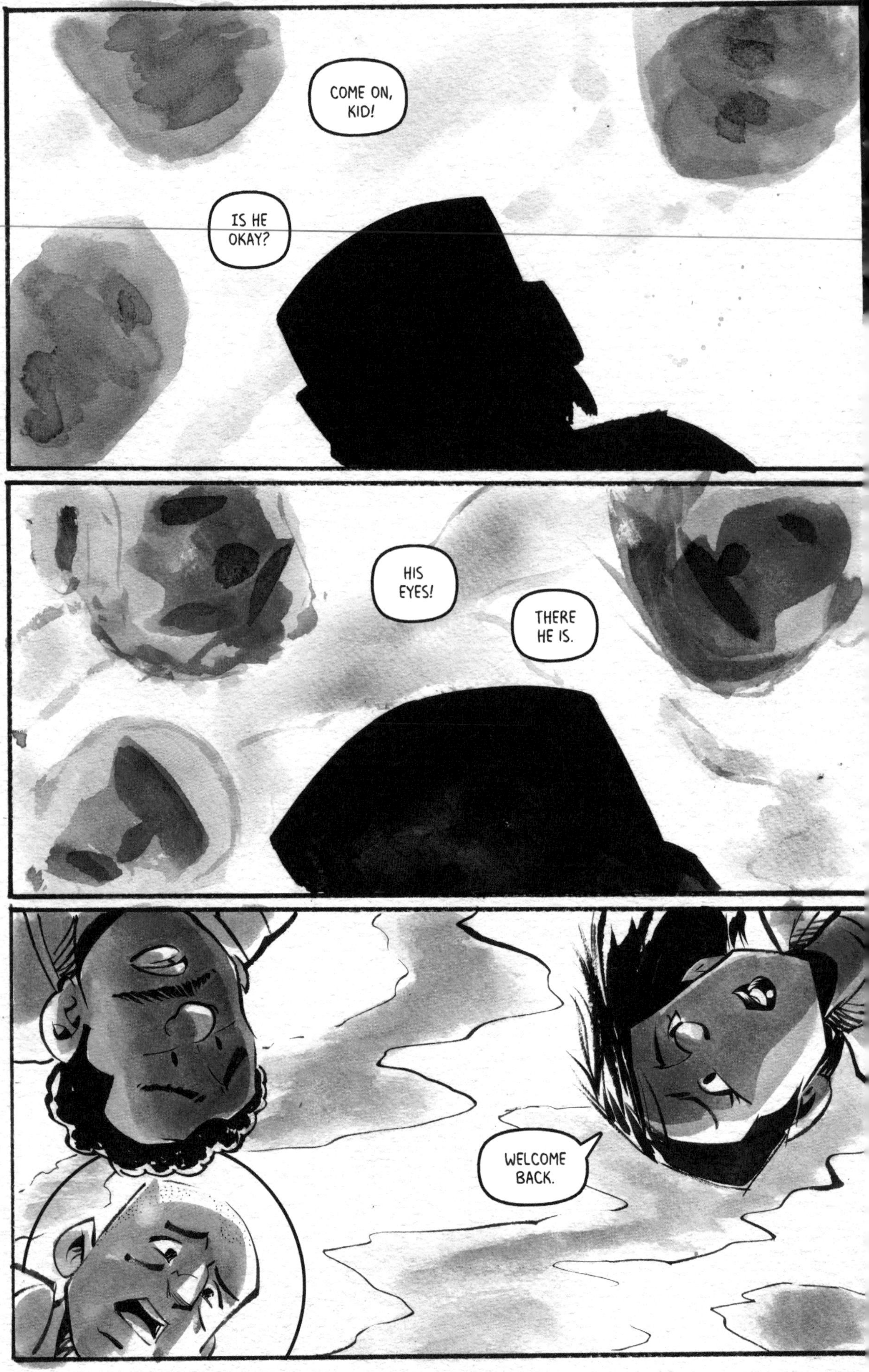
COME ON, KID!
IS HE OKAY?
HIS EYES!
THERE HE IS.
WELCOME BACK.

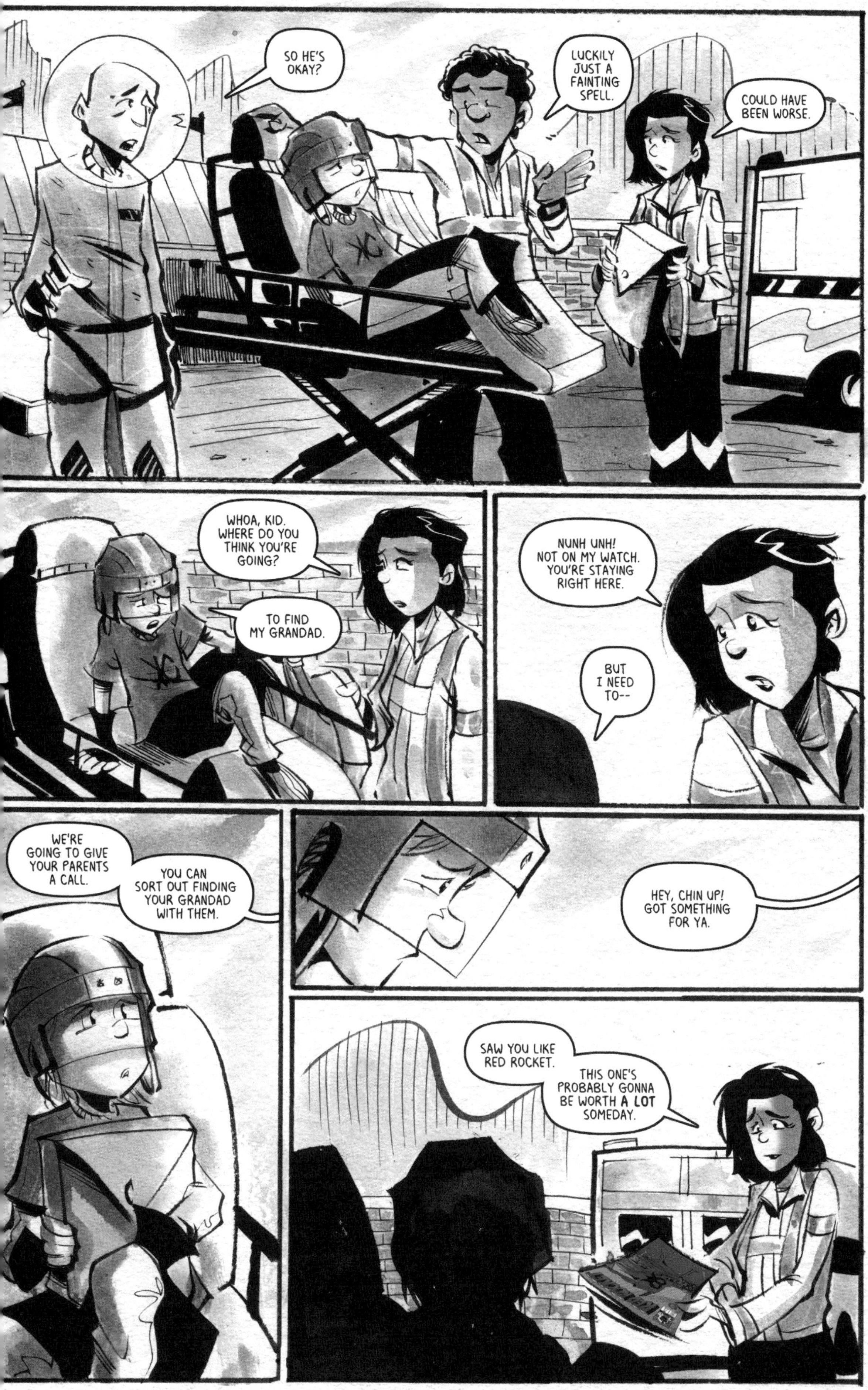
SO HE'S OKAY?
LUCKILY JUST A FAINTING SPELL.
COULD HAVE BEEN WORSE.
WHOA, KID. WHERE DO YOU THINK YOU'RE GOING?
TO FIND MY GRANDAD.
NUNH UNH! NOT ON MY WATCH. YOU'RE STAYING RIGHT HERE.
BUT I NEED TO--
WE'RE GOING TO GIVE YOUR PARENTS A CALL.
YOU CAN SORT OUT FINDING YOUR GRANDAD WITH THEM.
HEY, CHIN UP! GOT SOMETHING FOR YA.
SAW YOU LIKE RED ROCKET.
THIS ONE'S PROBABLY GONNA BE WORTH A LOT SOMEDAY.

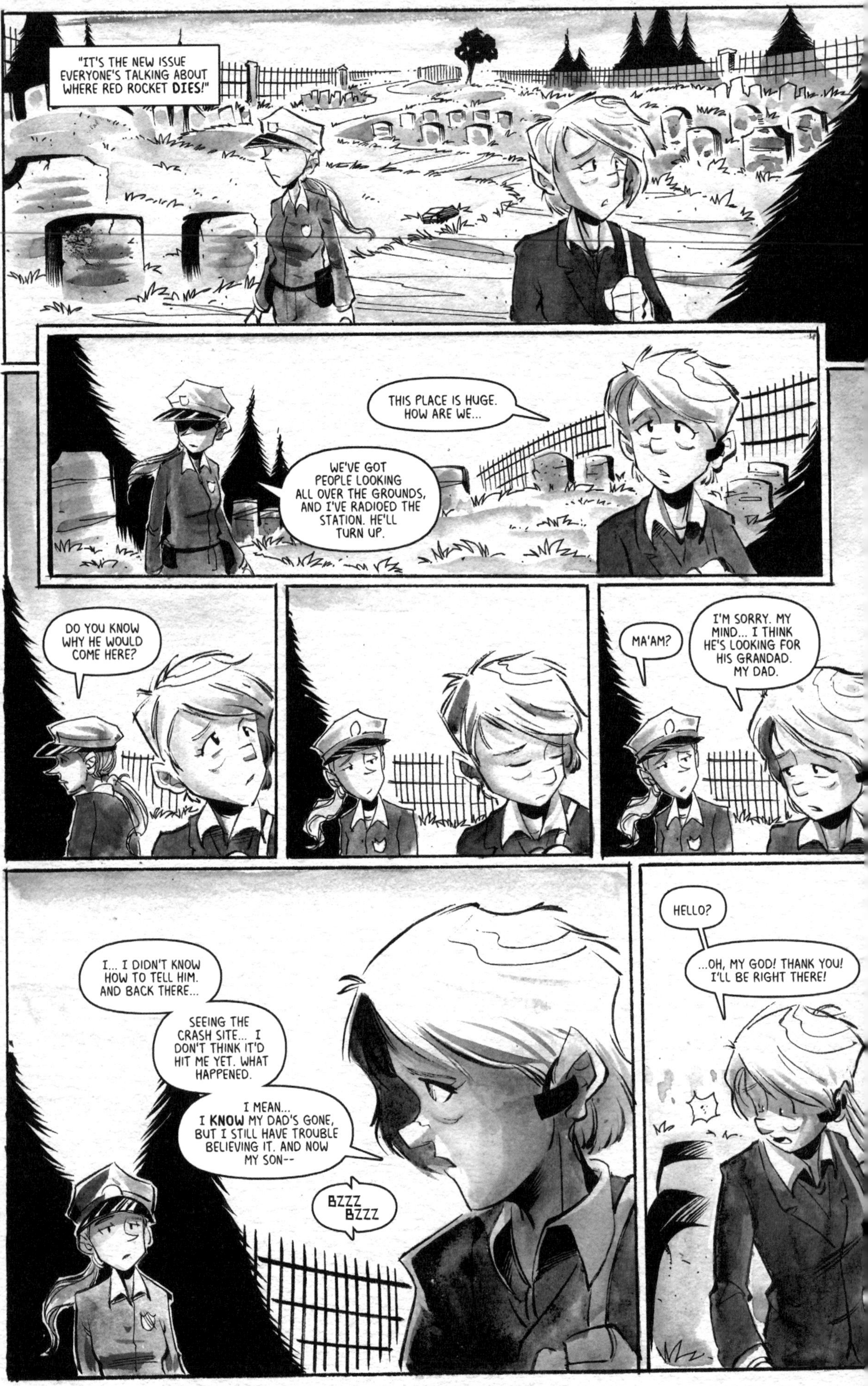
"IT'S THE NEW ISSUE EVERYONE'S TALKING ABOUT WHERE RED ROCKET DIES!"
THIS PLACE IS HUGE. HOW ARE WE...
WE'VE GOT PEOPLE LOOKING ALL OVER THE GROUNDS, AND I'VE RADIOED THE STATION. HE'LL TURN UP.
DO YOU KNOW WHY HE WOULD COME HERE?
MA'AM?
I'M SORRY. MY MIND... I THINK HE'S LOOKING FOR HIS GRANDAD. MY DAD.
I... I DIDN'T KNOW HOW TO TELL HIM. AND BACK THERE...
SEEING THE CRASH SITE... I DON'T THINK IT'D HIT ME YET. WHAT HAPPENED.
I MEAN... I **KNOW** MY DAD'S GONE, BUT I STILL HAVE TROUBLE BELIEVING IT. AND NOW MY SON--
BZZZ BZZZ
HELLO?
...OH, MY GOD! THANK YOU! I'LL BE RIGHT THERE!

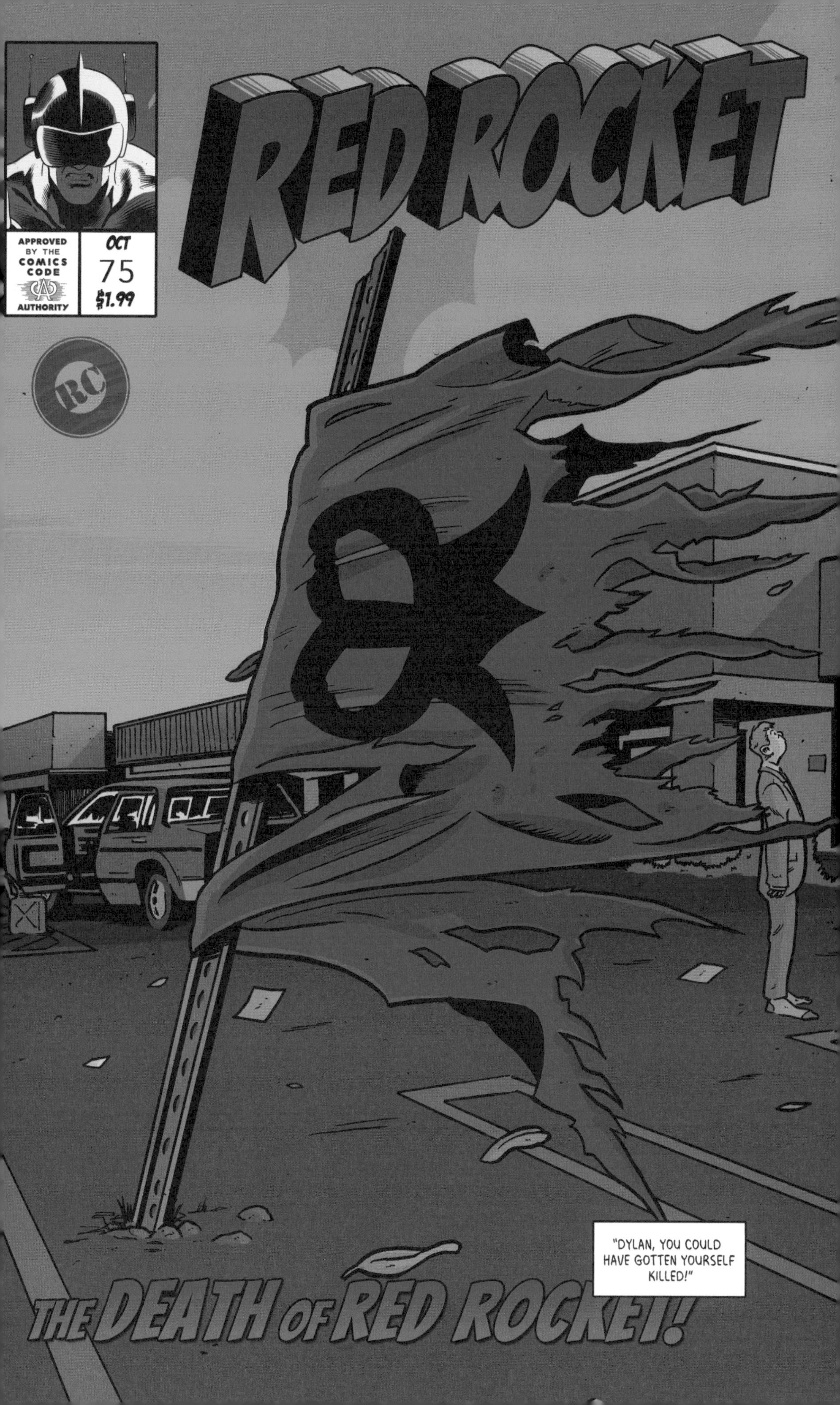
RED ROCKET
APPROVED BY THE COMICS CODE AUTHORITY
OCT
75
$1.99
RC
"DYLAN, YOU COULD HAVE GOTTEN YOURSELF KILLED!"
THE DEATH OF RED ROCKET!

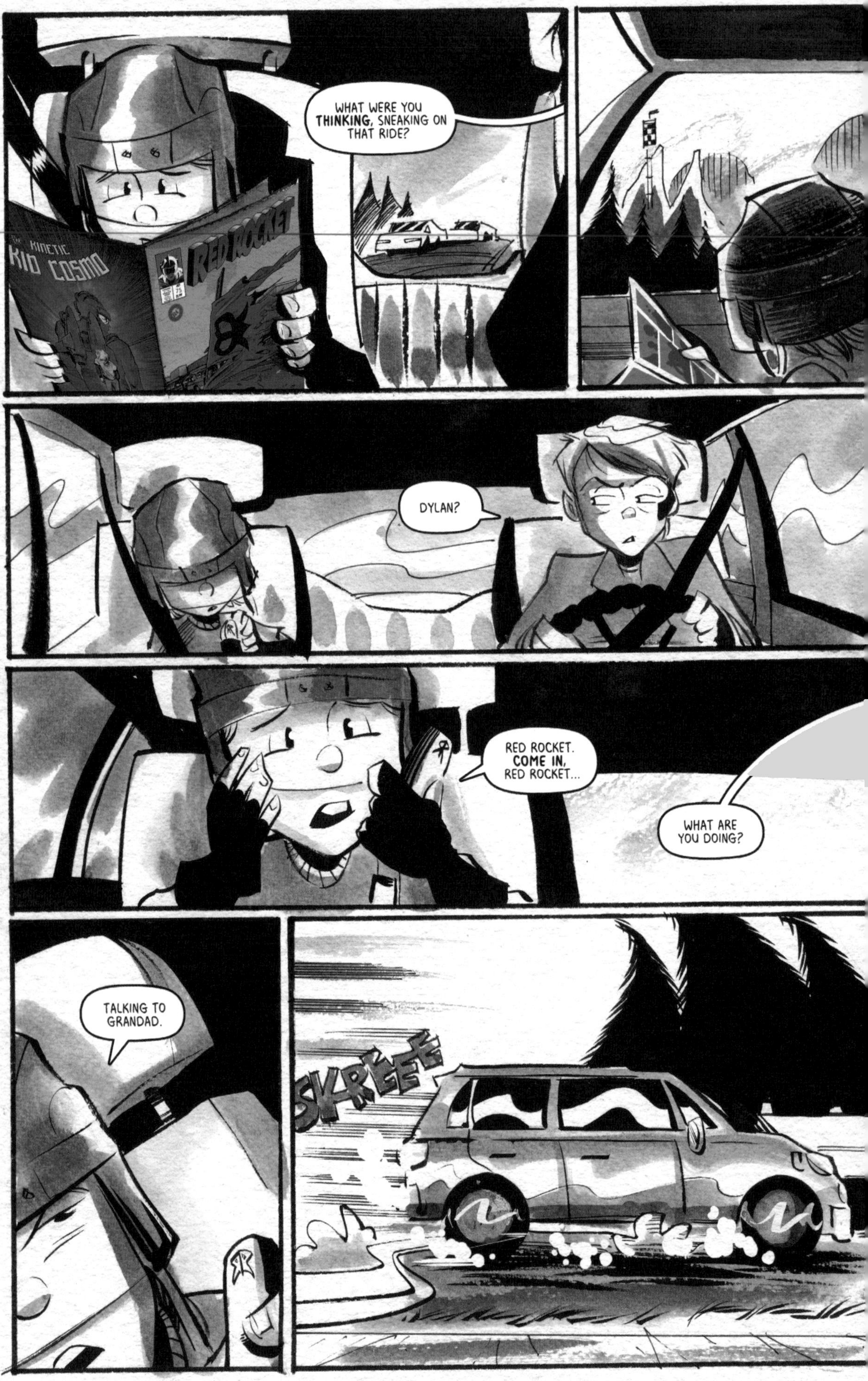

WHAT WERE YOU THINKING, SNEAKING ON THAT RIDE?
THE KINETIC KID COSMO
RED ROCKET
DYLAN?
RED ROCKET. COME IN, RED ROCKET...
WHAT ARE YOU DOING?
TALKING TO GRANDAD.
SKREEE

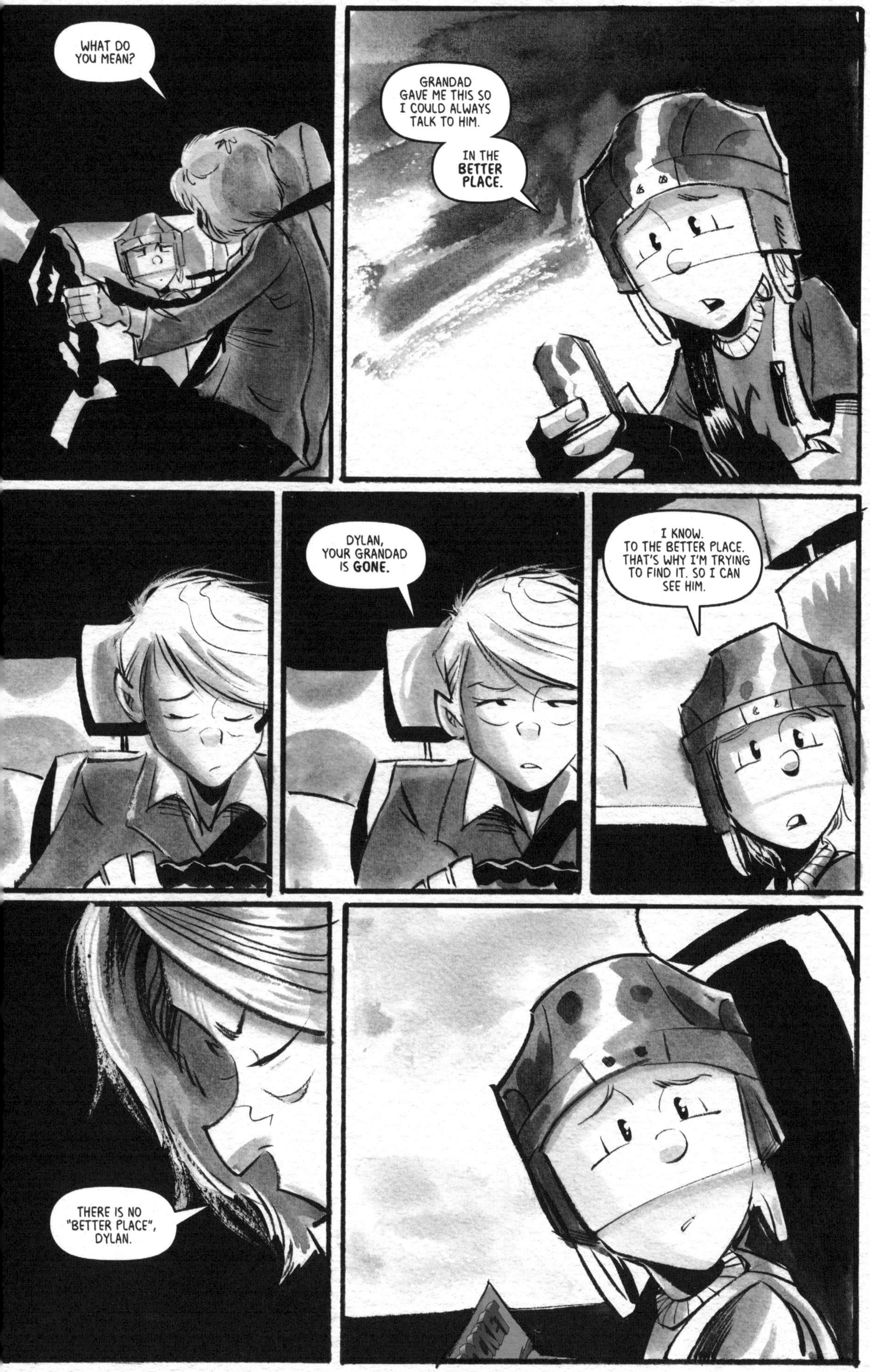
WHAT DO YOU MEAN?
GRANDAD GAVE ME THIS SO I COULD ALWAYS TALK TO HIM.
IN THE BETTER PLACE.
DYLAN, YOUR GRANDAD IS GONE.
I KNOW. TO THE BETTER PLACE. THAT'S WHY I'M TRYING TO FIND IT. SO I CAN SEE HIM.
THERE IS NO "BETTER PLACE", DYLAN.

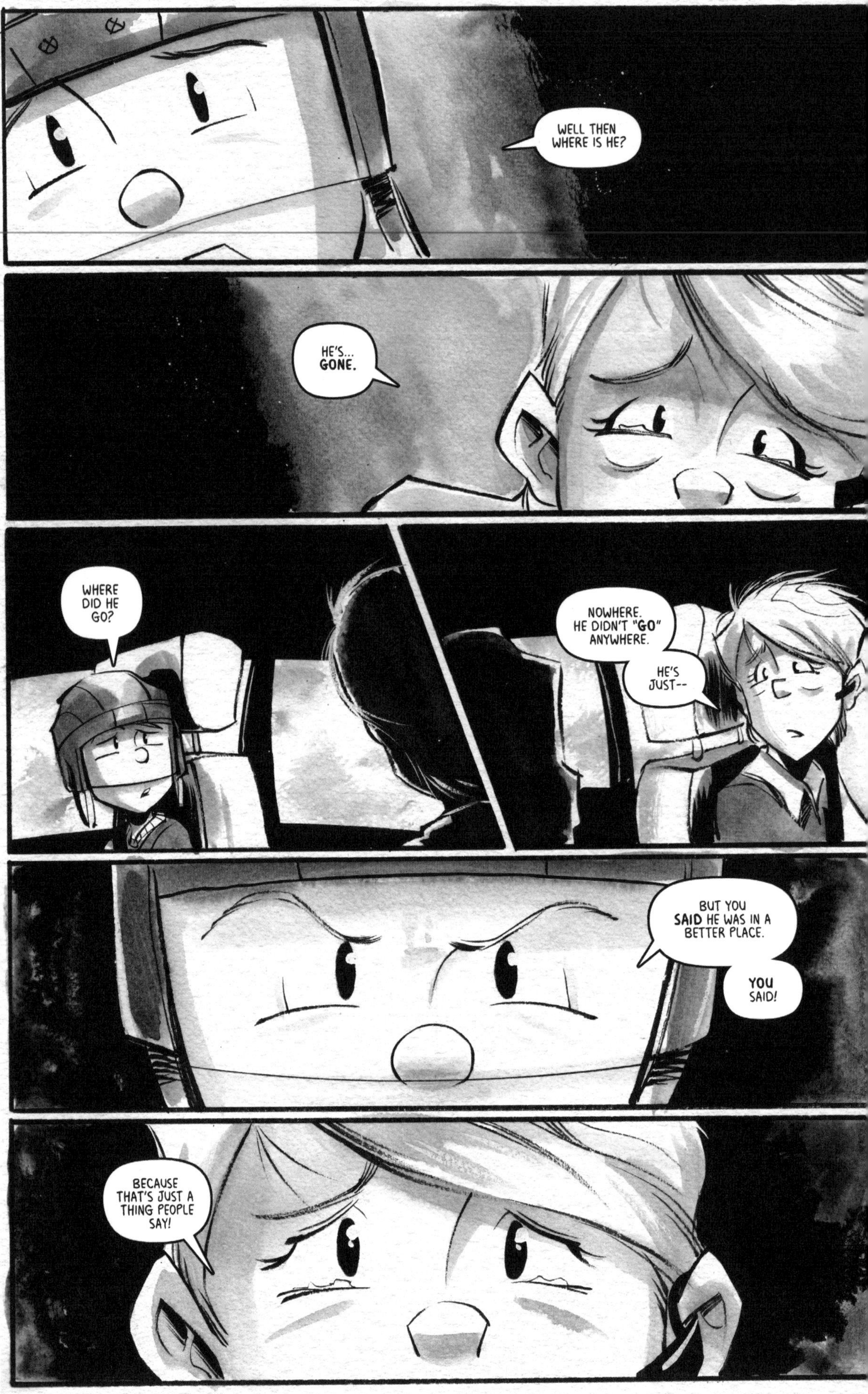
WELL THEN WHERE IS HE?
HE'S... **GONE.**
WHERE DID HE GO?
NOWHERE. HE DIDN'T "**GO**" ANYWHERE.
HE'S JUST--
BUT YOU **SAID** HE WAS IN A BETTER PLACE.
YOU SAID!
BECAUSE THAT'S JUST A THING PEOPLE SAY!

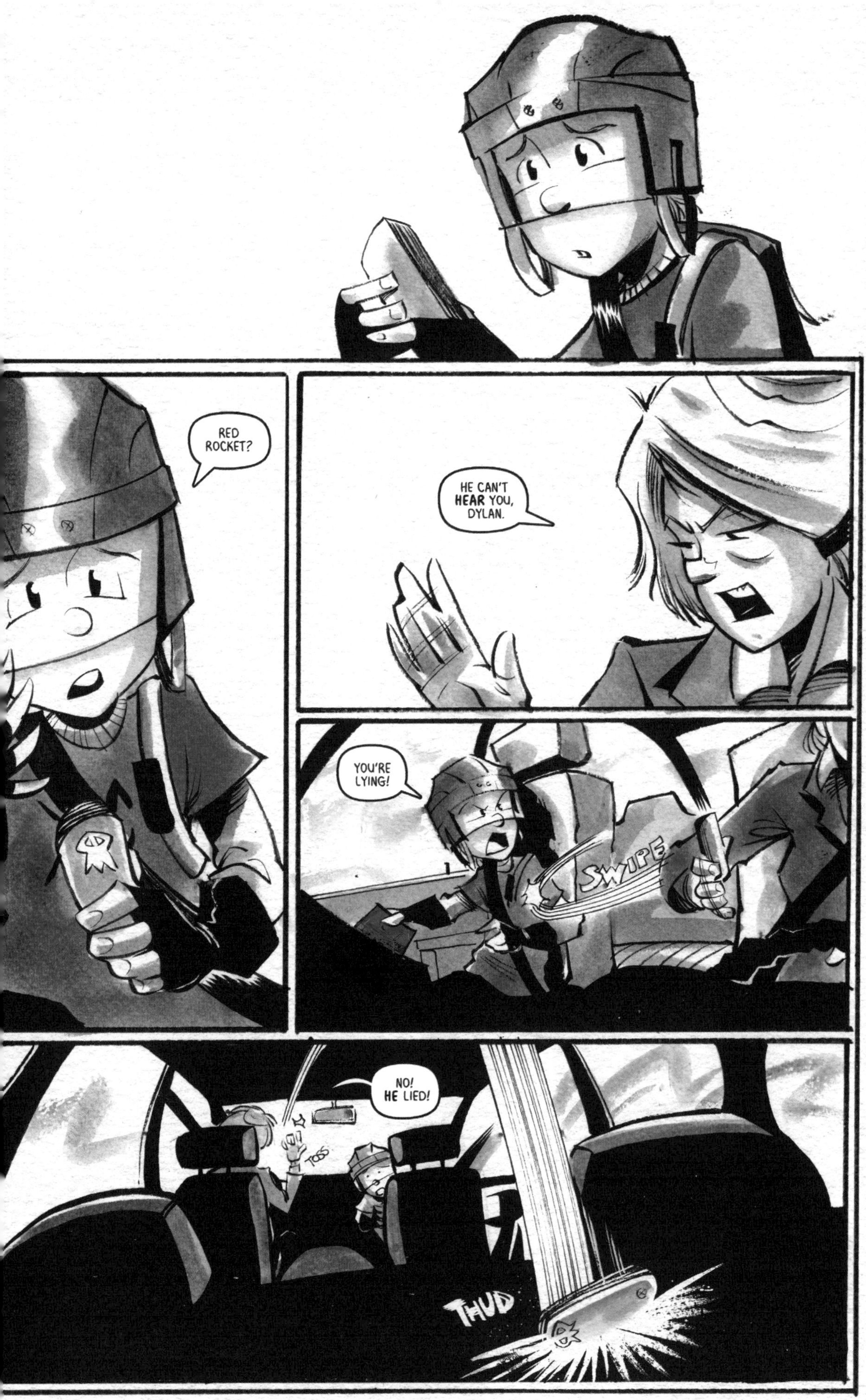
RED ROCKET?
HE CAN'T **HEAR** YOU, DYLAN.
YOU'RE LYING!
SWIPE
NO! **HE** LIED!
TOSS
THUD

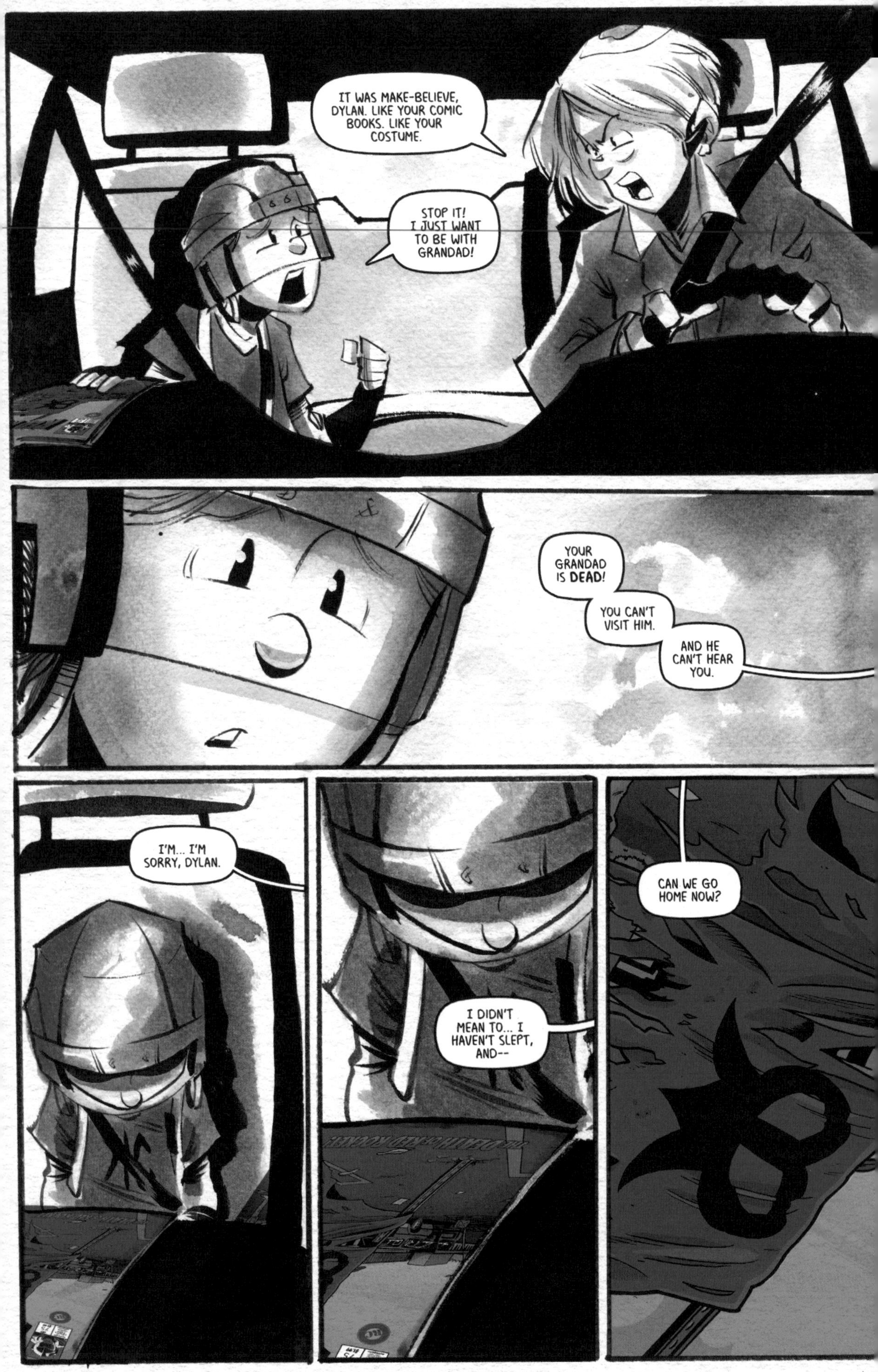
IT WAS MAKE-BELIEVE, DYLAN. LIKE YOUR COMIC BOOKS. LIKE YOUR COSTUME.
STOP IT! I JUST WANT TO BE WITH GRANDAD!
YOUR GRANDAD IS **DEAD**!
YOU CAN'T VISIT HIM.
AND HE CAN'T HEAR YOU.
I'M... I'M SORRY, DYLAN.
I DIDN'T MEAN TO... I HAVEN'T SLEPT, AND--
CAN WE GO HOME NOW?

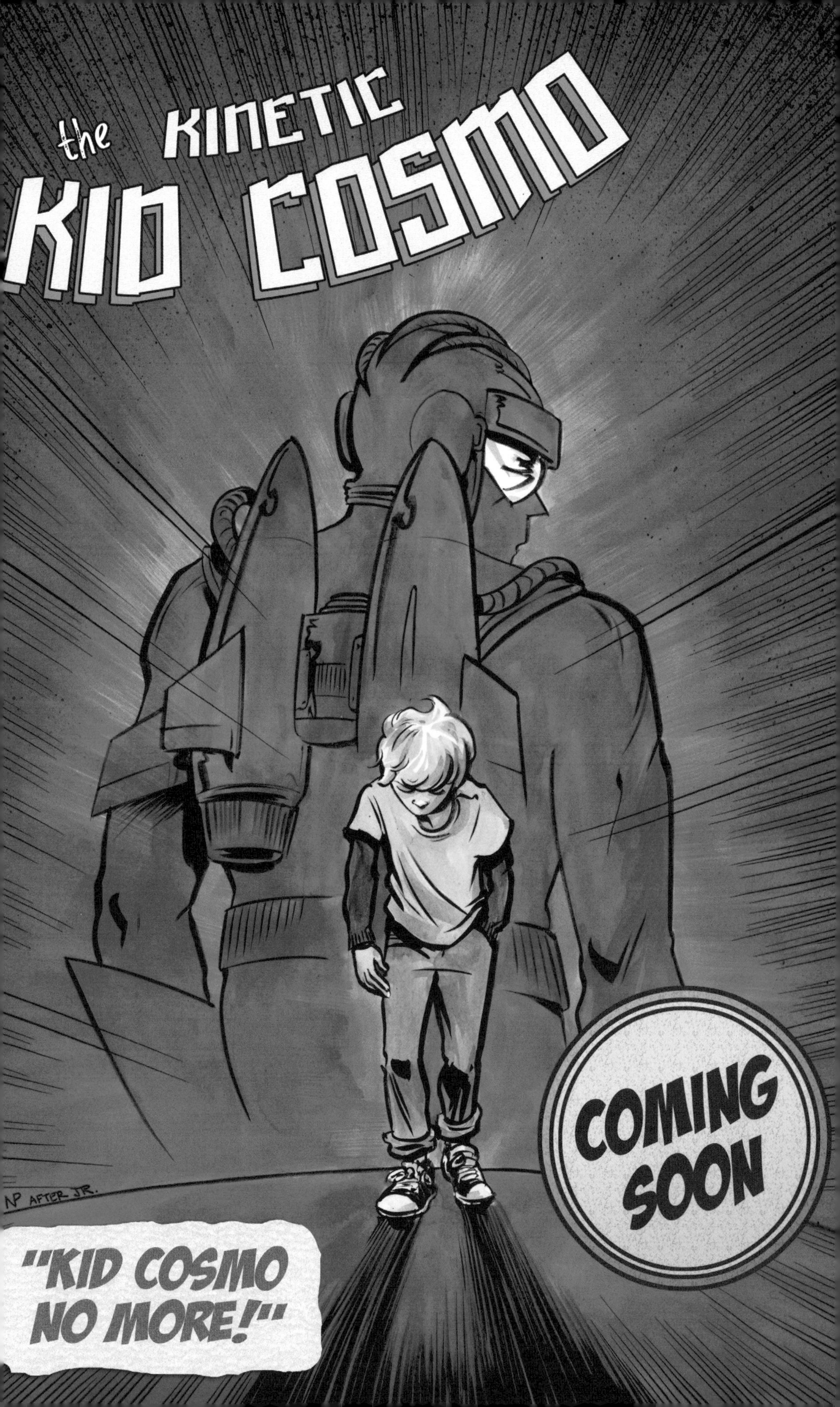
the KINETIC
KID COSMO
NP AFTER JR.
COMING SOON
"KID COSMO NO MORE!"

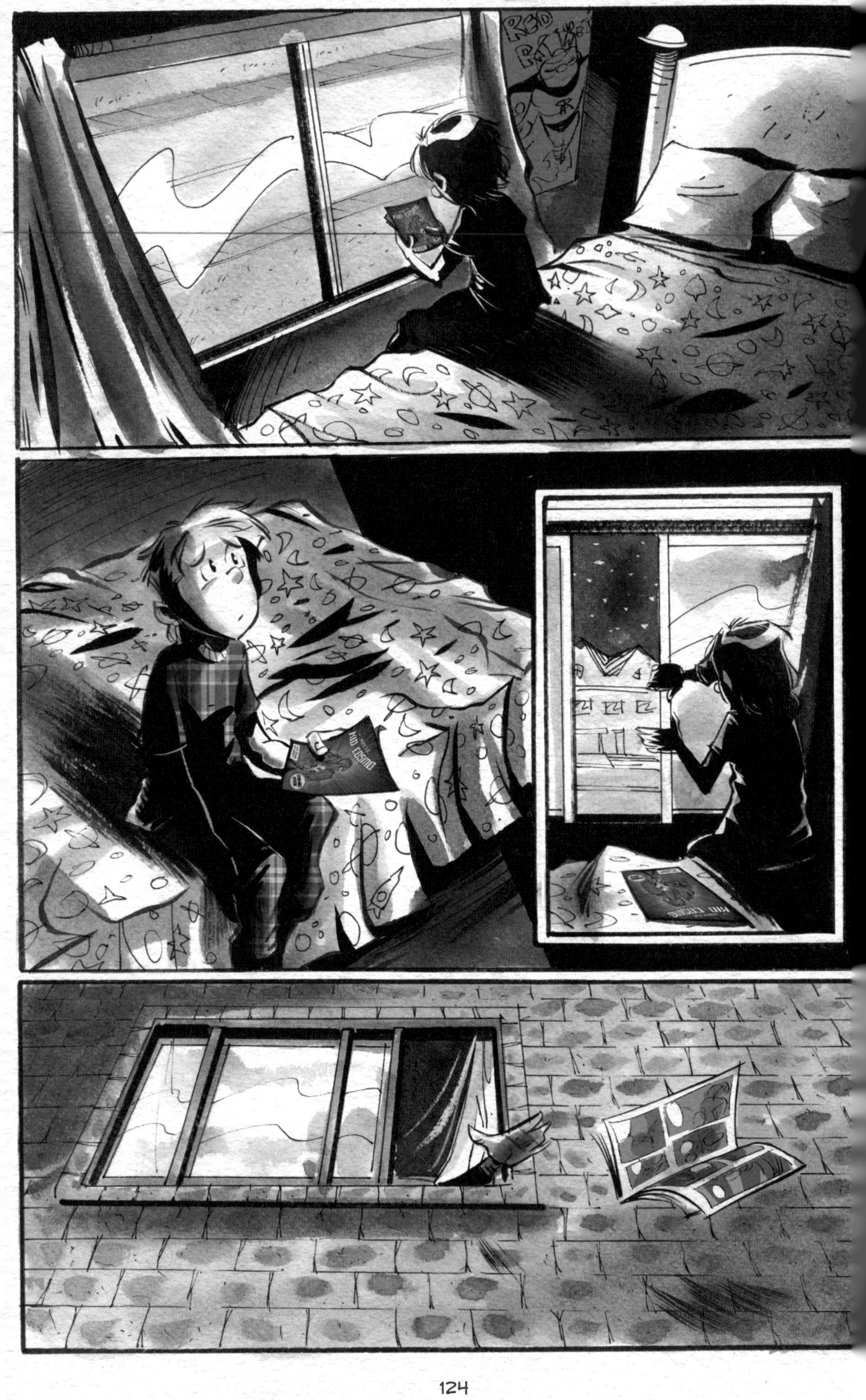

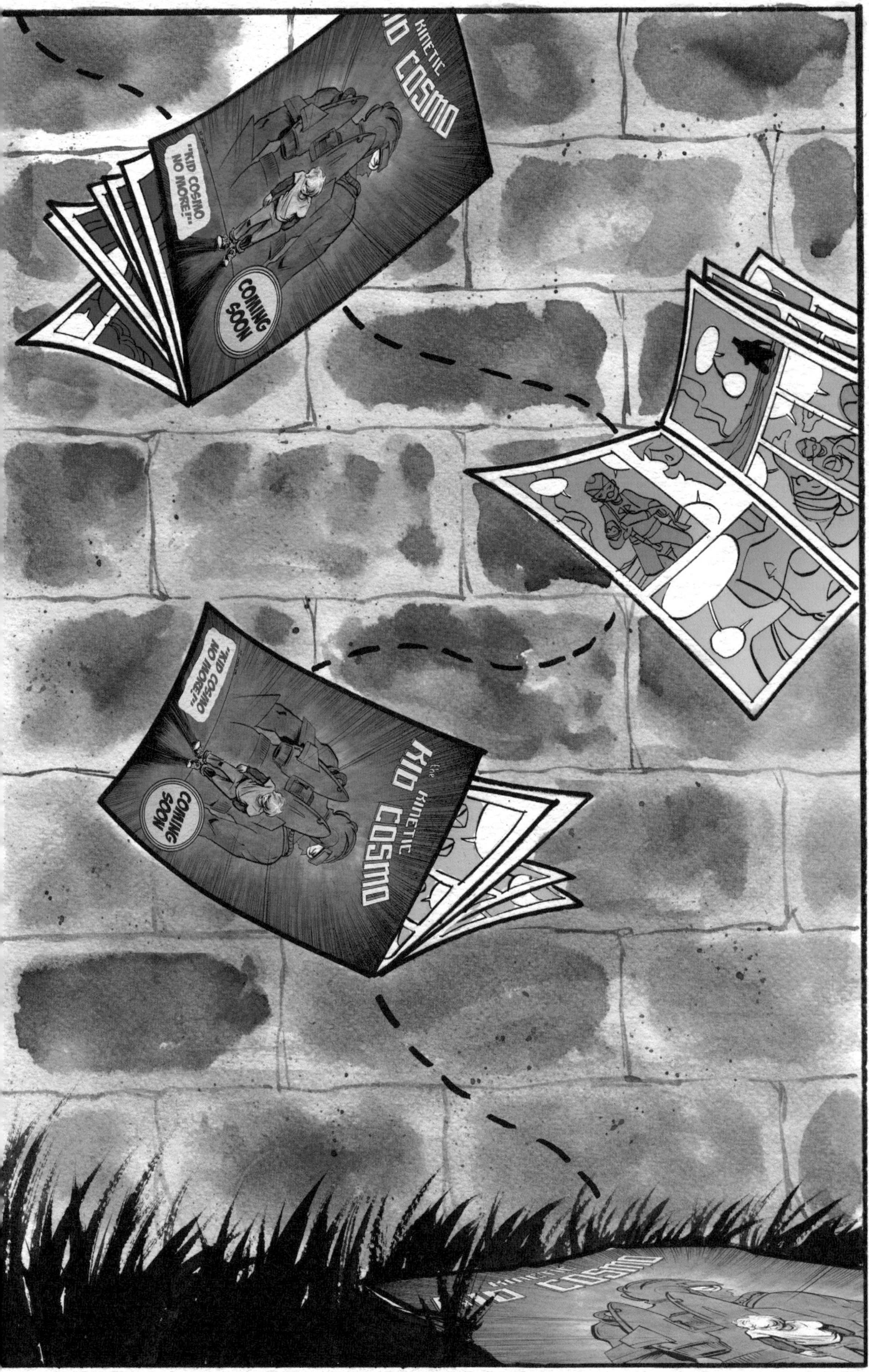
the KINETIC KID COSMO
"KID COSMO NO MORE!!"
COMING SOON
the KINETIC KID COSMO
"KID COSMO NO MORE!!"
COMING SOON
KINETIC KID COSMO

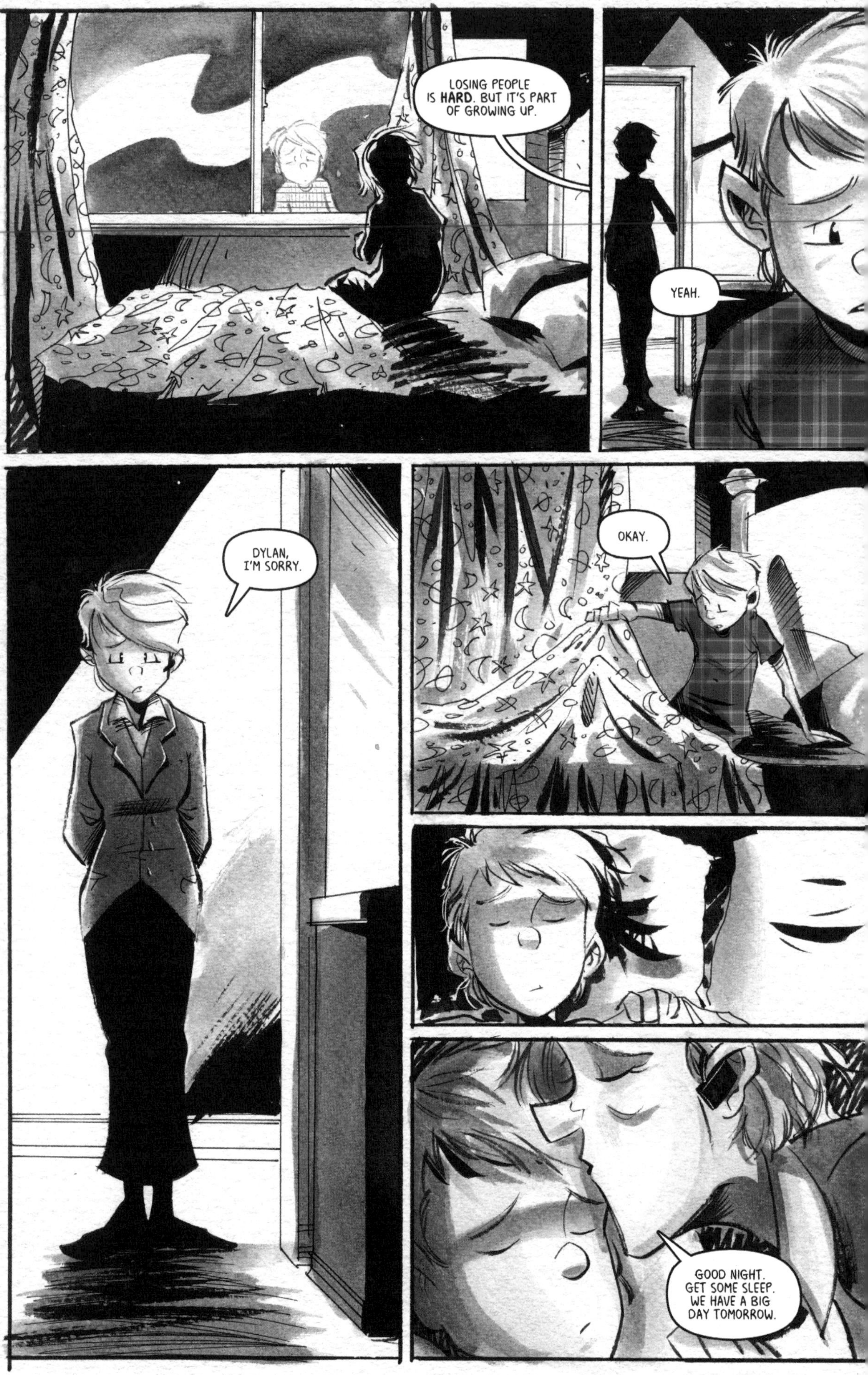
LOSING PEOPLE IS **HARD**. BUT IT'S PART OF GROWING UP.
YEAH.
DYLAN, I'M SORRY.
OKAY.
GOOD NIGHT. GET SOME SLEEP. WE HAVE A BIG DAY TOMORROW.

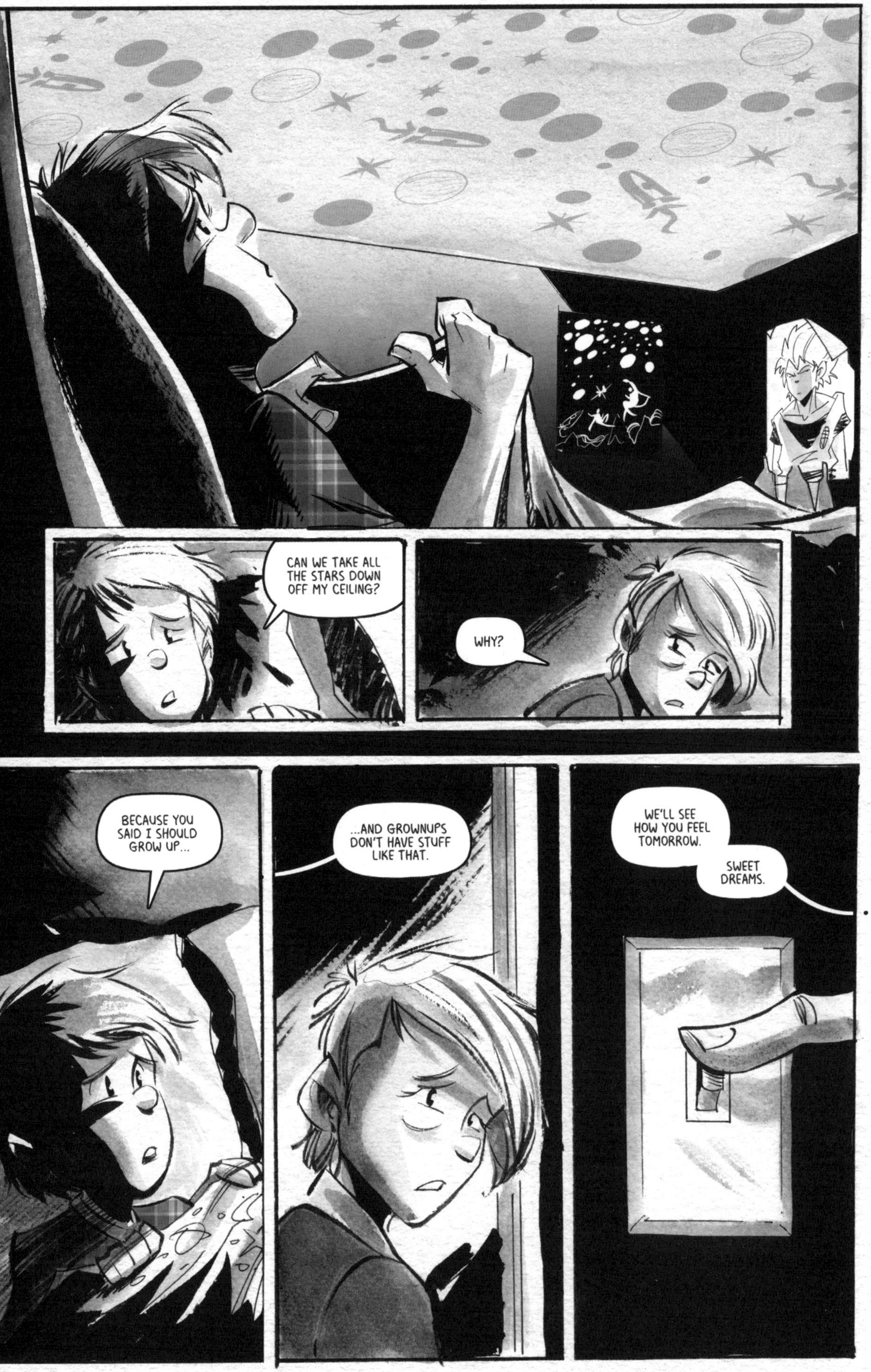
CAN WE TAKE ALL THE STARS DOWN OFF MY CEILING?
WHY?
BECAUSE YOU SAID I SHOULD GROW UP...
...AND GROWNUPS DON'T HAVE STUFF LIKE THAT.
WE'LL SEE HOW YOU FEEL TOMORROW.
SWEET DREAMS.

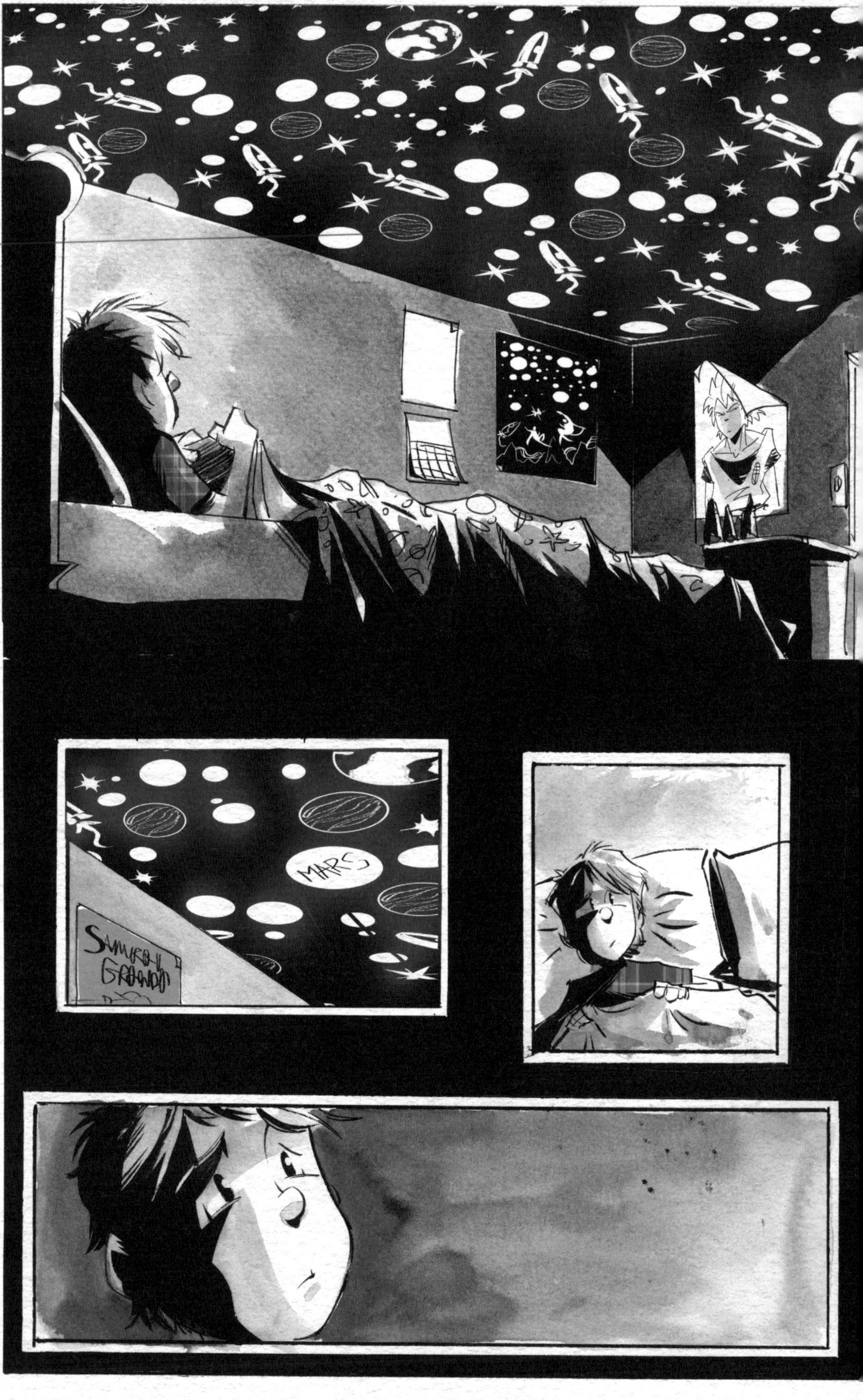
MARS

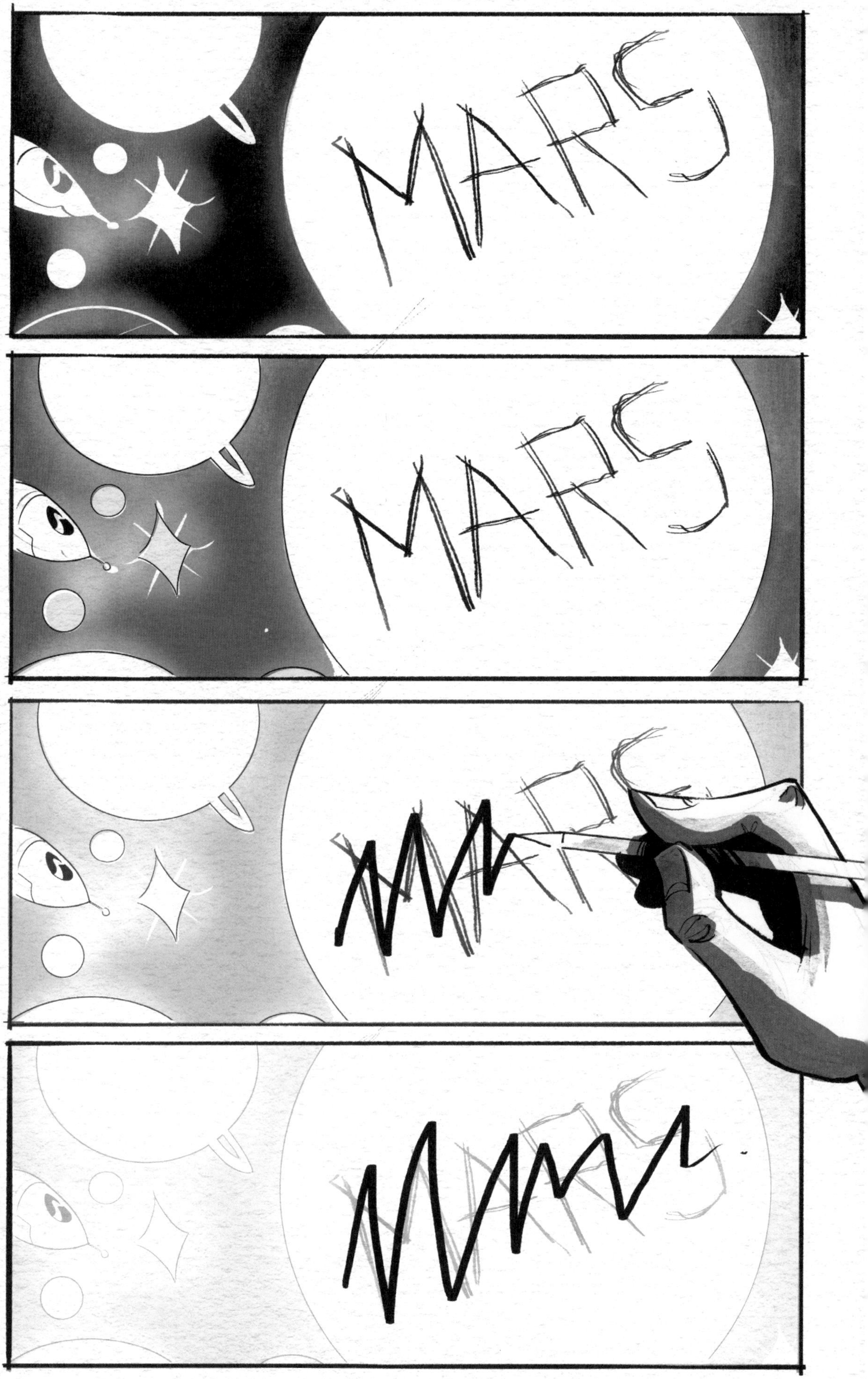
MARS
MARS
MARS

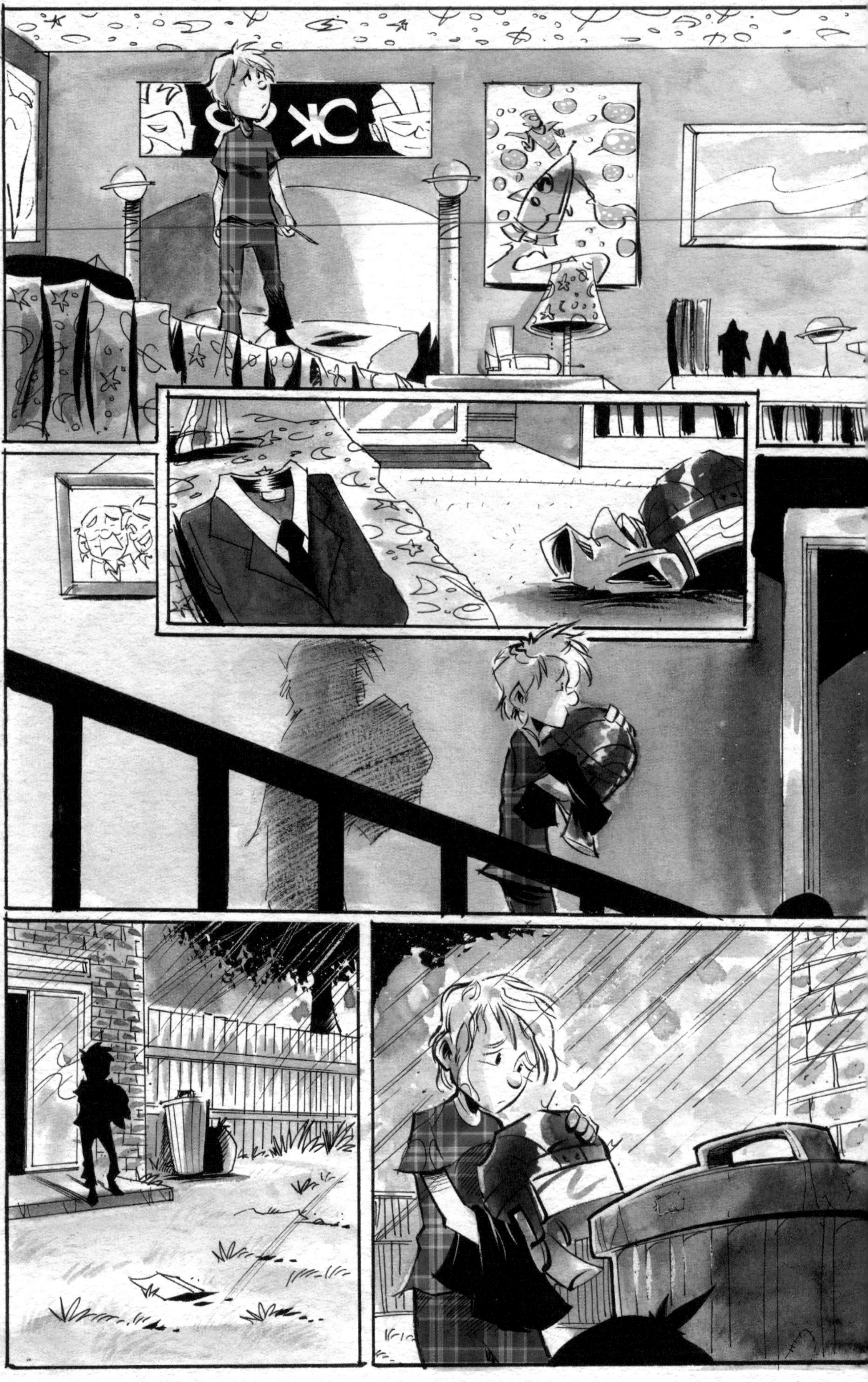
OK

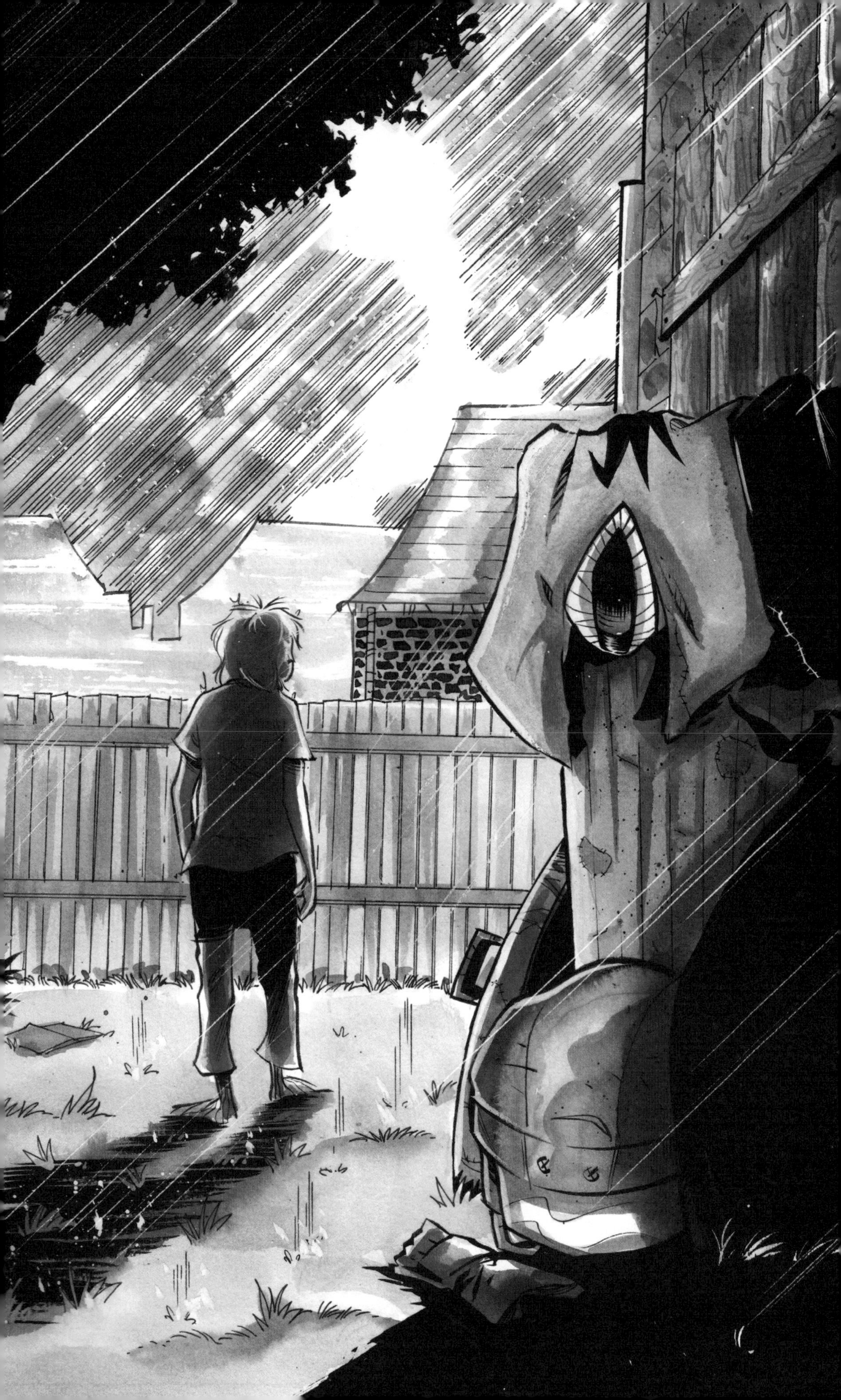

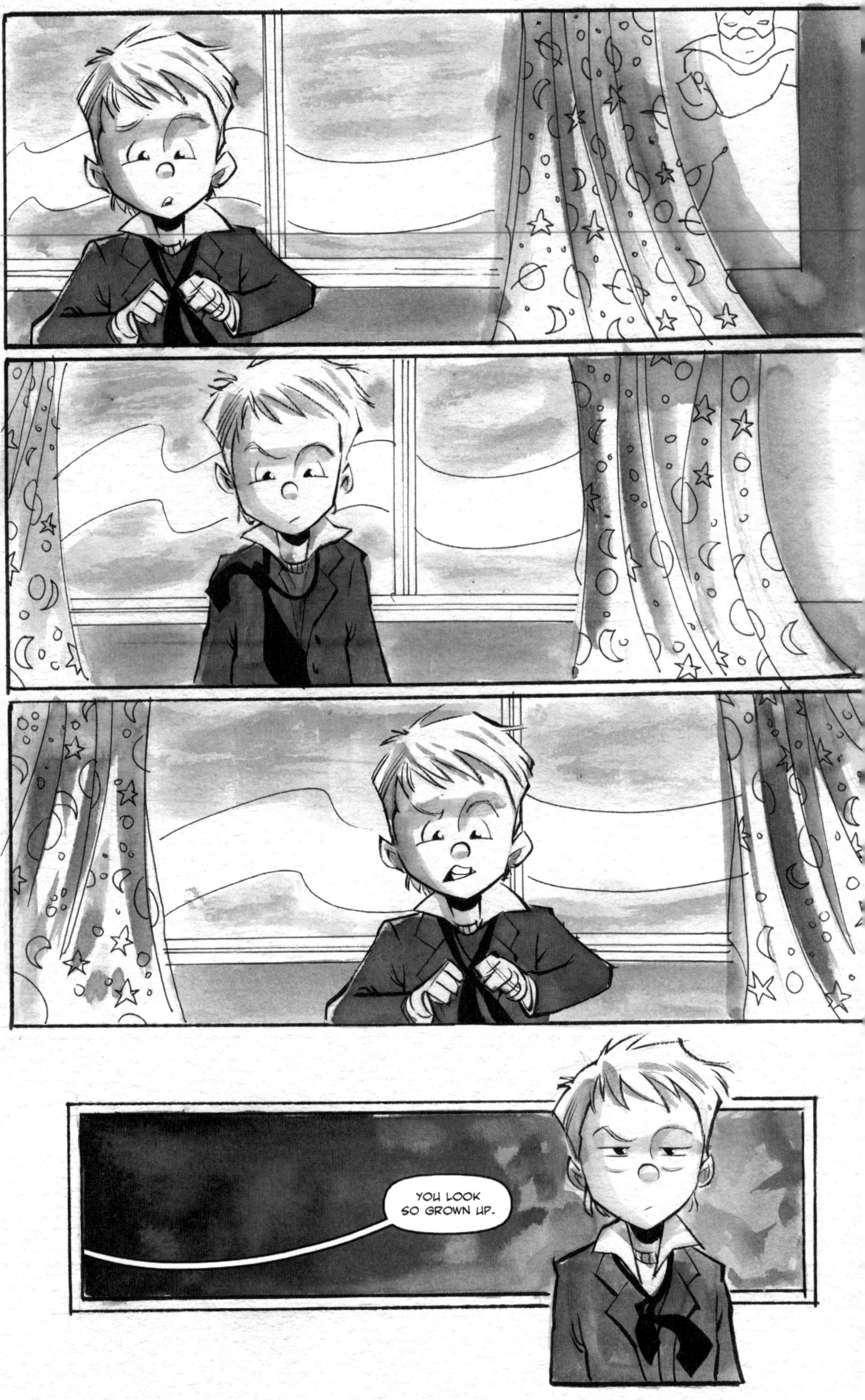
YOU LOOK SO GROWN UP.

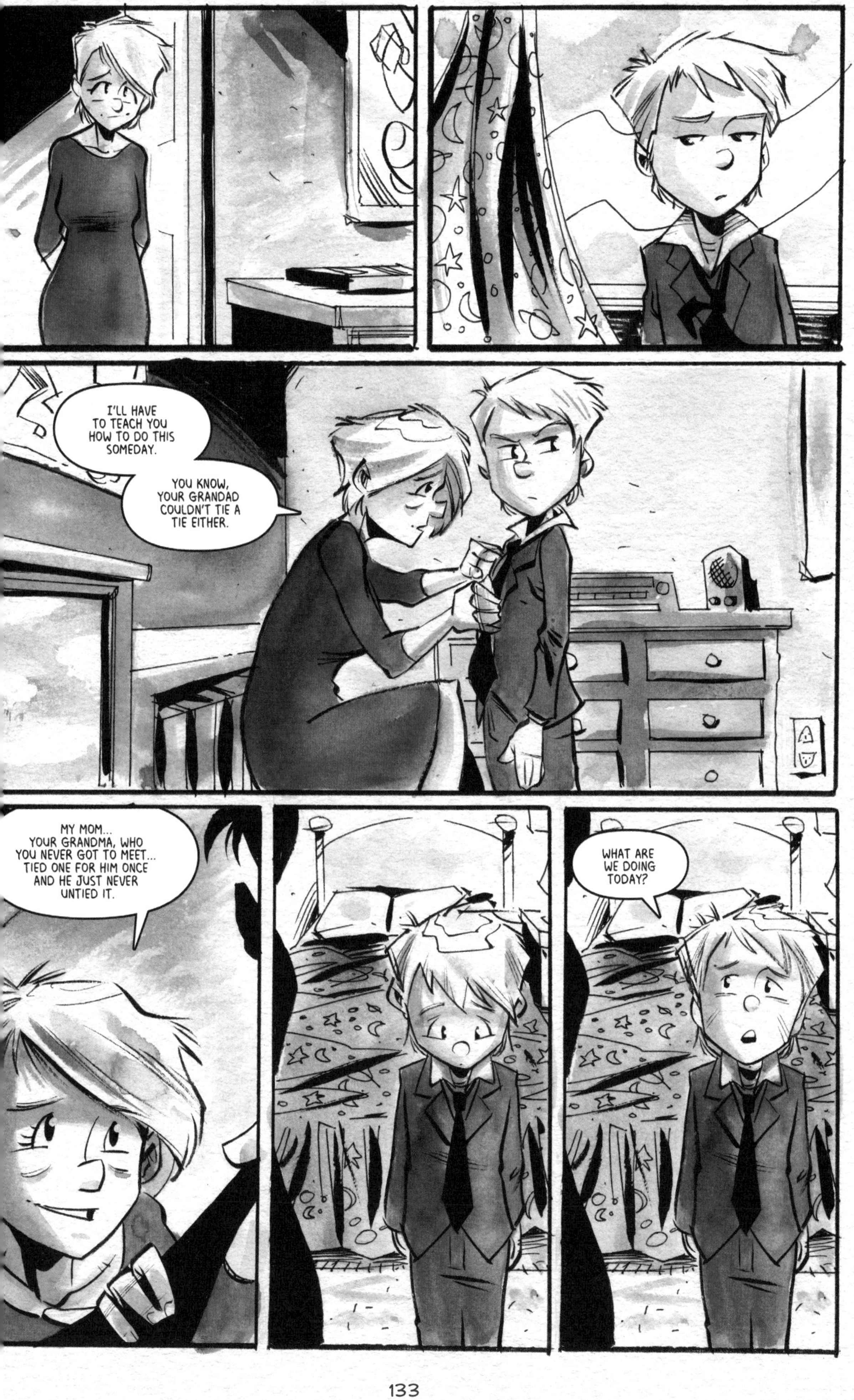

I'LL HAVE TO TEACH YOU HOW TO DO THIS SOMEDAY.
YOU KNOW, YOUR GRANDAD COULDN'T TIE A TIE EITHER.
MY MOM... YOUR GRANDMA, WHO YOU NEVER GOT TO MEET... TIED ONE FOR HIM ONCE AND HE JUST NEVER UNTIED IT.
WHAT ARE WE DOING TODAY?

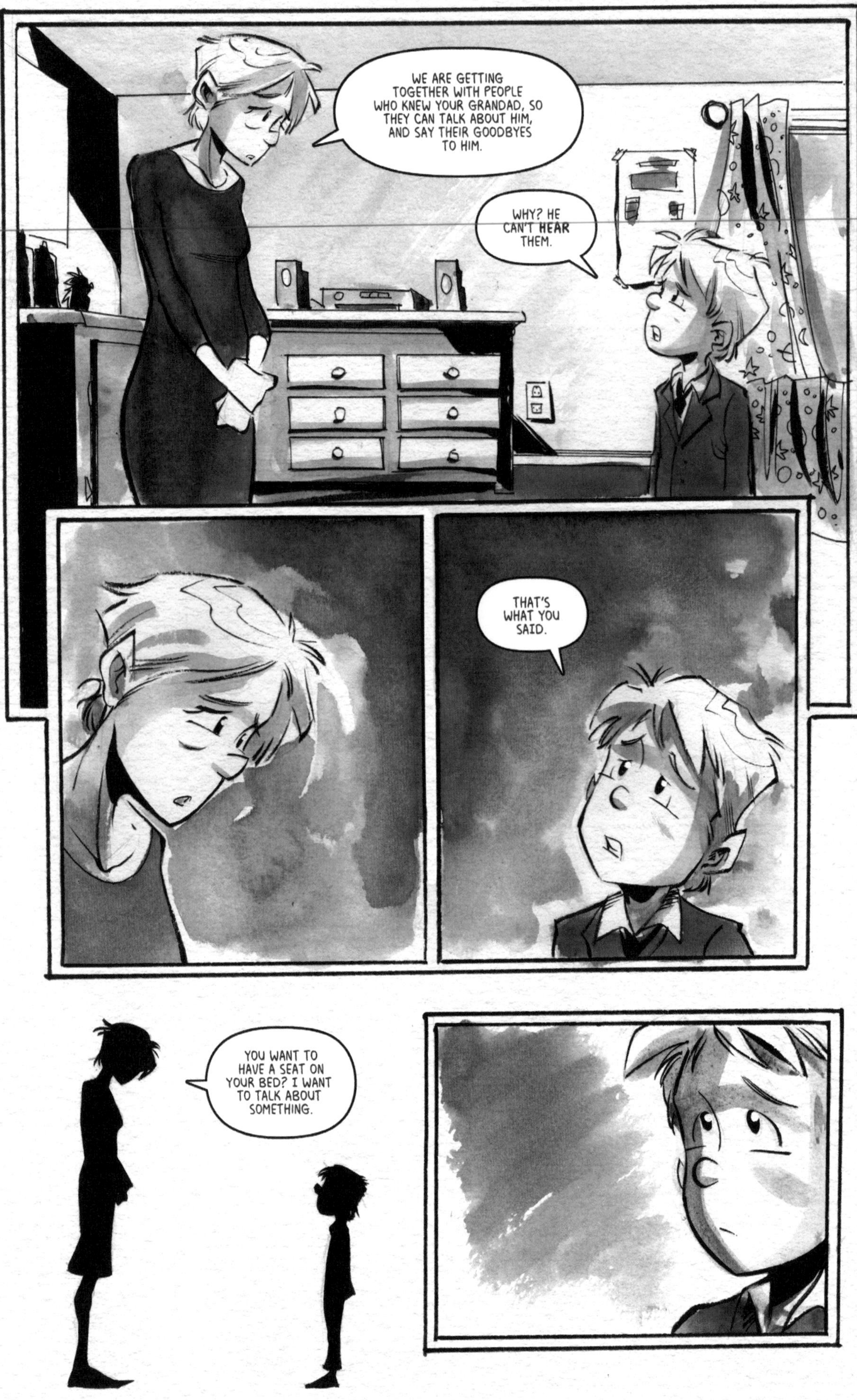

WE ARE GETTING TOGETHER WITH PEOPLE WHO KNEW YOUR GRANDAD, SO THEY CAN TALK ABOUT HIM, AND SAY THEIR GOODBYES TO HIM.
WHY? HE CAN'T **HEAR** THEM.
THAT'S WHAT YOU SAID.
YOU WANT TO HAVE A SEAT ON YOUR BED? I WANT TO TALK ABOUT SOMETHING.

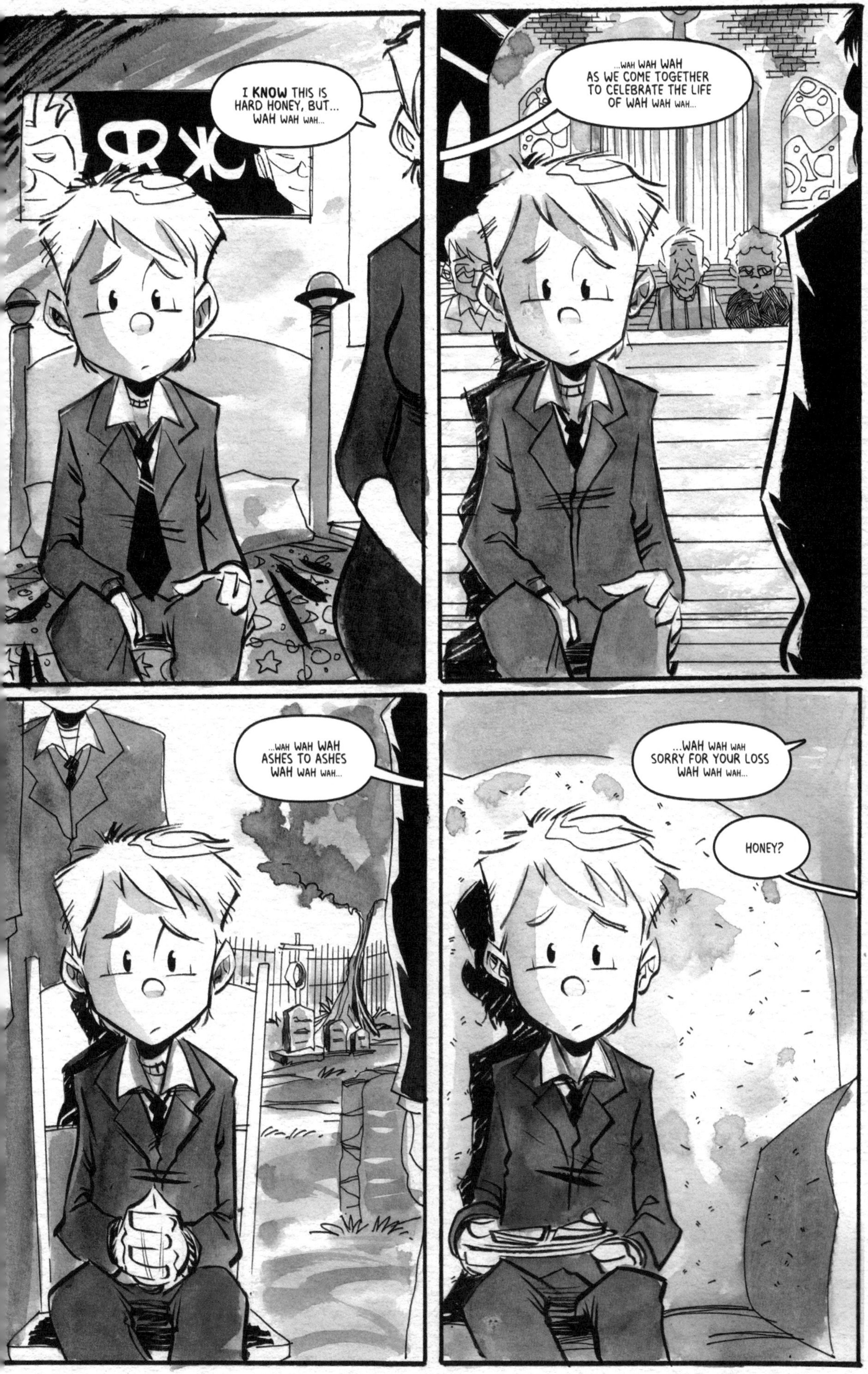
I KNOW THIS IS HARD HONEY, BUT... WAH WAH WAH...
...WAH WAH WAH AS WE COME TOGETHER TO CELEBRATE THE LIFE OF WAH WAH WAH...
...WAH WAH WAH ASHES TO ASHES WAH WAH WAH...
...WAH WAH WAH SORRY FOR YOUR LOSS WAH WAH WAH...
HONEY?

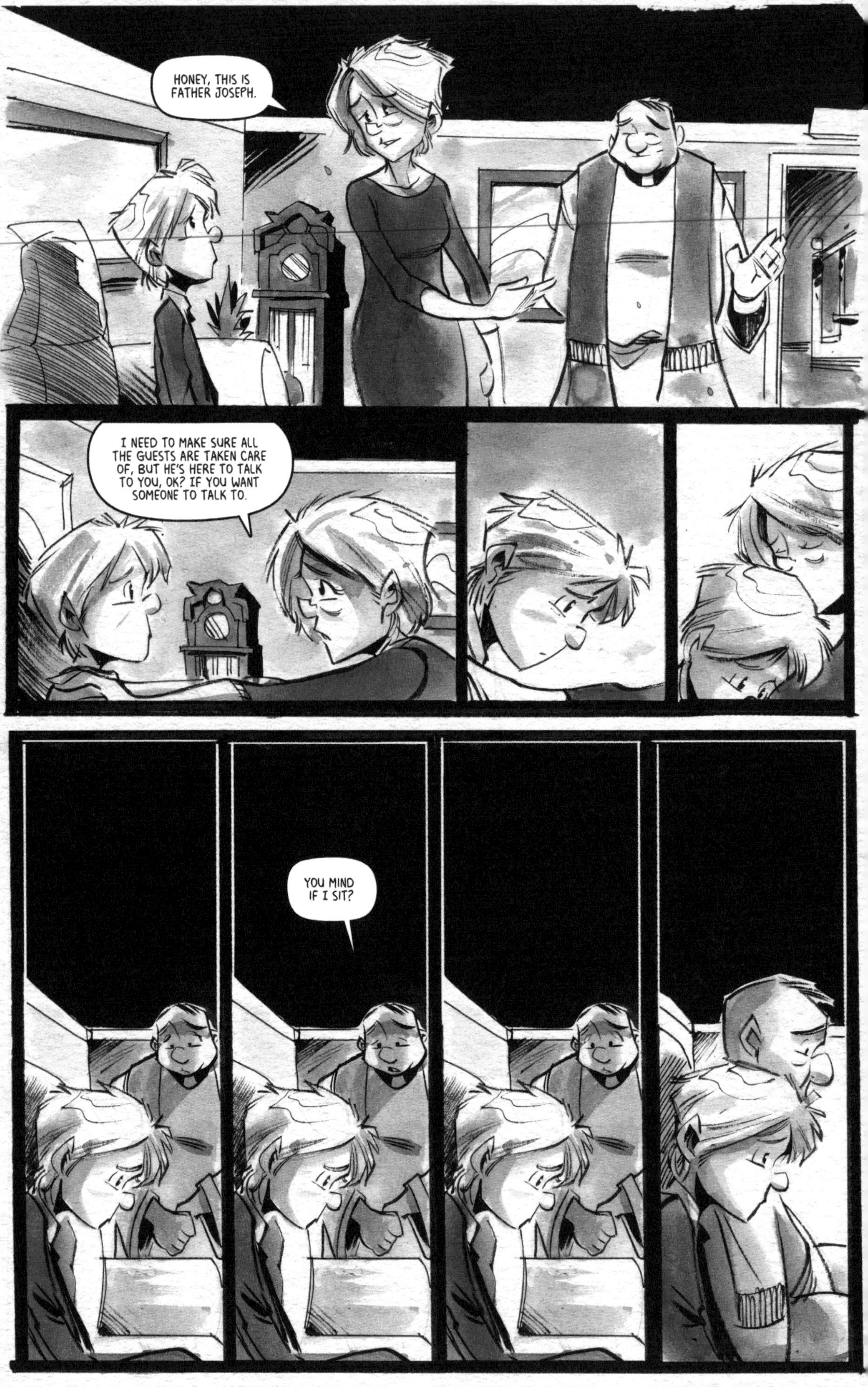
HONEY, THIS IS FATHER JOSEPH.
I NEED TO MAKE SURE ALL THE GUESTS ARE TAKEN CARE OF, BUT HE'S HERE TO TALK TO YOU, OK? IF YOU WANT SOMEONE TO TALK TO.
YOU MIND IF I SIT?

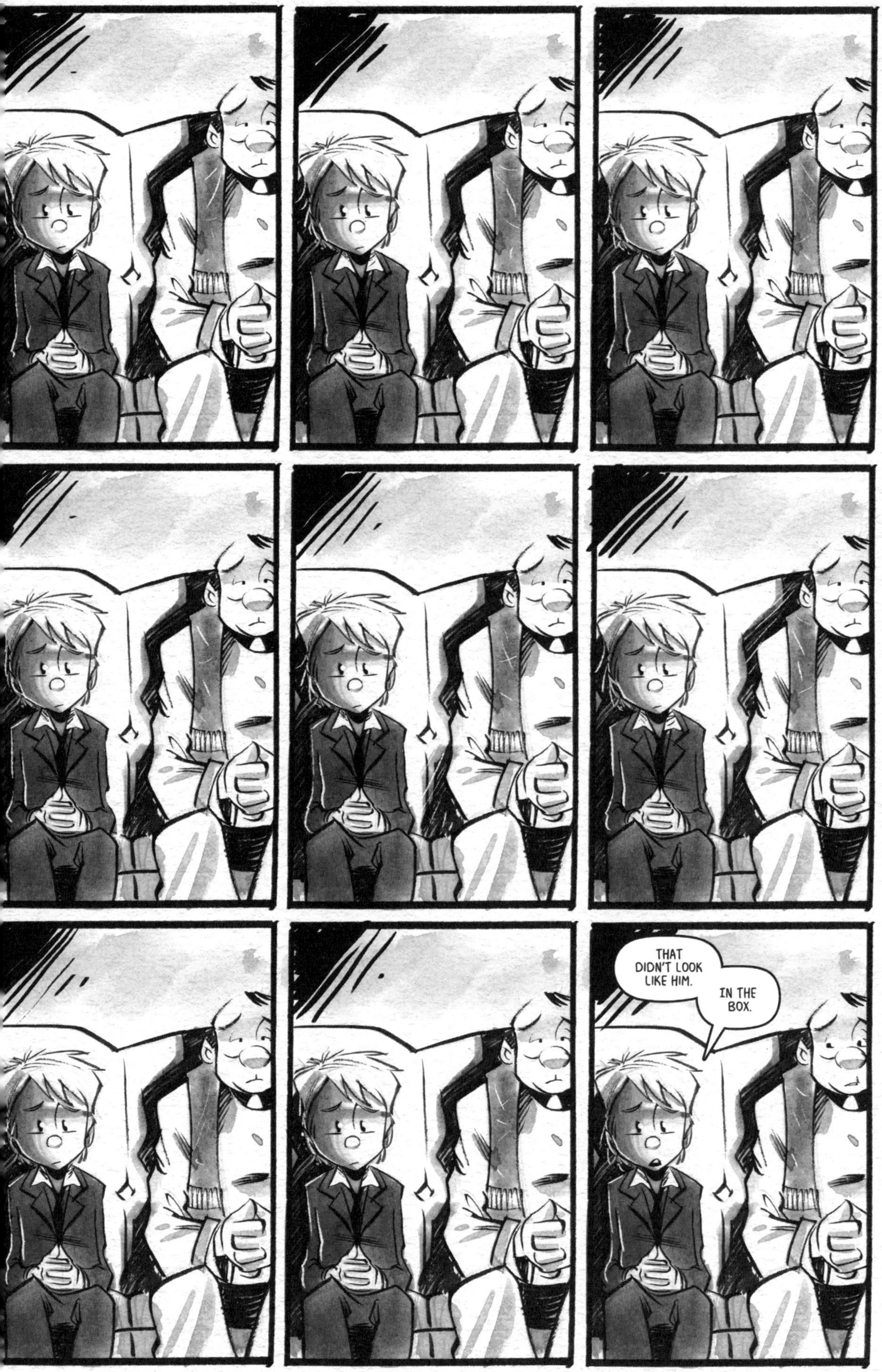
THAT DIDN'T LOOK LIKE HIM.
IN THE BOX.

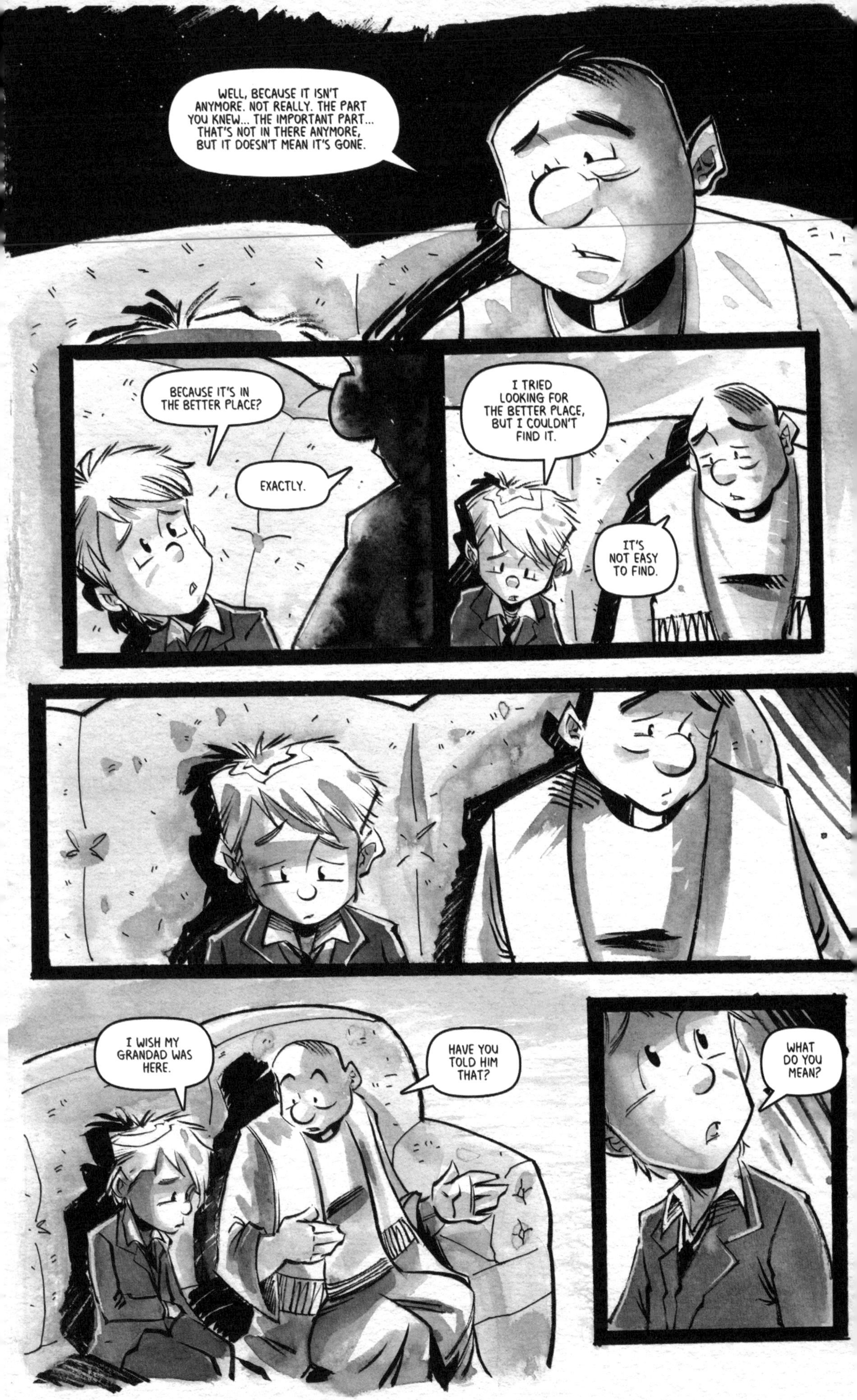
WELL, BECAUSE IT ISN'T ANYMORE. NOT REALLY. THE PART YOU KNEW... THE IMPORTANT PART... THAT'S NOT IN THERE ANYMORE, BUT IT DOESN'T MEAN IT'S GONE.
BECAUSE IT'S IN THE BETTER PLACE?
EXACTLY.
I TRIED LOOKING FOR THE BETTER PLACE, BUT I COULDN'T FIND IT.
IT'S NOT EASY TO FIND.
I WISH MY GRANDAD WAS HERE.
HAVE YOU TOLD HIM THAT?
WHAT DO YOU MEAN?

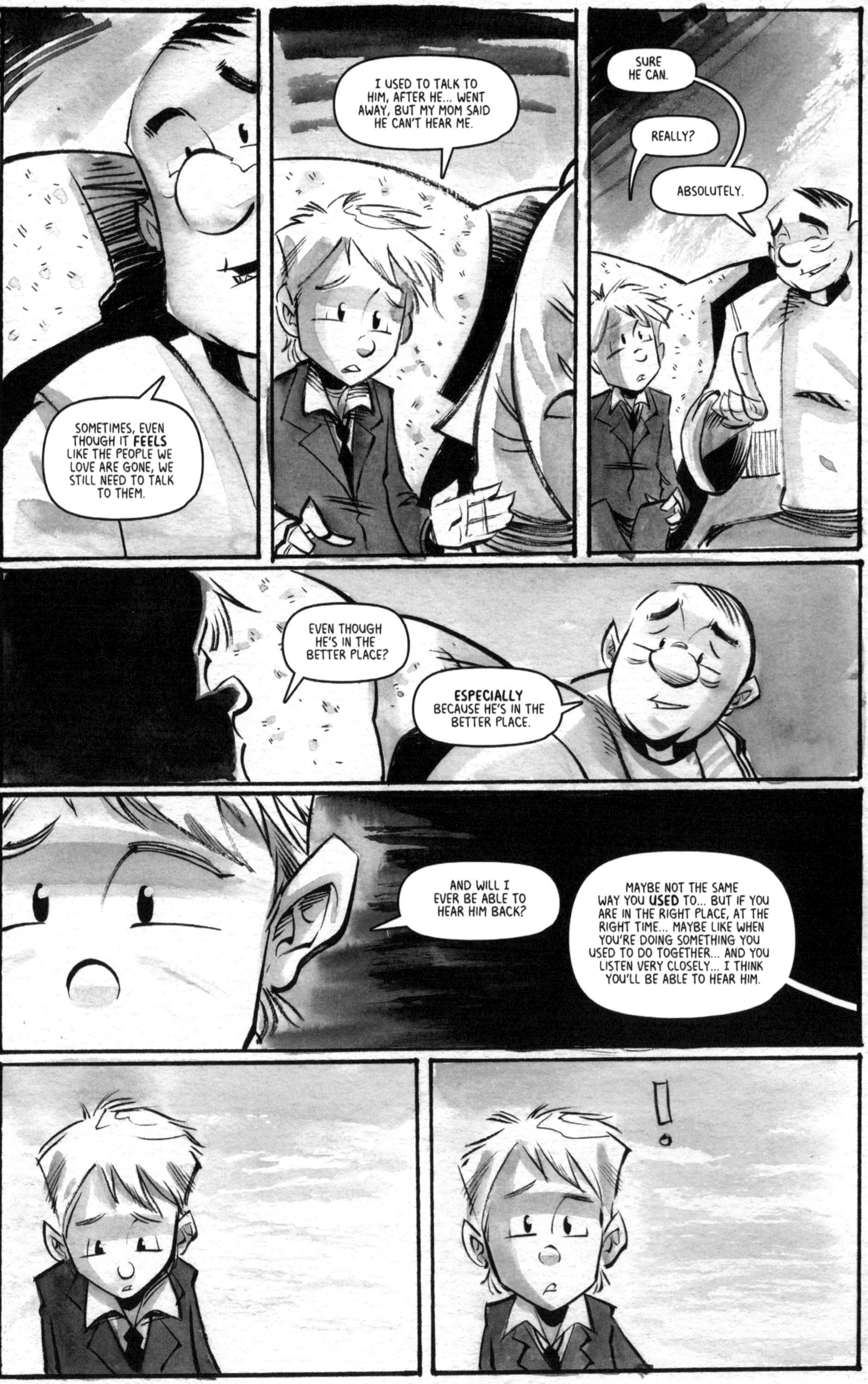
SOMETIMES, EVEN THOUGH IT **FEELS** LIKE THE PEOPLE WE LOVE ARE GONE, WE STILL NEED TO TALK TO THEM.
I USED TO TALK TO HIM, AFTER HE... WENT AWAY, BUT MY MOM SAID HE CAN'T HEAR ME.
SURE HE CAN.
REALLY?
ABSOLUTELY.
EVEN THOUGH HE'S IN THE BETTER PLACE?
ESPECIALLY BECAUSE HE'S IN THE BETTER PLACE.
AND WILL I EVER BE ABLE TO HEAR HIM BACK?
MAYBE NOT THE SAME WAY YOU **USED** TO... BUT IF YOU ARE IN THE RIGHT PLACE, AT THE RIGHT TIME... MAYBE LIKE WHEN YOU'RE DOING SOMETHING YOU USED TO DO TOGETHER... AND YOU LISTEN VERY CLOSELY... I THINK YOU'LL BE ABLE TO HEAR HIM.
!

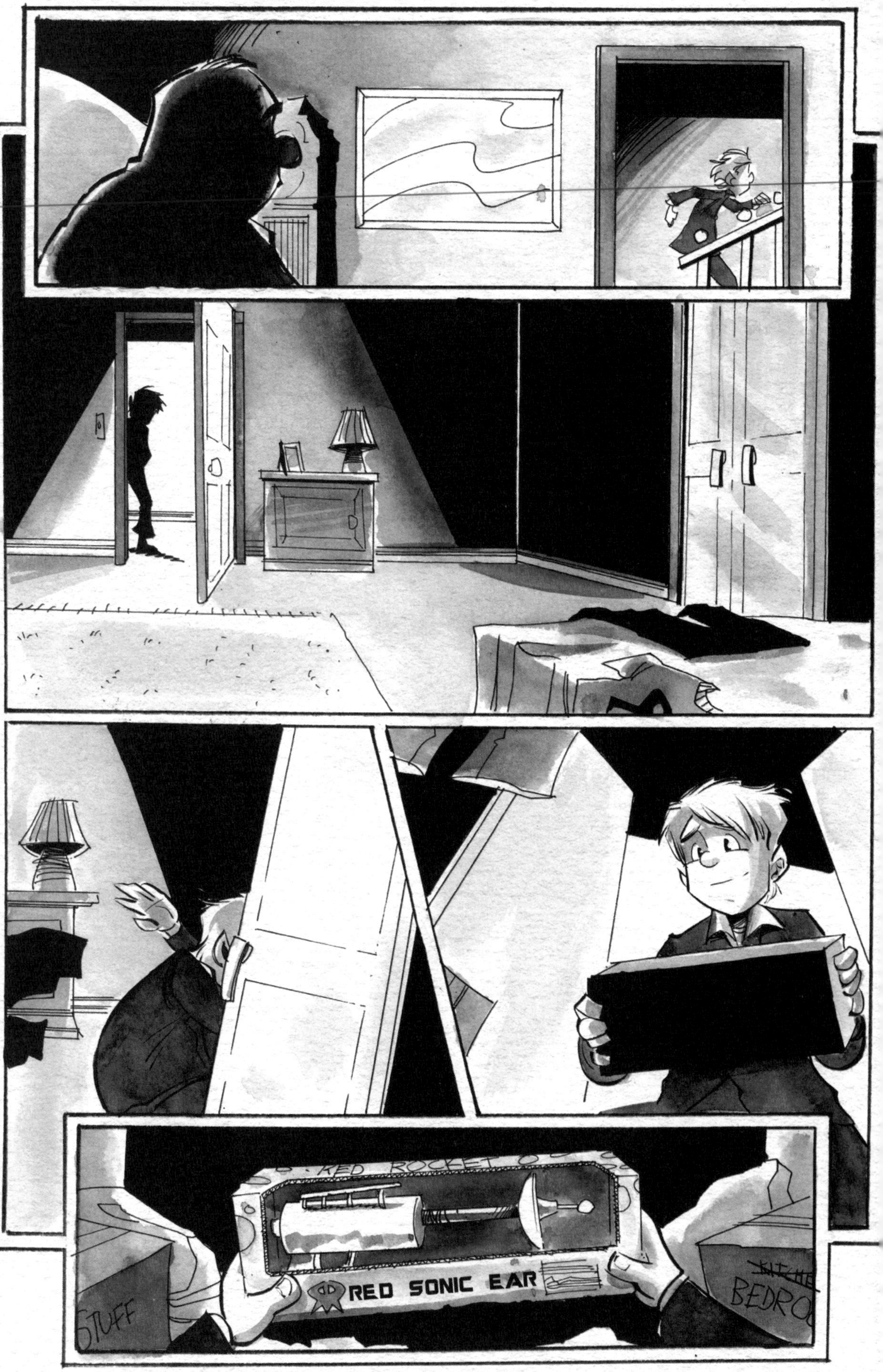
RED ROCKET
RED SONIC EAR
STUFF
BEDRO

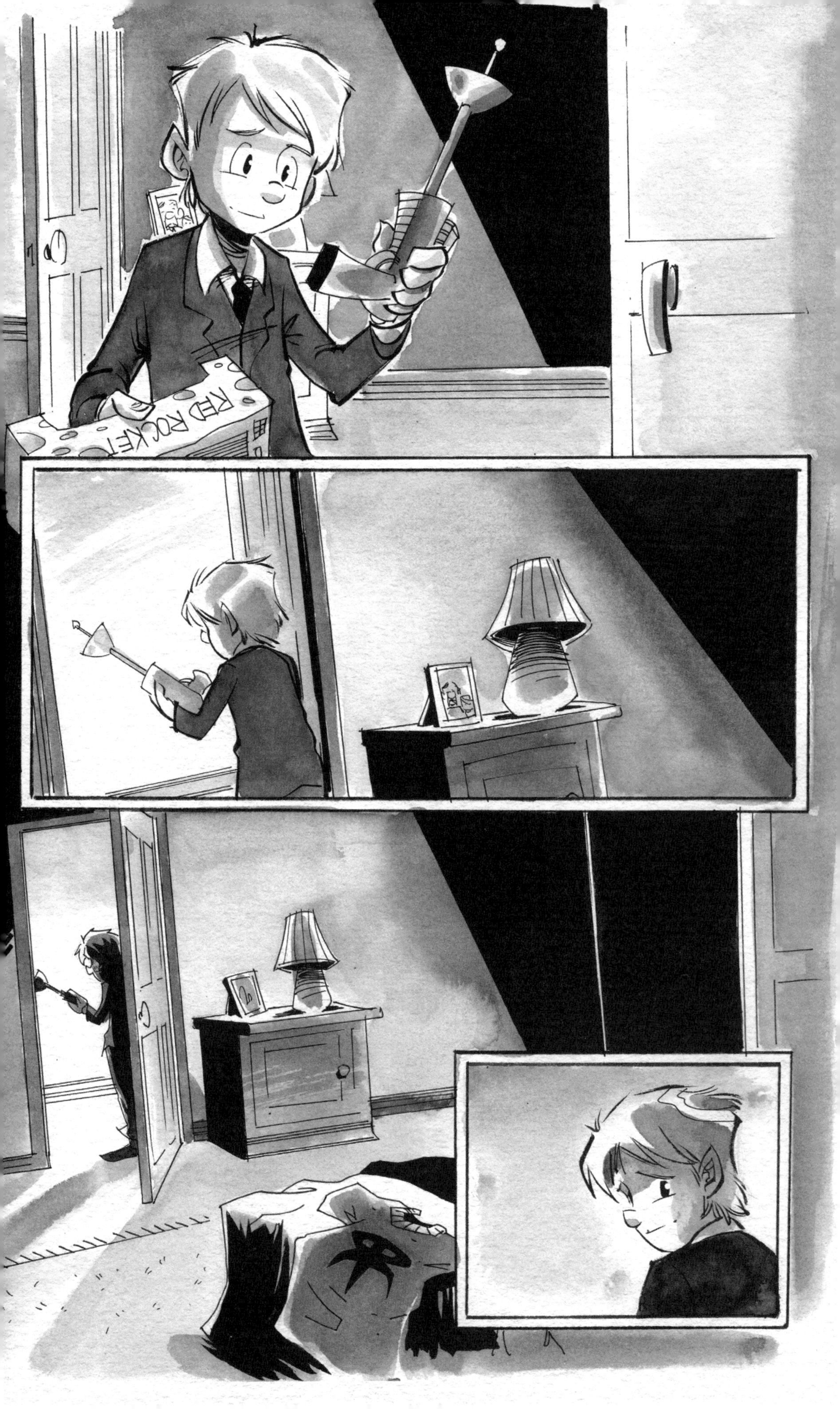
RED ROCKET

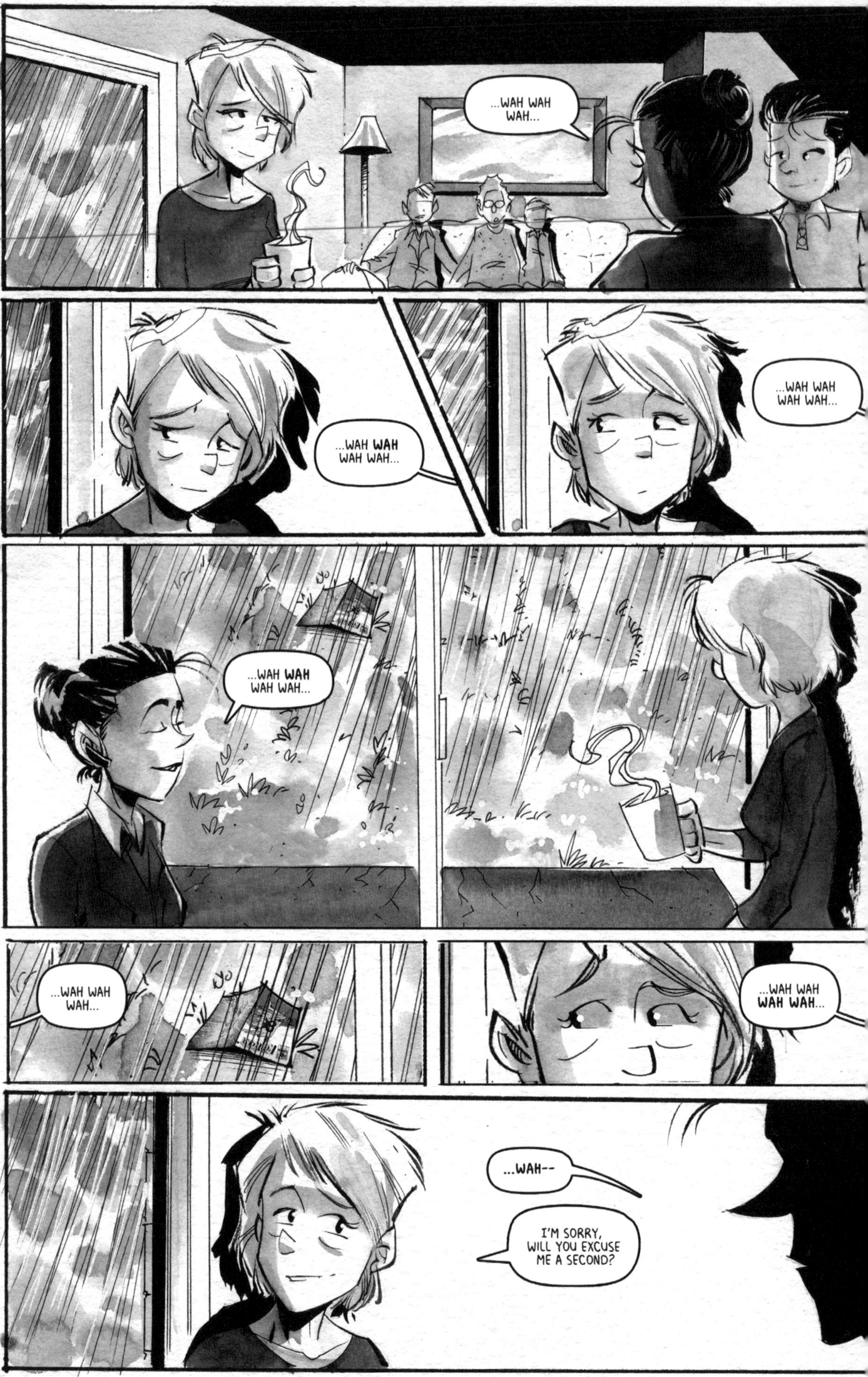
...WAH WAH WAH...
...WAH WAH WAH WAH...
...WAH WAH WAH WAH...
...WAH WAH WAH WAH...
...WAH WAH WAH...
...WAH WAH WAH WAH...
...WAH--
I'M SORRY, WILL YOU EXCUSE ME A SECOND?

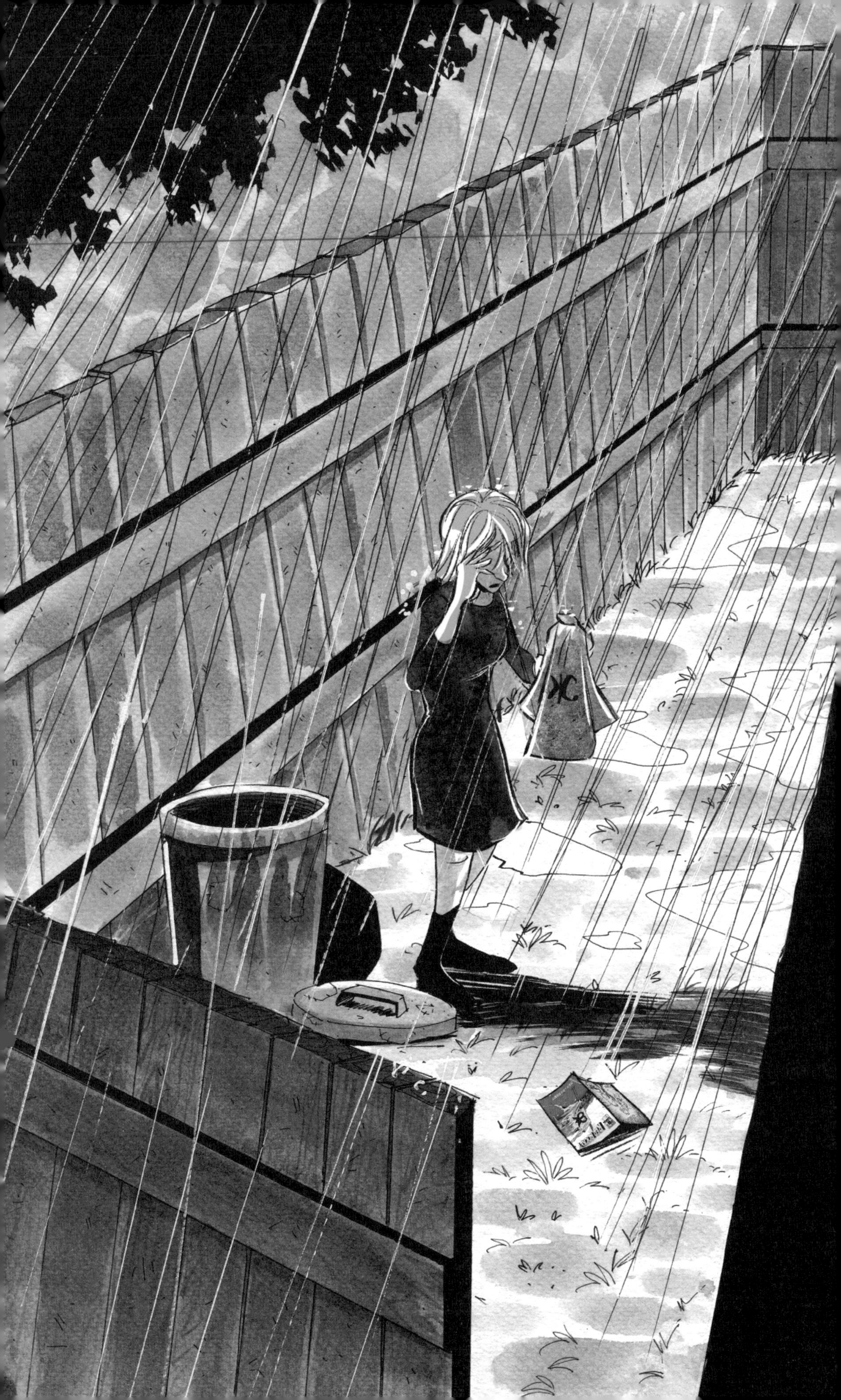

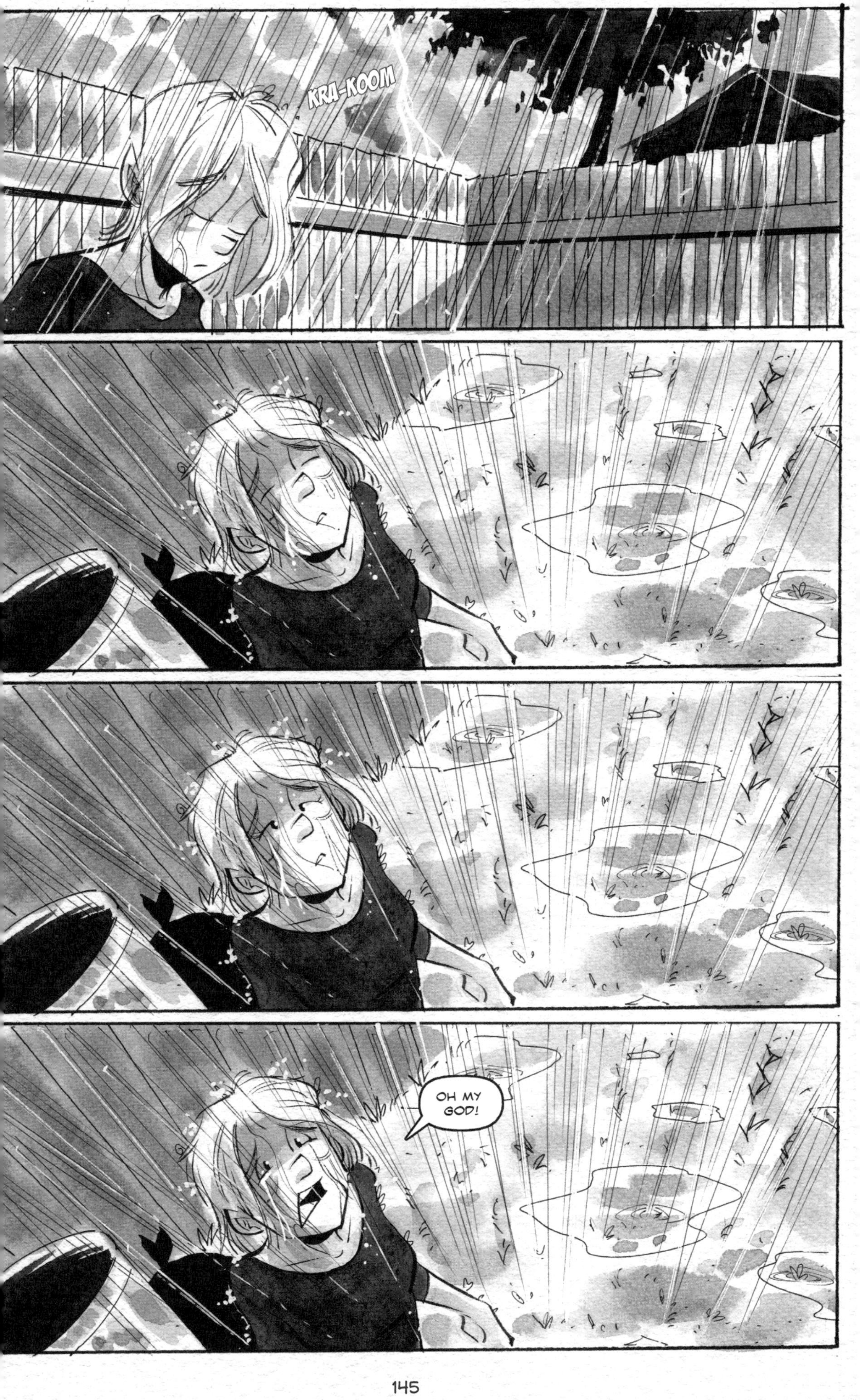
KRA-KOOM
OH MY GOD!

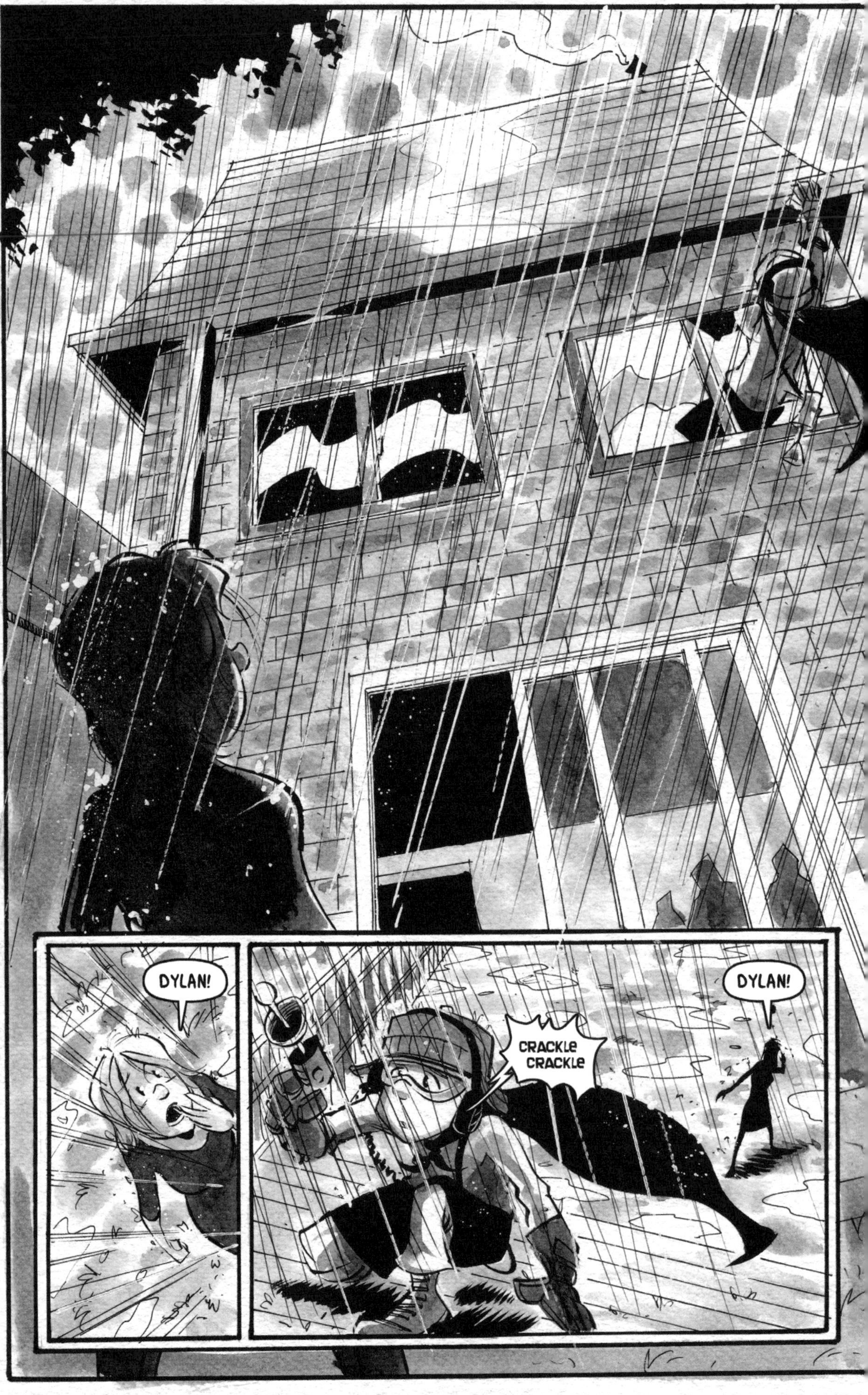
DYLAN!
CRACKLE CRACKLE
DYLAN!

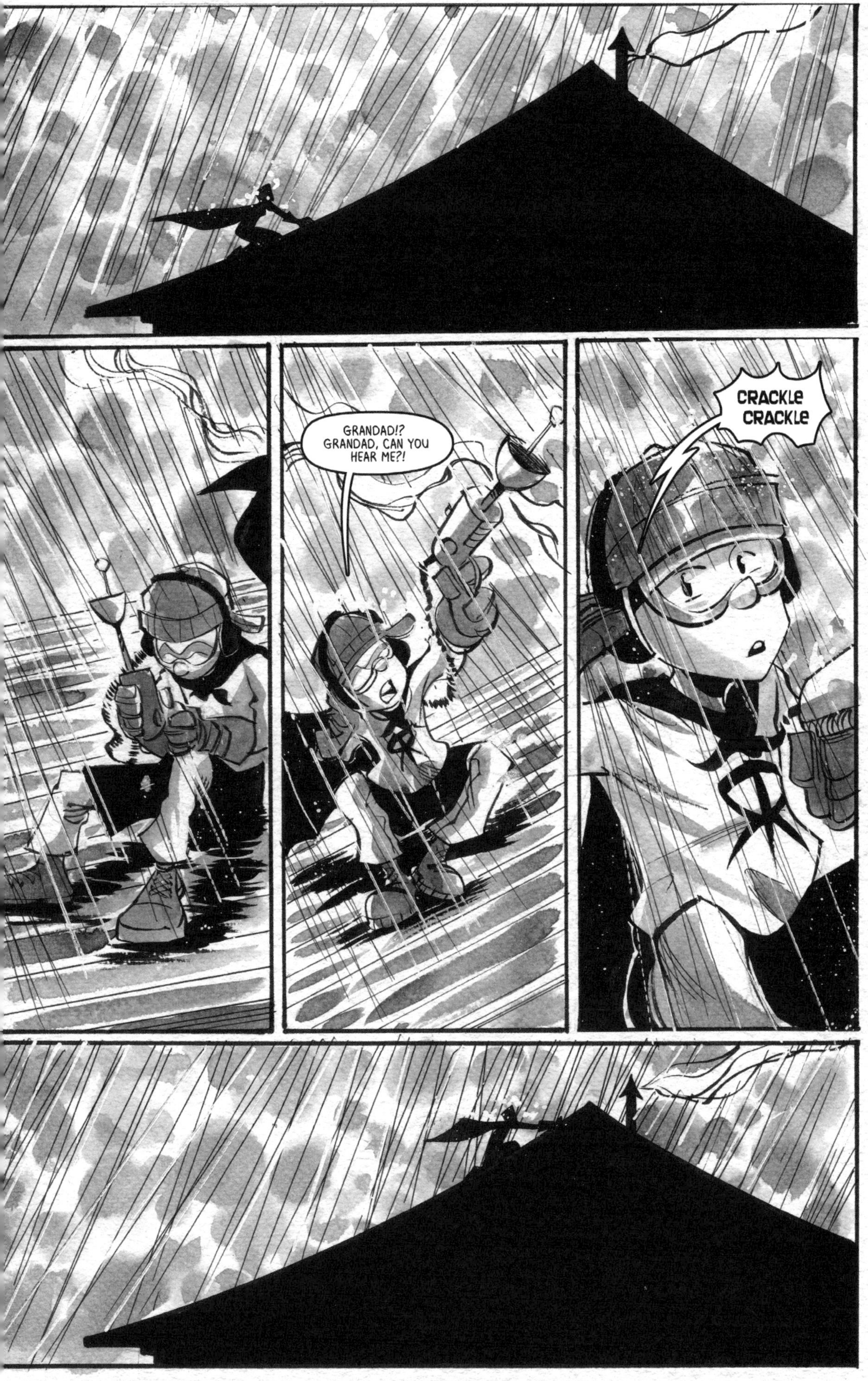
GRANDAD!? GRANDAD, CAN YOU HEAR ME?!
CRACKLE CRACKLE

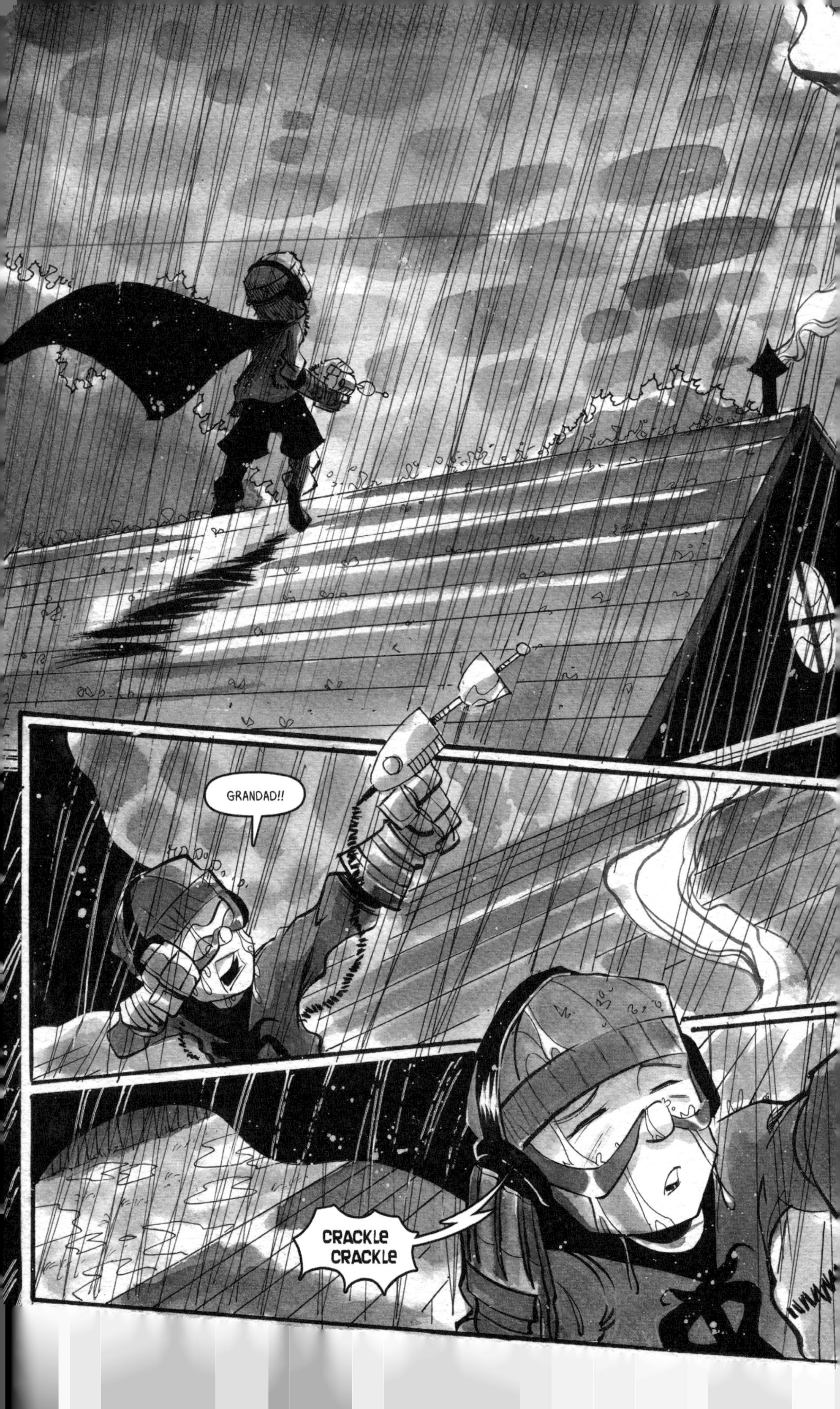
GRANDAD!!
CRACKLE CRACKLE

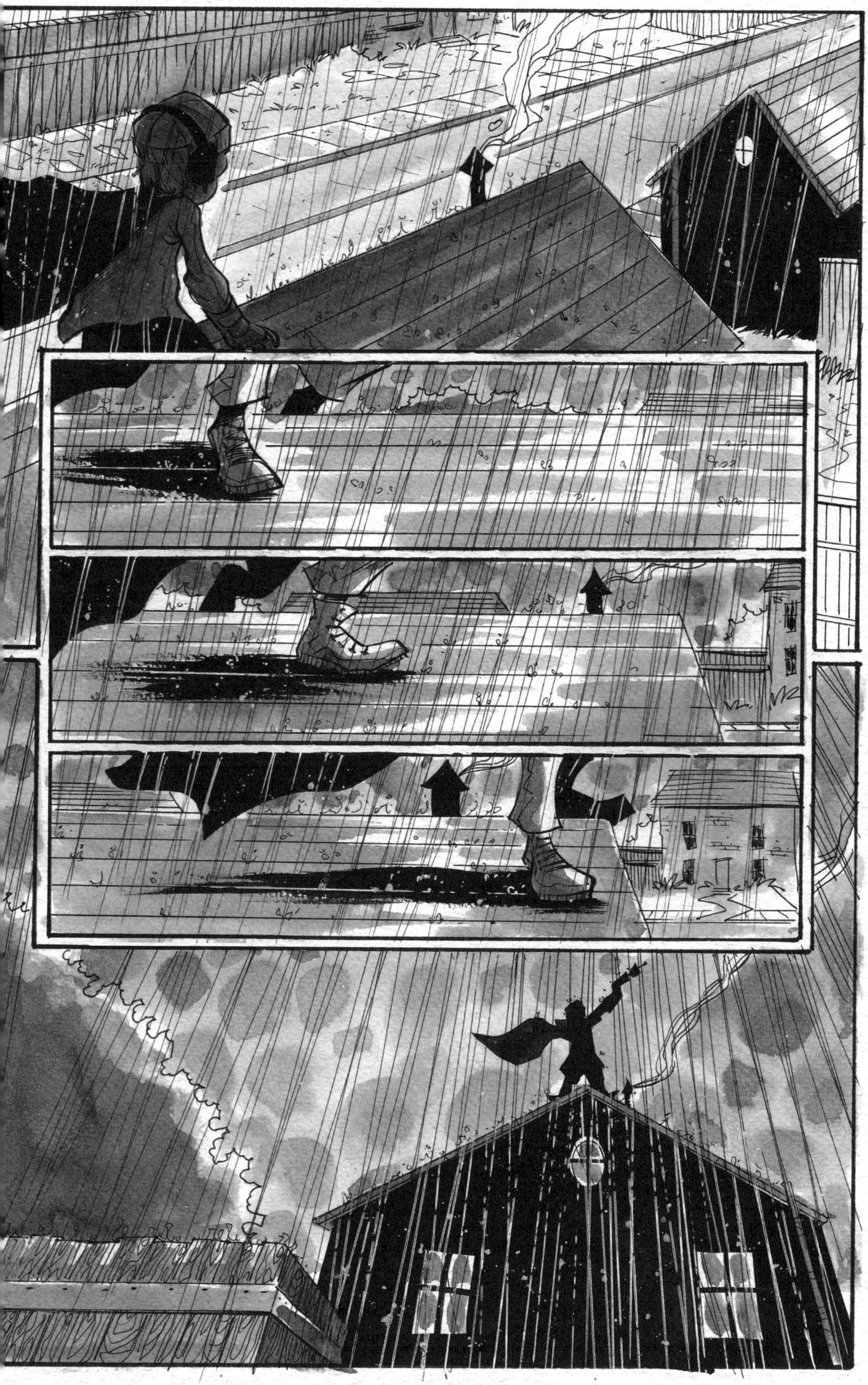

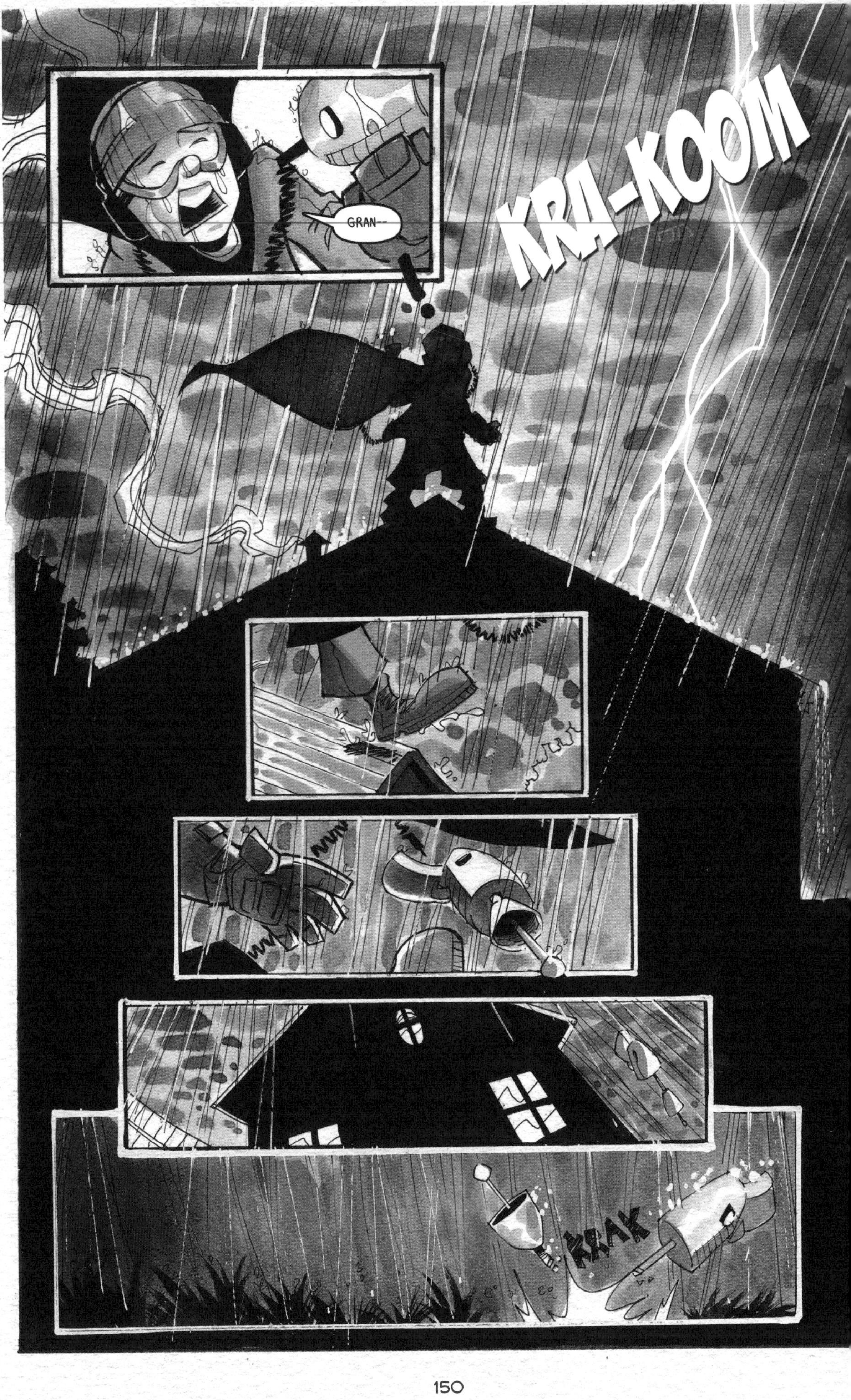

GRAN--
KRA-KOOM
KRAK

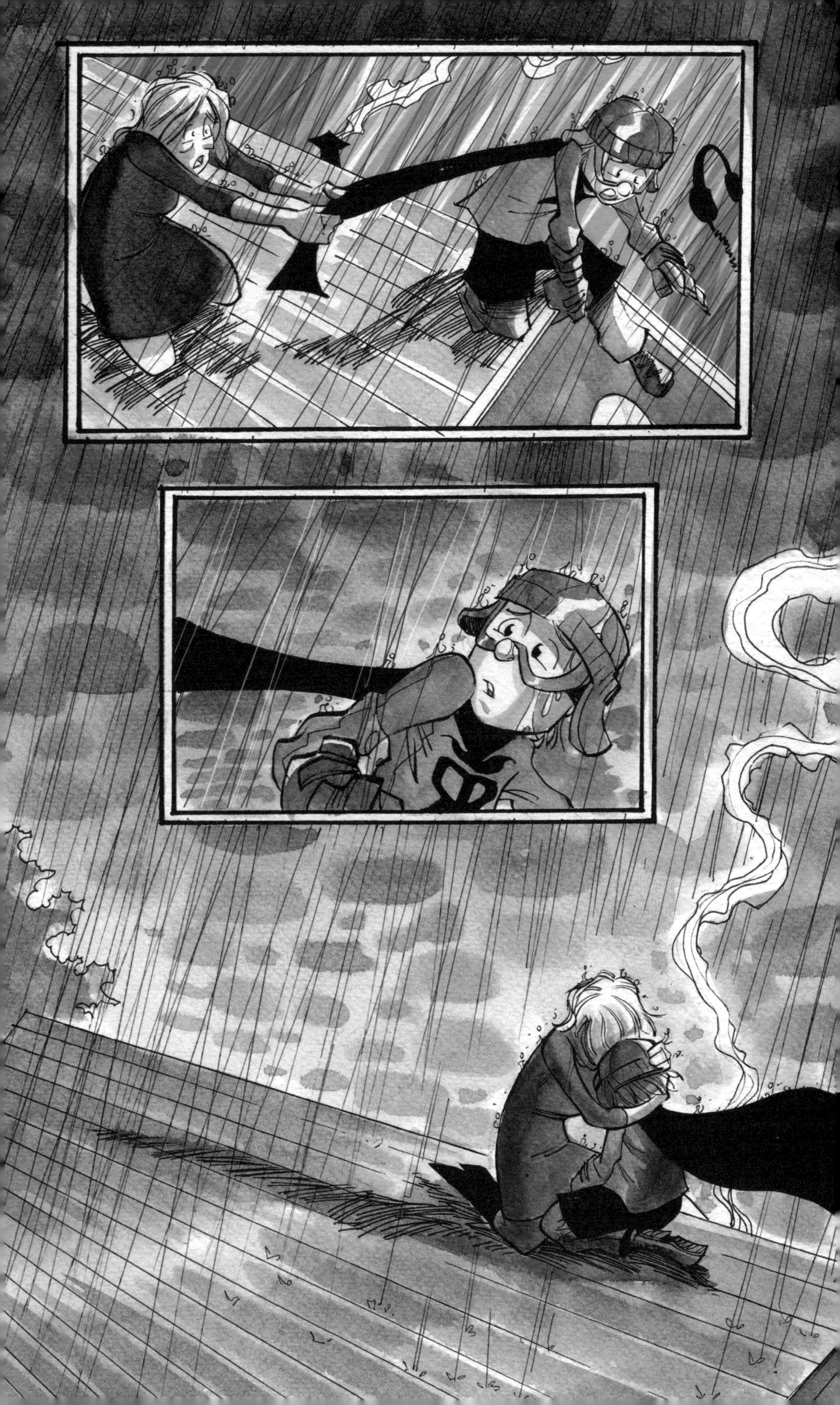

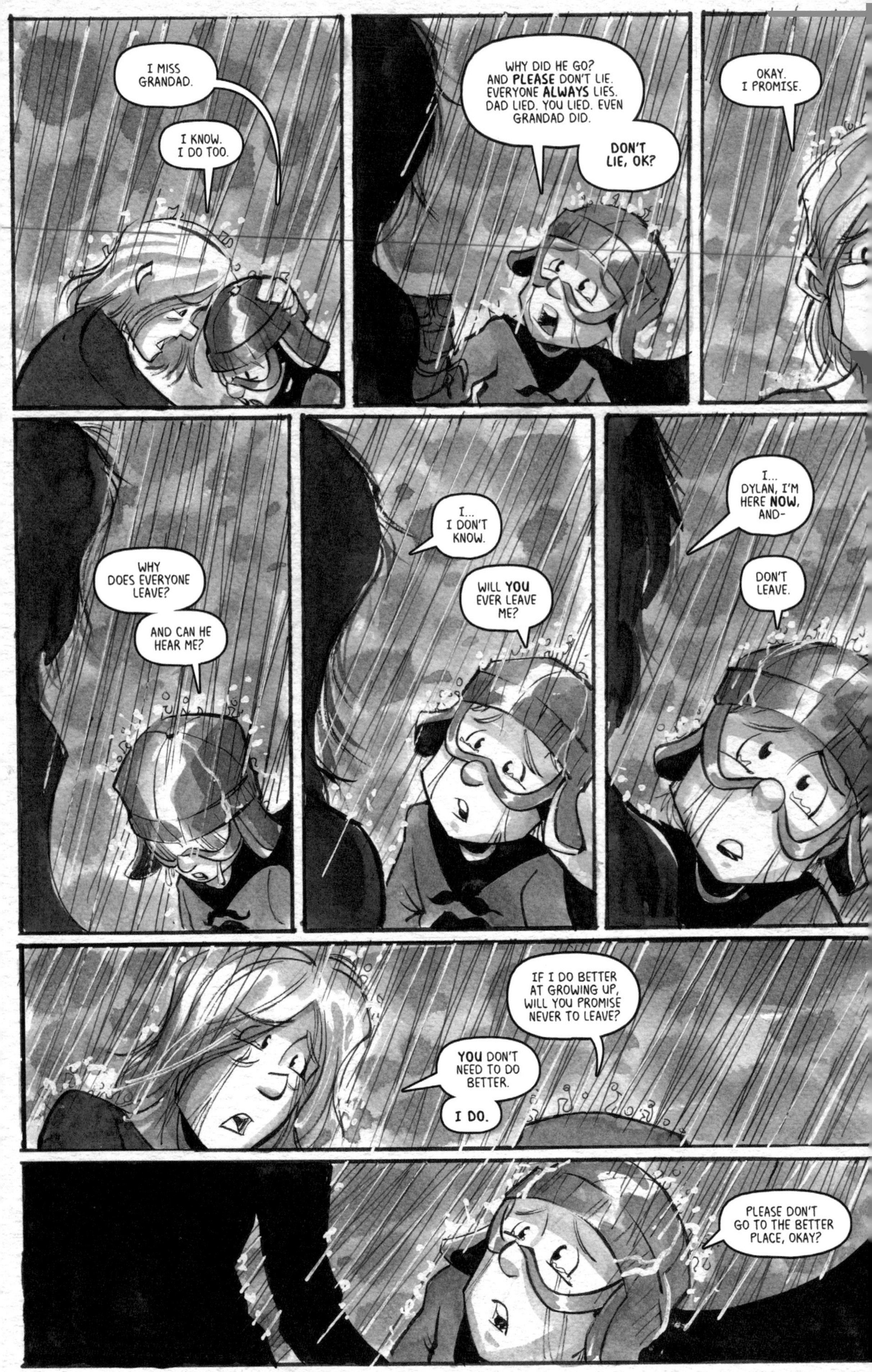
I MISS GRANDAD.
I KNOW. I DO TOO.
WHY DID HE GO? AND **PLEASE** DON'T LIE. EVERYONE **ALWAYS** LIES. DAD LIED. YOU LIED. EVEN GRANDAD DID.
DON'T LIE, OK?
OKAY. I PROMISE.
WHY DOES EVERYONE LEAVE?
AND CAN HE HEAR ME?
I... I DON'T KNOW.
WILL **YOU** EVER LEAVE ME?
I... DYLAN, I'M HERE **NOW**, AND-
DON'T LEAVE.
IF I DO BETTER AT GROWING UP, WILL YOU PROMISE NEVER TO LEAVE?
YOU DON'T NEED TO DO BETTER.
I DO.
PLEASE DON'T GO TO THE BETTER PLACE, OKAY?

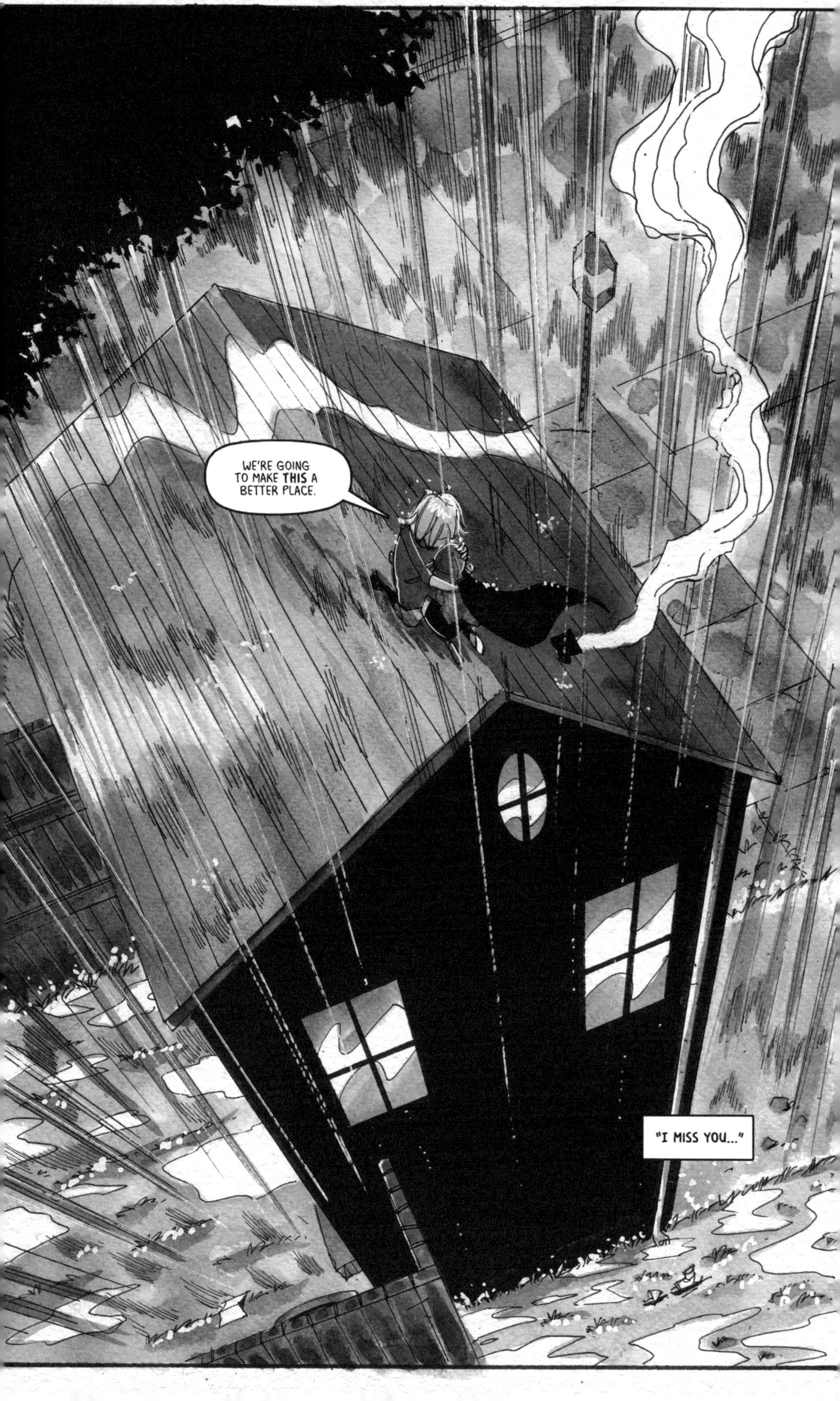
WE'RE GOING TO MAKE THIS A BETTER PLACE.
"I MISS YOU..."

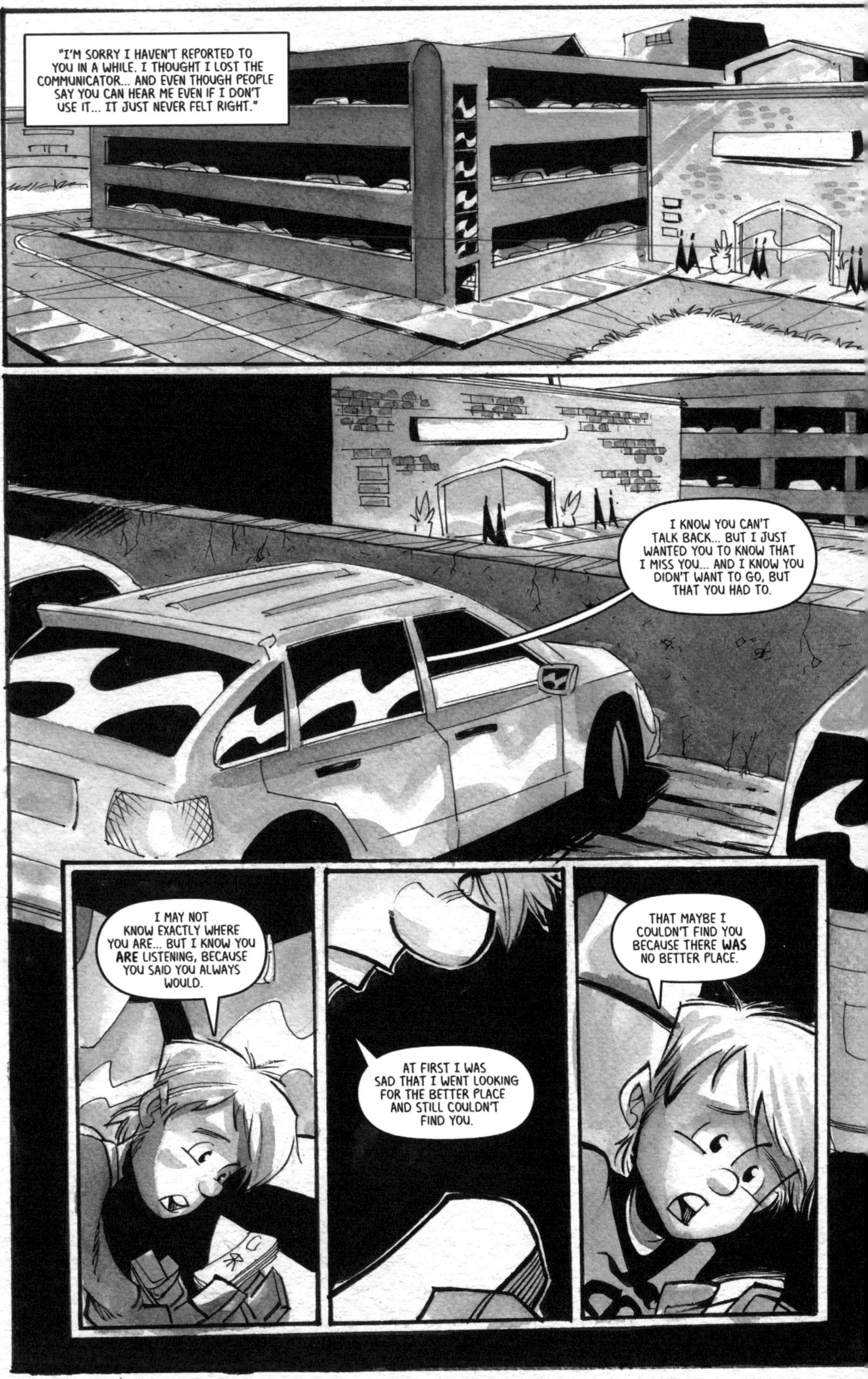
"I'M SORRY I HAVEN'T REPORTED TO YOU IN A WHILE. I THOUGHT I LOST THE COMMUNICATOR... AND EVEN THOUGH PEOPLE SAY YOU CAN HEAR ME EVEN IF I DON'T USE IT... IT JUST NEVER FELT RIGHT."
I KNOW YOU CAN'T TALK BACK... BUT I JUST WANTED YOU TO KNOW THAT I MISS YOU... AND I KNOW YOU DIDN'T WANT TO GO, BUT THAT YOU HAD TO.
I MAY NOT KNOW EXACTLY WHERE YOU ARE... BUT I KNOW YOU **ARE** LISTENING, BECAUSE YOU SAID YOU ALWAYS WOULD.
AT FIRST I WAS SAD THAT I WENT LOOKING FOR THE BETTER PLACE AND STILL COULDN'T FIND YOU.
THAT MAYBE I COULDN'T FIND YOU BECAUSE THERE **WAS** NO BETTER PLACE.

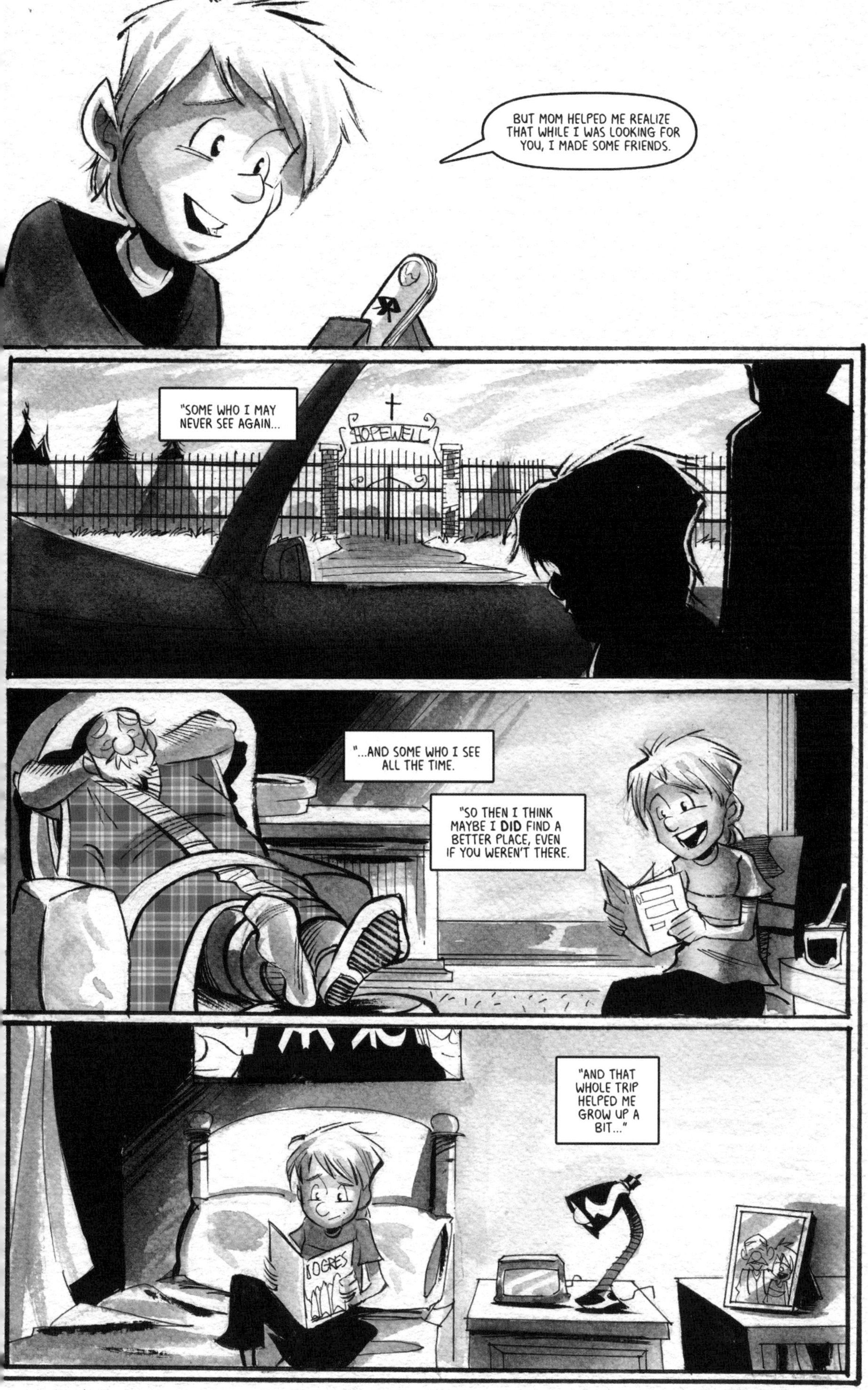

BUT MOM HELPED ME REALIZE THAT WHILE I WAS LOOKING FOR YOU, I MADE SOME FRIENDS.
"SOME WHO I MAY NEVER SEE AGAIN...
HOPEWELL
"...AND SOME WHO I SEE ALL THE TIME.
"SO THEN I THINK MAYBE I **DID** FIND A BETTER PLACE, EVEN IF YOU WEREN'T THERE.
"AND THAT WHOLE TRIP HELPED ME GROW UP A BIT..."
OGRES

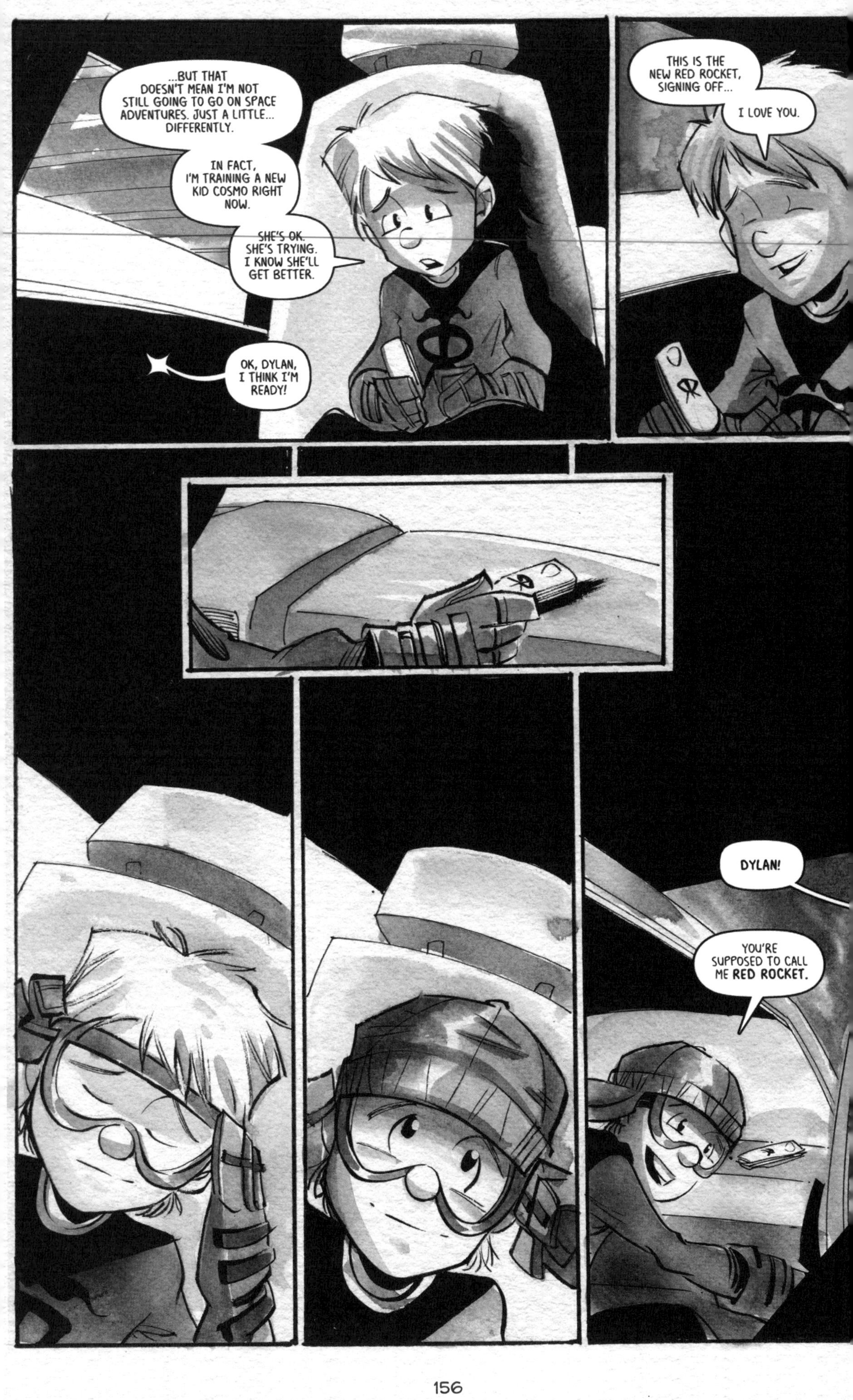
...BUT THAT DOESN'T MEAN I'M NOT STILL GOING TO GO ON SPACE ADVENTURES. JUST A LITTLE... DIFFERENTLY.
IN FACT, I'M TRAINING A NEW KID COSMO RIGHT NOW.
SHE'S OK. SHE'S TRYING. I KNOW SHE'LL GET BETTER.
OK, DYLAN, I THINK I'M READY!
THIS IS THE NEW RED ROCKET, SIGNING OFF...
I LOVE YOU.
DYLAN!
YOU'RE SUPPOSED TO CALL ME RED ROCKET.

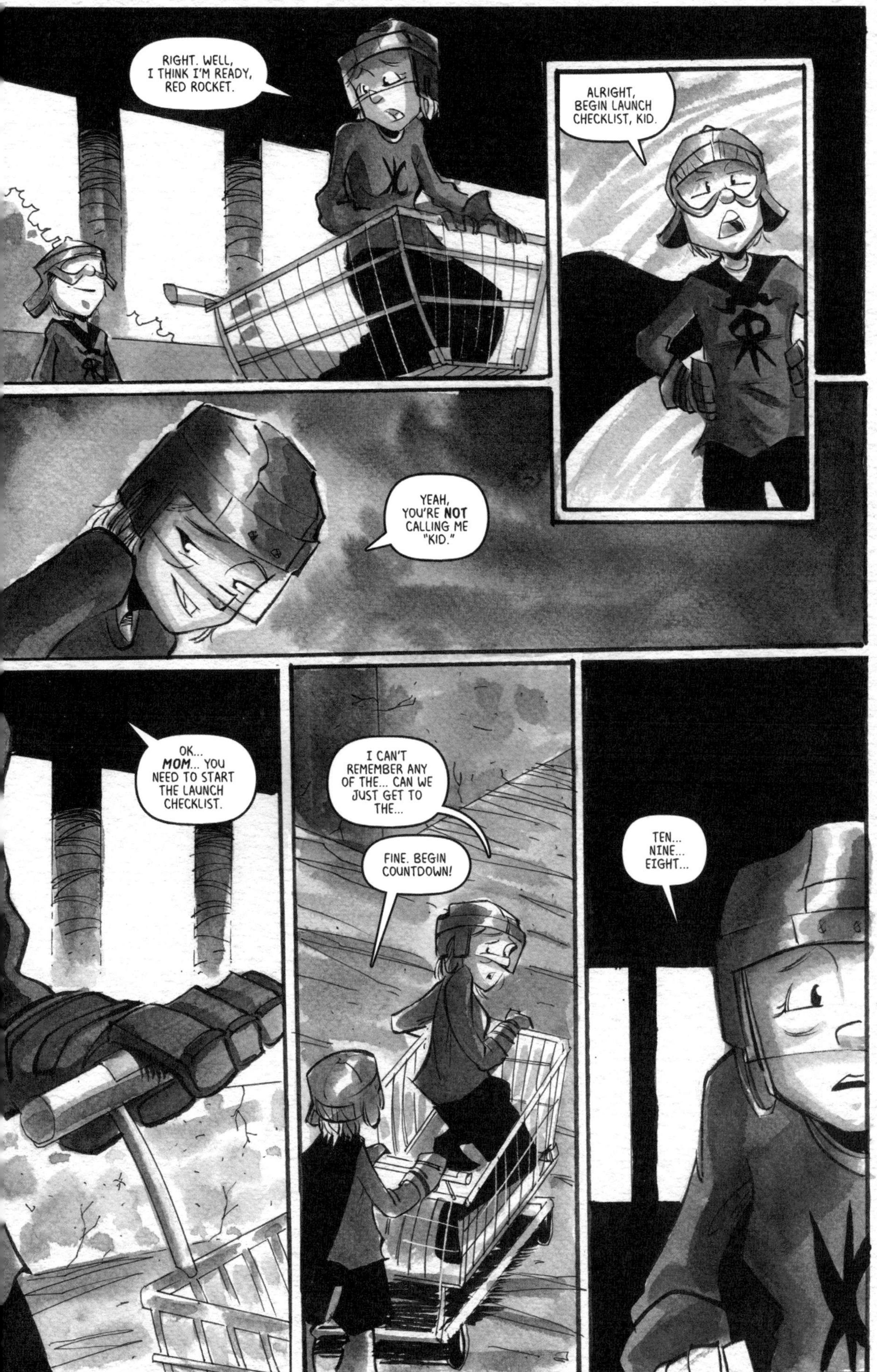
RIGHT. WELL, I THINK I'M READY, RED ROCKET.
ALRIGHT, BEGIN LAUNCH CHECKLIST, KID.
YEAH, YOU'RE **NOT** CALLING ME "KID."
OK... ***MOM***... YOU NEED TO START THE LAUNCH CHECKLIST.
I CAN'T REMEMBER ANY OF THE... CAN WE JUST GET TO THE...
FINE. BEGIN COUNTDOWN!
TEN... NINE... EIGHT...

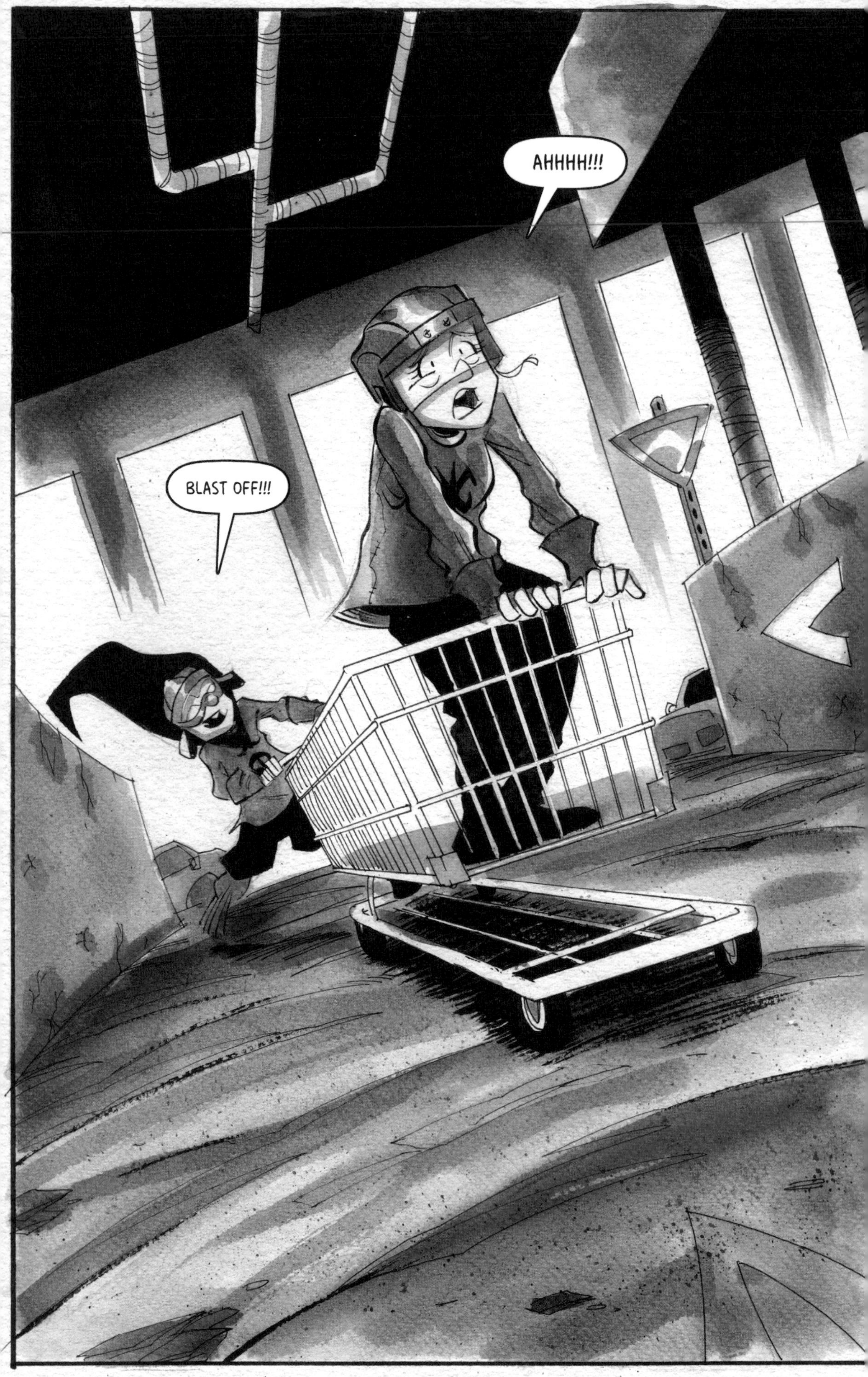
AHHHH!!!
BLAST OFF!!!

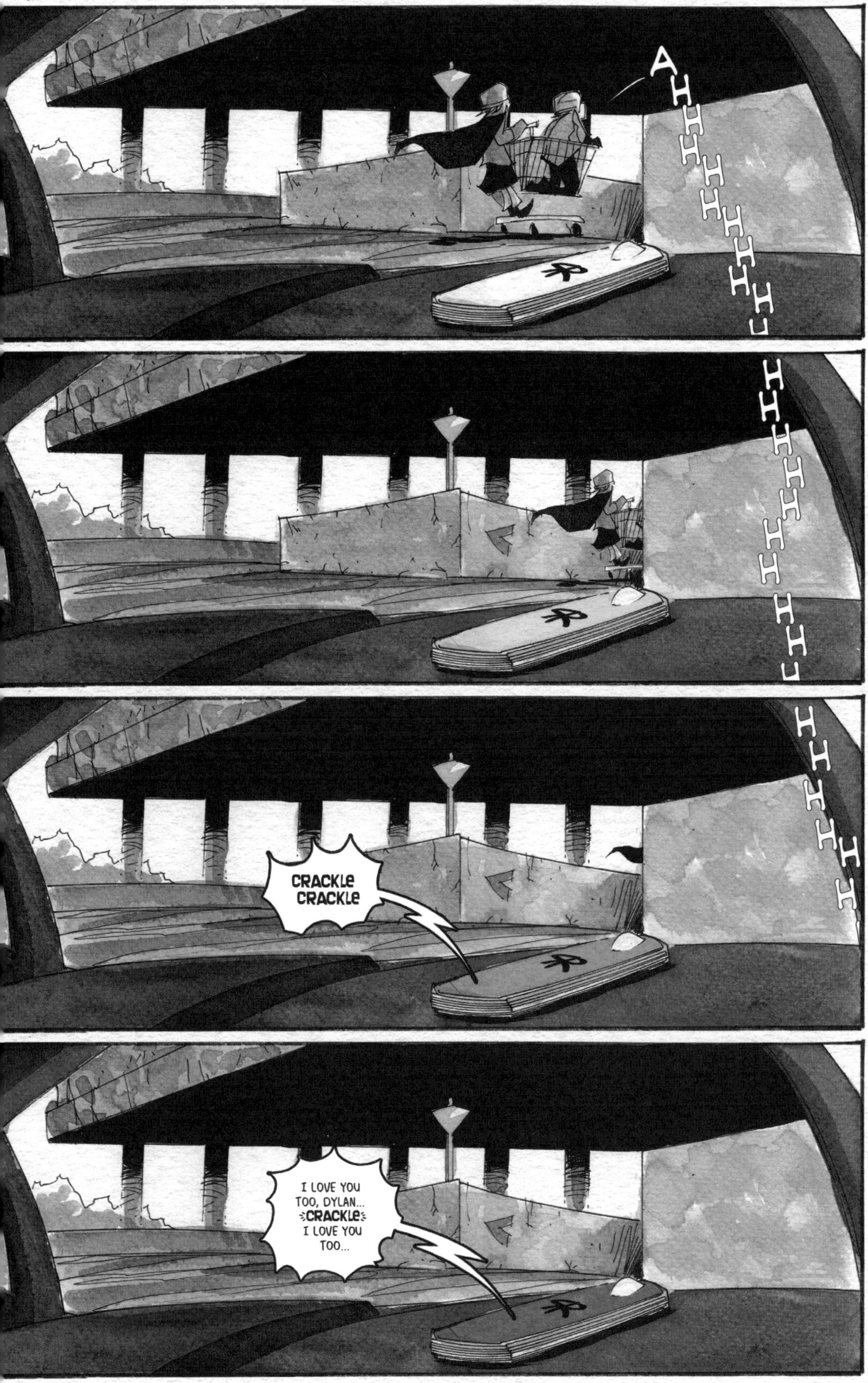
AHHHHHHHHHHH
HHHHHHHHHHH
HHHHHHHHH
CRACKLE CRACKLE
I LOVE YOU TOO, DYLAN... CRACKLE I LOVE YOU TOO...

Special Thanks:

To Shane, who helped me on this journey and supported me when I continued on my own to tell this story this way. To Chris Staros for giving this book a shot even after I sent an unsolicited email with a broken download link. To the superstar 'guest' artists, whose work not only inspired me to create this book, but who agreed to contribute to it, sight unseen and without hesitation. To Shawn, who came on board to not only draw my story but make it his own. To Leigh and everyone else at Top Shelf/IDW for their insight and expertise in helping the book cross the finish line and get it out there, and lastly to anyone who has given some of their valuable time to read it. Thank you all for making a dream come true.

–Duane Murray

To Kim, Laurence, Emily, Justin, and the family. I wouldn't have found my footing without you all helping me up. To the guest artists, for providing constant inspiration. You've all helped me grow as a cartoonist and storyteller. To Duane, for the unending artistic freedoms provided while drawing the book. I'll always treasure the experience, along with your trust and kindness. To the Top Shelf/IDW team, whose dedication and passion for comics is unrivaled. Working with you all has been an amazing experience. Finally, to the readers of *Better Place* and my other books. You all keep me going.

–Shawn Daley